It's Christmas in Twilight, Texas.

The town is decorated…

The kismet cookies are baked…

And 'tis the season…for love!

D0584158

"Are you asking me to kiss you . . . ?"

"Not me." She pointed upward. "The mistletoe."

"We're standing on the street in front of your house. In public. Where anyone and everyone can see."

"It's out of my hands," she said. "You have to kiss under the mistletoe at Christmas. It's the rules, and you don't break the rules."

"You might need mistletoe to justify wanting to kiss me," Shepherd growled. "But I don't."

Her eyes flew open. "Huh?"

He dipped his head closer, lowered his voice. "When I kiss you, woman, it's going to be because it's the right time and the right place. Not because you're standing under a clump of some parasitic plant. It's going to be hot and it's going to last a long time and your knees are going to buckle. No mistletoe required. Count on it."

By Lori Wilde

LORI WILDE

THE
CHRISTMAS
Key

A TWILIGHT, TEXAS NOVEL

AVONBOOKS

An Imprint of HarperCollinsPublishers

Excerpt from *To Tame a Wild Cowboy* copyright © 2019 by Laurie Vanzura.

THE CHRISTMAS KEY. Copyright © 2018 by Laurie Vanzura. All rights reserved. Printed in the United States of America. No part of this book may be used or reproduced in any manner whatsoever without written permission except in the case of brief quotations embodied in critical articles and reviews. For information, address HarperCollins Publishers, 195 Broadway, New York, NY 10007.

First Avon Books mass market printing: November 2018
First Avon Books hardcover printing: October 2018

Print Edition ISBN: 978-0-06-246827-7
Digital Edition ISBN: 978-0-06-246828-4

Cover art by Larry Rostant
Cover photographs © Shutterstock (six images)

Avon, Avon & logo, and Avon Books & logo are registered trademarks of HarperCollins Publishers in the United States of America and other countries.

HarperCollins is a registered trademark of HarperCollins Publishers in the United States of America and other countries.

FIRST EDITION

18 19 20 21 22   QGM   10 9 8 7 6 5 4 3 2 1

To Christine Evans. Because you turn the world on with your smile.

CHAPTER 1

November 26

Walter Reed National Military Medical Center, Bethesda, Maryland

Marine Gunnery Sergeant Mark Shepherd jerked awake. Disoriented, he lunged for the rifle that wasn't there.

He'd forgotten where his body was in time and space. In his head, he was still in Kandahar.

"Sir?" asked the bespectacled receptionist with kind eyes and a marshmallow voice. "Are you all right?"

He nodded, blinked. Straightened.

The psychiatrist's office, like most things military, was clean, efficient, and functional; metal folding chairs in the lobby instead of plush leather couches, unadorned white walls instead of framed artwork, cheap blinds instead of designer drapery, stained concrete floors polished to a high sheen instead of marble.

The austerity suited him.

He liked things neat, simple, and uncomplicated. Black and white. Liked having rules to obey. Protocol to follow. Liked the reliability of routine, the consistency of chain of command.

The military had given him direction when he'd had none. Had supplied a wild, undisciplined boy from Kentucky a firm place to land. He'd joined the Marines right out of high school, and for the past twelve years it had been the only life he'd ever known.

But now, the career he thought would last a lifetime had come to an abrupt end. He didn't know how he was going to adjust to the outside world. Or make peace with his sins. Either way, he couldn't stay in the military. He was no longer the best of the best.

And when it came to the Marines, it was either up or out.

He tapped his aching knee with the end of his cane, felt a sharp twinge in his lower back. The knee was a constant reminder of his mistakes. The pain a familiar old friend.

Definitely out. No further advancement. Not for a busted-up gunny who'd already risen through the ranks faster than most. He'd been lucky that the Marines had let him limp along for the past year while he healed. For that, he was grateful.

The door to the psychiatrist's office opened and a red-haired young man emerged. Dressed in black jeans and a black leather jacket, the kid scurried through the lobby. Head down.

A sense of inexplicable urgency seized Shepherd. Wrenched his gut.

The kid looked as if he'd gone through the wringer; blotchy skin, red-rimmed eyes, a runny nose.

"Private," Shepherd called.

The kid stopped, whirled. Stared at him with a haunted gaze. Snap-saluted.

"Forget that." Shepherd snorted. "My gunny days are over."

The kid looked uncertain, darted a glance at the exit.

"Don't run." Shepherd hadn't meant to sound so commanding. Habit.

The kid's nose twitched like a frightened rabbit.

Driven by impulse, Shepherd shuffled to his feet. "Listen—"

Panic flared in the kid's eyes. His chest heaved. Quick as a breath, he jumped forward, planted his palms against Shepherd's chest.

Shoved.

Hard.

Jolted, Shepherd's full weight landed on his bad leg. He fell back into the chair. Grunted at the searing burn.

"Stay away!" the kid yelled, terror in his eyes. "You stay away from me!"

Shepherd raised both hands. "Whoa, you're here. Now. Maryland."

The kid shook his head, appeared as dazed as Shepherd had felt a couple of minutes ago.

"It's okay, it's okay. You're safe," Shepherd soothed. "You're home."

"Am I?" The kid swiveled his head, eyes wide.

"Yes. Are you with me?"

The kid swallowed, bobbed his chin.

"Say it."

"I'm with you," the kid mumbled. "In Maryland."

"Good job, Private." Shepherd wanted to touch him, reassure him, but he didn't dare. "Whatever is going on, you'll get through this. I promise."

"Yeah?" The kid gave a skeptical laugh, his lip curling in a half sneer. "Any sage advice, Gunny?"

Shepherd drilled him with a don't-give-up stare. "Survive."

"I'm working on it." The kid ran for the exit.

"Wait."

He stopped, looked back. "Yeah?"

Shepherd reached for his duffel bag, took out a pearl-handled pocketknife and a flat block of cedar wood. Extended them toward the kid.

"What's this?"

"Take up woodcarving." Shepherd nodded. "It helps."

To his surprise, the kid took the carving supplies. "You mean like whittling?"

"Make something with your hands. Get lost in the art."

The kid fingered the wood. "I ain't artistic."

"It doesn't matter. Make crappy art. You'll get better as you go along."

"You're giving me this?" The kid clutched the pocket-knife and cedar to his chest.

"I am."

"Why?"

Shepherd met the kid's eyes. "*Semper fi.*"

"Thanks." The kid smiled for the first time. Skittish, but real. Slipped the knife and wood into his back pocket.

"You're welcome." A lump of emotion clawed at Shepherd's throat. Someone else unhinged by war.

"Good luck, Gunny."

"You too."

Hand touching his back pocket, the private disappeared out the door.

"He's had a tough row to hoe," the receptionist murmured. "That was sweet of you."

"That's me." Shepherd's laugh was as skeptical as the kid's. "A regular Tootsie Roll."

"Well, Tootsie, it's your turn." She nodded toward the psychiatrist's office.

Feeling both amused and grim, Shepherd used the cane to leverage himself to his feet again. Winced at the fresh river of pain rolling over him. The shove hadn't helped. Tightened his jaw and straightened his spine as best he could. Tried not to groan.

Turned the doorknob, and stepped over the threshold into the doctor's office.

The small digital clock on the wall read 11:01.

Fifty-nine minutes to go.

The psychiatrist stood at the coffeepot. Shepherd had seen him twice a week since he'd gotten out of the rehab hospital in April. Dr. Fox was filling a ceramic cup that read, "World's Greatest Granddad."

He nodded in greeting. "Want a cup?"

Edgy enough without throwing caffeine into the mix, Shepherd raised a palm. Bobbled with the weight shift. "I'm good."

"You're off balance."

"Wow, you're observant."

The psychiatrist flinched and his mouth flattened. He carried the cup to the desk and sat down. Didn't comment on Shepherd's snarkiness. He studied him from behind wire-rimmed glasses that made him look a bit like a plump John Lennon in a buzz cut.

"How are the nightmares?" Dr. Fox asked, his tone bland, but his eyes keen.

Shepherd shrugged off the question. Water from a duck's back. The nightmares were a regular occurrence. In fact, he'd had one every single night since he'd come out of the coma. Nothing new.

"Insomnia?"

Bored, Shepherd gritted his teeth, moved his head half an inch. Yeah, he was lucky if he got four hours of solid sleep a night.

"The sleeping pills aren't helping?"

"When I take them."

Dr. Fox's face pinched, exasperated. "So take the pills. That's why I prescribed them. You need the rest."

How could he explain that he didn't deserve a good night's sleep? That he'd earned those nightmares fair and square?

He *needed* to suffer. Pain was a good thing. It reminded him that he was alive. Unlike the Marine who'd died because of him. Without the pain, he feared he'd slide into oblivion.

As if on cue, both his knee and his head throbbed.

"Please." The doctor waved at the couch. "Sit down before you fall down. You don't have anything to prove to me. I know that standing for too long hurts like hell."

Was he that transparent?

Shepherd swallowed back the sarcastic retort on the end of his tongue. Sank down on the couch. Dropped his duffel bag. He wasn't sure why he was feeling so jittery. Of course, he hated talk therapy, but today the layer of anger was fresher, meatier.

He had to leave the Marines. But somewhere, deep inside, was he grieving the loss of the only family structure he'd ever known?

"It doesn't hurt that much," Shepherd denied.

"You don't have to lie to me."

"Pain is relative."

"Scale of one to ten?"

"The Marine scale or the civilian scale?"

"You're about to become a civilian, let's go with that."

"Ten," Shepherd said.

"Shit, son. That's bad."

"But it's only a five on the Marine scale."

"Did you talk to your doctor?"

"What's the point? I'm not swallowing fists full of painkillers. Not with my family history."

"What are you doing to manage the pain?"

"Sucking it up. Whittling."

Dr. Fox cleared his throat. Shepherd transferred his gaze to the windowsill. Three potted plants sat withered and neglected. The leaves turning brown, stalks drooping. Unsettled, he glanced down at his boots. Noticed a frayed shoelace. Picked at it.

"Have you tried yoga?"

Shepherd snorted and tapped his knee with the cane. As if he could handle downward dog with a bum leg. "My ass looks fat in leotards."

Dr. Fox hooted. "Ah, good to see that the classic Mark Shepherd humor is still in there somewhere."

Once upon a time, he had been a funny guy. Known for his ironic sense of humor and willingness to pull a prank when people least expected it.

But last Christmas changed everything. He was no longer a joker. Not after the ambush at the Kandahar orphanage. Nothing was funny after that.

Fixated, the memory tumbled in on him. He blew out his breath, shook it off.

"Shepherd?"

"Huh?" He glanced around the room, orienting himself in the here and now. A grounding technique he'd learned in group therapy. A trick to stop obsessive thoughts. Noticing and naming things kept him in the

present moment. Drafty vent. Olive green desk. Mr.
Coffee machine. Paper cups. Wilted poinsettias on the
windowsill.

It bugged him that the flowers were bone-dry.

Thirsty.

Neglected.

Calling out for help.

Perturbed, Shepherd couldn't sit still. Leaving his
cane propped up against the chair, he limped across the
room to the sink. Took a paper cup from the dispenser
and filled it with water. Moved toward the sickly plants.

"What are you doing?"

He could feel the heat of Dr. Fox's gaze on his back.
The wiry muscle fibers beneath his shoulder blades
twitched, the way they did when he was being watched.
He focused his attention on those plants. Cupped the
wilting blooms between his fingers. Felt a sense of loss
curl up inside him like the drying leaves.

"Your plants are dying."

"Why do you care?"

Irritated, Shepherd turned his head and rammed his
gaze smack into the psychiatrist. Growled. "Because
I've seen enough damn death."

Fox toyed with his ink pen, straightened his tie. Jotted
something down. "Want to talk about that?"

"No."

"Why not?"

"Why should I?"

"This is our last session. Feel free to say anything
that's on your mind," Dr. Fox prodded. "I'm listening."

"I don't feel like talking."

"Sitting in silence works too."

Shepherd knew the ploy. Create an uncomfortable quiet, and people couldn't stand it. They gabbed. He wasn't falling for the ruse. "I could sit."

Dr. Fox steepled his fingers, leaned back in his chair.

Feeling obstinate, Shepherd settled onto the couch. Tightened his hand around his cane. He tried not to think about Clayton Luther. The man he'd left behind.

The wall clock ticked off the seconds. Two minutes. Five. Ten. There was still a good half hour left in his session.

Finally, Dr. Fox let out an audible breath. "What's your biggest fear about leaving the military?"

"I thought we were just going to sit."

Dr. Fox gave a nonchalant shrug. "I thought you'd start talking by now."

"Silence *is* golden."

"Are we going to sit here for another thirty minutes?"

"Fine by me." But it wasn't fine. Nothing was fine.

"What's the first thing you're going to do when you get out?" The psychiatrist took off his glasses. Plucked a polishing cloth from his front shirt pocket. Rubbed the lenses.

Weary, Shepherd didn't even bother shrugging. "I thought about going to see Luther's grave."

"And his family?" Dr. Fox put his glasses back on, peered at him, treading on uneven emotional ground.

At a loss, Shepherd glanced away, unable to hold the man's penetrating stare. He didn't know if he had the guts for that. He wanted to apologize to the family, but how did he even start that conversation?

"Maybe," Shepherd mumbled.

"I don't think that's a good idea."

"Why not?"

"It doesn't matter whether Luther's family forgives you or not," Dr. Fox said.

"No?" Shepherd heard the gravelly sarcasm in his voice, wasn't the least bit apologetic for it. Dr. Fox was acting as if he knew everything there was to know about him. In reality, the man was clueless.

"Until *you* can forgive you, you'll never find the redemption you're looking for. Start there and you won't need the Luthers' absolution."

Wretched, Shepherd bit his bottom lip so hard he tasted blood. "How can I forgive myself when their son is dead because of me?"

"Is that really true?"

"If I'd gone to the orphanage with Luther as he'd wanted to pass out toys, I would have recognized Talid. I could have neutralized the threat."

"You were following the rules."

"That doesn't make me feel any better." Shepherd ground his teeth.

"From what I've gathered, the whole thing was on Luther." Dr. Fox's voice lowered, and his eyes softened. "He was impulsive—"

"FUBAR." The vein at Shepherd's right temple ticked. "That's all there was to it. But *I* was in charge, and *I* allowed Luther to fall into enemy hands."

"You've got to stop punishing yourself for something that was beyond your control."

"But that's the thing. Luther's death *wasn't* beyond my control," Shepherd insisted.

Dr. Fox shifted. The casters on his chair squeaked. "What do you mean?"

"I left him." Shepherd bit his lip again, tasted the

metallic warmth. "No man left behind. That's what the Marines drill into you. *No. Man. Left. Behind.*"

"But you *did* go back for him," Dr. Fox reminded him. "That's why you'll walk with a limp for the rest of your life."

"Too late. I went back too late."

"What you did was heroic. Driving the rest of your men out of harm's way. While you were bleeding profusely after taking bullets to your head and knee . . . Superhuman. Cut yourself some slack."

Shepherd closed his eyes and managed to fight off the flashback nibbling at the edge of his brain. Chalk one up for months of cognitive behavioral therapy. The flashbacks were much fewer and further between.

"Or," Shepherd said, "here's a thought. I *could* have saved him by going with him."

"If you'd gone with him, you would have been breaking protocol."

"I can't stop thinking about how I could have stopped it." Shepherd rubbed a hand over his jaw, felt the prickle of beard growth scrape his palm. "If I hadn't been so hidebound. I should have trusted my gut."

"If you'd gone, you could have been the one dead in the desert."

"That would have been better than this."

"Are you feeling suicidal?" Dr. Fox's tone turned arid.

"No. Not really." Shepherd chuffed. "I don't get to have that luxury. I have to live . . . for Luther's sake."

Dr. Fox said nothing. The sound of his pen scratching across paper was the only noise in the room.

"Don't write down that I'm suicidal." Shepherd glowered. "I'm not."

"You've been through a lot. It's understandable if

such thoughts cross your mind," Dr. Fox murmured. "You almost died."

"Part of me did die." Shepherd dug his nails into his palm.

"Maybe it did," Dr. Fox said. "But now you have room to become someone new."

It was an impossible thought. A fresh start. And yet, it was enticing. The idea that what went down in Kandahar did not have to define the rest of his life.

"When was the last time you remember being happy?" Dr. Fox asked.

Where did headshrinkers come up with these stupid questions? What did it matter when he last felt happy? He was alive. That was enough. Happiness wasn't even on the table.

"Mark?" Dr. Fox called him by his first name.

When was the last time he felt happy? Hmm, easy one. Last Christmas Eve, before what went down at the orphanage.

The barracks had been ablaze with celebration, decorations, and laughter. Red tinsel strung the length of the hallway. Cheerful music played. Eggnog downed over sentimental toasts.

The mail from home had arrived. Presents for everyone, except Shepherd. He didn't mind. A long time ago, he'd gotten used to not having any family.

Clayton Luther had strolled up. Wearing a big grin and a string of battery-powered blinking lights strung around his neck like a lei. The smell of rum lingered on his breath, and he had a jaunty bounce to his step. He carried a big green tin wrapped with a gold ribbon. Sparkly glitter trailed in his wake.

"Gunny, Gunny, it came, it came."

The sappy look on the twenty-two-year-old man's face punched Shepherd in the gut. Had he ever been that young? That naïve? That hopeful?

"What came?"

"The Christmas cookies." The eager private slipped the bow off the tin and opened it to reveal a wide array of cookies.

Shepherd didn't like to admit it, but he had a ferocious sweet tooth. Which was why he rarely indulged in sugary treats. Once he got started, he had a hard time stopping.

"Back home, each year some of the local ladies get together. Bake up huge batches of cookies, and mail them off to the troops. It's tradition," Clayton Luther chattered.

"Nice."

Luther surged forward to give him a cookie. Stumbled over his own shoelaces, and almost dropped the tin. The kid had had too much to drink, but it was Christmas Eve.

"You *gotta* try this." Luther fished out an oatmeal cookie embellished with cranberries and macadamia nuts. "It's called a kismet cookie. My big sister, Naomi, made this batch . . ." He paused, hiccupped, laughed.

Shepherd held up a hand. "No thanks. I'm good."

"C'mon." Luther shoved the tin of cookies at him. "Pick one. They're special."

"Are they spiked with rum?"

"Nope, spiked with love." Luther received more gifts and letters from his hometown than anyone else in the unit.

"If they came from your family and friends, I have no doubt about that."

"No, no." Luther gave an exaggerated shake of his head. "You don't get it. Kismet cookies can foretell the future."

Shepherd burst out laughing. Ridiculous.

"I mean it." Luther's eyes widened. "If you sleep with a kismet cookie under your pillow on Christmas Eve, you will dream of your one true love."

"You're drunk."

"Irregardless," Luther slurred, and pointed a wavering finger. "It works. The first time I slept with the kismet cookie under my pillow, I dreamed of my 'Mantha. Now she's my wife and the mother of my three-year-old son."

"That's ludicrous. How can a cookie predict who you're going to marry?"

"I dunno." Luther shrugged. "But it happens all the time in my hometown of Twilight."

"Sounds suspect to me."

"Who knows?" Luther went on. "Could be that your heart already knows who you love, even if your mind doesn't. And if you sleep with the cookie under your pillow it triggers subconscious dreams. Does it matter? Have a cookie, Gunny. Hell, have two, one to eat, and one to put under your pillow. What could it hurt? Your love life is as stale as a Ritz cracker in a survivalist's underground bunker."

He didn't know why he was humoring Luther. Even on Christmas Eve, enough was enough. But the cookies smelled delicious. And the kid looked so earnest. Shepherd couldn't find his hard-ass gunnery sergeant frown.

Shaking his head, Shepherd took two cookies. "Happy now?"

Luther chuckled. "You're gonna love 'em, Gunny, I swear."

"I'm sure they're good."

"Have you given any more thought to my idea of going to the orphanage to hand out toys?" Luther asked.

"I've tapped everyone for a donation, and I've got the cookies and my comic books."

"It's against regulations."

"The brass doesn't have to know. C'mon, the orphanage is only three miles down the road. We'll be in and out in under an hour." His voice hitched. "I miss my boy, Gunny. Since I can't be with him . . . It only seems right to make some orphan kids' Christmas merry and bright."

"No."

Luther had hardened his jaw. Shepherd should have known right then that the private was going to defy orders and go anyway. Luther was as stubborn as the day was long.

"You're an asshole, you know that?"

"And you're insubordinate, but you're drunk and it's Christmas Eve, so I'm going to let it slide. *This* time. Go get some coffee and sober up," Shepherd commanded with kindness in his voice. Much as he hated to admit it, he had a soft spot for the kid. "And that's a direct order."

"See if I give you any more of my cookies." Luther staggered away, light lei blinking. The dumb kid had no idea it was his last night on earth.

Neither had Shepherd.

Shepherd had eaten one cookie, and it was delicious. Luther's proclamation hadn't been a drunken brag. In fact, the cookie was so good that Shepherd almost ate the second one.

But something stopped him. Against all common sense, Shepherd had slipped the cookie underneath his pillow.

That night, he had the most vivid, experiential dream of his life.

He was standing beside an emerald green river. It was at twilight, the golden rays of the setting sun casting lush purple rays over the darkening sky. A great calmness came over him. He took a deep breath, inhaled the damp evening air, and then . . .

He saw her.

She was standing on the opposite side of the river. Dressed in white, a shimmering dark-haired angel, shining so bright. For a moment, he thought he had died and she'd come to ferry him to the other side.

He stared. Flabbergasted.

The dream angel raised her head. Met his gaze. It was as if a lightning bolt jumped from her stark blue eyes straight into his heart.

He gasped, startled and electric.

She looked at him . . . *into* him. As if she could see the contents of his soul and found him pleasing. A big, all-encompassing smile wreathed her sweet round face.

Shepherd's pulse galloped, and it was hard to breathe. If his heart stopped in that moment, he would die a happy man.

He woke bathed in sweat, the image of her beauty filling him with joy. Hope imprinted on his brain, a shiny coil of possibility.

"Clayton Luther was a silly romantic," Shepherd blurted to Dr. Fox. He clenched his hands against his thighs. "He had no business in the Marines."

"Wow," the psychiatrist said, staring at Shepherd's wadded fists. "Where did that come from?"

Had he said that out loud? Shepherd forced his hands to relax. Tucked them under his armpits.

"Post-traumatic stress syndrome is an insidious thing," Dr. Fox said. "It can slip up on you when you least expect it. You'll need to continue therapy once you're back home. Where will you be living? I can recommend some doctors in your area."

Uneasy, Shepherd itched to avoid the question. He had no idea where he would end up. He wasn't going back to Lexington. Bad memories there. His plan had been to keep renting his room here in Bethesda until he figured things out.

"Give it to me straight, Doc. Am I ready for the outside world?" he asked, being flippant.

But the psychiatrist took him seriously. "Do you mean are you strong enough to function in civilian life?" Dr. Fox scratched his chin. "Yes, you are . . ."

"But?" Shepherd prompted when the psychiatrist didn't go on.

"Are you free enough from guilt and self-loathing to pursue healthy personal relationships?" Dr. Fox met his gaze head-on, and didn't blink. "I don't know. You've got a lot of work ahead of you. If you can't love, trust, and forgive yourself, how can you expect anyone else to?"

Shepherd grunted. Scornful.

"Promise me you'll continue therapy," Dr. Fox went on. "Group therapy in particular."

He hated group therapy. It was the worst. "Okay."

"I mean it. Promise me. I know you're a man of your word."

Shepherd exhaled. "I promise to go to group therapy."

Dr. Fox leaned back into his chair. "All right then. I'm confident enough about your recovery to give you this now."

"Give me what?"

The psychiatrist reached into the bottom drawer of his desk. Pulled out a white legal-sized envelope with

Shepherd's name scrawled across it. He recognized
Clayton Luther's handwriting, and his breath left his
lungs.

A letter from a dead man?

Dr. Fox passed him the envelope.

"From Luther?" He curled his fingers around the stiff
white paper.

"It is."

"When? How?"

"They found it among Clayton Luther's personal
effects."

A chill ran through Shepherd, and the hairs lifted on
the back of his neck. A premonition. Like the one he'd
had last Christmas at the orphanage. A premonition
he'd ignored.

At their peril.

"Why am I getting this now?" Shepherd fought to
keep emotion out of his voice, but he heard the hard
steel, felt the punch of anger low in his gut. "It's dated
last Christmas Eve."

Dr. Fox's expression remained unruffled. "You were
in such dire straits for months. The coma. The rehab.
The decision was made to wait until your discharge
before giving you the envelope."

His entire body went rigid. *The decision was made.*

That was the military for you. His choices removed.
Presumably, the letter had languished in Dr. Fox's desk
all this time.

His chest was a vise. Tightening, thickening, squeezing
down on his heart until he could hardly draw in air.

"Are you going to open it?" Dr. Fox prodded.

Was he? Should he? What could be in it?

Part of him wanted to chuck the letter in the trash and walk away. But the part of him that carried the burden of guilt could not. Most likely the letter was Luther requesting leave, or something equally banal.

Dr. Fox extended a letter opener toward him.

He stared at the long slender paper cutter. His initial irritation and disapproval gave way to a sudden upwelling of fear. Finally, he accepted the opener.

Shepherd slipped the blade underneath the sealed flap, cut it free. Took out the piece of white copier paper dated the previous December twenty-fourth. Read the typewritten note.

> *Gunny,*
> *If I don't make it out of Kandahar, please deliver this key to my family in person. They'll know what to do with it.*
>
> *—Luther*

Goose bumps spread up Shepherd's arms. *If I don't make it.* Had Luther had a premonition about his death? Stunned, Shepherd read the note again, gulped, and turned the envelope upside down.

A decorative white key, tied up with a red velvet Christmas ribbon, dropped into his upturned palm.

CHAPTER 2

December 2

The Teal Peacock, Twilight, Texas

"Hon, if I put another thing on top of that pile, you're not going to be able to see where you're going."

Undaunted, Naomi Luther dropped her shoulders. The subtle move lowered the boxes stacked in her arms about half an inch. She was a pro. For the past five years, she'd owned Perfect Fit, a personal-shopping business. She had this.

"Lookee," Naomi said. "If you take that last box out of the bag, there's enough room to slide it right on top of the others. And I'll be able to hold it all down with my chin."

The older woman behind the counter, Patsy Crouch, looked skeptical. "One false move and the whole shebang will come crashing down."

"I'll be fine," Naomi reassured her with a jovial grin. "Go ahead. Stock it to me."

"Stock instead of sock. Hehe. You are so funny." Patsy laughed. "It's amazing the way you've bounced back after—"

"Gotta keep my spirits up for Hunter." Naomi polished her smile, brightening its sheen. Hoping to head Patsy off at the pass. This Christmas *must* be a happy one. Which, granted, was hard to pull off when everyone in town kept recounting her family's sorrows.

"How are things with Robert?" Patsy asked.

Naomi pressed her lips together. She didn't want to get into her love life. Or lack thereof. "Robert and I are . . ."

What was her situation with her long-distance boyfriend? She wished she knew. When Robert took the job in Denver, they'd had an understanding. Robert would get his life and career in Colorado established and then she would join him and they'd get married. It wasn't an official engagement. Nothing formal. He'd not asked for her hand in marriage. But she'd planned on marrying him since she was a junior in high school. She had a hope chest and a wedding idea book stuffed with dreams.

But since last Christmas, everything had changed. And Naomi was no longer quite sure where she and Robert stood. She hadn't seen him in four months. They texted, but it was not daily. They'd both been so busy. Shocked, she realized they hadn't even talked on the phone in over a month.

"It's complicated," she said, as much to herself as to Patsy. "All my focus is on Hunter right now. It has to be."

"Does that mean he's free to date other people?"

That pulled her up short. She hadn't really thought about it. Robert hadn't mentioned wanting to see other people. Was he seeing other people?

"How about you?"

Naomi made a dismissive sound. "If I had time for dating I could fly to Denver every few weeks and reconnect with Robert."

"Robert's not coming around to the idea of you adopting Hunter, is he?" Patsy looked at her over the rim of the reading glasses perched on the end of her nose. "That's the real issue."

Patsy made a good point, but Naomi wasn't going to discuss that. She, her parents, and Hunter's other set of grandparents had decided together that Naomi should be the one to adopt Hunter since her mother's health was fragile and her parents were both over sixty and the other grandparents still had five other children of their own to raise. Robert hadn't understood, and asked why her parents and the other grandparents were trying to "saddle" her with her dead brother's baby.

They'd had a huge fight over it. He didn't get that adopting Hunter had been *her* idea, not her folks' nor the Woolys'. In fact, they'd tried to dissuade her, telling her they didn't want her to give up her life to raise her nephew. But Hunter was her everything.

Her relationship with Robert had not been the same since, even though he'd apologized, and they'd smoothed things over.

On the surface, anyway.

"I'm sure everything will work out the way it's supposed to." Patsy took the box out of the shopping bag she'd just put it in.

"Hopefully." Naomi felt unsettled by Patsy's questions because she didn't know the answers, and she hated not being in control.

"How's your mother?" Patsy's voice lowered, knitting a sympathetic tone.

Naomi flinched at the pity, but kept the smile pasted on her face. Nothing was going to get her down. The family had been steeped in sorrow long enough. Being happy didn't mean they didn't still grieve their losses. But if she'd learned anything, it was that life was short and you had to make the most of it.

And hey, in high school she hadn't been a cheerleader for nothing. Rah, rah, Twilight Tigers.

"Mom's good."

"I know this is a rough time of year for your family. The holidays—"

"We're fine." Naomi's smile stiffened, but she kept her voice loose. A flag flapping in the breeze. *Oh, say can you see, life is good, good, good.* "We're doing great. Honest."

"You've all suffered a huge loss." Patsy added the box to the Leaning Tower of Pisa in Naomi's arms. "It's okay to grieve. I—"

"Could you open the door for me, please? Thank you." Naomi locked her elbows to help brace the load. Mashed her chin against the top package. Squelched the sad feelings rising up inside her.

None of that, missy.

"How far to your van?" Patsy asked.

"It's in the shop. Transmission overhaul. It'll be out of commission all week." But she wasn't letting the inconvenience get her down.

"So how are you getting all this home?"

"Jana's swinging around to pick me up at the curb."

"You sure you don't need help getting the packages into Jana's Jeep?" Patsy folded the empty bag emblazoned with a teal peacock and stuck it back inside the drawer.

"Juggling packages is all part of the Christmas fun, right?"

Patsy hustled across the old wooden floor to open the door, moving fast for a woman in her late sixties. "Do mind your step, hon, and watch out for the workmen setting up Dickens."

During the first weekend in December, tourists flocked to Twilight, looking for fun at the annual Dickens on the Square festival. Normally, Naomi loved this time of year. But after last year's tragedies . . .

Stop. No unwanted thoughts. Come hell or high water, this was going to be the best Christmas ever. No excuses.

With the packages blocking her view, Naomi inched down the stairs of the Teal Peacock. Workmen were stringing electrical cords and wiring. Two crew members carried neon orange sawhorses. They were using them to block off the cross streets.

Dang it. Now, Jana wouldn't be able to drive through that way and pick her up. She'd have to wait on the curb with her unwieldy load while Jana circled around to the back of the building.

No worries, no worries. Smile. Life is good. Yes, her arms were screaming at her to put down the packages, but she could ignore the burn for a little longer.

Hurry, Jana, hurry.

It was okay. Achy arms weren't going to kill her, and it wasn't as if she didn't have a loving community to help. Things were so much better than they were a year ago. She counted her blessings. She was healthy. Her business was turning a profit. She had parents who loved her. She lived in the best small town in Texas.

And she had the sweetest little boy who was about to become her son. Who could ask for anything more?

"Thank you," she murmured skyward. "Thank you, thank you, thank you."

Jana's black Jeep Grand Cherokee pulled up to the curb. Whew! Nick of time. Relieved, Naomi headed toward the back of the Jeep.

"Here, here," said one of the workmen. "Let me help." The man stretched out long, reached for the handle, and flung the door open.

"Thank you." Naomi breathed, offered him a harried smile. Nice man. Helpful. She dumped the packages in the backseat and slammed the door. Heard her cell phone ding from the bottom of her purse.

She wanted to ignore it, but with Hunter in preschool, she didn't dare. Digging in her purse for the phone, she hopped into the passenger seat. Without looking around, she clicked on her seat belt.

The workman shut the door behind her. She nodded at him, waved.

"Hello," she said into the phone, but the caller had hung up. She pulled the phone from her ear to see who'd called.

Jana.

Huh? Why was Jana calling her when she was sitting right here in the car with her? She turned to her best friend.

But it was not Jana sitting in the driver's seat.

Rather, it was a man. A tall man. A handsome man. A complete stranger. And . . .

Sweet
Holy
Mother
of
baby
Jesus . . .

He bore an uncanny resemblance to the dark-haired man she'd dreamed of last Christmas Eve, when she'd slept with a kismet cookie under her pillow. Not that she believed in the legend.

And yet, here he was.

Believe me now? taunted the legend.

"Eeep!" Naomi cried, scrambling for the door handle to jump out.

But the seat belt yanked her backward, tightening down on her chest. Which he must have noticed. Because he was staring at her breasts with an amused expression on his gorgeous mug.

Feeling like a ginormous idiot for getting into the wrong vehicle, she blurted, "Who are you?"

"Better question," he said in a voice as deep and dark as the Brazos River at midnight. "Who are *you*?"

And where did you come from, butterfly? Mark Shepherd stared at the beautiful bundle of electricity in his Jeep.

The woman gaped at him, openmouthed, and he felt the earth shift in a fundamental way. He'd never believed in fate or fairy tales. Myths and legends were for movies and children's books. He was logical, practical, down-to-earth.

But here she was. The big-eyed, dark-haired angel he'd dreamed of last Christmas Eve. After he'd put Luther's cookie under his pillow, and woke up with a bunk full of crumbs.

Could he still be asleep?

Snoozing in the last motel where he'd stayed the night in the Fort Worth Stockyards. Right next to Billy Bob's Texas, the world's largest honky-tonk. Country music had kept him awake until two DIP I

That had to be it.

He was still asleep, and it wasn't yet dawn. He hadn't grabbed a mediocre omelet for breakfast at a Yelp-recommended diner. Or programmed his GPS to Twilight, Texas. Hadn't turned on a prerecorded NPR podcast of *Wait, Wait, Don't Tell Me.* Or stopped to fill up the gas tank, and refresh his coffee when he hit Highway 377.

He was still sleeping, and she was a figment of his imagination.

Except that her chest rose and fell with an extended inhale, and a hissing release of air. Would a dream breathe?

The sound of Christmas music blared from somewhere. An up-tempo version of "We Three Kings." Sung by an artist he didn't recognize. In front of him, a workman climbed a ladder with a staple gun and green garland rope draped over his shoulder.

She looked as stunned to be in his vehicle as he was to have her there. She was studying him like he was an ugly baby swan in a nest of cute yellow ducklings. Now she was cocking her head at an endearing tilt as if she'd decided it was okay.

Gorgeous.

Enrapt by her eyes, he felt time stretch before him. It was as if eons had passed since she'd climbed into his Jeep. But in reality, it had been less than a minute.

How was it possible that his dream angel existed in the flesh?

He thought about the white metal key tied with a red ribbon shoved into the pocket of his black denim jeans. The Christmas key that had sent him on a solemn mission. The key that had led him to this town.

To her.

It was a lot for a skeptical man to swallow. Fear, as strong as anything he'd ever felt on a battlefield, gripped him.

In the perfect stillness of his Jeep, in the middle of the road, surrounded by workmen with Christmas wreaths and orange neon sawhorses, Mark Shepherd experienced the unedited terror of a man who knew he'd met his destiny.

And had learned too late that there was no escape.

Her cell phone rang and she answered it on a voice that flew high and thin. "Oh, Jana, where are you?"

There was a pause and she nibbled her bottom lip. "I see. Don't worry. You take care. I'll find another way home." She switched off the phone, glanced over at him.

And Shepherd heard himself say, "Do you need a ride, butterfly?"

"Did you just call me butterfly?"

He stared at her lips like he was spellbound. "What? No."

"You did."

"Did I?"

She covered her mouth with her palm. The awestruck look in his eyes freaked her out a little. "Yes, you did. You called me butterfly."

"I sincerely apologize if I offended you. I did not mean to say that out loud."

"Doesn't matter if you said it out loud or not, you thought it."

"Clearly, it does matter. If I had kept my mouth shut, you wouldn't be getting bent out of shape."

"I'm not getting bent out of shape." She smiled to prove it, and lowered her voice. "I just want to know why you would call me butterfly. Do you think I'm frivolous?"

"I—"

"Impulsive?"

"Well, you *did* get into the wrong—"

"Do you think I'm shallow?"

He looked flummoxed. "I don't even know you."

"Exactly." She clasped her hands together, realizing she was being weird. "Then why would you call me butterfly?"

"Because butterflies make me happy."

"Oh." She straightened. Blinked.

"They're pretty and delicate and bright. In a world that's often ugly and heavy and dark."

Well, that was a nice thing to say. She would have thought him slick if he didn't look so sincere. "So, it's a compliment?"

"It is to me. But I don't want to assign my values to anyone." The sparkle in his eyes told her he was teasing.

"I see."

"The offer for a ride is still open."

She didn't know this guy, and she wasn't going to let him give her a ride home. Allow a complete stranger to know where she lived. Not even a man who'd had the starring role in her dreams last Christmas.

No way. Not when she had Hunter to think about. Fantasy dream men were one thing, reality quite another.

"Thank you for the offer," she said, sounding overly prim even to her own ears. "But I couldn't possibly impose."

"No imposition." His smile was a blanket, soft and cuddly, his dark eyes kind. But behind that warm curtain of thick lashes, she saw a haunted emptiness. Her breath caught, and her chest pinched.

Clipped short hair, as if he'd started growing out a buzz cut. His shoulders were straight and broad, his spine erect. His black boots were polished to a high sheen.

Military, she thought. Sudden grief ambushed her in a hot, abrupt wave. She closed her eyes, exhaled. *Don't think about Clayton right now.*

She put her brother's memory in a box. Locked it up tight. Hid the key. Opened her eyes.

"Are you all right?" he asked.

"Fine," she said, forcing a rah-rah smile and unbuckling her seat belt. "I'm so sorry to have troubled you."

"No trouble."

She opened the door and tumbled from his Jeep. Turned to open the back door and retrieve her packages, but he was already getting out of the driver's seat.

"I don't need any help," she called, fumbling packages. Dropped three on the ground. "You can stay in your car."

She tucked several packages into the crook of her left arm. Squatted to retrieve the ones that had fallen onto the ground.

At the back of the Jeep, she spied a desert camouflage–colored cane. She glanced up. Handsome Dream Man limped toward her. Definitely military.

He squatted beside her.

"I've got this," she said.

They reached for a package at the same time. His big hand slid over the top of her small one.

Zing!

A current of awareness jolted through her. Sent tingles pulsating up her arm to her shoulder, and then to her heart. All the air escaped her body. Leaving her breathless and dizzy.

The pads of his fingertips, touching the back of her hand, were rough with calluses.

His energy lodged there. Poured into her. Throbbed. Full and heavy.

It was weird. Unexpected and hot.

I touched him. He touched me. We touched each other, she thought, and her heart floated into the clouds.

He was so close that she caught his scent. His aftershave was lovely. A delightful mix of cedar and basil, with soothing undertones of bergamot. Her nose twitched, eager to inhale more and absorb his intoxicating fragrance.

They both let go at the same time, and the package dropped back to the ground.

In unison, their gazes met and they laughed.

"I guess I'm more in the way than helpful," he said, and shifted his weight away from her. Grabbed the cane. Withdrew his warmth. The tingling faded away like the last note of a wistful song.

She scooped up the scattered packages. Rose to her feet. But she lost her grip, and all the packages fell topsy-turvy.

"Dang it," she muttered.

"You're trying to do too much. How about this. You pick up half of the packages, and I'll pick up half."

She almost questioned his ability to juggle both the packages and his cane. But her mother was in a wheelchair. Naomi understood the inherent clash between fierce pride and the urge to help.

Tread lightly.

She didn't want to dismiss his capabilities. Then again, she didn't want him to fall and break something.

He didn't wait for her approval. He'd already grabbed half the packages and was standing up. Rather adroitly, by the way, for a man with a cane.

Ha. She should be so adept. Her own knees were wobbling. She didn't know if it was from the wind that had just gusted around the Jeep or the presence of this man. But tremble she did.

He sized her up. "There's no way I can leave you on the curb with all this. Please, let me give you a ride."

"No, no," she chirped. She was both captivated and terrified. He was so handsome that she couldn't even look at him. The attraction was too much. *He* was too much. This was utterly crazy.

Robert, remember Robert.

Um, for the life of her she couldn't conjure up Robert's face.

"I get it," he said. "You don't know me from a hole in the ground—"

She laughed then, because that was a phrase her father used.

His eyes widened and his face brightened, and he said in a voice rich with sincerity, "You have the best laugh. I could hear a laugh like that for the rest of my life and die a happy man."

Their gazes met again.

Her heart skipped a beat. In that flicker of a moment, she felt a solid click. It was as if she didn't know the universe had been spinning off course, but one look into his brown eyes, and her world settled into its rightful groove.

Snap. Clack.

She let out a soft gasp.

He looked startled. The eternal timelessness evaporated. And she was back to normal. Feeling uncomfortable and awkward.

"Wow," he said. "That came out cheesier than I intended."

"It was a sweet thing to say."

It seemed as if he might say something else, but instead he buttoned up his lip and lowered his eyelids. Retreating.

Good. He was overwhelming.

She did not like overwhelming. Dad said it was because she had a knack for tuning into other people's emotions. Her quirky, mystical best friend, Jana, claimed Naomi was a natural empath. But she didn't know about any of that.

"Where do you want me to put the packages?" He glanced around.

Naomi had no idea what to do with the packages. She could call her father. But he had gone to the hospice center to pray for a longtime parishioner, Dotty Mae Densmore.

There was no Uber in Twilight, or even taxis for that matter. Just Jana's car service and medical transports.

"I do not mind giving you a ride," he said.

She hesitated. Torn between the ease of accepting his offer, and the inherent risk.

A horn honked.

They both turned to look.

An identical black Jeep pulled up behind his. A colorfully pierced and tattooed woman with dreadlocks waved from behind the steering wheel. Jana!

Her friend put the window down, called out, "Sorry I'm late. Got hung up with a client."

"Problem solved," Naomi told her dream man. "But thank you for your offer. See you around?"

"Not likely," he said. "I'm only in town for the day."

"That's too bad," she said, and meant it.

"You're the first stranger to ever jump into my Jeep by accident. What a happy mistake." His eyes danced with amusement. She had the distinct impression his happiness was a rare occurrence.

Jana parked her Jeep and got out. Came around to where they were standing.

He helped them transfer Naomi's packages to Jana's Jeep. Naomi explained her faux pas, mistaking his Jeep for hers.

"Fate's a strange thing," Jana said, sounding mysterious and cryptic. "You never know what she's going to dish up."

Once the boxes were all in Jana's vehicle, Naomi turned to thank him again. Tried not to think about fate and kismet cookies and Christmas Eve dreams.

"Good-bye," he said, and shook her hand one more time. "It's been a pleasure."

"Same here," she said, a melancholy sigh creeping up her throat. She'd just met him and he was leaving. But that was for the best. Her life was far too complicated. "Enjoy your stay in Twilight."

It was only after he'd gone that Naomi realized she'd forgotten to ask his name.

CHAPTER 3

Meeting the cheerful brunette threw Shepherd off his game.

It was as if by passing the "Welcome to Twilight" sign, he'd dropped into a portal to a different dimension. A place where it was possible for a man to dream of a soul mate, and have her materialize.

In those few minutes he'd been with her, he'd forgotten about war and suffering. Forgotten about mysterious Christmas keys, and Clayton Luther's death. Forgotten he was a battle-scarred warrior on a somber mission.

All he could think of was her blue eyes and the soft shape of her pink mouth, her round cheeks and sweet scent. A scent that reminded him of tiny purple flowers, rich vanilla beans, and happiness.

For that small window of time, he'd felt normal again. And he couldn't help wanting more. She hadn't been wearing a wedding or engagement ring, but that didn't mean she wasn't taken.

Forget it. Even if there were such things as soul mates, and she happened to be his, she deserved far better than the likes of him.

Soul mates? Gunny, you've lost your mind.

Shepherd had one purpose for being in Twilight. Visit Luther's family. Give them his condolences, and the key. Then be on his way.

To where?

Ambivalent, Shepherd shrugged. He hadn't figured that part out yet.

He drove through town. The whole place could have come from a made-for-TV movie. Charming. Quaint. Quirky. He cruised past a park into the center square surrounded by historical Old West–style buildings and old-fashioned lampposts. As he took a turn leading back to the outskirts, he saw a shimmering blue lake with sailboats bobbing on the waves even in December, white sails whipping in the breeze. Four houseboats sat moored in the marina.

The friendly waters called to him, inviting him to stay awhile.

He followed the GPS guidance down Ruby Street to the west side of town. Here, the houses were older. Craftsman bungalows. Sprawling Victorians. Tin-roofed farm-style houses. Was this place for real, with its picket fences, scrolled gates, and wide verandas? Almost all had holiday decorations in the yard. Nativity scenes. Rooftop Santas. North Pole workshops. Inflatable reindeer. The Grinch. Snoopy wearing a jaunty stocking cap.

Passing the First Presbyterian Church of Twilight, he felt his chest tighten. According to military records, Clayton Luther's father was the church pastor. The building was picturesque, and white. Tall, slender steeple. Built long on a short lot. Over a hundred years ago from the look of the architecture.

It had been years since Shepherd had been in a church. The last time he remembered going was with one of his foster families. For the sake of his soul, they'd insisted on baptism. They'd dunked him in the water for no discernible reason that a twelve-year-old could parse out. Held under far longer than was necessary by an overly enthusiastic preacher.

The church parking lot was empty, so he didn't stop. Instead he pulled into the driveway of a green Victorian two doors down.

Picket fence. Check. Nativity scene. Check. Christmas lights dangling from the eaves. Check. Predictable, considering how naïve and trusting Clayton Luther had been. The kid had grown up in a home full of hope and joy. He'd had no business in war.

Then again, who did?

Shepherd snorted past the sentimental feelings. He parked the Jeep and got out. His pulse rate kicked up, and his stomach flipped over. He shouldn't have stopped for that second cup of coffee.

Fallen leaves lay scattered across the lawn. A couple of the wet leaves wrapped around baby Jesus's cradle. He didn't know why he did it. To stall the inevitable? He limped across the yard. Removed the leaves from the cradle. Crumpled them into a damp ball and stuffed them into his pocket where he felt . . .

The key.

It was burning a hole in his pocket. The mystery intrigued him. What did the key open? What did it mean? Why was it so important to Clayton? These questions had circled his mind ever since Dr. Fox had given him the envelope.

Especially late at night when he couldn't sleep.

He swallowed, let go of the leaves, and wrapped his fingers around the key. How was he going to start this conversation? *Hello, Mr. and Mrs. Luther, you don't know me, but I'm the reason your son is dead.*

Dr. Fox's words blistered in his head. *It's not your fault.*

No? Then why did he feel so guilty?

Maybe this visit, hard as it might be, would ease his self-reproach. And he could let this go. Move forward. Maybe. It was a glimmer of hope in a year that had been pretty hopeless.

Shepherd eased up the steps to the wraparound porch. The weathered wood creaked underneath his weight. The front door, painted red and trimmed in white, welcomed visitors. Lace curtains hung in the window beside the door.

There was no doorbell. Only an iron door knocker. He lifted the knocker, and tapped it against the door. *Rap-tap-tap.*

Waited.

No answer.

In the backyard of the house next door, a dog barked at him, *yip, yip, yip.* He imagined this was the kind of place where neighbors were all up in your business.

He knocked again.

Nothing.

Shepherd dragged a palm down his face. Apparently, no one was home. He shouldn't be surprised. It *was* the middle of the morning.

Maybe the pastor was at the church. He returned to the church. Killed the Jeep. Sat listening to the engine tick as it cooled. The woman's delicate fragrance lingered in the air. He felt wistful and sad and then oddly hopeful again.

A few minutes later, he got out and walked the church grounds. Breathed, using the 4–7–8 pattern they'd taught him in therapy. A four-part inhale. Hold his breath to the count of seven. Followed by an eight-second exhale. Much as he didn't want to admit it, the pattern did calm his swift pulse and loosen his stiff chest muscles. It was a godsend when he was in the throes of PTSS symptoms.

Maybe he would take Dr. Fox's advice and sign up for a yoga class. He'd heard that yoga was as much about learning how to breathe as it was striking a pose.

Quieted, he rounded the side of the church and came upon a small cemetery.

Drawn by a morbid sense of curiosity, Shepherd pushed open the black wrought-iron gate. The rusty hinges creaked in greeting.

He wandered the perimeter.

Most of the graves were those of people who'd died during the settling of North Central Texas. But at the far corner of the square plot, Shepherd spied newer tombstones.

Fresh. White. Stark.

His blood chilled.

His heart wasn't in this. His head told him to go back to the Jeep. But his feet beelined straight for the new graves.

Two white marble markers side by side. Even before he got close enough to read them, he knew that one belonged to Clayton Luther.

He limped closer. The pulse at the hollow of his throat jumped hard. His boots bogged in the damp earth.

Shepherd stopped, overwhelmed.

Read the name on the tombstone.

Sure enough, here were the remains of the naïve American kid who'd died far too young in Kandahar. Breaking all the rules and getting himself killed just to brighten some orphan's day.

A hard shake of grief grabbed hold of Shepherd in sharp, jagged teeth. His vision dimmed and his chest squeezed.

He dropped to his knees beside Luther's grave. Ignored the burst of pain shooting through his bad leg. Tucked his chin to his chest and bit down on the inside of his cheek. Tasted salt and blood.

"I'm sorry, I'm sorry," he mumbled. "So damn sorry."

A crow cawed overhead. An acorn dropped from a nearby oak. It hit the fence and skittered off into the grass beyond the cemetery. He raised his head, peered at the tombstone next to Luther's. Realized the markers were almost identical.

Blinking, he read:

Samantha Wooly Luther, beloved wife of Clayton, devoted mother to Hunter.

Stunned, Shepherd stared at the engraving on the tombstone. The letters and numbers started to blur. Unshed tears filled his throat. How was it possible that Clayton's young wife had died seven days after her husband?

Inconceivable.

His heart stuttered, fear jamming up his arteries, until he couldn't breathe.

Life was damn unfair.

Grief and guilt mingled together. What had Samantha Luther died of? And what had happened to Clayton and Samantha's son?

The ache inside him was unbearable. He tried the 4–7–8 breathing. It didn't work. He couldn't stop thinking about Clayton and Samantha, and how he'd ruined their lives.

Kids. Just kids, the both of them.

He dropped his head into his hands. Wanted to weep. Couldn't.

A loud crack of a twig breaking snapped him alert.

He jumped up and spun around as fast as his bum knee would allow. Lurching and grabbing for his cane.

And came face-to-face with a man who looked the way Clayton Luther would have looked in thirty years if he had lived.

"There you are," the elder Mr. Luther said, as if he'd just been waiting for Shepherd to appear.

Pushing against the ground with his cane, Shepherd straightened his spine. The cane's tip sank into the moist earth, and he lost his balance. Would have toppled if Mr. Luther hadn't grabbed his elbow.

The older man's eyes were gentle and kind. He didn't mention the cane or Shepherd's unsteadiness. Just held him up.

Heat burned Shepherd's throat. He hated looking weak. He stepped away from Mr. Luther and his helpful grip.

"Glad you finally made it," Clayton's father said.

Huh? Had Dr. Fox called ahead and told the Luthers that Shepherd was coming? What had he said?

"Don't worry about being late. Everything happens in divine timing."

Shepherd eyed him. Late? For what? Something was going on here. Cautiously, he waited, saying nothing.

"But where are my manners? Let me introduce myself." He stuck out his hand. "I'm Pastor Tom Luther."

"Mark Shepherd," he said, shaking the other man's hand.

He studied Tom's face to see if the older man recognized his name. He had no idea if the military had mentioned him when they'd told the Luthers what had happened to Clayton. Most likely not. The military stance on dissemination of wartime information was to reveal as little as possible. But Clayton might have written to his family about their friendship. Had he?

Tom's expression didn't change one whit. His smile stayed warm, still welcoming. "I am glad you're here. Joe told me you were the best handyman he ever met."

Shepherd frowned. "Joe?"

"Joe also said that you were modest, but there's no need in hiding your light under a bushel, son."

Son.

The word was a dagger straight to Shepherd's heart. "Sir, there's been—"

"Happy to have you."

Obviously, the man had him confused with someone else. "Mr. Luther, I'm not—"

"Whole," Tom Luther said, nodding at Shepherd's cane. "That's okay. We all have our difficulties. You come highly recommended, and I'm sure you'll do a great job despite your challenges. Heck, I imagine you'll work harder because of them."

What was going on here? "A mistake's—"

"Follow me," Tom said. "I'll let you see what you're up against."

"Mr. Luther." Shepherd braced his cane against the sidewalk. "I'm not who you think I am."

"I'm not here to judge you," Tom said. "You're welcome just as you are."

"But—"

"Please." Tom held up both hands. "You have nothing to explain. You owe me nothing. Whatever is troubling you belongs between you and the Lord."

"I'm not—"

The pastor clapped his hands in a gesture so startling that Shepherd lurched backward. "You showed up. That's all I need to know. God's divine timing. Remember? You're right where you're supposed to be. Doing exactly what you're supposed to be doing. Believe it. I do."

Tom beamed at him. "Now . . . this way."

Bewildered, Shepherd tottered after the pastor. His knee throbbed from kneeling on the damp ground beside Clayton's grave. He glanced back at the twin tombstones, felt his stomach lurch.

Pastor Tom tracked his gaze. He stopped. His smile faded, and his gray eyes misted. "That was my boy."

Shepherd gulped, nodded, cut into pieces by the pain in Tom's eyes.

"We lost him last year. He was military." Tom scrutinized Shepherd. "Like you."

Shepherd got that same weird feeling he had when the pretty brunette had jumped into his Jeep. Like he'd fallen through a portal to another dimension and ended up in the Twilight Zone.

Landed in a place where people believed in crazy things. Like divine timing and cookies that could predict soul mates.

"How do you know I'm military?" Shepherd asked.

"The haircut. Your bearing. Plus, I must confess, Joe told me. That's why I'm so glad you showed up."

"Because I'm military?"

An enigmatic expression crossed Tom's face. "Among other things."

Shepherd wanted to ask, *What other things?* But Tom Luther was still looking at the graves.

"Losing Clayton was hard enough." The senior Luther blinked. "But when Samantha took her own life . . ." He pressed his lips together. "It was almost too much for us to bear."

"She committed suicide?"

Tom put a hand to his mouth.

"How *did* you bear it?" Shepherd whispered.

"God got us through." Tom pushed his hands into the depths of his pockets. "And of course, we had the boy to think of. That little ray of sunshine is the reason I'm still standing."

Shepherd stared at Samantha's tombstone. Thought about a young woman so heartbroken over losing her husband that she might have taken her own life. Left her small boy behind.

"She took too many of the sedatives the doctor prescribed to get her through the funeral." The older man's voice broke. "I like to think it was more accidental than intentional. Otherwise why didn't she make provisions for her baby if she meant to do it?"

"I . . . I . . ." Shepherd had no words. He clamped his mouth shut.

The news was a blow. Clayton's death wasn't the only one weighing on his conscience. Now he had to add Samantha Luther to the list.

And their little boy.

And Clayton's parents.

All permanently wounded because Shepherd had made an error in judgment.

Shepherd and the pastor inhaled simultaneously. It was a tandem sound of sorrow. Sharp and deep in the quiet morning.

He couldn't let this case of mistaken identity continue. He had to come clean. Absorb the hatred he knew he would see in the older man's eyes when he realized who Shepherd was. "Sir, this is important. I have something to tell you."

"Come along." Tom motioned with a crook of his finger. "Let's see the church first. Let me show you what work needs doing. Then we can talk."

Shepherd wasn't sure why he followed. Why he didn't blurt out who he was right then and there. Maybe it was Tom Luther's kindness. Or maybe it was because he was searching for a gentler way to break the news to a grieving father. Or maybe the honest reason he kept his mouth shut?

He needed a place to be for the holidays, and Tom Luther was offering it to him.

But only if he pretended to be their handyman. No, he couldn't do that. Shepherd might be a lot of things, but he wasn't a liar.

Tom stopped underneath the eaves of the back porch. Glanced up at the weathered, weakened wood of the overhang. The entire exterior paint job was peeling. Carpenter ants tracked inside the cracks between boards where the caulking had eroded.

"The wooden awning needs replacing before it falls in on someone," Tom fretted, furrowing his brow and running a palm along his jaw. "Clayton used to do these repairs for the church. But now that he's gone . . ." Tom cleared his throat, his Adam's apple bobbing as if he were gulping back a lump of tears. "I do what I can, but

I'm no spring chicken. But that's why you're here, isn't it? To fix things."

Fix things.

That phrase resonated, plucking a chord deep within Shepherd's chest. He could never make amends for leaving Clayton behind, but he could fix an overhang. He was good with his hands. Had aced woodworking in high school. Whittled as a hobby. He didn't mind physical labor. Even with his bum knee, it shouldn't take him more than a couple of weeks to repair the awning, do the caulking, and repaint the church.

Here was a plan. He could be their handyman, do the work, and confess after Christmas. When he thought about it, helping out was the least he could do for the loss of the man's son. He didn't expect forgiveness anyway.

"This way." Tom opened the back door. "I'll show you the rest of the work that needs doing and then you can get started tomorrow. You've had a long journey."

He had.

Tom paused at the threshold, looked back at him. "I can't tell you how happy I am that you're here."

Fresh remorse rolled through Shepherd. He almost confessed then.

But the older man was bending over to show him baseboards that were pulling away from the wall. More cracks that needed caulking. Burned-out lightbulbs. Unbalanced ceiling fans.

"And if you could erect the nativity scene this weekend, I would be so grateful." Tom Luther ran a hand through his thick silver mane. "I have a longtime parishioner in hospice and she needs my full attention these last few days. I don't have the time, and my wife is pretty much confined to a wheelchair."

"I'm sorry to hear that," Shepherd said, because it seemed the right thing to say. He was lousy at comforting people.

"My daughter was going to put up the manger, but she's got her hands full with our grandson. That little rascal keeps her on her toes." Tom chuckled.

"Sure thing." Shepherd nodded, getting sucked in.

Was he really doing this? Was it smart? Shepherd placed a palm to the nape of his neck, his conscience warring. On the one hand, he shouldn't deceive the Luthers, but couldn't this be a small way to start making amends?

And what happened when the real handyman showed up? What then?

"You'll get a small stipend for your breakfast and lunch on top of your salary," Tom said. "But you'll take your dinners with my family and me. We live in the green Victorian two doors down."

Yes, Shepherd already knew that.

"Well." Tom dusted his palms together. "I'll let you look around. Tools are in the barn at the back of the property. You'll find everything you need in there. Dinner is at six sharp." His face brightened. "We're having pot roast tonight. My favorite. You'll love it. My daughter is a wonderful cook."

"I'm sure she is," Shepherd mumbled, because he didn't know what else to say, and just like that, he'd committed.

CHAPTER 4

"Yoo-hoo, anybody home?"

Naomi was in the kitchen, cutting up potatoes for dinner. From her vantage point, she could see her mother in her wheelchair in the breakfast nook. Mom was plucking dried leaves from the Benjamin ficus. The poor plant had gone into shock.

Two days ago, Hunter had decided to whack it with his toy plastic hammer. At the kitchen table, the boy colored in a Pokémon coloring book. He was humming and swinging his legs against the stool.

"Terri," her mother called to their neighbor poking her head in the front door. "Come on in here."

Raven-haired Terri Longoria strolled into the room. She carried a covered pie pan and wore a satisfied smile. Terri owned Hot Legs Gym and it showed. Tanned. Toned. Well muscled. She was still trim in her late forties. Her husband was the chief of staff at Twilight General Hospital. And they had a fourteen-year-old son, Gerald. Gerald was the talk of the town, praised for his talent in junior varsity football. A decade ago, Terri had appeared on a reality show called *Fear Nothing*. She'd gamely downed a bucket of earthworms to win ten thousand dollars. The stunt had earned her admiration from the town's teenage boys, which she had to this day, but she did endure a lot of earthworm jokes.

She was also on the First Love Cookie Club's charity ball committee with Naomi.

"I had some pumpkins from my fall garden that I needed to use up," Terri said. "I spent the day baking pies. Brought one over for you."

"Oh, thank you, Terri. You do know pumpkin is my favorite." With a gnarled fist, Mom pushed the controls on her electric wheelchair and propelled herself into the kitchen.

"How sweet of you." Naomi took the pie and set it on the counter. She was grateful for the dessert. She hadn't had time to bake or pick something up from the store. She knew how blessed she was to have such good neighbors, and said a silent prayer. *Thank you.*

As Dad liked to say, divine timing.

Naomi put the potatoes in a Dutch oven, added enough salted water to cover the spuds, and put them on the stove to boil.

"You are so welcome," Terri said. "I just wanted to drop off the pie and let you know everything is shipshape on the dance committee. If this event goes as well as planned, the club members want to make the ball an annual Christmas tradition."

"I just want to get through this party," Naomi admitted.

"One day at a time," Terri said.

Yes. That had been her motto for the past year.

"Don't worry. I know the ball is going to be a huge success with you at the helm. How could it not? You're such a planner. Y'all enjoy the pie." Terri wriggled her fingers. "Toodle-oo."

Once Terri had gone, Mom wheeled around to Naomi. "That was nice of her to bring us a pie."

"We are blessed to have such good neighbors."

"I know." Mom bowed her head. "I don't know how we would have gotten through this past year without them."

Naomi looked at her.

Tears streamed down her mother's face.

She steeled herself, and sank to her knees beside the wheelchair. Wrapped her arms around her mom and squeezed her tight.

She couldn't think of words to ease her pain. She couldn't begin to imagine what it was like to lose a child. Two children, if you counted Samantha as theirs. Which they had. It was horrible enough losing a brother and a sister-in-law.

"We have to put on a brave face for Hunter," she whispered in her mother's ear. The little boy had been the only thing that had pulled their family out of shock and depression.

"You're right." Mom tugged a tissue from her pocket, dabbed her eyes.

Naomi leaned over to get Hunter in her line of sight. The boy was no longer in his chair at the table, but rather he squatted on the floor, coloring on the wall.

Oh no! Sometimes she felt so helpless at the mothering thing.

"Honey, honey." She hopped to her feet and sprang over to the four-year-old.

Hunter tilted his dear face. He looked so much like his daddy that it wrenched Naomi's heart. He grinned as if to say, *Aren't I a great artist?*

She plopped down on the floor beside him. "That is

such a pretty picture, Hunter, but instead of coloring on MeeMaw's wall, let's use the coloring book. Okay?"

"Okay." Hunter bobbed his little blond head, stuck the crayon in his mouth, and started chewing.

She eased the crayon from his hand. Was his habit of chewing nonedible things normal childhood development? Or was it anxiety from losing his parents? She tried her best to create a calm, loving environment. But nothing could make up for not having a father and mother.

"Why don't we eat some string cheese instead?" She fished a chunk of blue crayon off his bottom tooth. Later, she'd clean the crayon marks off the wall.

"String cheese." Hunter jumped up and ran to the refrigerator, his socked feet padding against the tile.

He yanked the door open so hard a jar of homemade bread-and-butter pickles fell off the shelf. The jar shattered against the floor, surrounding the little boy in broken glass and sticky juice.

At the same moment, the potatoes on the stove boiled over. Hissing hot water onto the burner and dousing the gas flame.

"Hunter," Naomi commanded, a little harsher than she intended. She was terrified he might cut himself on the glass. "Do *not* move."

At the sound of her stern tone, her nephew burst into tears.

"I'll get him," her mother volunteered, hitting the controls on her wheelchair.

"No, Mom, your wheels will track the glass and pickle juice."

"I'm just trying to help." Her mother sounded hurt.

"I know, I know." Oh Lord. She was stomping on everyone's feelings without meaning to.

Naomi zipped to the stove and switched off the gas. Zoomed over to where little Hunter had turned into a sobbing statue, gazing at the lake of pickle juice. Picking her way around the sticky liquid and glass shards, she leaned forward to pluck him up and plunked him down onto her hip.

"You are such a good boy," she said, and kissed his head.

"I brokeded the pickles." Tears tracked down his round cheeks.

"It's okay, it's okay."

The refrigerator door was still hanging open. With her free hand, she grabbed a package of string cheese from the dairy compartment. Bumped the door closed with her knee and made her way back to the kitchen table. Settled Hunter into a chair and mollified him with the cheese.

"You make that look easy," her mother said.

"Hardly." Naomi snorted, returned to the mess. Sank her hands on her hips as she tried to figure out how best to tackle it.

"How can I help?" her mother asked.

"Keep an eye on the wee one." Naomi turned the fire back on under the potatoes, gathered up paper towels and a trash can, and went to work.

She picked up the glass first. Luckily, it had broken into big chunks, and she threw those away. She was elbow deep in sopping up pickle juice when the back door opened. She heard the sound of boots scraping against the welcome mat.

Oh dear, it was almost six and she was nowhere near ready to put dinner on the table.

"There's a hack for that," a deep male voice said.

"What?" Naomi looked up.

It was the man from the Jeep. Standing in her parents' kitchen staring down at her.

All the air left her lungs. Every nerve ending in her body roared to life. Sang. Spun. Electric. A fire station of heat.

He met her gaze. His dark eyes mysterious. The set to his mouth amused and intrigued. He wore the same brown leather jacket and black jeans he'd had on earlier. Same red plaid flannel shirt that stretched so nicely over his broad chest.

Dumbfounded, Naomi couldn't look away. Didn't *want* to look away. It was as if the two of them had teleported to a whole other planet. Nothing around them. No one else in the room.

The air crackled from the energy that surged from him to her, and back again.

"And what hack is that?" she asked, amused and lured in, oddly anxious to hear him speak again. She wanted to luxuriate in the sound of his sexy voice. Which was not like her. Not at all.

"Baking soda."

"Um, okay."

"I'm serious." His smile was like a light coming in underneath the door of a dark room, full of hope and relief from an endless night. "Got any? I'll show you."

They kept a box of baking soda in the fridge to absorb odors. Naomi cracked open the fridge, grabbed the orange box of baking soda, and handed it to him.

Their fingertips touched.

The briefest of brushings. But that same electrical impulse passed through her again. The one that had shot up her arm and into her heart when he touched her fingers on the package she'd dropped.

She stared at him.

In a blur of inexplicable white light, she saw him as she had in her kismet cookie dream. Standing before her, wearing a Marine uniform.

Her jaw unhinged. Her heart was an elevator. Plummeting to the ground. Hitting. Splitting. Breaking open.

What *was* this feeling? Her hand was trembling, and she stuffed it into her armpit so he wouldn't see.

"Naomi?"

Someone said her name. Not the stranger, though. He was still staring at her, eyes narrowed, lips thinning out.

"Naomi?" her father repeated.

She blushed, half expecting to wake up in bed. Hoping that she would wake up to discover the past terrible year was nothing but a dream. That Clayton and Samantha were both still alive and they were all a happy, intact family.

Wake up to learn that she and her parents hadn't had to sit Hunter down and try to explain as best they could to a three-year-old boy why he would never see his mommy and daddy again.

The memory of that awful time was burned into her brain. Hunter had cried for his mommy every night for weeks, even as Naomi and her parents promised him they would always love him and care for him. No matter what.

Somehow, they'd all made it through.

She inhaled, pulling herself back to the crush of reality.

"This is Mark Shepherd," her father said. "He's our new handyman."

"Oh," Naomi said, and then, because she didn't have time to process what that meant, she said again, "Oh."

"You can call me Shepherd." His smile was a cushion, as if he understood her confusion. "All my friends do."

Was he telling Naomi that he considered her a friend?

Aww shucks, said a recalcitrant part of her brain. *Friend-zoned*.

Shocked by her silly, wayward thoughts, she stepped back. Embarrassment flamed her cheeks hot. Why was her mind misbehaving? She was already in a relationship.

Sort of.

Shepherd was smiling at her, his eyes tender and gentle. An easy, open smile that belied the severity of his clipped haircut and the regimented way he moved. Erect spine. Stiff shoulders. Even with the limp, he exuded a regal bearing.

Her pulse leapfrogged, took off. She felt dizzy. Thrown, she jammed one hand in her pocket, waved the other at the spilled juice and the baking soda in his hand. "Have at it."

He sprinkled baking soda over the floor, and it absorbed the juice. "Broom?" He raised one inquisitive eyebrow. "Dustpan?"

Naomi stepped over the carpet of baking soda drying into a paste. Snagged a broom and dustpan from the closet in the mudroom. Brought it back to him. Stood closer than she should have. Wished she could back up but didn't know how without being obvious. She couldn't let him know how much he threw her for a loop.

She didn't like feeling so out of control.

With smooth, efficient movements, Shepherd bent over and swept up the crumbly powder, whisking it into the dustpan. Mesmerized, she watched. Fascinated by the veins on the backs of his hands. The thickness of his wrists. The length of his long fingers.

"The paste picks up any lingering broken glass too," he said.

"You're right. It's a great hack." Her breathing was shallow and too fast. *Slow your roll, Naomi.*

"We'll need to mop, of course." His gaze was direct. Steady. Here was a man that a woman could count on.

"Of course," she echoed, unable to hold on to that gaze. *We'll.* As if they were a team. Big question. Why did the idea of them being a team appeal to her so much?

"*I'll* mop," she said, surprised by how much emphasis she put on *I'll.*

They weren't a team. She did not know him. Okay, yes, she'd had a dream about a man who looked a lot like him last Christmas Eve, but it didn't mean anything.

How could it?

But what if it did? a voice at the back of her mind whispered.

For the first time in twelve long months, her illogical ragtag heart opened a crack. Aching to let someone new in.

Encouraged, but nervous, she stepped into the mudroom. Retrieved a mop and a bucket. Returned to find that Hunter had slipped back into the kitchen.

He stood eyeing Shepherd. Tilting his head as if puzzling out something. Then his face dissolved into a happy smile. The boy flung himself across the room, tackled the stranger in a bear hug around his knees.

Cried, "Daddy!"

CHAPTER 5

Staggered, Shepherd sucked in his breath. Stared down at the little boy wrapped around his legs. The impulse to turn tail and run ate him alive.

What should he do? Crouch down to the child's eye level? Tell him who he was? Would the child understand? He knew nothing about kids. Except this one was yanking at every heartstring inside him.

Should he wait and see what Naomi would do? He shot her a glance, but her eyes were on the kid.

Thrown, Shepherd just stood there, listening to his pulse pounding through his ears. Feeling the boy's body against him. His battle-weary heart skipped, skittered.

He'd come to dinner with a solid plan. Over the meal, he would tell Tom Luther and his family who he was. Take his licks. Give them the Christmas key. Be on his way.

Duty done.

But that was before he locked eyes with the breathtaking beauty. The same dark-haired, blue-eyed beauty who had jumped into his Jeep by mistake that morning.

What were the mind-blowing odds that she was the woman he'd dreamed about last Christmas Eve and she was his buddy's sister? His angelic dream woman who'd been his sole comfort this past miserable year as he recovered.

One in a billion?

C'mon. The dream was a year ago. How could he remember the tiny details of a dream woman's face?

How? Because that sweet face was right in front of him now.

He met her eyes.

Eyes the color of a Kentucky summer sky. Gently curving, well-shaped eyebrows. Long, thick lashes. A celestial nose, petite and pretty, the tip turned slightly upward to heaven. Soft, round face. Small, firm chin. Saintly cheekbones. Balanced, harmonious features.

She stood transfixed.

Unchained lightning blasted through his body. It was as if he'd touched a downed power line and lived to tell about it. And was grateful to be alive. His feet welded to the spot, and his heart liquefied in his chest. Was this what fate felt like? Foregone and inescapable.

Yes. This felt like the truest truth he'd ever known.

She was one in a billion.

He didn't know her, and yet her scent was already familiar to him. As if imprinted in his brain millennia ago. As if she was the very thing he'd never known he'd spent his entire life searching for.

Indelible.

Enduring.

His breath was shallow, and no matter how hard he tried, Shepherd could not deepen it.

Naomi looked as surprised as he felt. Her eyes burned fever-bright flame. The tip of her pink tongue brushed her upper lip.

If only he had met her under different circumstances. If only she wasn't the sister of the man he'd left behind to die. If only the little boy wasn't her dead brother's child. Who, apparently, she was helping raise. If only he wasn't busted and lame with nothing to offer her.

If only, if only, if only.

Worthless words. Things were what they were, and no amount of wishing could change it.

And then that amazing little kid had wrapped his arms around Shepherd's legs and called him Daddy.

The boy was still holding on. Looking up at him as if some prayer had been answered. The child's adoration was too much to process. He gulped, unnerved.

Everyone was staring at him. The room filled with clumsy silence. They were waiting for him to react.

Holding on to his cane, Shepherd squatted in front of the boy. Met the child's big blue eyes, the same color as his gorgeous aunt's. And his late father's.

"You must be Hunter," he said. "My name is Shepherd."

The little boy interlaced his fingers. Tucked his joined hands underneath his chin, and studied Shepherd with somber eyes. "Daddy?"

A question this time.

The child was so young. He probably couldn't remember what his father looked like. Shepherd and Clayton had been the same height. Similar build. They had the same color hair and military cut.

Naomi knelt beside Hunter, wrapped her arm around his waist. "Daddy's in heaven, remember? We talked about this."

Hunter grinned shyly and shook his head. He placed a hand on Shepherd's shoulder. Beamed at Naomi, said emphatically, "Daddy."

"I'm sorry about this." Naomi raised her eyes to meet Shepherd's gaze. "Sometimes, he mistakes other men for his father. His dad died in the war last Christmas."

"Your father told me," Shepherd said, swallowing a boulder of guilt for not being honest with her. "It's okay if Hunter wants to call me Daddy." His heart broke for the kid. "I don't mind."

"No, it'll just confuse him." Her tone was firm. To the boy she said, "Hunter, this is Mark Shepherd."

Hunter cocked his head, wrinkled his brow. "Shepherd?"

"Shepherd," he and Naomi said in unison. They shared a look. It felt weighted and intimate. Weird. But nice. He wanted more looks like that from her.

"Not Daddy?"

"No, sweetheart. Not Daddy," Naomi murmured and extended her hand to the boy. "Let's go wash up for dinner, okay?"

"O. K." Hunter took her hand and followed her from the room. But he glanced over his shoulder at Shepherd.

Breathless and befuddled by the child's sweet look, and charmed by the way he said *O. K.* instead of *okay*, Shepherd wiped away the sweat that popped up on his brow.

"I'll mop the floor while you're gone." He levered himself to his feet with his cane. Reached for the mop and bucket that Naomi had gotten from the mudroom.

Watched by the curious gazes of Clayton Luther's surviving family members, Shepherd mopped their kitchen floor.

He was aware of the mother in a wheelchair. The joints of her misshapen hands twisted into distorted fists. She had what appeared to be a severe case of rheumatoid arthritis. He winced. She couldn't be more than sixty, far too young for such a disability.

He was aware of Pastor Tom standing in the doorway. Observing him with a keen eye and a bewildered tilt to his head, as if he were expecting a different Marine, his son, to be working in the kitchen.

He was aware of the little boy who'd come back into the room with Naomi, studying Shepherd with an unabashed stare.

But most of all, he was aware of *her*.

The woman he'd dreamed about. The woman he'd been unable to get out of his head. The woman he'd believed imaginary. Until this morning when he'd stopped at the detour around the town square and she'd climbed into his Jeep.

Naomi.

Winsome, gorgeous Naomi Luther. Her dark hair pulled back off her forehead with a festive red-and-white-striped barrette. As if she had a bit of peppermint candy cane caught in her hair. The sides tumbling to her shoulders in big, soft curls.

Clayton Luther's older sister.

What cruel trick of fate was this?

If she knew who he was, it would destroy any blooming hope he had of getting to know her.

As if.

A deep sense of yearning spiraled through him. A poignant longing for something he could not have. Shepherd continued mopping. Cleaning an area bigger than where the pickle juice had spilled. As long as he was mopping, he didn't have to talk.

For a moment, it seemed they were all caught in the same web. Suspended in time and space, the five of them. Destinies intersected. Lives crossed. Even though the Luthers did not yet know it.

He felt his apprehension mount. Felt the weight of the white key in his pocket. The special key that had brought him here. Would they know the key when they saw it? What did it open? What did the key symbolize?

So many questions that needed answering. And he didn't know how or when to broach the topic.

"Looks like you got it all," Tom Luther said, breaking the spell by clamping a hand on Shepherd's shoulder. "I don't believe that floor has ever been so clean."

Shepherd straightened.

Naomi took the mop and disappeared without looking back.

Mrs. Luther welcomed him. Introduced herself as Irene. Apologized for not being able to shake his hand, or get up from her wheelchair.

"It's been a rough day for the arthritis," she said. "A cold front blew in this morning."

For the life of him, Shepherd couldn't help thinking that *he* was that cold front.

"You've been in the military," Irene said, peering at him with a sorrow-filled gaze. "That's why Hunter thought you were his daddy."

"I was. The Marines."

"Like our boy." Irene's eyes watered, and she blinked away the tears.

Now was the time. An opening. He should say what he came here to say. Show them the key. All he had to do was open his mouth, and let the words drop out.

"Thank you for your service," Naomi said. The light shone off her curls, creating a halo effect above her head.

He knew people meant well when they said that, but he hated it. He didn't want thanks. It felt wrong. "Thank you for yours."

An awkward pause.

A long silence.

He darted a glance at Naomi. Caught her studying him with wistful eyes. His heart chugged as he felt a corresponding hankering. What was going on here?

Tom gripped Shepherd's shoulder again. "Let me show you where you can wash up for dinner."

"Thanks," he mumbled, and followed the pastor down the hallway to the washroom.

Once inside, he closed and locked the door. Sank his head against the wall beside a shelf filled with cheerful seashells. He took several long, deep breaths.

As he breathed, his head steadied. He glanced down. Focused on his boots. Black. Military issue. He stared at his feet. Pretended he was a tree. Solid roots extending into the earth. Grounding down. Warding off the influx of memories waiting to tumble in on him, and send him to the floor.

He would *not* have a PTSS flashback at the Luthers'. He gritted his teeth. Changed his breathing pattern again. Sucked in cooling air through clenched teeth. Hissing as if burned. Exhaling through his nose.

Even now, his past still troubled his restless dreams. *Forgive yourself.* Shepherd stared at his reflection. *Let it go.*

Peering into his own dark eyes, he struggled against the dogged riptide . . . that current that towed him down into the muck of memories. Caging him in the despair of his childhood. The loss flooded over him as it often did. In a tidal wave of sensory overload. The smell of cheap whiskey on his father's breath. The sight of his mother in handcuffs. The sounds of the traffic whizzing by the highway apartment where he shivered alone and forgotten for days before policemen knocked at the door and he let them in.

Turning to the sink, he spied more seashells. Pretty, cheerful things. Met his eyes in the mirror. Dark eyes. Accusatory eyes. He clenched his jaw. Splashed water in his face.

The very last thing he wanted to do was sit at the Luthers' dining room table, eat pot roast, and make idle chitchat.

You owe *them.*

You let their boy die.

You left a man behind.

Shepherd gulped. He was still caught in that horrible dilemma. Trapped between the Marine motto and following orders.

Guilt was an anchor tied around his neck, and he couldn't saw it loose.

Get in your Jeep. Drive away. Get out now.

"Shepherd?" There was a knock at the door. Pastor Tom's voice. "You okay? Dinner's on the table."

Dammit. The man was too considerate. Too caring. He saw where Naomi got it. The kindness. The sincerity.

"Fine," he mumbled. "Be right out."

"Take your time. No rush."

He heard Tom's footsteps pad away. Splashed more water into his face. Got a grip. Returned to the kitchen. Found the family sitting around the dining room table, waiting on him.

He slipped into the spot across from Naomi. He could feel her energy surging across the space, melding with his. Eerie. Weird. This sense of instant connection. As if they'd known each other in another life.

Except that he didn't believe in such stuff.

Shepherd settled a cloth napkin in his lap. It had been a long time since he'd sat at a dinner table with a family. Used a napkin that wasn't paper. It felt unfamiliar, but nice.

"Mark, would you please say grace?" Tom asked.

Grace? Fear clutched him. Shepherd had no idea how to say grace. He looked over at the pastor and shook his head. *Thanks, but no thanks.*

But Tom had already closed his eyes, brought his hands together, and bowed his head. Irene closed her eyes and bowed her head as well, her misshapen hands clenched at her heart in two fists. Naomi lowered her head too. Followed by little Hunter.

A pious family.

He didn't belong here with these good people.

They waited on him to start the prayer. Not opening their eyes. Not peeking. Not even the kid.

Shepherd shifted, stared down at his hands. Finally pressed them together in a gesture that felt so foreign he wasn't sure he was doing it right. He mimicked the Luthers, pressed the knuckles of his thumbs against his sternum. Heaved in a deep breath. Exhaled. Cleared his throat.

Stalling.

He had no idea what to say or how to sound reverent.

"Just speak from the heart, son," Tom murmured.

Son.

That word again. A barb. A burning sting. A sharp reminder. He was here and their son was not.

A bitter taste filled his mouth, like the astringent chalkiness of persimmon skin. One of the foster homes where he'd lived had had a fruit orchard. The children were forbidden to eat the produce without permission.

One September afternoon, lured by the bright orange fruits, he'd scaled a tree. Picked one of the soft ripe persimmons and bit into it. The sour residue of the peel coated his tongue. He spat it out so forcefully that he'd fallen backward off the tree limb. Landed hard on his back. Breathless and in pain from a broken rib.

Staring up at his foster mother's angry face. "Maybe next time you'll listen to me," she scolded. "Follow the rules and you won't end up in prison like your parents."

Follow the rules.

Toe the line.

Do what you're told.

Time after time, he'd received that message—from foster families, from his teachers, from the military. He'd had it drilled into his head. And he'd learned his lesson well. *If you don't buck the system, you won't get punished. Keep your head down. Don't make waves. Obey orders.*

For the most part, that winning strategy had defined his life. The Marines had loved him for it. He'd been so good at following orders that he'd gotten promoted above men who'd been in the service far longer than he. Shepherd had found his credo. *Don't color outside the lines.*

Until last Christmas morning when that credo he'd come to rely on failed him. He'd lost his moral compass then, and he was still adrift. Uncertain of what to do with the rest of his life now that he was out of the military.

Across the table, Naomi made a noise of encouragement, sweet and supportive.

Oh yeah, he was supposed to pray.

He wanted to open his eyes and look at her. Study her face in the glow of the chandelier. To admire the fall of soft chestnut-colored hair over her slender shoulders. To meet those intelligent blue eyes and get lost in them.

To stare at those pink lips he wanted so badly to kiss.

But he did not.

"Dear Lord," he began, his voice sounding as creaky as the rusty cemetery gate. *Dear Lord, what now?* His foot tapped fast, itching to run. He quelled the urge, marshaled up the Marine. "Um, thank you for the roast beef."

Lame.

Say something more. But what?

"And the mashed potatoes and the gravy and green peas and rolls." *Officially the worst prayer in the history of prayers, Gunny.*

"And um . . . thanks for the good company at the table."

Better. Marginally.

"Thank you for . . . thank you for . . ." He was unable to think of anything else he was thankful for. How did you know to end the prayer?

Just say what's in your heart, Tom had told him. Fine. He could do that. "Dear Lord, thank you for putting a woman as pretty as Naomi here on earth."

Ugh! Had he actually said that out loud? Shepherd swallowed a groan, and his eyes flew open.

Naomi's eyes were open too and they stared at each other. Wrapped in a strange magnetic force field. The same strange pull that ensnared them when she'd landed in the passenger seat of his Jeep. Breathless and red-cheeked.

When was the last time he wanted something as much as he wanted her? He couldn't remember.

Unnerved, he squeezed his eyes shut. How did he end this freakish prayer?

"Thanks for everything," he blurted. "Amen."

"Amen," the family echoed.

Shepherd dropped his hands to his lap. His fingers going for the comfort of the cane propped against his chair. If he needed to, he could push up from the table, walk out the door, and never come back.

But he didn't do that.

Slowly, he opened his eyes again, but this time, he avoided looking at Naomi.

Platters and bowls went around the table. Naomi dishing up food for both Hunter and Irene. She carried a lot of responsibility on those slender shoulders. But she handled it with grace, and a quiet dignity that stirred something inside him.

He hungered for what he could not have. It was an overwhelming throb of need that began in the center of his chest and pulsed outward. A woman like her. A family like this. A place to call home.

Stop it, Marine.

"So, Mark," Tom said, apparently not inclined to call him Shepherd as he'd requested. "Where are you from?"

"All over." It was true enough. Once he'd left Kentucky.

"You're a Southern boy." Irene managed to slip a spoon between her gnarled fingers. "I can hear it in your drawl. I'm originally from North Carolina myself. Mecklenburg."

"No kidding." He wasn't sure what to say.

Irene tossed him a conspiratorial wink and a we're-gonna-be-great-friends smile. He could see where Naomi got her upbeat spirit. "You can take the boy out of the South, but you can't take the South out of the boy."

"No, ma'am." He shot a look in Naomi's direction. He noticed the small pearl earrings nestled in her lobes. The gold cross on a chain around her neck. She was dishing up a spoonful of peas on Hunter's plate.

The four-year-old wrinkled his nose. "No peas, please."

"Just a few bites." Naomi chomped the air, pretending to chew. "And I'll read you *The Magic Christmas Cookie* before bed."

Hunter smashed a pea with an index finger, peered up at Naomi from beneath long eyelashes. Gauging her reaction.

In the home that Shepherd had grown up in before foster care, he would have gotten whacked for such defiance.

Naomi laughed, a light and happy sound.

A sound that wrapped around his spine and pulled him headlong toward her. Engulfed. He felt engulfed. Surrounded. Enveloped by desire and pining. He *yearned* for her. On the cellular level. Each atom in his body vibrated with need. What would it feel like to hold her in his arms? To taste her? Bury his face in her hair?

"Okay, wee one. I get the message. Peas are not your fave. Tell you what. For each pea you eat, you get to smash one. I'll do it too, and whoever has the most smashed peas at the end wins." Naomi squashed a pea with her thumb, and then popped one into her mouth.

Hunter giggled and stuffed three peas in his mouth. Then he pounded three peas in succession—smash, smash, smash. Giggled again.

Fascinated and impressed, Shepherd watched Naomi beguile the boy into eating half the peas on his plate.

"She is so good with him," Tom murmured. "I don't know what we'd do without her."

Naomi beamed. "Luckily, you'll never have to find out."

Irene and Tom shared a look that Shepherd couldn't decipher. An uneasy glance. Was it related to having tragically lost their son and daughter-in-law?

"Is something wrong with your food?" Naomi asked him.

"Huh?" Shepherd blinked.

"You haven't touched a thing on your plate."

"Nothing wrong, sorry." Shepherd smiled. Or tried to. It felt crunchy. Brittle. Fragile. "I was watching you charm the boy. You're amazing. Do you work with children?"

"No," she said.

"Well, you've got a knack."

"Naomi runs her own business," Irene said, pride combing her voice. "She's a personal shopper. This time of year, she's hopping."

Ahh, that explained all the boxes she'd dumped into the backseat of his Jeep. He thought she'd been on one heck of a shopping spree.

Her cheeks pinked and she lowered her eyelashes. She leaned over to ruffle Hunter's hair. Light from the Christmas decorations on the porch came in through the dining room window. Chandelier prisms threw rainbows over the table. It felt to Shepherd as if Naomi was bathing her nephew in happiness. Gilding him with her golden smile, nourishing him with her caring touch. Wrapping him in a protective cocoon of love.

Woman and child looked into each other's eyes and laughed together. Naomi kissed his forehead and murmured, "Such a good boy."

Nostalgic for something he'd never had, Shepherd thought, *She's a born mother.*

Naomi and Hunter were so lost in each other that he couldn't help feeling like a voyeur. He shifted his gaze to his plate, speared a piece of roast beef. Chewed. It was delicious, but he barely tasted it.

He didn't belong here. He was an interloper. Why was he here? Oh yes, to deliver a key. A key that opened what? And for what? To stir up the past when the Luthers were working so hard to let go of their pain? He felt small and selfish. He'd come here not for them, but rather to ease his own guilt.

And he was jealous.

Of their connection. Of their faith. Of the peace they'd found in the face of so much tragedy. Of the fact that he'd had no one like Naomi in his life when he was growing up.

Shame bit into him. A hard, cold bite.

Let it go. Water under the bridge.

Forget about the past.

Sweep it under the rug.

Tamping down his feelings had worked for thirty years; why change tactics now? Trouble was, shoving the past into the past left him with . . .

Now.

And right now, he should be telling the Luthers who he was and why he was here. Give them the key. Brace for their condemnation and outrage.

He was responsible for the death of their son, and he had the audacity to sit at their table and break bread with them. *It's not your fault,* Dr. Fox had told him. But he wasn't sure the Luthers would buy the argument. *He* didn't buy it.

"The food is delicious," Shepherd said. "I don't often get home-cooked meals."

"Stick around." Tom winked. "Naomi is an excellent cook."

"Where do you find the time?" Shepherd asked her, falling back on polite chitchat. Scrambling to figure out a way to bring up the topic he'd come here to discuss. "Between running after this little guy, and shopping for other people." He nodded at Hunter, who was mixing the smashed peas with the mashed potatoes on his plate.

"Oh, that's not all she does. Naomi is the current president of the First Love Cookie Club, and spearheading their first annual Christmas charity dance to benefit military men and women suffering from post-traumatic stress."

"The First Love Cookie Club?" Shepherd asked, picking up the easy part of that topic.

"Our little town has lots of clubs," Irene explained. "We're joiners. Each year, the First Love Cookie Club has a cookie swap the second Friday in December. Their mission is to preserve, perpetuate, and celebrate Twilight's traditions."

"Um," Shepherd said, not getting it at all. "Okay."

"The club sends cookies to our troops overseas every Christmas," Irene said. "That's what the club is really all about. Making sure our military personnel don't get forgotten."

Shepherd should keep them talking about cookies. It was the easy way out. Leave his confession to another day.

But the time had come. The meal was almost done. Soon the family would be doing dishes, winding down, getting ready for bed. Shepherd couldn't delay this any longer. He steeled himself. Ignored the dread tromping up his spine.

Once he said this, any hope of kissing Naomi was gone. *As if you had any hope to begin with.*

He was a Marine. Man up.

Shepherd placed both palms on the table, framing his plate. "Mr. and Mrs. Luther . . . Naomi."

Everyone turned to him, smiles pregnant with possibilities. Kindness in their eyes.

"Yes?" Tom set down his fork.

Shepherd cleared his throat. "There's something I must tell you."

"What's wrong?" Irene sank back in her wheelchair. "You look so serious."

This was harder than he thought it was going to be. "I'm not who you think I am."

"Hold it right there." Tom held up a stop-sign hand. "You don't need to confess anything to us."

"Yes, sir, I do," Shepherd corrected. "You need to hear what I have to say."

"We don't judge people," Tom said. "In our church, we strive to practice unconditional love and acceptance."

"How is that possible?" Shepherd asked, incredulous.

"We're not perfect. We slip up." Tom's rueful headshake was humble. "But then we remember who we are, and do better."

"I—"

"If Joe vetted you, we know you're on the up and up."

"But Joe—"

"I'm guessing that a man of your bearing doesn't become an itinerant handyman without a hard-luck story. But this is what I want you to understand. The past is the past. It's gone. And *you* are *not* your story."

Oh, but he was. The Luthers just didn't know it yet.

"You don't know the things I've done," he whispered.

The room went silent.

Tom inhaled and said in a reverential tone, "It doesn't matter. We're all sinners here. Forgiveness is absolute in this house."

The pastor said it as if such a thing was possible. Shepherd didn't believe him. Not for a second.

"Mark." Irene leaned across the table to rest her knobby fist over his hand. "Do you have a place to stay while you are in Twilight?"

"No," he said, because it was true. He figured he'd crash at the closest motel. "Not yet."

"Then it's settled. You'll stay in the rectory."

"But—"

"It's not fancy," Irene went on, her tone brooking no argument. "It's old and small. But it's clean and furnished and free. You're welcome to live there and work for us as long as it takes you to get back on your feet."

"It's too much," Shepherd said, wretched guilt twisting up his gut. He wanted to tell them the truth. Needed to get it off his chest. These were good people. The best people. And he was deceiving them. "I'm not—"

"You're staying in the rectory," Irene said, starch coming into her voice. The strong look in her eyes belying the weakness of her wheelchair. "And I won't hear another word about it. Now who is ready for dessert? Terri brought over pumpkin pie this afternoon."

He needed to refute her. Stake his claim. Shepherd pushed back his chair and stood up.

"Oh, thank you for helping me clear the table," Naomi said, and stuck a stack of dirty plates in his hands.

And that ended his confession before it ever began.

CHAPTER 6

Naomi needed to move. Sitting at the table across from Shepherd had her insides knotted up like sweater yarn. And when he said that he had something to confess, goose bumps had spread up her arms.

Chilled her.

His jaw was tense. His eyes dark and unfathomable. His shoulder blades pulled down. She couldn't help wondering what in the world he had done.

Like her parents, she believed in forgiveness and unconditional love. But believing something and acting on those beliefs were two different things. She wasn't as good a person as she longed to be.

She was afraid.

And at the root of her fear was her intense attraction to him. She had dreamed of this man. Wanted to believe in fate and kismet cookie true love. But the hazards were as clear as a giant red neon sign blinking in a pitch-black night.

Slow down. Caution. Danger ahead.

He was a total stranger. She did not know him at all. And yet, she wanted him.

Her heart was an emergency vehicle racing to a fire, flashing lights and screaming sirens. *Warning! Warning! Here lies trouble.*

He could turn her ordinary life upside down, in ways she couldn't begin to image. Never mind the gentle expression on his face when he had looked at Hunter. Or the kindness that lay heavy in his voice when he spoke to her mother. Or the respect in his eyes when he listened to her father.

The man had something to confess. He'd said so, plain as day. He had a secret.

She shivered. Gathered up the gravy boat and the bowl of mashed potatoes and carried them into the kitchen.

The new handyman had come recommended from another church. But that didn't mean much. Mark Shepherd could have pulled the wool over their eyes. Was he a wolf in sheep's clothing?

She studied him. No. That was wrong. There was nothing sheepish about this man. He was at least six foot two and full of muscles. Testosterone oozed from his pores. He possessed a perfect Greek nose. Straight and proud. Broad shoulders that could make angels weep.

And there was that butt. Not too big. Not too small. Just right. Firm and high.

Dear Lord, please let me stop this. She did not want to be so consumed. It wasn't smart. But every part of her body was aware of him. Her toes curled. Her knees weakened. Her nipples tightened. Her mouth went dry.

What secret was he keeping?

Bigger question, did she really want to know?

He followed her into the kitchen. "Where should I put these?"

"The sink." She turned toward him.

He met her eyes over the glow of the kitchen lamp, and in that brief exchange she saw it. The wildness he kept on a short leash. A primal animal lurked inside the man.

She sucked in air at her body's response. Her nipples turned rock hard, and her stomach softened. And heaven help her, she *wanted* him. Wanted him with an urgency that terrified her. *He* was not the dangerous one.

She was.

Mark ducked his head, dropped her gaze. Limped to the sink. What had happened to him? Wounded in the war, she supposed. Did the limp have anything to do with the secret he was keeping?

She went across the room to the sideboard where the pumpkin pie sat. Her heart tapped out a ragged rhythm, pushing blood through her ears in a roaring rush. She could hardly hear anything else.

"Need some help?" Shepherd asked.

Naomi jumped.

He was right behind her. Standing so close they were almost touching.

Her pulse shot even higher, sprinting like a jackrabbit from a coyote's sharp teeth. Running until the frantic pace left her staggered and dizzy.

"I . . . I . . ."

"Yes?" He leaned in closer, and she lost her voice. Lost her breath. Lost all common sense. His eyes glistened, going from chocolate brown to almost midnight black.

"Take this to the table." She thrust the pie into his hands. Cut off his gaze. "Dad, you want coffee?"

"Decaf, please," her father called from the dining room.

"Do *you* want coffee?" she forced herself to ask Shepherd. As if everything were nice and normal.

"Yes," he said. "But I want the real deal."

There was nothing sexual in his tone of voice or in his expression. But the words lit her up as hotly as if he'd licked the nape of her neck. Tingles surfed from her belly straight down between her legs.

What was going on? What was *wrong* with her? Why did this man turn her on like no other man ever had? She had never felt this level of sexual desire with Robert. If she had, she would have moved with him when he first got that job in Denver. Except that he'd never come out and asked her to go with him.

One glance from Shepherd started a brushfire inside her. And she didn't even know him.

Soul mate, whispered a voice in the recesses of her mind. *This is how it is with soul mates.*

Nonsense. This feeling was insanity. Bats. Looney tunes. Loopy.

And yet, it was as if a magnetic current was hauling her toward him. Terrifying. Exhilarating.

Magical.

What *was* happening?

Because she didn't want these feelings, didn't want them at all. And she needed to learn how to make them stop.

The bedroom was cell-like. The wrought-iron framed single bed adorned by a plain, well-worn quilt. The picture of Jesus on the wall reminded him that this was a rectory, as if he could have forgotten.

Its sparseness suited him. The picture made him nervous. He wasn't a religious man, but that the room reminded him of military barracks—simple, sparse, and clean—did bring him a certain comfort.

Even so, Shepherd feared he would not sleep well tonight. He hadn't slept well in a year. He was in a strange place to begin with, and his dreams were haunted by the nightmares of his mistakes. And unless he wanted to go for the sleeping pills at the bottom of his duffel bag, tonight wouldn't be any different.

For a moment, he considered the pills, but decided against them. He'd had enough of feeling fuzzy-headed. He lay down. Did his breathing routine.

It didn't work.

The place was new to him. The smells and sounds were new. Wind blew through the sycamore tree outside the window. The musty scent of hymnals. The creak of old floorboards of the house settling. But he'd fallen asleep in all kinds of unusual and uncomfortable places. Pool tables. Rocky ground. A rooftop, once.

But since last Christmas, even the finest mattress could not coax him to sleep easy.

And this was not the finest mattress. It was too thin. The pillow too fat. The room too warm.

He flopped one way.

His knee ached.

Flopped to the other side.

His neck got a crick. He sighed and shifted onto his back. Stared up at a crack in the ceiling. Thought of Naomi. The terrific way she smelled, the gentleness of her smile, the loving way she dealt with her nephew, the cheerfulness that seemed an innate part of her character.

The feelings churning around in his body were foreign, but pleasant. So very pleasant. He wanted to feel like this more often. Wanted to be around Naomi as much as he could. She fed his spirits, hopes, and dreams.

But it was dangerous to feel this way. To long for a life that could not be his.

An hour passed. Ten-thirty.

Finally, he threw off the covers. Got up. Got dressed. Sat on the edge of the bed staring at his knee. Thought of Clayton.

The kid was an ache in his heart. Guilt was a flame burning him up inside. Why hadn't he told the Luthers who he was? Why hadn't Clayton given them the key himself? Why was he pretending to be their handyman? Why had he agreed to live in the rectory?

Because you're a coward, snarled the ugly voice in his head. The one that sounded like his father.

He picked up the Christmas key he'd left lying on the bedside table beside his wallet and car keys. Traced his fingers over the bumps and ridges. "Why did you leave this for me, Luther?" he mumbled. "Why send me on this mission when you could have just mailed it to your family?"

Shepherd gulped. He'd probably never know the answer to that question. But clearly, Luther must have had some kind of premonition he was going to die if he left the key for him.

Feeling as if he were suffocating, Shepherd stuffed the key into his pocket. Reached for his cane. Limped across the floor. Walked out of the room. Out of the house. Pulled the door closed behind him.

Out on the front porch, he took a deep breath of the cool night air, looked up and down the street.

Total silence.

He paused, listening. The military had sharpened his senses, and he strained for the sounds beyond the sound. Faintly, he heard the faraway whinny of a horse. On the interstate, the rumbling of big rig tires.

And music.

It was faint, and low. Coming from his left, toward the town square. Apparently, the music was being piped through the outdoor speakers the workmen had set up for the Dickens festival. "Joy to the World."

His heart sloshed up against his chest, messy and wet. He wanted to believe in joy to the world. Agreed with the sentiment. But he knew no such thing existed.

Shepherd pulled up the collar of his coat, snuggled deeper inside. With intent and focus, he placed the tip of the cane onto the step below him. Eased down. He took another step and then another. Finally, he was on the sidewalk.

The elderly concrete buckled in places. It was uneven and cracked. He navigated his way toward the street, passing more quaint houses like the Luthers', all looking as if they had been built in the 1910s and 1920s, with wide, inviting front lawns.

Many of the homes still had their Christmas lights on, and he suspected they'd be on all night. Walking through the darkness, but still surrounded by light, felt surreal to him. He shook his head, trying to empty it. Walked. Since his knee injury, he had a hard time walking any great distance and thinking at the same time. Walking required focus. It was a gift, if he let himself see it that way.

Land solidly. Push off with the cane. Let the momentum propel him to the next step. *Look, Ma, I'm walking.*

Except his mother was long gone. Out of his life when he wasn't much older than Hunter. He barely remembered her. Knew she'd had dark brown hair and blue eyes from the single photo he had of her. In the photograph, she was sitting on a carousel horse, riding a merry-go-round. Shepherd on the painted pony with her. His little boy hands on the reins. His head tossed back. Joy on his face.

That was long ago and far away.

His gut tightened.

He kept walking.

The deserted town square was lit up. Christmas lights aglow. Red, green, white. Big old-fashioned bulbs and twinkle lights. Flashing lights. Blinking lights. Flameless candles.

Each store window held a lavish display. One boutique featured Santa's elves wrapping gifts. In the window of the tearoom, a table was laden with a wide assortment of cookies.

The sight of the cookies stirred his memory.

He saw Naomi as he'd seen her in his dreams last Christmas, and then today in his Jeep. Recalled the shocked look on her pretty face when she realized her mistake. The surprise in her eyes when she'd met his gaze.

And then again, in her kitchen, when she'd looked up from cleaning up a jar of broken pickles. That moment had been pretty monumental for him too.

It took Shepherd ten minutes to walk the square. It calmed him. The walk. This town. The place was too good to be true. It felt like something from a schmaltzy black and white Christmas movie. But he liked it.

Too bad he didn't belong here.

His knee was throbbing, but the pain reminded him

that he was alive. Clayton Luther wasn't lucky enough to feel pain.

He left the town square going east. Ambling along a path that led down to the lake. The air was much colder here. Boats bobbed in the slips. Metal moorings clanked. The dampness tightened his knee, kicking the pain up a notch.

Good.

Shepherd clenched his jaw. He needed to hurt. Needed to feel something, anything. Numbness was a luxury he could ill afford.

When he reached the lake, he circled back, making a loop. About halfway around the lake, his knee was hurting too much for him to continue and he stopped.

Near a bar called the Horny Toad Tavern. He'd seen the bar on his way to the Luthers' that morning. The perfect place for a bar, away from the residential zoning, but near enough to the town square to allow for pub crawls, and with the only signs of life at this hour. Vehicles were parked in the lot. Honky-tonk music spilled out, and when the door opened he heard an old Hank Williams tune, "Lovesick Blues."

He stood there, debating whether to go in or not. His knee told him he needed a drink. A big stiff drink. But his heart wasn't in it.

How was he going to get back to the church? He had to be at least a mile away from the Luthers' by now, and his knee was ready to collapse. No way he could walk back under his own steam. Why hadn't he thought this through?

In the city, he would call for an Uber. But he knew before he ever checked his phone app that there was no such thing in Twilight.

He had to go into the bar. Or he was going to end up sitting down in the parking lot, and he wasn't sure he could get back up again if he did.

Reaching deep for his reserve energy, he headed toward the bar.

"Yo, Gunny!"

He stopped. Turned. Saw a man standing across the road at a twenty-four-hour diner called Waffle-O-Rama. Waving.

At him.

Shepherd squinted. Did he know this guy?

The man trotted over.

Shepherd studied him—early to mid-forties. Shaggy hair. Goatee. Peacoat. Military bearing. Watchful eyes.

No. He didn't know him, but his instincts told him this guy was navy.

"Ah," the guy said. "You *are* a gunny."

"Do I know you?" Shepherd kept his voice neutral.

"Name's Nate Deavers." He stuck out a hand.

Shepherd didn't want to shake the man's hand. It was after midnight and they were standing outside a bar. The scenario had mugging written all over it. He swept his gaze over the perimeter, searching for accomplices. But the man appeared to be alone.

The guy kept standing there, hand extended, gave his rank and serial number, ended with "SEAL Team Six."

The magic words. That broke Shepherd's resistance. He clasped the man's hand. "Mark Shepherd. How did you know I was a gunny?"

"You look the part." Nate grinned, and inclined his head toward the bar. "You going in?"

"Debating it."

"If you're on the fence, and don't have your heart set on a drink, why don't you join us?" Nate waved at the diner.

Shepherd looked back across the street to the plate-glass window of the restaurant. A group of men sat around a table. From the looks of them, all ex-military.

They met Shepherd's gaze, raised their coffee mugs in invitation, and he knew at once what was going on. They'd been sitting in the window and watched him lope up. Saw him hesitate outside the bar.

"I don't need an intervention." Shepherd scowled.

"No one said you did." Nate's smile was mild, but his eyes were razors. He didn't miss a trick.

Shepherd looked from the Waffle-O-Rama to the bar, back to Nate. "I don't have a drinking problem."

"No one said you did," Nate repeated.

"You friends of Bill Wilson?" Shepherd asked, referring to the code name for an AA meeting.

"Some of us," Nate said. "But mostly, we're here to support each other through the shit."

"Good for you," Shepherd said, hearing his voice drip sarcasm.

"PTSD?" Nate grunted.

"They're calling it PTSS these days."

"Doesn't matter what acronym they stick on it. Results are the same. Shellshock. Battle fatigue. Seen and done too many gawdawful things in service to our country."

Shepherd nodded, but didn't speak.

"Having trouble sleeping?"

"No more than you."

"Point taken." Nate laughed.

Shepherd jammed his hands in his pockets, his cane hooked around his elbow.

"If you want to talk about it, we've got big ears and closed mouths."

Did he want to talk? To strangers? That was a big N-O.

Nate waited. Patiently. Not going anywhere. From the bar, Hank gave way to the Rolling Stones, "Honky-Tonk Women."

Then again, why not strangers? Might be easier than with friends. He considered it a moment. Nope. He'd had enough of running his gob with Dr. Fox.

Yeah, but Dr. Fox hadn't been where Nate Deavers had been. He had a safe position behind a desk. The psychiatrist had no idea what it was like to get shot at. No clue what it's like to have a man die in your arms.

Nate held out his hand, an ushering gesture that said, *Come with me.*

Shepherd leaned on his cane. He'd promised Dr. Fox he'd go to group therapy, and Shepherd always tried to keep his word. Even if this bunch wasn't an officially sanctioned group, it qualified.

"No pressure," Nate said. "We get how hard it is to integrate back into polite society. You can come sit with us. You don't have to say a thing. Or not."

A longing gripped him. The old need to belong to a group was strong. The Marines had been everything to him. But here in the cold, it felt too much like weakness.

"No man left behind, right?" Nate murmured, beckoned with his fingers.

Those words, solid as steel on the December night, cut right into Shepherd. He tightened his jaw and his grip on the cane.

"C'mon, Gunny. There's a hot cup of coffee, and a warm piece of apple pie with your name on it. That's all. Nothing more."

Shepherd shook his head. "I'm fine."

"Maybe." Nate's smile was kind. "But your knee's not."

He was right about that. Part of him wanted to peel off and follow Nate like a puppy. But another part, the self-loathing part, wanted to go into the bar and order a boilermaker.

"I'll give you a ride home," Nate said, looking at Shepherd's leg. "No matter which building you walk into."

That cinched it.

Shepherd nodded again and followed Nate Deavers into the Waffle-O-Rama.

CHAPTER 7

After her father took Mark Shepherd over to the rectory, Naomi got Hunter ready for bed and he went down easy. She read him *The Magic Christmas Cookie* as promised. Afterward, he slipped his sweet little arms around her neck for a good-night hug. Whispered, "Night, night, N'omi."

Her heart cracked open, bursting with both joy and sadness. The boy was a constant reminder of why she could not give in to her grief. He needed stability. He needed her.

And she would be there for him.

Always.

She texted Robert good night, and sent a fun little animated gif. He did not text back. She told herself he was probably already asleep.

It was a little after ten when she crawled under the covers. Normally, Naomi worked so hard she had no trouble falling asleep.

But not tonight.

Tonight, she felt oddly restless, as if her skin were too

tight. She threw off the blanket. Got cold. Put it back on again. Got hot.

She went down to the kitchen for a glass of water. Stopped in the living room to stare out the window. Watched the neighbor's roof angel wink off. Stepped out onto the porch in her bathrobe. Shivered. Crossed her arms over her chest.

Then she saw something surprising—someone was limping down the sidewalk toward the town square. Her pulse quickened. It had to be Mark. But what was he doing roaming the town this late at night?

She had almost chased after him. Almost called his name. But didn't. The Marine was a stranger, she reminded herself. She had no business running after him. She had enough baggage of her own.

So instead she stayed silent, listening only to the blood thumping through her ears, feeling bewildered and overwhelmingly sad as she watched him disappear from view.

Naomi stepped back inside. Closed the door and padded to bed. But she still couldn't sleep. Tossing and turning, she thought instead about Mark Shepherd. The man practically oozed loneliness, and the nurturer in her wanted so badly to fix him. But she couldn't afford those feelings.

Not now. Not ever, really.

She wasn't free. She had a long-distance boyfriend. She was adopting her nephew. She was a pastor's daughter. A good girl. Her parents depended on her, even though they insisted she should not give up her life for them. She didn't see it that way. To her, you sacrificed for family. Period. Besides, she actually enjoyed living with her folks.

The periods of time she'd lived alone—during college and afterward—were the loneliest times of her life. Robert was off getting his graduate degree and not around much. She was a people person. Needed to be with others. In fact, after Clayton and Samantha died it had been *her* idea to move back in with her parents. It had also been her idea to adopt Hunter—the child she loved with every beat of her heart. Her family was not a burden.

Even so, her life wasn't her own. Her actions had repercussions on her family.

All the more reason to avoid Mark Shepherd.

After thrashing around for half an hour, she got back up. Made chamomile tea and ate a kismet cookie.

Her father came into the kitchen, yawning. "It's almost midnight, sunshine."

"I know."

"Can't sleep?"

She shook her head. "You?"

"Your mom is snoring," he said, his voice filled with affection.

"I'll make you a cup of tea with warm milk."

He sat down at the kitchen table. "Thank you."

She put on a saucer to heat the milk.

"What do you think about Mark Shepherd?" her father asked.

"He seems nice." She bit her bottom lip, a little horrified that her own father might have picked up on the sexual attraction between her and Mark. "How long is he going to be here?"

"Just through the holidays," her father said.

"Oh." Naomi wondered why she felt disappointed. Why should she care how long the handyman hung around?

The milk started to simmer and she added it to the hot

tea. Brought it to her father, and sat down beside him. Gave him the full brunt of her smile.

He did not smile back.

Her stomach ached. "Thinking of Clayton?"

Dad tapped a restless finger against his cup. "He's never off my mind."

"Mine either."

He laid a hand on top of hers, said with conviction that didn't stick, "It'll get better."

"It already has."

"But sometimes that old swat of grief bats you right back down the dark hole. This time of year, I . . ."

"I'm trying not to let grief get at me." Happy is as happy does. Right? She had to stay positive. Because if she didn't, she was terrified she would lose control and everything would fall apart. "That's why we have to give Hunter the best Christmas ever. He might have lost his parents, but he's still loved. Still has us."

"Your mom and I worry that you're giving up your own life for your nephew."

"Oh no, no!" She splayed a palm to her chest. "Hunter *is* my life. I couldn't love him more if he were mine."

"I know, but Robert—"

"Robert will come around." Naomi bobbed her head as if all she had to do was think it and she could make it so.

Her father held her gaze, his darkening with concern. "And if he doesn't?"

Naomi notched her chin up. "Hunter comes first. *Always.*"

"Even if that means breaking up with Robert?" Her father ran his thumb over her knuckles.

She didn't hesitate. The answer rolled right off her tongue. "Yes."

"You've been with Robert since high school. He's the only boyfriend you've ever had. Are you sure you're prepared to lose him?"

She couldn't help feeling she'd lost him already and had just been too busy to address it.

"And yet, he's never asked me to marry him."

"But you have an understanding."

"That's not enough." She bit her bottom lip. "Not anymore. If Robert wants me, he's got to want Hunter too. We're a package deal."

Her dad shook his head, a regretful expression plunking at the corners of his mouth, but he said nothing.

"What is it?" she prodded, gripped by an unknown anxiety.

"From the time you were little, you sacrificed yourself for others. I still remember how generous you were with your brother. If there were five M&M's you would give him three and keep two for yourself."

"He was my baby brother."

"Most kids are all about themselves. It's normal. Natural to be selfish when you're six. You weren't."

"I guess I just like giving. It makes me feel good the way nothing else does. I don't feel as if I'm missing out on anything. I feel like so much love is being added to my life. Hunter enriches me in countless ways. He's not a burden. Besides, I always knew I wanted kids. Now I have one."

"But not in quite the way you planned."

"It's part of God's plan." She bowed her head. "I believe that with all my heart."

Her father looked relieved. They'd discussed the issue before but not to this degree. "And you're certain this is what you want?"

"It's not just what I want, but what God wants for my life."

His soft smile turned wry. "Maybe you should deliver Sunday's sermon. You sound far wiser than me."

"Daddy," she said. "You and Mom lead by example. You give so much to others, how could I not follow in your footsteps? It's my best way to honor you and Mom, Clayton and Samantha."

"Your mother and I could adopt Hunter. It's still an option."

"We've been over this before, Dad. Mom is in no shape to take care of an active boy, and you are busy with your congregation."

Her father nodded. The same reluctant nod he'd given her when they hashed this over with Samantha's parents after Samantha's death. "Your mom and I and the Woolys just want to make sure you know what you're getting into. Raising a child isn't easy."

"I know." She straightened her shoulders, buffed her smile. A shiny, polished, I-just-won-an-Oscar kind of smile. But she knew neither one of them was buying it. "But I'm prepared."

"Samantha fell down that dark hole of grief we were talking about . . ." Her father trailed off again.

"She was hurting."

"We all were."

The cookie Naomi was eating turned to dirt in her mouth. They all wanted to believe that Samantha's death was accidental, but in her heart of hearts, Naomi *knew* it had been intentional. The coroner had put down that the cause of death was accidental because he was friends with her parents and wanted to blunt their pain, but Samantha had swallowed a whole bottle of sleeping pills that she'd had filled at the pharmacy the week before. No way that could have been an accident. Although it was hard to imagine how a mother could leave her child without making provisions, the truth was what it was. After much soul searching, Naomi had come to understand how the emotional pain of losing her husband, and Samantha's delicate mental constitution, had led her to end her life and abandon her son. Naomi could only pray that God understood too. That was why Naomi was so determined to raise Hunter. He deserved a stable, strong, happy mother who would be there for him no matter what.

It was her job to get her father back on cheerier topics. This had to be a happy Christmas, *no matter what*. As the oldest child, and a pastor's daughter, giving to others was ingrained in her. Service was as much a part of her as her hair color. It was up to her to make this Christmas the merriest of all, for herself as much as anyone else. She needed to be needed. And talking about Clayton and Samantha was taking them in the opposite direction.

"Tomorrow," she said, "let's take Hunter to see the new Disney movie."

"I forgive Sam, and I know God does too. We all miss her terribly," Dad went on, ignoring Naomi's attempt to shift topics, and letting her know that he too realized Samantha had indeed killed herself. "But she's left us with a tough row to hoe." He nodded in the direction of Hunter's bedroom.

"I don't mind. I love the little guy to pieces. But I wish . . ." She caught herself, pulled her chin up. "Well, there's no use in wishing for things that can't happen. All we can do is move forward with a smile on our faces and hope in our hearts."

"I'm so proud of you, sunshine." Her father squeezed her hand and looked into her eyes. When she was a little girl and felt sad, he would bounce her on his knee and sing "You Are My Sunshine" to cheer her up.

"Thanks, Daddy."

"You are so strong."

"No stronger than you." She squeezed his hand right back. Since her mother had been diagnosed with RA, their bond had strengthened. They were the caretakers now. "I love you, Daddy."

Tears misted her father's eyes. "I love you more than words can say, sunshine. Never doubt it."

They sat for a moment. Father and daughter. Holding hands. Steeped in grief. Naomi was lucky. So very lucky to have loving parents. Parents who'd taught her that service to others was the most rewarding of life's paths. Not everyone was as lucky as she. She sent up a prayer of gratitude, thankful for her blessings.

The image of Mark Shepherd popped into her mind. He didn't have to tell her about his past for her to understand that he was one of the unlucky ones. The clouded look of yearning in his eyes when he'd watched them at the dinner table spoke volumes.

What had he been like as a boy? she wondered. What conditions had he grown up in? Who was he deep down inside?

"It was weird," she said. "Wasn't it? About Hunter calling Mark Daddy."

"Yes," her father agreed. "It was awkward, but you handled the situation well."

"You hired Mark as our handyman because he's a Marine."

Her father nodded. "Like Clayton."

"By taking him in, it's like you're saving Clayton."

"Things aren't as cut and dried as that."

"You're too softhearted, Daddy."

"So are you." He smiled at her, a foggy smile. Weary. Stared off into the distance as if peering into the past. "You get that from me. Your mother is a lovely soul, but she's much better at keeping her heart out of business decisions."

"You and Mom make a great team."

"Things were easier before the arthritis took over," he said. "But all growth comes with challenges."

"It would be nice if God slowed down on the challenges a bit," she said. "I've had enough growth for one year."

"He never gives us more than we can handle."

Naomi wasn't so sure about that, but it was too late at night to get into a philosophical discussion. "Do you know what you're going to talk about for Sunday's sermon?"

"I do." He finished off his tea. Her father often read his sermons to her for feedback.

"Are you going to make me wait until Sunday to find out?"

"Forgiveness," he said. "I want to talk about forgiveness. Forgiving others. Forgiving ourselves. Forgiving our misunderstandings of God's plan for our lives."

"We can't lay everything at God's feet," Naomi said, getting agitated. "He wasn't the one who killed Clayton."

"Forgiveness," her father murmured.

"You're directing the sermon at me?" She let go of her father's hand, ran her palms over her upper thighs.

"I'm directing it at anyone who needs forgiveness. Both giving it and getting it."

"And what about the Marines? Why didn't they rescue Clayton? *No man left behind.* That's the motto, right? Yet they left him behind."

"Others' lives were at stake. More would have died if they'd gone back after your brother."

"When I imagine what Clayton went through . . ." Naomi shuddered. Dropped her face into her hands.

Her father massaged her shoulder. "Shh, shh. Don't think about it."

"But that's the trick, isn't it? How do you *not* think about it?"

"Prayer helps."

"But sometimes prayer fails."

"*Seems* to fail," he corrected. "We have to be patient."

"And when you can't be patient?"

"That's when I chop firewood," he said. "Or go box at the gym."

"Maybe *I* should take up boxing," she mused, and feigned punches.

"Perhaps you should." His tone said he meant it.

Naomi laughed at the idea of taking up boxing.

Her father yawned, pushed back his chair. "We should try and get some sleep."

"I'll give it a shot." She got up, kissed her father's cheek, went back to bed. And finally managed to fall asleep.

Only to dream of Clayton. That terrible, recurring dream when he begged her to rescue him. In the dream, she kept trying to get to him, but she couldn't run. Mired in gooey glue that stuck to her shoes. Held her down.

She woke, bathed in sweat. Trembling. Tears filling her eyes. Swamped with a terrible knowledge. If she lived to be a hundred, she didn't think she could ever forgive the evil man who'd killed her baby brother.

Or the Marines who'd left him to die in enemy hands.

CHAPTER 8

The men at the table introduced themselves to Shepherd. Gideon Garza, former Army Ranger, Ryder Southerland, army military police, and Hutch Hutcherson, retired Delta Force. There was a lot of collective military experience in the Twilight Waffle-O-Rama.

And a lot of pain.

These men had seen things, done things that civilians couldn't begin to understand.

Gideon was missing a hand. Hutch was the sole survivor of a guerrilla attack on his team in Afghanistan. And Ryder had witnessed a good friend die in front of him during a training exercise.

"I gotta make a call," Nate said after he'd introduced Shepherd to the group, and he disappeared.

"His wife's pregnant again," Hutch explained. "Shannon's over forty now and Nate's as fussy as an old hen about her. They got a late start on love."

"But they've made up for lost time." Ryder chuckled. "This is baby number four."

"You got kids?" Gideon asked Shepherd.

He shook his head.

"You married?" Ryder asked.

"No."

"Ever been close?" Hutch inclined his head.

Shepherd shrugged. "Married to the Marines. Does that count?"

"This must feel like a divorce." Gideon poured maple syrup over a stack of blueberry waffles.

"It's a change." Shepherd ran a hand over his head, and started wishing he'd gone into the bar.

"No girlfriend?" Ryder asked.

What was with the twenty questions? Shepherd glanced around. Where had Nate gone? The former SEAL had promised him there was no pressure to talk.

"Something wrong with your pie?" asked the waitress who'd dropped by the table to refill coffee cups.

Shepherd stared down at the plate in front of him. Realized he hadn't even taken a bite. "Sorry," he said. "I got distracted."

"By these old lions and their war stories?" The waitress, who was of an age when her prettiness was starting to fade, nudged Hutch's shoulder with her elbow.

"Hey, hey, Allie June," Hutch said, shifting away from her. "I'm younger than you are."

"I may not be twenty anymore," Gideon threw in, "but I can still roar."

"Yes, your roar is quite impressive," Allie June purred, and lowered her lashes.

"I'm a happily married man," Gideon reminded her. "All you'll get from flirting is a twenty percent tip."

"Why do you think I do it?" Allie June winked again. "Give the pie a try," she told Shepherd. "I promise you'll like it."

He picked up his fork and took a bite of pie. The crust

was flaky, the filling sweet, but not too sugary. "Mmm," he said for Allie June's benefit, and she wandered off with a mollified smile.

Once she was gone, the conversation shifted back to their war experiences. Shepherd didn't contribute. Listening, he took a pocketknife from his jeans. Claimed the piece of wood he carried in his coat, and began whittling.

"What are you making?" Hutch asked several minutes later.

"A nutcracker."

"From the ballet?" Hutch asked.

"Yes."

"So, you're like Drosselmeyer."

It surprised Shepherd that the former Delta Force operator knew who Drosselmeyer was. "You know *The Nutcracker*?"

"It's my daughter Kimmie's favorite Christmas story. I've seen it half a bazillion times."

"You're really good at whittling, Gunny," Gideon observed.

"And quick." Ryder nodded at the curlicues of wood peeling off Shepherd's knife.

"Woodworking calms my mind."

"You should give us lessons," Hutch said.

"I'm a doer, not a teacher." Shepherd didn't look up from his work. Concentrated on forming the nutcracker's uniform. He'd carved the figure so many times it was second nature. He carved things and gave them away.

"What's your story?" Ryder leaned forward on his elbows.

Shepherd glanced up to find the three men staring at his knee.

Should he be as open with them as they'd been with

him? Shepherd's instinct was to withdraw. Clam up. Keep everything locked tight.

The three men were staring at him. Waiting.

Shepherd closed the knife. Passed the carved nut-cracker to Hutch. "For your daughter."

"Hey, thanks." Hutch beamed. "She'll love this."

Shepherd pocketed the knife, swept the wood shavings into a paper napkin.

"Nothing you want to tell us, Gunny?" Ryder prodded. "Why are you in Twilight?"

Nate wandered back to the table, sat down.

"I came to bring this to Clayton Luther's family." Shepherd took the key from his coat, put it in the middle of the table.

"Why?" Hutch asked.

"Because I'm responsible for Clayton's death," Shepherd shocked himself by blurting out in the Waffle-O-Rama to men he did not know.

They studied him with even expressions. None of them reacted. Or judged him.

Shepherd felt a rush of acceptance that he needed, but couldn't quite embrace. They might be fellow military men. They might have shared similar experiences. But he was the stranger in their midst and Clayton had been one of them.

"What do you mean?" Gideon ventured. "We understood that a terrorist took Clayton hostage after he went AWOL to deliver toys to kids at an orphanage."

"That's true," Shepherd admitted. "But here's the kicker. Clayton asked my permission to go. Asked me to go with him. But I wouldn't break protocol. I didn't have the stones to go against the rules. If I had, I would have saved his life. I knew what the terrorist looked like.

He was wounded and hiding out in the orphanage. If I'd seen him I would have dealt with him before he could harm anyone."

The men stayed silent. Emotionless. Waited.

"But Clayton, the dumb kid, had no idea what he was walking into. If only I had followed my gut instead of the rules." Shepherd gulped and told the rest of what went down last Christmas morning in Kandahar. How he'd taken a team to go find Clayton, and they'd been set upon by the terrorists who'd come after their injured man. How he'd left Clayton behind in order to save his other men.

His voice cracked. "I'm not supposed to leave a man behind."

"Gunny," Hutch said. "You gotta stop beating yourself up. You were rank-and-file. Following orders is drilled into your brain. Black and white. It's only when you get into Special Forces that, hey, wait, you discover there's twelve hundred shades of gray."

Shepherd ran a hand over his head. "Well, guys, I'm breaking the rules now."

"What do you mean?" Nate asked.

Shepherd told them the significance of the key. How he'd come to Twilight to confess to his role in Clayton's death to the Luthers. How he'd gotten mistaken for the church's new handyman. How he'd gone along with it.

"I let the Luthers believe what they wanted to believe." Shepherd steepled his fingers, shook his head. Still not quite certain how he'd ended up here.

Until Clayton, he hadn't lost a single man under his command. The kid's death was a yoke around his neck that he could not shake off.

"Why do you think that is?" Hutch asked.

"I don't really know." Shepherd raised his shoulders to his ears. Let them flop back down. "Hoping to make some kind of amends I suppose."

It sounded like a lame excuse, hearing it out loud.

"Maybe doing some repairs around the place will make a difference. Help out any way I can. But if I do that, the more time that passes, the harder it's going to be to come clean." Shepherd drummed his fingers on the table.

"Don't do it," Ryder said. "Don't tell them who you are."

Shepherd eyed the former military policeman. "Why not?"

"Your impulse to confess is about clearing *your* conscience." Hutch dumped a spoonful of sugar into the coffee that Allie June had refreshed. He stirred in lazy circles. "That's what *you* need. Been there. Done that. I stirred things up for the families. Brought their grief back. I felt better for confessing, but at what cost?"

Shepherd bobbed his head. His palm was sweaty against the warm coffee cup. Yes. Hutch was right.

"The pastor and his family have been through hell and back," Gideon said. "What they need is to heal. They're trying their best to move on."

"If you lay your soul bare, you're going to rip off the bandage, and expose their wounds." Ryder took the motorcycle jacket off the coat hook beside their table and slipped it on.

"If you feel compelled to tell them," Hutch said, his dark eyes unreadable, "at least wait until after Christmas."

"How do I make up for what I did?" Shepherd asked, disturbed at the thought of upsetting the Luthers. The men were right. If he confessed, he'd be doing it for selfish reasons, not because it was what the Luthers needed to hear right now.

"You're being too hard on yourself." Ryder took a twenty-dollar bill from his wallet and laid it on the table.

"Terrorists killed Clayton," Hutch said. "But we get why you feel responsible. It's impossible not to feel responsible when you lose men under your charge."

"I have to make amends." Shepherd tightened his hand around the coffee cup.

The three other men exchanged a look. As if they were giving Shepherd some kind of test that he was on the verge of failing.

"So then be the Luthers' handyman. Stay through the holidays. Fix things up for them. Donate the money they pay you back to the church. Then be on your way." Gideon rested his artificial hand on the table.

"And if you feel the need to talk, come find one of us," Hutch offered. "We get what you're going through."

"You're not alone." Ryder met Shepherd's gaze head-on. "Remember that."

"What happens when the real handyman shows up?" Shepherd wanted to believe them.

Hutch winced. "Then you cross that bridge when you come to it. And who knows? Maybe he won't show."

Shepherd didn't like that option. It left too much to chance. He wished now that he hadn't opened up to this group. Wished that he wasn't stuck waiting for Nate to give him a ride to the church. Wished he'd stayed in bed and dealt with his insomnia.

Shepherd glanced outside. A slow spiral of snow-flakes had started to fall. The ground was too warm for it to stick, but he thought of Naomi. She lifted his hopes like the promise of snow.

And that was a dangerous thing. For them both.

"You're ready to go?" Nate asked, speaking for the first time since he'd returned to the table.

Shepherd exhaled, relieved. He'd appreciated being with the group for a time, but now he yearned to be alone.

"Hey, Nate, did you see what Shepherd made for Kimmie?" Hutch bragged, showing off the nutcracker.

Nate eyed Shepherd with new respect. "You carved that?"

"While you were yakking on the phone with your fine wife." Hutch snapped his fingers. "Just that quick."

"It's a stress-relieving hobby." Shepherd shifted, uncomfortable with the attention. He'd started whittling when he was eight, with the knife his father gave him. Done it to pass the time on the drive to the Kentucky Correctional Institute for Women in Shelby County.

"Impressive." Nate examined the nutcracker Hutch passed him. "Do you paint them too?"

"When I have the time."

"You could do this professionally," Nate said.

"Not much of a market for hand-carved toys," Shepherd said.

"What do you plan to do now that you're out of the military?" Hutch asked.

"Haven't thought that far ahead."

"I gotta get home, fellas. It's been real." Nate left money on the table. Shrugged into his peacoat.

Shepherd, chilled from the long walk over, hadn't even taken off his coat. He left cash for his pie and coffee, stood up, shook hands. "Nice to meet you all."

The men bid him good night, welcomed him back anytime. Reminded him not to tell the Luthers who he was.

Shepherd followed Nate to a late-model minivan. Raised an eyebrow.

"Don't laugh." Nate laughed himself. "Minivans are awesome."

"You've got kids."

"Three," Nate bragged. "Four-year-old twin boys and a two-year-old girl and another one on the way."

"You're lucky."

"I wasn't always. It takes some of us a while to find the people we belong with. But man, on the other side of the shit." Nate laughed like he'd won the Powerball. "There's heaven."

"For some people, I guess."

"For you too, if you want it." Nate said it as if life were that simple. Decide what you want. Go after it. Get it.

Shepherd didn't even bother commenting. Climbed into the passenger seat. The minivan smelled of kids. Juice boxes. Cheerios. There were three car seats in the back. Two blue. One pink.

As he looked at the car seats, a strange yearning pierced Shepherd's chest. What was this? A kid was the last thing he needed.

Nate started the minivan, sat there letting it idle.

Shepherd glanced over.

The older man was studying him with a level gaze, half curiosity, half wariness. "You serious about getting rid of those nightmares?"

"Yes." Shepherd swallowed his pride. He needed help and it was being offered to him. "More than anything."

"Then stop thinking about yourself."

"What?" That caught Shepherd by surprise. He was *not* thinking about himself. He'd been thinking of Clayton Luther nonstop for the past year. "I'm not—"

"You are." Nate's voice cut sharp, no-nonsense. "Your guilt is going around and around in your head like a carousel. You're telling yourself what you did wrong. How you failed Luther. What a terrible gunny you are."

Shepherd stared at the vet, both stunned at his insight and offended by it. He dropped his gaze, rubbed his knee. Nate was right.

"Beating yourself up isn't going to change what happened. Your guilt is tripping you up. Holding you back from healing. As long as you're wrapped up in it, you're not ever going to be happy."

Wow. It was as if Nate had peeled off the top of his skull and peered down into his brain. How did he know?

"I know," Nate said, leaving Shepherd to wonder if he'd spoken out loud. "Because I was the same way when I came back."

"You were?"

"If it hadn't been for other military men in this town offering me a hand up . . ." He shook his head. "And the people of Twilight. Let's just say they know how to forgive and forget. If not for them, I don't know if I could have snapped out of the self-recrimination in time . . ."

"Time for what?" Shepherd asked when Nate didn't go on.

"To save my life."

Shepherd studied the craggy vet who was being open and honest with him. "You were suicidal?"

"War screws with a man's head."

"Amen," Shepherd muttered.

"Get the hell out of your head and do something for someone else. We need all hands on deck for the annual Angel Tree and toy drive for needy kids. You game?"

Noncommittal, Shepherd fiddled with the zipper on his coat. "I don't know if I'll still be here by Christmas."

"You will if you give your word."

Shepherd raised his chin. "How do you know that?"

"You're a Marine. You keep your promises."

"What would I have to do?"

"Collect the donated toys. Or hell, you're a cracker-jack whittler. Make some toys. Sort 'em, wrap 'em, then on Christmas Eve, put on a Santa suit and hand 'em out." Nate eyed Shepherd's flat belly. "We'll have to stuff you with pillows, but you can pull it off."

The idea brought last Christmas into sharp focus again. How Clayton had begged Shepherd to go with him to the orphanage to hand out gifts. He should have gone. Clayton would be alive if he'd been brave enough to break the rules and go. Shepherd was certain of that.

"I know it's tough, considering your history," Nate went on. "But being among kids might just be what you need to get over this."

Feeling contrary, Shepherd said, "I don't need help."

"All right. You might not need help, but the kids do. Are you in?"

"Thanks for the vote of confidence, but—"

"You'll do it. Great." Nate kept one hand on the wheel, stuck out the other one. "Handshake's a binding contract in this town."

Shepherd hesitated. "I—"

"Do you want to stop feeling like shit or not?"

"I do."

Nate kept his hand extended. "Can we count on you, Santa?"

It seemed as if Nate was not going to retract his hand until Shepherd shook it.

"I'm in." Shepherd hoisted a sheepish grin, took the man's hand. Sealed the deal.

For a flash of a second, he felt like his old self again.

CHAPTER 9

The next morning, Naomi got up at six as usual. Immediately, she thought of Mark Shepherd and wondered if he'd come back last night.

But she didn't have time to keep track of him. She had a full schedule.

Except her silly mind wouldn't obey. It kept conjuring images of that moment when their hands had touched— the look in his eyes, his enticing scent, the curve of his cheekbones, the shape of his mouth.

Enough.

She woke Hunter. Helped the boy get dressed. Fed him breakfast. Overnight oatmeal with bananas and brown sugar. Combed his hair. Walked him to the side- walk with his backpack. Practiced his colors with him while they waited for Sarah Walker to pick him up for preschool carpool. Sarah was the author of *The Magic Christmas Cookie*. She was also the granddaughter of the woman who'd created the kismet cookie recipe. Naomi needed to talk to her about those cookies . . . and the dreams.

"What color is Santa's suit?"

"Wed," Hunter sang out, hoisting his backpack up on his shoulder.

"What color is Frosty the Snowman's nose?"

"Cawwot!"

"And what color are carrots?"

"*Ow*-ange." He drew out the first syllable and grinned. "Like Goldfish cwackews."

"Smart boy!" She kissed the top of his head.

Sarah pulled to the curb, her four-year-old son, Justice, strapped into the backseat. Hunter and Justice were the best of friends.

Naomi approached the minivan and Sarah rolled the window down. "Good morning."

"Morning, do you have a second?"

"Sure. What's up?"

It seemed silly in the light of day talking about kismet cookies and midnight dreams of handsome men. Plus they didn't have much time. But Naomi took a deep breath and forged ahead.

Naomi leaned into the car. Kept her voice low. "Remember last year? When you and the First Love Cookie Club persuaded me to sleep with a kismet cookie under my pillow on Christmas Eve?"

"I do. You wanted to find out if Robert really was your true love."

"Yes."

"We never talked about it, because of, well . . ." Sarah didn't mention Clayton's name. "But I'm guessing you did *not* dream of Robert."

"I did not."

"You dreamed of someone new?"

"Yes." This conversation was tougher than she thought it would be.

"And?" Sarah raised her eyebrows, obviously intrigued.

"Well . . ." Naomi cleared her throat. It felt goofy even saying it out loud. "I met *him*."

Sarah squealed, plastered a palm to her chest. "OMG! The man you dreamed about?"

"Or someone who looks a lot like he did in the dream."

"Does it feel . . ." Sarah whispered, "*fated*?"

"It does, but that's so illogical."

"I know, I know." Sarah bobbed her head. "I get it. Cookies can't *really* foretell your soul mate."

"No."

"But you know it's not Robert. You feel that in your heart."

Naomi held her breath, and said out loud something she hadn't even admitted to herself. "I do know he's not my soul mate."

Sarah rubbed her palms together. "So spill. Who did you dream about?"

"The handyman my dad just hired. His name is Mark Shepherd."

"Interesting." Sarah adjusted her sunglasses, and Naomi wasn't sure what to make of that comment.

"Confusing," Naomi clarified.

"Hey." Sarah laughed. "Love is a great mystery. If it feels right, I say roll the dice. What have you got to lose?"

"N'omi." Hunter tugged on her hand, bringing her back to earth. "We gotta go."

She looked down at the boy. She couldn't be taking risks. Not now. Not with Hunter to consider. Feeling utterly devoted, she ruffled his hair and leaned down to kiss his forehead. "Be cool in school."

"I always cool."

"Yes, you are." She helped him into the backseat. Buckled him up. Waved as Sarah drove away. Her heart filled with love. He was the most important thing in her life.

Period.

If she ever had a child of her own, she knew she could not love that baby any more than she loved Hunter. He was hers, one hundred percent, even if the adoption wasn't yet final. In her heart, she was already his mother.

Resolved to ignore her attraction to Mark Shepherd, she went back up the sidewalk. Her house slippers crunched the sweep of fallen leaves. Inside her pocket, her cell phone buzzed.

She checked the caller ID. Jana. "S'up?"

Jana clucked, a frustrated sound. "I can't give you a ride today. My mom fell and broke her hip and I'm headed to Austin right now."

"I'm so sorry. Is there anything I can do?" Concerned for her friend, Naomi nibbled her thumbnail.

"Prayers would be good."

"I'm on it."

"Thank you." Jana's voice was wavy, full of unshed tears.

"Please let me know if you need anything at all. Do you want me to look after your pets?"

"Sesty's got that covered," Jana said, referring to one of her bosses, Sesty Langtree.

"I really hate that this is happening. I wish I could be there to give you a hug."

"Thanks."

"Let me know how it goes."

"I'm sorry about leaving you stranded."

"Don't worry about me. You concentrate on your mom."

"You're the bomb, Luther." Jana wasn't the sentimental type. But Naomi heard gratitude in her voice "Call you when I get to Austin."

"Drive safely." Naomi switched off her phone and went back into the house.

Her parents were in the kitchen having breakfast. She waved and called good morning on the way to her room to get ready for the day. She didn't want to linger. They'd take one look at her and figure out there was a glitch. Her parents were pretty perceptive, and she couldn't always fool them by flipping the big-smile switch.

They had enough on their plate without worrying about her. Naomi got dressed. Styled her hair and put on a little makeup. By the time she finished, her parents had left. She said a prayer for Jana's mother and for Mom's appointment to go smoothly, then got down to business.

She brewed a cup of blueberry tea and pulled up the printout of Mrs. Beauchamp's shopping list. Plotted store visits for the most efficient route. She'd already bought some things online wholesale. But her true talent lay in ferreting out unique, handmade products tailored to her specific clients. Luckily, Twilight had a thriving artist community.

First order of business, find a ride.

She stood at the kitchen window, sipping her tea. Flipped through her mental files, considering and discarding possible names. Her gaze landed on the roof of the rectory two doors down.

Cocking her head, she could see a yellow metal ladder braced against the side of the building. The man atop the ladder wore blue jeans, sneakers, and a red flannel shirt.

It was the man of her dreams.

Mark Shepherd.

Warmth filled Naomi's stomach, and she caught herself smiling over the brim of her cup. Wow, but the man could fill out a pair of jeans.

Heat lit up her cheeks. What was wrong with her?

Mark made it up another rung.

First-name basis, huh, Naomi? He'd told her family to call him Shepherd. But it sounded too formal, and he seemed like a man in need of hearing his first name.

He moved his cane, hooking it around the rung above him. How in the world could he climb a ladder when he walked with a cane? Or, even more important, why had her father hired a handyman who could hardly get around? Well, she already knew the answer: her father had a soft spot for people in need. But that was the pot calling the kettle black, she knew. As she poured hot tea into a thermos, she wondered if Mark would want something to drink.

Okay, now this seemed like a bad idea. She should go back home. Do her shopping when her parents returned with their van.

Except she had to have Mrs. Beauchamp's order delivered to her house by five. Gift-wrapped. Darn it.

Straightening, she tucked the thermos under her arm, smiled brightly, and sauntered down the sidewalk toward the church.

At the rectory, she found him pulling old nails out of the loose boards that formed the back-porch awning. She assumed he was taking down the old rotting boards so he could put up new ones. He leaned over to the side; his body braced against the ladder. The muscles in his shoulder bunched underneath his long-sleeved flannel shirt.

Her heart skipped a beat, and she found it hard to breathe.

The urge to run came over her. She had no logical explanation for it. But her stomach clenched and her throat clogged. And she felt . . . *overtaken*.

"Good morning," he said, peering down at her.

There went her chance for a clean getaway.

Clearing her throat, she strolled to the foot of the ladder. Looked up. Lost her breath at the sight of his hot body. Settled her hands on her hips and smiled, smiled, smiled. "Good morning."

She'd hoped to sound crisp and efficient. And not at all like a woman who was ogling his butt. Not that she meant to ogle, but it was a nice butt.

Very nice.

His jeans cupped against him. Snug but not too snug. The perfect fit to showcase the perfect butt.

Good grief, Naomi, stop it!

The morning sun was in her eyes and she couldn't see his face from this angle. She shielded her eyes with the flat of her hand.

He studied her from underneath his armpit. He had a hammer in one hand, and new boards resting on the roof above him.

"Do you need something?" His tone was stiff, but polite. As if he really wanted to say, *Go away*.

Um, why yes. You.

The thought popped into her head. Irrational and sticky. The idea shocked her to her bones. But there it was, raw and stark, this chemical attraction. She felt tingly in places that hadn't tingled in a very long time.

Whoa!

Naomi held up the thermos. "I brought you some blueberry tea."

He grunted.

Well, hello, Mr. Conversational.

"Just brewed it. Piping hot," she said, knowing full well she was chattering because she was nervous. "I hope you like hot tea. Do you like hot tea? And blueberries?"

"I like hot tea." Neither his tone nor the look in his dark eyes gave anything away. "And blueberries. Although I can't claim I've ever had blueberry tea."

She extended the thermos.

He hooked the hammer through his belt loop. Started down the ladder, moving with care, each step slow and painstaking. He kept a hand on the rungs for support, even when he landed on the ground beside her.

His scent filled her nose. Nice. Soap and sunshine and cedar. It was a homey scent, and she was surprised how much it attracted her. Then again, everything about him surprised her.

"Hello," she said, her voice coming out husky. Dang it.

"Hello." A shadow of a smile lifted his lips. Faint. Not halfhearted, really. More cautious than lacking.

The morning sun was in his face, glinting off his dark eyes, rich as melted chocolate. Accentuating his angular jawline. She noticed the slight laugh lines at the corners of his eyes. He hadn't always been so serious. He had the potential for laughter. That lightened her heart.

"How did you sleep?" She rubbed the toe of her right fashion boot against the calf of her left leg. Swayed in the light breeze.

His shrug was a small shoulder roll, those broad shoulders barely moving. "Strange town. Strange bed."

Bed.

The simple three-letter word spun an image of him lying naked against a plethora of pillows, a sheet draped strategically across his waist. Arms up, cradling the back of his head in his palms, revealing manly armpits and a bare, well-muscled chest.

Sweat pearled between her breasts. "Not well, then."

He shook his head, a man of minimal words. He opened the thermos. Took a sip of tea. Smiled bigger.

Curiosity nudged her. "Do you have nightmares?"

His gaze was a laser beam, searing into her. "Sometimes."

From the way he said it, she had a feeling it was a lot more often than sometimes. "If you'd like, I'll make you some chamomile tea before you go to bed at night."

"I appreciate the offer, but chamomile's not going to cut it." He gave her a you-sweet-naïve-thing smile.

A wiggle of irritation squirmed through her. Because she had a sunny disposition, and she was a minister's daughter, people often mistook her for a Goody-Two-Shoes.

"We could always tipple bourbon in the tea," she teased.

He shook his head, a sharp movement. Propped his cane against the building. "I've got enough crutches. Thanks."

"You have a real problem with insomnia?" She ran two fingers along her brow, worried about him. That image of him naked in bed flashed through her mind again. *Stop it!* What time had he come back from his late-night wanderings?

He leveled her a cool stare. "Is there a reason you came over besides the tea?"

In other words, state your need or be gone. Okay, he wasn't the friendliest person in the universe. No problem. She had lots of friends. The only thing she needed from him was a ride.

"What do you want?" Mark Shepherd asked, his tone lowering on the word "want."

Her stomach jumped and she almost told him never mind. Almost scurried away. It would have been the wise thing. But she did not.

"Lightbulb replaced? Jar lid opened? Drawer un-stuck?" he asked.

"A vehicle with a big backseat." A new image popped into her head. This time, he was bare-chested in the backseat of his Jeep, beckoning her with a come-to-me finger.

Ack!

"Is that all?" He sounded relieved. "Here." He pulled the Jeep keys from his pocket, dangled them from his index finger. "It's a stick. Can you drive a stick?"

"No."

"All right." He pocketed the keys, turned back to the ladder.

"Wait." She held up a hand, not sure what to make of him. The stranger was challenging.

And intriguing.

He paused, swung around, a guarded expression on his face. "Yes?"

Her throat seized up. "Umm . . . could you drive me?"

One dark eyebrow went up on his forehead, his gaze piercing hot. And she thought illogically, *Heathcliff.*

Wuthering Heights was her favorite classic novel. While other women went gaga over Jane Austen, *Pride and Prejudice*, and Mr. Darcy, she was more of a Brontë girl. Give her *Jane Eyre* and *Wuthering Heights*, Mr. Rochester and Heathcliff, any day of the week.

Perhaps her darker taste in literature was a counter-balance to her cheerful nature. Or maybe she had a thing for brooding loners. Itching with the need to bring them out of the darkness into the light.

"You mean like a chauffeur?"

She cringed, afraid that she'd offended him. "I'm spending the morning shopping, but my friend who was going to give me a ride . . . well, her mom broke her hip and she had to drive to Austin to be with her. I need a vehicle big enough to haul my packages. Can you do it?"

He picked up his cane. Was that a yes or a no?

"You'll give me a ride?" she asked.

"I'll do better than that. I'll carry your packages and watch your purse while you concentrate on shopping. I've seen how you load yourself down. How distracted you get."

"Wow, Mr. Judgy Judgerson."

"You're the one who jumped into the wrong Jeep."

He had a point, but she didn't want to admit it. She was about to tell him to forget the whole thing. He'd been hired to work at the rectory, after all, not ferry her around. But it would be nice to have someone deal with the packages and watch her purse while she shopped.

Not that Twilight was a high crime area. But this time of year, tourists packed the town. No reason to lead people into temptation.

"Thank you for your offer. That would be nice." Her heart was doing a Snoopy dance. A squiggle of happiness swam around in her stomach.

"Are you ready to go right now?" he asked.

"Yes."

"Let me take down this ladder," he said. "We don't want some kid wandering up and climbing on the roof."

"Kids should be in school."

"'Should' being the operative word. Kids play hooky."

"I didn't."

"Of course not." He gave her a corner of a smile and a bounce of his eyebrows. Half smug. Half not.

"I'm assuming you did." She plaited her fingers together, clasped her hands at her chest.

"At least once a week."

"Wow. A bad boy, huh?" A prickling of delight lifted the hairs on her arms. Oh, this chemical attraction nonsense was delicious agony.

"Not bad," he said. "Misguided."

"What did you do when you skipped school?" She held her breath. Half expected him to say he shot pool or smoked pot or drag-raced or hooked up with girls. Those thoughts set her heart pounding faster.

"There were caves near where I lived. I went there to hide out. Be by myself."

Brooding loner, indeed. Move over, Heathcliff.

He reached for the ladder, pushed a mechanism that truncated it. Tucked the ladder under his arm and limped to the back of the house.

Wincing, Naomi followed. Did his leg hurt as much as it looked like it did?

He put the ladder in the barn, dusted his palm on the seat of his jeans, and came back to where she stood. Retrieved his cane, and led the way to his Jeep.

CHAPTER 10

"Where to?" he asked, once they were inside.

"Town square." She smoothed down her skirt.

He started the engine. The inside of the cab was quiet. Cozy. It smelled like him. Piney. Outdoorsy. Earthy.

She tried not to notice the provocative scent. Wondered why the smell hadn't clued her in yesterday that she'd slipped into the wrong vehicle. Distracted. It was her only excuse.

The square remained blocked to through traffic. It would be until after the Dickens festival was over.

Shepherd stopped the Jeep before he reached the saw-horse blockade, and glanced around, looking for a place to parallel-park on the street. No free spots.

"Just drop me off. You can swing back around and pick me up here in . . ." She peeped at her phone. "Let's say forty minutes."

"I'm going in with you." His tone was firm. Brooking no argument. His eyes half-lidded and sultry.

Yipes! "There's no need."

He pulled the Jeep into an alley, backed up. "There's

all the need in the world. You asked for my help. I'm giving it to you."

"I'm giving you an out. You don't have to come." That sounded too suggestive. Oh gosh. Ulp. "With me. You don't have to come with me." Sweet heavens, she was making it worse.

"I'm going. End of discussion." He spun the Jeep around.

She clutched her hands to her heart. Thrilling to his firm but kind tone. She sneaked a peek over at him. Noticed how strong his broad hands looked on the steering wheel. Felt her pulse throb at the hollow of her throat.

He drove in the opposite direction until he found a parking spot on a residential side street.

Whoa, Mr. Take Charge. She wasn't quite sure she liked this alpha male baloney. But a secret part of her quivered with joy, and she wasn't quite sure why.

"It'll be boring," she said.

He turned his head, stared her straight in the eyes, his eyes flaring with interest. "*Nothing* is boring where you're concerned."

Butterflies fluttered in her stomach. Naomi gulped from the heat of his stare. His tone was sincere, the look in his eyes determined and sexy. Far too sexy. He *wanted* to go shopping with her? Well, okay then. She'd hush up trying to dissuade him.

A helpless, look-what-I-found-under-the-tree-on-Christmas-morning smile stole her lips.

Oh my, but she liked him.

Shepherd watched Naomi flit around the first store they entered. It was a feminine boutique, and a diffuser misted the scent of roses into the air, making him feel a little light-headed. He didn't know if his dizziness was from the scent, from skipping breakfast, or from his closeness to Naomi. Maybe it was all three, he thought ruefully.

"What do you think?" Naomi wrapped a luxurious shawl around her shoulders, twirled. She beamed at him, her face aglow. The brightly colored material enhanced her Snow White complexion. Dark hair. Blue eyes. Ivory skin.

He thought *she* was magnificent. Warm tingles started in his stomach, spread out through his body. Forcefully, he ignored the sensation. "It suits you. You should buy it."

Her smile drifted away, and she caressed the fine weave of golden threads on the shawl's hem. "Oh no, I couldn't ever afford something like this. It's for a client."

The wistful disappointment on her face stirred his soul. It was all he could do not to reach for his wallet and buy the shawl for her. No matter what number was on the price tag.

Give it to her for Christmas, a voice in his head whispered.

But that was an impulsive thought. Would he even be in Twilight by Christmas? Yes, he'd promised Nate he'd hang around for the Angel Tree and toy drive. But nothing was holding him to that beyond a handshake.

And his moral compass.

Here was the kicker. Even if he stayed through Christmas, he'd eventually have to give her family Clayton's key and tell his story. And that would be that. He doubted she'd ever speak to him again once she knew the truth.

The familiar guilt was a weight, tightening around his neck. He thought about why he was here. To give them the key Clayton had left behind for him. To bring closure to the family. And himself. Then he thought about what the military men had told him last night. Felt pulled like taffy in two opposing directions.

"Well?"

Shepherd stood near a rack of dresses, stared at her in bewilderment. He'd already forgotten what they'd been talking about. His head—and heart—wrapped up in the mess he was making of things. All he wanted was for her to be happy. Yet all he had to offer her was sorrow.

Her smile was a joyous thing, cloaking him in holiday nostalgia. She bounced on the balls of her feet, excited as a kid. Her breasts swayed provocatively beneath the drape of the shawl.

Every masculine part of him yearned for her.

He liked it here. He liked *her*.

Too bad he was who he was. And she was Clayton Luther's sister. His mouth tasted like chalk. He knotted his hands.

Naomi waited in front of him. Her cheeks pink, her eyes welcoming. "I can tell from the look on your face that you approve." She turned to the hovering clerk. "I'll take it. Put it on my account, please."

"How does that work?" Shepherd asked.

"What?"

"Your business model."

"Oh." Her eyes lit and he saw the passion for her work reflected on her face. "I consult with the client, getting a sense of what they like, don't like, who they're buying for. We create a shopping list and a total budget. I buy the items. If my client lives within twenty-five miles I'll hand deliver everything, if they're farther away I'll ship it, and at Christmas I'll wrap the presents for an extra charge. My service fee is ten percent of the total."

"Interesting."

"You think so?" She gave him a look that said, *You're full of bullshit, buddy*, except she probably didn't use profanity.

He ran a hand over his chin, studied her in the prism of light shining off the nearby Christmas tree. Noticed how good she looked in that red sweater, short black skirt, black leggings, and black-heeled boots. Stylish. But understated. Elegant and classy.

Today, little gold stars replaced the pearl earrings. She still wore the gold cross. Not just as a fashion statement, he realized, but as a symbol of her devotion to her beliefs.

"How did you get started as a personal shopper?" he asked.

"Quite by accident." She laid the shawl on the counter so the clerk could ring it up. "My parents couldn't afford to pay for my college tuition so I looked around for ways to make money part-time while I went to school."

"Enterprising." He studied her face, charmed. She had the softest lips. He couldn't seem to stop thinking about kissing them.

"I was already doing all the shopping for my mom by then, and I added some of the people in her RA support group." She signed the receipt the clerk passed across the counter to her. "Turns out I had a knack for finding just the right items at good prices. When I expanded to Fort Worth, my business skyrocketed. I ended up dropping out of college because the business was doing so well."

"What were you studying?" He admired the way her hair curled over her shoulders, soft and silky. Ached to run his fingers through it.

"Fashion merchandising." Her eyes crinkled up in a lovely way, inviting him to join her in a smile.

"So it was a natural fit." Irresistibly drawn to her, he stepped closer. "Where did you go to school?"

She leaned in, and he caught a whiff of her peppermint scent. "The University of North Texas in Denton."

He didn't know much about Texas. "Is Denton near here?"

She gestured in a northerly direction. "About seventy-five miles north."

He studied her face, noticed a small sprinkling of freckles across the top of her pert little nose. "Did you live on campus?"

"Actually, I commuted on Tuesdays and Thursdays."

"That seems like a long commute."

"People in Texas are used to driving long distances. We're a big state." She chuckled. "Besides, it was only two days a week."

"How come you didn't go to school in Fort Worth?"

She rubbed two fingers against her thumb. "Both of the four-year universities in Fort Worth are private schools. Too pricey for my blood."

"So have you always lived with your parents?"

"I did have a little apartment just down the road to be close to the folks after Mom got sick instead of moving on up to Denton. But then after Clayton and Samantha—" She broke off, hoisted up a half smile. "I moved back in with them to help with Hunter. Samantha's parents didn't take him because they had five other children and they were living in a three-bedroom house. There was simply no room for him over there. Besides, Samantha and Hunter had already been living with Mom and Dad while Clayton was deployed. It worked out all the way around.

No risk of a custody battle if that's what you're thinking. Hunter is mine. Everyone agrees."

"Will you stay with them once you adopt Hunter?"

She hesitated, bit her lip, and looked as if she was trying to decide whether to tell him something or not. Finally, she said, "I'm just trying to make it through the holidays. I haven't had time to think much beyond that."

He had a feeling she was hiding something, but it was her right to keep her secrets. She didn't owe him an explanation. "Do you ever feel like you gave your life up for your family?"

"Oh no! My parents are great."

He liked that she had a strong nuclear family. He didn't get it, but he liked it. Wondered if she'd had any men in her life. She was a pastor's daughter. Was she a virgin? But she was in her late twenties and gorgeous. Surely, she'd had boyfriends. Lovers?

"What is the secret to your success? What makes you so good at your job?" he asked.

"I ask a lot of questions." She accepted the bag the clerk passed to her. Thanked her. "And I really try to listen to the client. It's often as much about what they don't say as what they do. You have to read between the lines."

"She *is* awesome," the clerk confirmed. "Naomi is fifteen percent of my business."

"It does help that I live in a town full of quirky, creative artists." Naomi winked at the clerk. "I buy handmade artisan products whenever possible."

"Here." Shepherd reached for the bag. "I'll carry that."

"My." Naomi grinned and relinquished it. "This is nice."

She headed for the door, and he took three steps after her before he realized he'd forgotten his cane. He was slowly getting stronger, and starting to rely on the cane less, but he wasn't taking chances. The last thing he wanted was to end up on the ground in front of Naomi.

He found the cane where he'd propped it against the counter. Caught up with her as the bell over the door jangled.

A cool blast of air greeted them. She laughed, a sweet sound that unbuttoned his reserve.

"I smell snow," she said, her cute little nose wriggling.

"And what does snow smell like?" he asked, captivated.

"Wet." There was that laugh again.

Outdoor speakers were playing Andy Williams, "It's the Most Wonderful Time of the Year." Naomi bobbed her head in time to the music, sang along. Adorable. She was freaking adorable. Full of heart and happiness, despite all she'd suffered. He admired her so much he felt a pinch dead center in his chest.

People stared at her. She didn't care. She sang for the sheer joy of it. Infectious. The woman had an irrepressible spirit that made him long to know her better.

"Let's go in here." She pushed open the door to the next boutique. This one was a yarn store that also carried hand-knitted clothing.

Shepherd watched her flutter around the store, and he thought of butterflies. Floating. Brightly colored. Filled with beauty and grace. Cheering up the world.

"What do you think?" She held up two fluffy sweaters. One purple. One green.

"For you?"

She gave a shake of her head and a minor eye roll. "No, silly, for Matilda Muckraker."

"That's a real name?" Shepherd chuckled.

"Don't make fun." She slanted her eyes coyly. "Matilda has suffered horribly over it."

"Why doesn't she just change her name?"

"And get rid of a noble family moniker? Her ancestors were some of the first settlers in Texas."

"Oh well, then. Muck away, Muckrakers."

"You're a bit sarcastic, aren't you?" Amusement lit up her eyes.

He lifted a shoulder. "I can crack wise."

"I like that about you." She winked, held up both sweaters again. "Now which one?"

"I like green."

"Purple it is." Naomi handed the sweater to the check-out girl. "Put this in the pile."

"If you were going to do the opposite of what I said, why did you ask my opinion?"

Naomi's smile was honey on hot biscuits. "I wanted you to feel needed."

Shepherd snorted, laughed. Damn, but he liked her.

"You're hanging around with nothing to do. I thought I'd liven things up." She poked him playfully in the ribs with her elbow.

Oh, she livened things up all right. And it had nothing to do with sweaters. Um, beyond the one she was wearing and filling out so nicely.

"Onward and upward," Naomi chirped, a delightful sound that bounced off the high ceilings of the old building, a sound that left him feeling special and included. "Next stop, Perks."

"What do they sell there?"

"Coffee. Shopping is hard work. I need caffeine."

"You sure about that?" he asked. "I can barely keep up with you now."

Immediately, her brows dipped in concern. "Oh my, I didn't think. I am so sorry. Is it your leg? Are you in pain?"

"I'm fine," he said, putting gravel in his voice. He hated to call attention to his damn knee. Wished he hadn't made that joke. "I was talking about your boundless energy. You're a force of nature."

Naomi patted his shoulder and leaned close to whisper, "Oh that. Don't worry. We'll get you a double shot of espresso so you can keep up."

And Shepherd couldn't have been more bowled over if she'd reached up and kissed him.

CHAPTER II

"Welcome to Perks!" said the girl behind the counter wearing a green elf hat. A jingle bell jangled from the end of it every time she bobbed her head. Which was often. The cheery barista was as bubbly as Naomi.

"Hi, Mia." Naomi wriggled her fingers at the elfish blonde.

"Hey." Mia's eyes lit up at Shepherd, and she licked her lips. "Who is your handsome new friend?"

"Mark." Naomi turned to him with a flourish of her hand. "This is Mia. Mia, Mark."

"Hello, Mark." Mia took a Tic Tac box from her pocket, popped a mint into her mouth. "Where did *you* come from?"

"He's our church's new handyman," Naomi explained.

"Nice to meetcha, Mark." Mia went up on her toes to lean over the counter and offer him her hand.

"You can call me Shepherd." He shook her hand. His shoulder was still tingly from where Naomi had touched him. "Everyone does."

"Except me," Naomi piped up. "Last names used as first names seem so cold."

"I think it's sexy." Mia didn't let go of his hand or his gaze. "Anyone ever call you Shep?"

"Not and lived to tell about it." Shepherd reappropriated his hand.

Mia laughed, but looked disappointed. "Wanna sample the new coffee flavor?"

"What's it called?" Naomi asked.

"Mistletoe Mocha."

"Sounds, um . . . interesting. What's in it?"

Mia wrinkled her nose. "I'm not sure. Mocha definitely. Other than that . . ." She shrugged. "I've got the recipe here somewhere."

"Did Evelyn make it up?"

"Yes." Mia rolled her eyes. "You know how Evelyn is when she's got a wild hair."

"Evelyn's the owner," Naomi explained to Shepherd. "She puts together some weird flavor combos. Some of them turn out great, others not so—"

"Like the Fourth of July Watermelon Latte." Mia shuddered.

"That didn't work out so well," Naomi finished.

Shepherd rested his arm against the counter. Enjoying the exchange between the two women.

"So, you want the Mistletoe Mocha?" Mia asked.

"I'll stick with my usual cappuccino. Add an extra shot of espresso."

"Extra shot, huh?" Mia inclined her head toward Shepherd. "This guy wearing you out? If he is, just say the word. I'll take him off your hands."

Shepherd braced himself against the sassy barista's words.

"If anything," Naomi quipped, "I'm wearing him out."

"Ooh-la-la. Fun day."

"We're just getting started."

"What's *up* for the afternoon?" Mia stared pointedly at the zipper of Shepherd's jeans. "You can leave him here with me if he's slowing you down."

Naomi slid a sidelong glance his way. *Sorry*, she mouthed.

He shrugged, sent her a quick, good-natured smile. Not her fault that Mia was an outrageous flirt.

"My loyalties lie with Naomi," he told Mia.

"Damn the luck." Mia laughed and punched Naomi lightly on the shoulder with a knuckle. "Look at you go, girl."

"I'm not going anywhere," Naomi said. "There's no-where to go. Shepherd and I are just . . ."

"Just what?" Mia prompted, retying the strings on her apron.

"He's helping me."

"Sure he is." Mia winked.

Naomi blushed.

"No worries." Mia waved a hand. "I'm just poking fun. Makes the day go by quicker. What'll you have, cowboy?"

"Cowboy?" Shepherd echoed.

"She calls every guy that," Naomi explained. "She has a Western fetish. I blame *Longmire*."

"Well," Shepherd said, "she does live in Texas."

"Thank you." Mia fluttered her eyelashes at him. "You want the Mistletoe Mocha?"

"I'll pass on the fancy coffee," Shepherd said. "I take plain black."

"With sugar?" she asked.

"No."

"Cream?"

"Black."

"Any flavorings?"

"Black."

"Watch out for him. He's weird," Mia whispered to Naomi. "But cute."

"Cute goes a long way in making up for the weird." Naomi chuckled.

Shepherd lifted his shoulders to his ears, the collar of his coat brushing his lobes. If he didn't think Naomi was the cutest thing since baby kittens, he might have walked right out of the coffee shop.

"Still. Plain black coffee? When he could have any of this." Mia swept her arm at the overhead chalkboard filled with elaborate drink offerings. She clucked her tongue and sent Shepherd a *tsk-tsk* glance. "You could have a Royal Flush."

"I'm not even gonna ask what that is," he mumbled.

"Pumpkin flavoring. Caramel. Vanilla. Hazelnut cream. Sprinkled with cinnamon and nutmeg," Mia said.

"Pass."

"You don't know what you're missing . . ." Mia shook her head as if he were a lost cause. "It's yummy. Earthy and frothy, sweet and complex."

"I like things simple." Shepherd paused, and cast a glance at Naomi. "Uncomplicated."

"Translation, *boring*."

"I'm good with that." Shepherd took a ten-dollar bill from his wallet and stuck it in the tip jar.

"Woo, a big tipper. He's a keeper. Okay, I'm back to liking him again." Mia grinned at Naomi. "Unless he's trying to buy my affection." She narrowed her eyes at Shepherd. "Is that what you're up to?"

"You want me to take the ten bucks back?"

"No, no." She placed her hand over the tip jar. "I'm good with having my affections bought. How long you in town for, cowboy?"

"Just through the holidays," Shepherd answered.

"Too bad." Mia licked her lips. "If you ever get a hankering to get out of your boring rut . . ." She leaned over the counter, grabbed his hand.

Taken aback, Shepherd sucked in air. Battled his Marine's instincts to fight when caught unaware.

Mia flipped a ballpoint pen from the pocket of her apron and wrote her phone number in his palm. "Don't wash it off."

Laughing, Mia turned to make their coffees.

"Does that happen to you a lot?" Naomi murmured as they waited in line to pay for their drinks.

"It's the limp," he said. "Brings out the nurturer in women."

"Right. And it has nothing to do with how hot your butt looks in jeans."

"You think my butt looks hot?"

"Don't let it go to your head," she quipped. "Hot butts are a dime a dozen."

"Who's got a hot butt?" asked a voice from behind them, followed by an audible inhale. "Oh . . . I *see*."

Shepherd turned to see a woman about Naomi's age. She had long, straight red hair and wore stylish dark-wash blue jeans, a black turtleneck sweater, and far too much makeup in Shepherd's estimation.

"Lily!" Naomi squealed, and wrapped the woman in her embrace.

Lily hugged Naomi, but over her shoulder gave Shepherd the stink eye. This one was protective of her friend. "Who's this?"

"Dad's new handyman."

"Handyman, huh?" Lily narrowed her eyes. "He doesn't look like any handyman I ever knew."

"Oh you." Naomi patted Lily's arms. "You're so suspicious of strangers."

"He walks with a limp. What handyman limps?"

"One who got injured." Shepherd met Lily's hard-edged stare. Dealt one right back at her.

"Don't let the limp fool you," Naomi said, sticking up for him. "He's very capable."

"Really?" Lily sent him a she-wolf stare. "I've got a loose floorboard in my kitchen. Would you mind taking a look at it?"

She was testing him. No question.

"I'm committed to the Luthers, sorry," he said.

"Just my luck. Handsome stranger rolls into town, and he's already in a committed relationship."

"Mark," Naomi said. "This is Lily Hanson, one of my best clients."

Lily faked a pout. "I thought I was your *best* client."

"Shh." Naomi giggled and pressed a finger to her lips. "You are."

"*Best* client." Lily slung her arm around Naomi's shoulder, pulled her closer.

Shepherd blinked and stared at the two women. Light and dark. Night and day. And he wasn't talking about their coloring. From her clothes to her stance to the look in her eyes, Lily was tough and sharp, all rough edges and angular lines. By comparison, Naomi was soft and round, smooth curves and gentle circles.

"Where are you from?" Lily asked, stepping closer and narrowing her eyes. "You don't sound like a Texan."

"Kentucky."

"Where in Kentucky?"

"You a private investigator in your spare time?" Shepherd asked.

"When it comes to my friends, I am." Lily raised two fingers to her eyes, and then pointed those same two fingers at him. "I'm watching you, buddy."

"Lexington." He cracked a smile. Lily was all right.

Lily's eyes squinted even narrower. "You any kin to Raylan Givens? You look kinda like him."

"Raylan Givens is a fictional character." Entertained and intrigued by Naomi's choice of friend, he smiled. Whatever Lily lacked in couth and decorum she made up for in loyalty.

"I know that," Lily said.

"Raylan Givens can't live in Kentucky," he said.

"Of course he can. He's a fictional character. He can live anywhere he wants." Lily scowled at him as if he were a total idiot.

"She has a thing for Timothy Olyphant," Naomi explained.

"Not Timothy Olyphant," Lily corrected. "*Raylan Givens.*"

"Good luck with that," Shepherd said.

Lily laughed. "I like him." To Shepherd she said, "You get a pass for today. But you mess with my friend, and you die."

"Yes, ma'am," he said, and saluted her.

"I'm not kidding."

"Have you ever been in the military?" Shepherd asked her.

Lily got a weird look on her face as if she'd had a major

run-in with the military. "I have to be somewhere." She hugged Naomi. "See you later." She turned and scooted out the back door of Perks.

"Your friend is . . ." He paused, searching for the right word.

"Colorful?" Naomi supplied.

"Yes," he said. "That."

"Cappuccino," called out the young man behind the cash register. "And . . ." He looked confused at the drinks Mia had put in front of him. "Plain black coffee?"

"He's a Marine. No nonsense." Naomi whipped out her debit card to pay for the coffee before Shepherd had a chance to get out his wallet.

"I see," said the kid behind the counter.

"I was going to pay for the coffee," Shepherd protested.

"You got the tip. I got the java. Plus you're driving me around all day. Buying your coffee is the least I can do." She picked up her cappuccino. "Do you want to sit or walk?"

His knee needed to sit, but Shepherd wanted out of the noisy, crowded café. "Walk."

"This way." Naomi led him out the back door where Lily had gone and into a cobblestone courtyard.

Wrought-iron picnic tables were on a little patio area, but it was too cold to sit outside. The ubiquitous Christmas lights had made their way back here too. Draped over the live oak trees, and down the sides of a pergola arbor.

They strolled the gentrified alleyway toward the town square. The tourist traffic was light. It was still early, and a Tuesday morning to boot. Banners for the Dickens festival flapped overhead in the breeze. Vendors were setting up a food kiosk, including a booth selling roasted chestnuts.

"I've never eaten a chestnut," Shepherd said.

"Really?" She looked surprised, as if roasted chestnuts were as common as salt. "We've got to get you some once Randy gets them toasting." She raised her cup in greeting. "Morning, Randy."

"Hi, Naomi," called the paunchy middle-aged man. He had two different colored eyes. One brown. One green. He sported a handlebar mustache and a wide-brimmed cowboy hat. "How are your folks?"

"Fine. Doing well."

"And little Hunter?" Randy said. "How's he?"

"Running me ragged." She chuckled. "He's a lively four-year-old."

"I get that. We raised four of our own and now the grandkids keep coming. Charlene is expecting her second in May."

"Oh, Randy." The tension eased from Naomi's voice. "That's so awesome."

"Yep. It's a boy this time. She's gonna name him after me." The chestnut vendor puffed out his chest with pride.

"What a lovely honor," Naomi said, but the comment wasn't perfunctory. Her tone was warm and genuine. She meant it. "You must be so proud."

"As a peacock." Randy laughed.

"We'll be back later when the chestnuts are ready." Her smile was a Christmas present all by itself. Shiny and bright, but beneath it, Shepherd saw a thick layer of unexpressed sorrow. She was still holding on to a lot of grief. He detected it in the stiffness of her shoulders, the deepening hollow of her cheeks.

Randy sidled a glance at Shepherd. "We?"

"Where are my manners?" Naomi clucked her tongue. "This is the church's new handyman, Mark Shepherd. My van is in the shop so he's escorting me today."

Randy stuck out his hand to shake Shepherd's. "Welcome to Twilight."

"Thank you," Shepherd said. "It's a friendly place."

"You ain't seen nothing yet." Randy smoothed his mustache. "Come back in an hour. Any friend of Naomi's is a friend of mine. The chestnuts are on the house."

Naomi slipped her arm through Shepherd's. The contact was electric.

Startled, he jumped. What the heck? But then he realized she was guiding him around a gnarled tree root that had grown up through the sidewalk.

"Trip hazard," she said, and released him. "With your knee, I didn't want to take chances."

Too late.

She'd already taken a huge chance by touching him. Damage done. Those soft fingers had curled around his upper arm. Her fresh, honest scent—like vanilla, peppermint, and starched linen—had gotten tangled up in his nose. His body instantly responded to her touch, growing hot and tingly.

She leaned forward to toss her empty coffee cup into a nearby trash can. Her camel-colored coat swung against the curve of her hip.

He could not stop staring at her. It wasn't just her beauty that mesmerized him, or her sweetness. He'd dreamed of her, of moments like this. He'd longed for a woman like her—friendly and open and trusting, with a smile as wide as the sky.

Now that she was here with him, he didn't know what to do. Naomi and her sunbeam eyes. Her tipped-up mouth offered him a life preserver. He knew in his heart of hearts that he did not deserve her. She was too special, too precious, too sweet and pure for the likes of him.

Lily knew it.

From the look Randy had given him, and the tight, slightly threatening squeeze of his handshake, the chestnut vendor knew it too.

Shepherd finished off the last of his coffee, and put the cup in the trash receptacle. Stepped back. Stepped away from her.

Breathing room.

He needed breathing room.

"Onward and upward," she said in her gung-ho singsong. "Next stop, the toy store!"

She headed for a building on the opposite side of the square, cutting across the courthouse lawn. Her dark hair bounced silkily over her shoulders.

He watched her move, awed by her lithe grace.

She paused when she realized she'd outpaced him. Turned to look at him over her shoulder. The clouds parted overhead and the morning sun streamed down in fingers of warm, rich light.

Stunned, he could only stare at her golden perfection and wonder how he'd come to be in the presence of such an angel.

"Where's your cane?"

"Huh?" He blinked, realizing for the first time he was without the cane. "I must have left it in the coffee shop."

She came back for him. "Take my arm."

"I'm fine." He held his hands behind his back.

She sent him a funny look. "Then why were you standing there just staring after me?"

He wanted to say, *Because you are so beautiful I can*

hardly bear it. But that would be weird, so he pointed to the sign on the courthouse lawn.

"Keep Off the Grass."

"Oh that." She waved a dismissive hand at the sign. Pointed to the foot traffic trail right through the middle of the grass. "C'mon."

Shepherd shook his head. "The sign says not to."

She sank her hands on her hips. "Are you kidding me right now?"

"Rules are rules."

"The grass is dead. There's a dirt trail through it. No reason to keep off."

"Not dead," he said. "Just dormant for the winter. It'll come back in the spring if we don't trample it."

"If we don't cut across the lawn, we have to go the long way. The workmen have that whole side of the square blocked off. Detour through Sweetheart Park."

"I'm good with that."

"Even without your cane?"

He hardened his chin. "I'm not walking on the grass."

"You are such a Boy Scout," she teased.

"And you are a minister's daughter. You should know better than to disobey the law," he joked right back.

"Haven't you heard? Preachers' kids are the worst." Her face was so full of glee that he wanted to take a snapshot to remember this moment.

"You don't strike me as a stereotype."

"It's just a 'Keep Off the Grass' sign."

"It's a rule."

"Sometimes you have to know when a rule isn't really a rule, but more of a suggestion. Sometimes you just have to trust your gut."

Trust your gut.

Those words made him think of last Christmas. When he should have trusted his gut and gone to the orphanage with Clayton. He paused. Debating. It was just walking on the grass. What was the big deal?

His lips twitched. The urge to tell her who he was swept through him. He wanted to blurt it. Clear his conscience of everything. Confess that he was not a handyman. Give her the Christmas key in his pocket. Beg her forgiveness.

But he thought about what Nate and the other military men had told him the night before. Recalled how Lily had playfully threatened him if he hurt Naomi. Not that he was scared of Lily, but the last thing he wanted was to hurt Naomi.

No getting around it. He was going to hurt her. Whether now or later, whenever the truth came out, it wouldn't matter if he slept with a hundred cookies under his pillow and had a hundred dreams of her. She wouldn't be able to forgive him.

How could she?

Her family had been destroyed because of him.

The pain of what he could not have was powerful and poignant. He yearned for her like a hungry kid with his nose pressed against a bakery store window.

She snorted an exasperated breath, but her lively eyes were kind. "Okay, we'll do it your way. Stroll through the park it is. C'mon."

Turning, she skirted the cherry-picker truck, parked in the middle of the road. Hoisting light-stringing workmen up to the treetops.

Shepherd caught up to Naomi as she stepped down off the curb, and headed for the entrance to Sweetheart Park.

She stopped, swung back toward him. "Oh, do mind your ste—"

But she didn't get to finish her sentence. The toe of Shepherd's boot hung in a deep, wide crack in the cobblestones and his knee collapsed inward. He stumbled forward.

Naomi grabbed him as he fell. Good-naturedly whispered, "Bet you wish you'd cut across the grass now, huh?"

You couldn't tell it from the way she dressed. Or the gold cross hanging around her neck. But this one had a saucy side to her. Oh yes, she did.

CHAPTER 12

At the contact of Mark's chest against her breasts, Naomi sucked in air. Lots of it. She had her arms around him and was leaning forward to keep him from hitting the concrete. He was a good nine inches taller than her five-foot-five height. And at least sixty pounds heavier. He was lean, but stacked with muscles.

She crouched beside him, trying to lever him up. Wished he had his cane. She almost had him to his feet. But then her foot slipped out from underneath her at the shift in his weight. And they both ended up on the ground.

Shepherd on his back. Somehow Naomi was straddling him.

She just *had* to be in a skirt, didn't she? Yes, she had on leggings, but they were little protection. Her thighs were on either side of him. Her pelvis perilously close to his.

And the zipper of his jeans was straining. He had an erection.

Because of her.

Holy moly.

Naomi was twenty-seven years old. Yes, she was a preacher's daughter. But she wasn't a prude, and she'd had the same boyfriend since she was sixteen. She wasn't innocent. She wasn't virginal. She'd given herself to Robert knowing in her heart of hearts they would one day marry.

Or so she believed at the time.

No, she wasn't chaste. But boy, did she blush.

Red-hot heat swamped her. Bathing her entire body in blood-roasting flames. Her internal temperature felt shoved to a hundred and ten degrees Fahrenheit.

In the desert.

In August.

The cool wind blowing up her skirt did nothing to cool her. Nor did the molten look in Mark Shepherd's eyes. This man wanted *her*.

And she wanted him.

The spot between her legs, where she was straddling him, burned and ached with crazy mad desire.

She had no time to process that look or her feelings. People were rushing over. Exclaiming in alarm. Reaching out. Helping them up.

Naomi didn't dare look at Mark. And when she finally did hazard a quick glance his way, he wasn't looking at her. Thank heavens.

"You took quite a tumble," a woman said to Mark.

"Are you okay?" a man asked Naomi.

"I'm getting after the mayor about these sidewalks," said Patsy Crouch. She'd hurried over from the Teal Peacock. Patsy was on the town council. Plus, Sheriff Hondo Crouch was her husband. More than one board member quaked in their boots whenever she walked into the room. "These cobblestones might be quaint, but they're a liability."

"Shh," another business owner hushed Patsy. "Don't give him any ideas."

"I'm not suing anyone," Mark assured them. He straightened his shoulders and pulled away from a clutch of women who were dusting off his coat. "It's my own fault. I have a trick knee, and I should have been more careful. I should have listened to Naomi, and cut across the courthouse lawn."

"Blindly following the rules can get you into trouble," Patsy said.

Naomi dredged up the courage to meet his gaze. Her pulse was still galloping. "Are you all right?"

"I'm fine." His lips were tight, his eyes flat. Embarrassed.

She imagined he hated all this focus on his mobility. She understood because of her mother's battle with rheumatoid arthritis. Independence versus the need for help. It was a fine line to walk. No one wanted to look weak. Then again, being unwilling to accept help was a weakness of another kind.

Or so people told her. Often, friends and family scolded her for trying to shoulder too many burdens alone.

"Can you walk on it?" she asked.

He tested his knee. Winced.

"It's hurting you."

"Nothing out of the ordinary." People were still hovering. That seemed to bother him. He waved them away. "I'm fine, I'm fine. Please go on about your lives."

People started drifting away. A few lingered, giving advice.

Better ice it.

Keep it elevated.

Make a run to minor emergency.

"Should we do any of those things?" Naomi fretted, nibbling her bottom lip.

"Look," Mark said. "This is normal for me. My knee gives way all the time. I shouldn't have been vain and left my cane."

"Vanity?" she said. "You left it behind on purpose?"

"Yeah." He gave her a rueful, don't-judge-me smile. "How can I be strong for you if I'm bumbling around on a cane?"

"Aww," she said. "That's so sweet. And weird. Don't do it again."

"Gotcha."

"Cane or no cane, you're plenty he-man enough for me."

"Oh really?" He wriggled an eyebrow. "You don't say."

"You're awfully cocky for a guy who just took a header off the curb. Here." She slipped her shoulder underneath his armpit. "Let's get you over to the park bench and regroup."

"You don't need to support me. I can walk."

"Humor me, okay?"

He didn't shake her off, but she noticed he did not put any weight on her shoulder either. She got him settled on the nearest park bench underneath the Sweetheart Tree. Went after his duffel bag lying on the ground where he'd lost it in the fall.

When she got back, she found him tapping around his knee with his fingertips. "What are you doing?"

"Coaxing blood supply to the knee. It goes numb from time to time."

"You sure we don't need to take you to minor emergency?"

"I didn't hurt it. You broke my fall." He looked chagrined. "Thanks for that."

"My pleasure."

They sat in silence. The day had warmed as the sun crept toward noon. More people were on the square, but cedar trees lining the path secluded them from the hustle and bustle.

"Did you injure your leg in the war?" Naomi asked.

Mark stuck his left hand in the pocket of his jacket. Looked as if he had something he wanted to tell her. Opened his mouth. Closed it again. Nodded. "Yeah."

Should she ask him more questions? It seemed like he wanted to talk about it. "Were you in Afghanistan?"

"Yes."

"That's where my brother died." Oh gosh, why had she said that? What if he *wanted* to talk about the war? That was the *last* thing she wanted to talk about. This was going to be a happy Christmas. No more tears.

A bird flitted by.

"Look." She pointed at a bird. "Was that a woodpecker?"

He blew out his breath through his teeth, and his shoulders slumped. He looked in the direction she'd pointed. "It might have been."

Awkward silence.

Naomi cleared her throat. Smiled. A sunshine, rainbows, unicorns smile. A let's-join-hands-and-sing-"Kumbaya" smile. But it felt too phony, so she dialed it down.

"Well," she said, planted her palms on her knees. "Well."

His face was bland. Expressionless. But there was nothing bland about this man. He had the countenance of a warrior—strong and stalwart, solid and steady, dependable and determined.

And brave.

So brave. He'd been in battle. Come out scarred. And she knew the scars were much more than physical. That was quite clear.

He was not big on small talk. Where did she go from here that would keep the conversation light and cheery?

Apparently, he was grasping for conversational straws too. He leaned over to look at the sign over the entrance to the park. "Sweetheart Park. What's up with that?"

"Town legend," she explained.

"Like knights-of-the-round-table legend?"

"Not history that ancient, but along those lines. It's some pretty romantic stuff."

"No kidding?" He glanced over at the fountain. It was a statue of a couple in Western clothing, enveloped in a passionate embrace. "Who are those two?"

"Two of the town founders," Naomi said. "Rebekka Nash and Jon Grant. We named the town in honor of them."

"How so?"

Relieved to have a safe topic, Naomi launched into the story. "Rebekka and Jon were from Missouri, but the Civil War broke them up. Jon joined the Union Army. Rebekka's family were farmers and they sided with the South."

"Star-crossed lovers."

"Exactly. The war came. Jon went into battle. Rebekka's family moved to Texas to escape the conflict. Fifteen years passed. Each assumed the other was dead, but neither had married. After the war was over, Jon served the military in Fort Worth. They sent him west on a scouting expedition."

Shepherd shifted on the bench, turning closer toward

her. He'd stopped tapping on his knee and was watching her face. "Go on."

"One evening, at twilight, Jon wandered down to the banks of the Brazos. And there on the other side stood Rebekka watering her horse. They recognized each other immediately. They could never forget their true love. They fell into each other's arms. Soon after, they married. The town was built on the spot where Jon and Rebekka met again. And named Twilight in honor of their auspicious reunion."

"Aww."

"It's a bit sappy." Naomi shrugged. She loved the legend anyway. "But true. Mostly."

"I think it's an amazing story," Shepherd said.

"A lot of additional lore sprang up around the tale. Especially since it stokes tourism. In particular the sweetheart legend." Naomi leaned over. Planted a hand against the bark of the nearby two-hundred-year-old pecan tree.

A white picket fence surrounded the pecan. Beneath it, a white wooden sign read: "Do Not Deface the Sweetheart Tree." Carved into the bark were hundreds of names. *Jon loves Rebekka. Sarah Loves Travis 4 Ever. Earl + Raylene. Hondo & Patsy.*

"This town likes signs that tell you what to do," Mark mused, running his fingers along his firm jawline.

"Rules," she said. "That should agree with you."

"Don't make fun of my values." His eyes teased. He wasn't offended.

"What else do you value?" She cocked her head to study him. Felt the ends of her hair skim along her shoulder.

A fox-in-the-henhouse smile slid from his lips all the way up to his eyes. For the first time since she'd met him, he seemed to be enjoying himself. His delight was hers. She loved it when people were happy.

His fetching smile made her think of hot chocolate with marshmallows, sipped in front of a roaring fire on a cold winter morning. Of fuzzy fleece blankets and Perry Como holiday songs. Of cinnamon-scented pinecones, and sugar cookies left out for Santa on Christmas Eve.

"Woodworking," he said. "Whittling. It calms me."

"Whittling? What are you? Sixty-two? Next thing you know, you'll tell me you value yodeling too."

His tone was dry, but his eyes were lively. "Don't dis yodeling."

Naomi beamed, pleased. "So, whittling. How did that happen?"

"I like working with my hands."

She looked down at his broad, square hands resting on his upper thighs. Sturdy, reliable hands. Her throat heated and her lips tingled. And she thought, *I like him too much*.

From his jacket pocket, he pulled a pocketknife and a piece of wood. Opened the knife. Started whittling. Deftly guiding the blade over the tinder.

"I can see why you find it calming," she said, distracted by his fingers, and then he stopped. Curled one hand around the knife handle, and the other around the wood, and she added, "It's very Zen."

He raised an eyebrow. "You've studied Buddhism?"

"I'm not closed-minded." She sniffed, fingered the cross at her neck.

"I never said you were."

"I read *Zen and the Art of Motorcycle Maintenance* in high school," she said. "That's my nutshell knowledge."

"Me too," he said, and went back to whittling.

"Mindfulness is in the Bible too, you know."

"I suspected."

"Have you read the Bible?"

"Parts of it." His shoulders bunched. Tensing.

"And?"

"What's there to say? It's the Bible."

She backed off the topic. Leaned in, watched the wood quickly taking on a shape. "What are you making?"

"Christmas ornament." His eyes met hers. "For you."

Flattered, she pressed a hand to her heart. "I don't even have our tree up yet."

"I can help with that." He paused. "If you like."

"We'll see," she hedged. "You've got a lot to do for the church, and I've already taken up a big chunk of your time."

He whittled a face into the wood. A beatific smile. Wings. A halo.

"You're carving an angel." She clapped her hands, leaned in closer. "Oh! She looks like me."

He dusted the wood shavings off the angel, passed it to her. Smiled. Simple. Straightforward. An offering. In that moment, he looked like a small boy who'd picked a little wild bouquet.

"She's beautiful." Naomi clutched the wooden angel to her chest, touched beyond words. And impressed. Her hands trembled. His skill astounded her. "Thank you so much. I love it."

"You're welcome." He pocketed the knife, and stood up. Full-grown, badass Marine. She loved the contrast. He was a complex guy.

Nervous in case his knee collapsed on him again, Naomi hopped up too. She didn't want him standing there without something to lean on.

He moved toward the Sweetheart Tree, his gaze scanning the names. She stayed at his side, the angel clasped in her hand.

"Judging by the names carved in the tree . . ." His laugh was light, breezy. "People in Twilight aren't very good at following the rules."

"Many were there before the sign went up in the 1980s," Naomi explained. "Some weren't."

Mark stepped closer to the tree. "*Cody loves Piper 11/12/17.* Cody's a little rebel." He circled the trunk, reading off names.

Naomi rubbed the knuckles of the hand clutching the angel against her other palm. There were a lot of names carved into the bark. Would he find *Robert + Naomi 4 Life*? Did she want him to?

If he found it, he would ask about Robert and then she'd have to talk about that. Over the past eleven years, she and Robert had broken up and gotten back together at least half a dozen times. They'd been high school sweethearts. Their love affair had been encouraged by the romantic town legends. She admired Robert's work ethic and his impeccable table manners, and they had shared tastes in music and literature.

But Twilight had not been enough for Robert. He wanted to conquer the world. Which was fine. But he wanted her to do it with him.

Problem was, Naomi liked living in Twilight. She enjoyed being around her family and friends. Loved the security of her tight-knit community. Granted, Twilightites were not the most sophisticated or erudite, but neither was she. She liked how down-to-earth people were here. How kind and bighearted.

The more time Robert spent in Denver, the more judgmental he'd become of their hometown. Naomi had almost ended their relationship the previous summer because of the changes in him, but he'd sweet-talked her into hanging on. Promised once she moved to Denver everything would be okay.

But then Clayton died and Samantha took too many pills on New Year's Eve.

Robert had flown home to comfort Naomi. He'd stayed in Twilight for a month to be with her, and it had been so easy to fall into their old pattern. He was safe and familiar in a time when her world turned upside down, even though their relationship was long distance. She urged him to look for a job in Dallas or Fort Worth. He urged her to come to Denver. The same old clash they'd had before.

They were currently at a stalemate. He wanted her to come to Denver alone. Let her parents or Hunter's other grandparents adopt the boy, and she just couldn't do that. She truly *wanted* Hunter, and Robert didn't understand that. And he still hadn't answered her text from last night.

But now, her body thrilled over this handsome stranger.

She shoved those thoughts aside. It wasn't as if anything was going to happen between her and Mark Shepherd. Despite the fact she had dreamed of him. It was silly to base affairs of the heart on a cookie dream.

Putting the angel he'd carved her into her purse, she moved away from the Sweetheart Tree, and led Mark deeper into the park.

But her nerve endings were hyperaware of the walking power line behind her. His body exuded heat and energy. *Her* body vibrated like a tuning fork.

He must have sensed she was wound up. He strayed over to the side, giving her breathing room. She inhaled purposefully. Exhaled. Did it two more times.

"And here we have the Twilight wishing well." She wandered over to a pond that branched off from a tributary of the Brazos River. The bottom of the pond was dark with coins. Mostly pennies.

He stepped closer. Peered down into the wishing well.

She studied the proud tilt of his head. The breadth of his shoulders. The way his dark hair swirled to the right at his crown. Her breathing grew shallow again, faster.

What was it about this man that so compelled her?

Yes, he was good-looking. Yes, he was sexy. Yes, he smelled great.

But he tugged at her heartstrings. There was a loneliness that fanned her nurturing flames. There was an invisible wall around him. A protective force field that held him at arm's length.

A sudden impression of him as a child climbed into her mind, and she could not shake it. Someone had hurt him to his core. And he'd decided a long time ago not to ever let anyone get close.

A lump of sadness filled her throat.

Naomi had an overwhelming urge to pull him into her embrace. Squeeze him tight. Tell him everything was going to be just fine. Of course, she didn't. Couldn't.

"Rumor has it if you throw a coin into the wishing well, your high school sweetheart will reunite with you," she said.

"Your town has some interesting customs." His eyebrows flew up. "What if you don't want your high school sweetheart?"

"Then don't throw a coin into the well."

"What if you were never separated from your high school sweetheart?" His eyes were full of mischief. He was enjoying teasing and she loved seeing this light-hearted side of him. "What then?"

She'd only been with *her* high school sweetheart. She'd gone on a few dates the times she and Robert had broken up, but not with anyone more than once. "Again, don't throw a coin."

"What if you didn't have a high school sweetheart?"

"You are taking this way too literally," she teased back, batting her eyelashes for good measure. "The whole thing is a fable to sell tourists on Twilight. Roll with it."

"I keep thinking about those poor wallflowers with no high school sweethearts." He shook his head, feigned a mournful face. "Oh, the humanity."

Naomi laughed at his dry wit. "That's why we have the kismet cookie legend."

"The what?" His voice changed. Tone lowering. Pitch sharpening. "Another legend." He cupped his palms behind his ears. "All ears."

"It goes like this. If you sleep with a kismet cookie underneath your pillow on Christmas Eve, you'll dream of your one true love." She heard her own vocal quality shift. The man had no idea that she'd slept with a cookie under her pillow last Christmas Eve and dreamed of him.

But she knew it.

She wouldn't tell him. How could she? It sounded completely bonkers.

"Do you believe in soul mates?" His eyes met hers. Darkened. The expression on his face, mysterious and foreign, took her breath.

"The kismet cookies are blarney too." Naomi waved a flippant hand, despite her quickening pulse. "I mean, c'mon, how could a cookie predict your soul mate? But the cookies *are* tasty and people have fun with it, so why not?"

"You *don't* believe in soul mates?" His eyes locked onto hers and she could not glance away.

Something passed between them. A certain look. A shared understanding. Was he sending her a message with his stare? *Yes, we have something going here.*

Or was it all in her crazy imagination? Her feelings were out of control, and that scared her. Her entire life she'd made plans and stuck to them for the most part. She was a planner, a rule follower. It gave her a sense of control.

Her attraction to him knocked her control for a loop. Leaving her feeling as if all her circuits were broken.

"Do you?" she whispered, and moistened her lips. Her heart rattled inside her rib cage. Terrified if she allowed herself to fully experience the feelings bubbling up inside her, she would implode.

"I—"

"There you are, Naomi," a woman's voice called from behind them. "I've been looking all over town for you."

Relieved and grateful for the interruption, Naomi turned away. Breaking the enigmatic spell Mark Shepherd had cast over her.

CHAPTER 13

Naomi introduced Shepherd to Terri Longoria. Told him that Terri was a longtime neighbor, owner of the local gym and day spa, and a member of the charity ball committee that Naomi was heading. There was a snafu with the catering for the event, and Terri wanted to catch her up to speed.

While Naomi and Terri confabbed about how to solve the problem, he went back to Perks and retrieved his cane, then returned to the park bench. He wasn't much of a sitter. Wouldn't have done it if it hadn't been for the damn knee. He wanted to pace. *Needed* to pace.

Hell, he needed to run.

Why was he here? Oh yeah, he'd agreed to chauffer Naomi around. Speaking of . . .

He cleared his throat. Tapped his watch face. "We're burning daylight, butterfly. You got a five ᴘ ᴍ deadline."

"Yes, right." Naomi's cheeks reddened. She told Terri she'd sort things out and call her later.

Terri nodded to Shepherd on her way past. Eyed him suspiciously. Shepherd got that. He was a stranger in a small town.

"Nice to meet you," he said, raising a palm as Terri went past.

Naomi rejoined him. "Thanks for getting me out of that conversation."

"Soup sandwich?" he said, referring to the military slang that meant someone or something wasn't as it should be.

Naomi laughed. "That's one of Clayton's favorite military sayings."

Clayton. Present tense.

At the mention of her brother and her painful slip of the tongue, her smile dried up, and her eyelashes lowered. He watched her shake her spine. Draw back her shoulders. Thrust her chin up. Bolster her emotions. Paint on another smile.

"I've got a few more stores to hit," she said. "Are you up for it?"

He stood up. "I've got your six."

Another military term. Each time he used those words, it reminded her of her brother.

"That means you've got my back, right?" Naomi asked.

"Yes."

Her smile returned. A little tighter than before, but there. "Well," she said. "Let's do this."

In under an hour, Naomi managed to buy everything remaining on her list. And stay within budget.

Impressed, Shepherd eyed her as they left the final store. The woman knew what she was doing.

But he was a mess. Whenever he got within a foot of her, his body buzzed with energy. Muscle memory recalled what her supple thighs had felt like when she'd straddled him on the street.

Laden with packages, they walked back to his Jeep. She chattered about her Christmas plans for Hunter. Take him to the Dickens festival that weekend. Get him in to see Santa. Catch a matinee of *The Nutcracker* at the Twilight Playhouse. Ride around the courthouse square in a horse-drawn carriage. Bake Christmas cookies. Go caroling. Open the Advent calendar every day.

"Whoa." Shepherd laughed. "That's a lot to shoehorn into one holiday season."

"It'll be fun!"

"I don't mean to criticize. But from what I've seen today, you're taking on water."

"My plate is a little loaded, but I've got it under control."

"If you cross a few things off your list, the boy isn't going to know."

Naomi hardened her chin. "*I'll* know."

"You could give him the best Christmas any kid ever had," Shepherd said. "But it's not going to make up for losing his parents."

"I'm aware of that." Her voice grew icy. "I don't need your input."

Crunch. Toes stepped on. Got it.

"Please drive me home," she said. "I've got packages to wrap."

"It's almost two. You need lunch."

"No time."

"Listen, I don't mean to tell you what to do—"

"Then don't," she cut him off.

He opened the passenger side door for her and she flounced inside. Gorgeous hair floating past him. "You have to take care of yourself. If something happens to you, who's going to take care of Hunter?"

Shepherd shut the door, went around to get inside the Jeep.

"Okay, fine," she snapped. "Drive through the Burger Barn."

"That stuff's not good for you."

"Make up your mind. Do you want me to eat or not?"

"I'll make you something healthy when we get to your house."

"You can cook?"

"Hide and watch." He laughed and took off.

Back at the Luthers' house, they brought in Naomi's purchases and noticed that her parents still weren't home from Fort Worth.

"They probably decided to do a little Christmas shopping," Naomi said.

"Are you worried about them?"

"They were supposed to be home over an hour ago."

"Go ahead and check on them." Shepherd shrugged out of his coat and rolled up his sleeves. "I'll see what you've got in the fridge."

"Thanks." Naomi took her phone into the other room.

He voice-activated the electronic virtual assistant docked on the bar. Asked it to play Christmas music.

The device surprised him with Louis Armstrong's "Cool Yule." Perfect music for whipping up an omelet and green salad. He whistled along, happy to do this for her.

Naomi reappeared, all smiles. He was flipping eggs in the omelet pan with an adroit flick of his wrist.

"Ooh, don't you look all Julia Child."

"Your parents?" he asked, grinding cracked black pepper into the eggs.

"They ran into some old friends and went out for

a long lunch. They'll be home in an hour or so." She scooted closer, leaned over the stove. "Nice. I'm not used to anyone cooking for me."

Naomi stood so close that if he turned half an inch, his hip would bump into hers. He felt trapped, but it was his own doing. He *wanted* to turn into her. Bump hips. Touch her.

She tilted her head, slanted her gaze up until she found his. He wanted to believe the light in her eyes flared a little when she looked at him. But that might just be wishful thinking.

They ate across from each other at the kitchen table.

"This is delicious," she said. "I wish I didn't have to eat and run, but I've got to get those packages wrapped."

"I'll help you," he said. "So, you'll make your five s ɪp ɪdelivery deadline."

"You don't have to do that. You missed a whole day working on the church." She polished off her eggs. Patted her tummy. "Yum."

It pleased him that she liked his cooking. "I can kick it into high gear tomorrow."

"Really, it's okay." She tucked into the salad. "I can handle this."

"You don't have to do everything on your own."

"I don't want to be a bother."

"That's the last thing you are, butterfly."

Her cheeks pinked and she dropped her gaze. Focused on her plate.

He'd embarrassed her. Dammit, why couldn't he have kept his mouth shut? This thing surging between them didn't stand a chance. He knew that and yet he kept pushing.

"Thanks for the food," she said. "It was delicious, and you're right. I'm fortified and ready to tackle the world."

"Then let's hit it."

She didn't turn him down again. They did the dishes together, standing side by side at the sink. He rinsed the plates, handed them to her. She tucked them into the dishwasher. Then she led the way into the living room where they'd left the packages.

Smiling to himself, Shepherd followed her. Admired the soft sway of her fanny.

Naomi sank her hands on her hips. Stared at the pile of sacks and boxes. "Did I just say I was ready to tackle the world? I don't see how we're going to get these wrapped in time to make my deadline. Even with your help."

"Food for fuel can only take you so far," he agreed. "What we need is a system."

"Meaning?"

"You can't eat the whole enchilada at once. Bite by bite. Step by step. It's the only way anything gets done."

"Agreed. So what's step one?"

"First," he said. "You clear your A.O."

Her brow furrowed. "My what?"

"Area of operation," he explained.

"Oh boy," she said. "Another military term. How do you guys memorize all that?"

Only someone who'd been through the military milieu could understand the answer. Could know what it was like to strip off your personal identity and submerge in the group mentality. The ability to do that was what made Shepherd perfect for the military. In his childhood, he'd been solitary for so long that being part of a team had salved his deepest longing.

But now? The military was nothing but a memory. Gone. Leaving him without a tether. He had a new longing now.

And she was sitting right in front of him—beautiful, sexy, happy, fun.

A woman he had no business yearning for. Yet here he was, yearning with a need so profound it floored him. His body ached and his soul burned for her.

He organized the items. Stacking boxes to the right and slightly behind them. Wrapping paper, bows, ribbons, tape, and scissors to the left. The area in front of them kept clear for the packages they were wrapping at the time.

Naomi sat on the floor, tucked her shapely slender legs beneath, bobbed her head in approval at the setup. "I can see how this makes the process easier."

"Streamlined. Clears the confusion."

"I *am* getting muddled," she said. "With everything I have on my to-do list stacking up like cord wood."

"I wasn't judging the way you do things." He folded a crisp edge on the paper. "Just offering a suggestion."

"I get that." She treaded a watery smile. "I'm ticked that I didn't already think of it."

"Don't be so hard on Naomi," he said. "She's a good person, and she has a lot on her plate."

She was watching him, and their eyes met. They sure liked each other. And that was unsettling, because this couldn't go anywhere. Wouldn't go anywhere once she knew the truth.

"No more than any other single mom." She pressed her lips together, gave a quick shake of her head. "And I have more help than most."

"If you have more help it's because you have more friends, and you have more friends because you are a good friend. I've been watching you with people. They light up when they're around you." *I light up when I'm around you.*

"Ah." She laughed. "That's sweet . . . and maybe slightly creepy."

Ah crap, he'd stuck his foot in that one. "You're infinitely watchable, butterfly."

Her cheeks pinked again. "These packages aren't going to wrap themselves . . ."

Message received. Shut up and work. Fair enough.

"Hand me that purple sweater," he said, and got down to business.

After a few minutes of oddly comfortable silence, she said, "Tell me about your family."

"Nothing to tell."

She looked confused, glancing at him with those big blue eyes. One hand went up to smooth away an errant strand of hair that had fallen across her forehead. "What do you mean?"

"I don't have a family."

Twin emotions flickered in her eyes, alarm and pity. "No one?" Her voice was a breathless whisper, as if the idea totally shocked her.

"Nope. Pass me the tape, will you?" He wanted to tell her everything, share the details of his childhood traumas. But he knew better. Telling her his darkest secrets, his deepest fears would only bind him more tightly to his growing feelings for her. He shouldn't let himself fall for her.

She pushed the tape toward him. But did not resume wrapping the package in front of her. It was pink cashmere pajamas.

"Those pajamas have me confused," he said.

"How so?" She crinkled her adorable little nose with her grin.

They were getting too close. He needed to get away.

From her smile, from her perky scent, from the way he longed to run his thumb along her bottom lip before he kissed it.

But he didn't run as every nerve in his body was urging him to do. Instead, he answered her question. "Doesn't cashmere have to be dry cleaned? Who wears pajamas that have to be dry cleaned?"

"The pajamas are hand washable with gentle liquid detergent," she explained with a soft laugh.

"Sounds like a pain in the as—er, backside," he said, remembering she was a pastor's daughter.

"Oh, don't worry about that. Women don't mind washing out their delicates."

"Learn something new every day," he murmured.

"Back to your family—"

"Don't have one."

"No siblings?"

"Not that I know of." She was a persistent little thing.

"No grandmothers?"

"Both dead before I was born."

Naomi hissed in a breath. "That's way sad."

He shrugged. "Such is life."

"Both my grandmothers are still alive. Grammie Luther lives in Santa Fe and Mawmaw Parker lives just down the road in Jubilee."

"You're lucky."

"I know. Grandfathers?"

"Dead."

"Aunts? Uncles?"

"Dead, dead, dead, dead."

She cringed with each "dead," batting her eyes as if it could protect her from his personal shrapnel. "Your parents are both dead too?"

"My dad's dead."

"How?"

Shepherd didn't want to get into it. "Hard living."

"Addiction?" she guessed.

"Something like that." He taped up the package, tied it up with a silver ribbon. Added it to the pile. Did not meet those gorgeous blue eyes.

"Nice job." She admired his handiwork. "Precision."

"Comes from making beds with military corners."

"What about your mom?" Naomi asked, her smile softening, her eyes inviting him to spill his guts.

He let out a long breath. "It really doesn't matter."

"It does to me," she said.

He finally met her gaze full-on. Added a challenging stare. "Why?"

"Because how can I understand you if I don't know where you come from?"

"The past is the past. It's over."

"But it lingers. It affects us all." Pain crept into her voice and her eyes grew shiny. Was she thinking about Clayton and Samantha?

"Only if we let it." He put steel into his voice. Not for her sake, but for his. He could feel himself falling under her spell—it was that moment on the town square when he'd fallen and she'd ended up straddling him when she'd seemed just as bewitched by him as he was by her.

"Spoken like a man who's sweeping it all under the rug," she challenged.

"What's wrong with that?"

"Nothing at first. You take the hit. But instead of dealing with the emotional fallout, you just pick up the corner of the rug. Brush the dirt underneath it. No one else can see it and the room looks tidy, right?"

He watched her long, slender fingers fuss with the wrapping paper, but he didn't answer. It seemed to be a rhetorical question.

"Then you take another hit from life, and you get out your broom again, and sweep, sweep, sweep." She gestured, pantomimed sweeping under a rug. "And then that little pile of dirt gets a little bigger. Then life hits you again. Instead of flipping back that rug and doing some spring cleaning, you slip in more dirt. But the pile is getting thicker and now when other people walk over the rug they can feel the lump."

"Where is this analogy going?" Shepherd narrowed his eyes, studied the soft glint of the light off her clean, shiny hair.

She dropped the wrapping paper she was mangling, reached over to grasp his wrist with both hands. Her palms were warm and damp. "If you don't deal with the emotional fallout, that dirt pile underneath the rug gets bigger and bigger. Until one day, someone trips over it. Falls and breaks their neck and then where will you be?"

"Calling an ambulance," he mused.

"Exactly!" She clapped both hands as if dusting chalk off them.

"Um . . . okay." She amused him. Here she was lecturing him on sweeping emotions under the rug. The same woman who so desperately wanted to paint a happy face on Christmas that she pushed away any darker emotions. Was she projecting her fears onto him? Was the lecture really for her?

Gunny, you've been in too many therapy sessions. Dr. Fox would be so proud of his insight. "So, stop sweeping dirt under the rug. Problem solved."

"All right."

She waited, eyes locked on his. A second passed. Then two. Three. Ten. A whole minute. "Well?"

"Well what?"

"What happened to your mother?"

She wanted to know? Fine. He'd tell her. "She's in prison."

Naomi absorbed that news, bit down on her bottom lip. Her eyes growing wider, lashes blinking rapidly.

He studied her. What was she thinking? Did knowing that Virginia Shepherd was a hardened criminal change the way she thought of him?

"For a crime that she didn't commit?" Naomi ventured.

"No." Shepherd bobbed his head. "She committed them."

"Oh." She had a look in her eye that said she maybe wished she hadn't opened this can of worms. He'd tried to tell her. "What did she do?"

"Swindled elderly people out of their life's savings. Mail fraud. Identity theft. Among other things."

"Did she have a substance abuse problem?"

"She did, as did my father. They were quite a team. Grifters."

"Grifters?"

Naomi was so innocent she didn't even know what that word meant. It occurred to him that he shouldn't be here. Contaminating this fine, upstanding young woman with sordid tales of his no-good family. He should just pick up his things from the rectory and go. Why didn't he?

Why? The key in his pocket. His guilt over Clayton. The desire not to ruin her Christmas. Truth? He was hooked. Deceiving himself into thinking her cheery happiness could rub off on him if he hung around her enough.

"Professional con men," he explained.

"I see."

No, she didn't. She couldn't see less if she were legally blind. At night. Far off in the country. If she really wanted to understand him, she needed to hear it all.

"When I was five, they went off on a grift and left me alone."

"By yourself?" She sounded shocked.

"That's the general definition of alone."

"At five?"

"They left me with some food and the TV as a baby-sitter. In their defense, they thought they'd only be gone for a few hours. They had no idea they were buying tainted smack with the money they'd gotten from their grift."

"Smack?" Her eyes were saucers now. He didn't know if they could get any bigger. "You mean heroin?"

"Yep." The word popped out, weirdly peppy for the topic.

"Dear heavens." Her eyes misted.

"They ended up almost dying. They were both in comas for several days—"

"And you were all alone in the house."

"It was an apartment, but yes."

"Dear Lord." Naomi pressed a hand to her heart as if to keep it from jumping from her chest. "You could have died."

"Not really," he said. "I had food, water, and shelter."

"You could have turned the oven on and burned down the house. You could have stuck a metal toy in a light socket. You could have—"

"None of those things happened."

"No," she said. "But it could have."

"It didn't."

"Did you get taken away from them?"

"Not that time."

"But at some point, you did go into the foster care system."

"Yes."

"That's terrible."

Her distress touched him. He could see how upset she was over his childhood. It was bonding her to him, just as he feared it would. "I survived."

"It's not fair."

"Butterfly," he said, "haven't you learned by now that there's nothing fair about life?"

CHAPTER 14

God had brought this man into their lives. She didn't know how or why, she only knew it was so. Mark Shepherd needed Naomi, and her family, as much as they needed him.

Never mind that he rocked her sense of control to the core. She'd have to find a way to make peace with the chaos while he was there, because Mark deserved a happy holiday as surely as the rest of them. No matter what it took, Naomi was going to make that happen. And if that meant shakily overcoming her fear of taking risks, she'd do it.

Mentally, she added him to her Christmas list.

Her parents got home in time to watch Hunter, and Mark drove her to deliver the packages in time to make her deadline. Mrs. Beauchamp was so impressed with Naomi's service, she insisted on tipping her fifty dollars and promised to spread the word about her services.

After they left Mrs. Beauchamp's house, Naomi tried to pass the fifty-dollar bill on to Mark.

"No, ma'am." He shook his head. "That's yours."

"I wouldn't have made my deadline without you. I'd still be elbow-deep in ribbons and wrapping paper."

"You forget I caused your delay when I fell off the sidewalk because I was too proud to use my cane."

"No, you forget, I wouldn't even have been able to get the packages home if you hadn't given me a ride. Please take the money."

He held up a stop-sign palm. "Use it to buy Hunter a gift."

She sat there, holding out the fifty-dollar bill. "I insist."

"Insist all you want. I'm not taking it."

"Where did you come from?" She studied him.

"What?" He looked startled, eyes widening.

"How did you end up being so honorable? The Marines?"

"Yes, but more so my parents."

"What?" she asked, confused.

"They showed me the path *not* to take."

She cocked her head, studied him in the illumination of the dashboard light. "You're not like any man I've ever met. It's like you're from another planet."

"Are you saying other guys would have taken the fifty?"

"Not that part, per se."

"What part?" The corner of his mouth quirked up. A humble half smile that endeared him to her even more.

"You were generous with your time. Spending your whole day helping me out."

His mouth flattened as if she'd said something wrong. "Don't idealize me, Naomi," he warned. "I'm fallible as hell."

"Aren't we all?"

"I'm not the man you think I am." He growled low and fierce. His eyebrows dipped down in a scowl.

Goose bumps spiked up her arms. His mysteriousness and the flicker of pain in his eyes unraveled her. Left her with an all-too-familiar need to turn herself inside-out for him. Win his love. Oh, the folly of the nurturer who thought she could cure every wounded bird.

"Are you thinking about all the things you had to do in the war?" she whispered.

He didn't answer her. Pulled up to a stoplight. In profile, he looked so tough, so badass. His dark aura was both sexy and alarming.

"What's it really like?" she whispered, thinking of Clayton. "On the front line?"

The look he threw her was cold steel. "Trust me, butterfly, you have no idea. And you *do not* want to know. You just keep doing what you do best. Smiling and making things pretty."

She couldn't tell if he was being condescending or not, but her feelings were hurt. She wasn't all sweetness and light. Far from it. That was the very reason she tried so hard to be cheerful and optimistic. She knew how low she could sink if she didn't.

"I . . . I . . ." What could she say? He was right. She was clueless about what went on outside the borders of her safe little world.

"Yes?" In profile, his jaw tightened, cheekbone hardened.

"You seem to think I'm shallow. I'm not *shallow*." She knotted her fists against her thighs, felt her pulse throb through the sides of her hands.

"Not shallow." His tone softened. "Innocent. Naïve."

"I'm not either one of those things. I just care deeply about people, and I want to help as much as I can. I want to help *you*."

"I don't need your help." He was gruff again. Staring out the windshield, his knuckles tightening on the steering wheel.

Her heart slammed into her chest and she regretted asking him. He'd been so nice to her today. So kind and considerate. But there was this other side to him that she knew nothing about.

"Why?" he said.

"Why what?"

"Why do you want to help me? I'm nothing to you." Behind the coldness of his words, she heard the hurt little boy. The child who hadn't been loved the way all children deserve to be loved.

"You're a human being."

"But why do you feel it's your place to alleviate all suffering?"

"I don't think it's my place to alleviate all suffering."

"No, just everyone you come into contact with."

"Are you trying to push me away?" she asked, realization dawning. He was as terrified of their surging attraction as she was. That softened her knees and her heart.

"You don't get to turn this around on me," he said. "We're talking about you. Why are you such a giver?"

"You make it sound like it's a bad thing."

"It is if you're ignoring your own needs in favor of everyone else's."

She paused, the question nagging at her. In this world there were givers and there were takers. She'd come hardwired to be a giver. And yes, she got taken advantage of at times, but she was who she was.

"It's also the way I was brought up," she admitted. "It's better to give than receive. Pastors' kids hear that a lot."

"Do you realize that if you're always giving in a relationship, it becomes inequitable and the other person starts to feel uncomfortable always being on the receiving end?"

Robert popped into her head. She thought of how she'd liked to give him shoulder rubs, but never let him give her one in return. He'd complained once that it wasn't fair, but she'd waved off his complaint with, "I like doing it."

"If you don't allow other people to give to you in exchange, you're robbing them of the pleasure of giving."

"I've never thought of it that way."

"Life is about balance," Mark said. "There needs to be an equal flow of giving and receiving for relationships to be healthy."

Was that what was wrong between her and Robert? She gave and Robert took? Uneasiness moved up her spine. She needed to call Robert. Nibbling her bottom lip, she stared out the window at the passing farmland. What was she going to say?

She wondered why she hadn't told Mark she had a boyfriend. Yes, she barely knew him. Yes, he was only in town until he got the church repaired. Yes, they couldn't explore this thing between them for a dozen other reasons. But she should have made it clear up front she was in a relationship—albeit long distance—but she hadn't.

Why not?

Because she was thinking about breaking up with Robert for good.

She'd been tiptoeing around that idea ever since she and Robert had fought over her adopting Hunter. But now it was here, in the forefront of her mind. How could she be with a man who did not want her adoptive son?

"You were the 'good' child," Mark guessed. "To make up for Clayton being the impulsive one."

Naomi jerked her head around to stare at him. "How do you know that about Clayton?"

Mark glanced over, and shot her a guilty expression. Looked as if he'd been caught in a lie. Why? Or was she misreading his face? "I assumed that's why you give so much, and take care of everybody. Part of being the oldest child, I'm guessing."

"It's true," she said, feeling put on the spot. "Clayton was a bit wild in his younger days. Not in a criminal way, but he experimented with drugs and alcohol, ran with the wrong crowd in high school, got lousy grades, had too many girlfriends. I felt like I had to make up for his behavior."

"The good girl got ingrained in you early on."

She shrugged, accepting it. "By the time Clayton grew up and found his footing, he went off to the Marines just as Mom's RA got truly debilitating. I was the only one around at that point . . ."

"So you just naturally slid into the role of caretaker, supporter, family champion," he finished for her.

"Yes."

Mark nodded, his gaze straight ahead on the road. "Then Clayton gets killed and Samantha does what she does and there's this boy . . ."

She felt tears burn at her eyes. Blinked them back. She was not going to cry in front of him. It was a pit of self-pity. Not something to which she was prone, but his words dredged up the thoughts of all she'd lost. She'd had to put her marriage dreams into "park" to take care of Hunter, and her mom needed help . . . Without even meaning to, she'd ridden the wave of life situations and ended up trying so damn hard to make this good for her family.

Until Mark pointed it out, she'd not really taken the time to acknowledge what had happened. It had been gradual. Not something done to her by other people in any deliberate way, but here she was, taking care of everyone. And since her dad was busy with his flock, she often felt she couldn't go to him with her problems the way she might want to.

"In a way," Mark said, eerily reading her thoughts, "you're just echoing what you've been taught by your dad. Other people come first. It's not a bad thing, but you gotta have balance."

Balance.

That word again.

"My parents do worry about me trying so hard to make everything right," she mumbled. "But how can I let go of the reins? How could I possibly step back now?"

"You've got a determined streak a mile wide." He turned to look at her again, his gentle smile kind and uplifting. "Don't you?"

Nailed it. She did.

They were at another stoplight and he was watching her, his eyes intense. Head tilted as if he didn't know what to make of her. That made two of them. She had no idea what to make of him either. Yes, she was attracted to him, but she knew nothing about him.

It was time to take a big step back. She and Mark had fun today. They'd shared a lot. But maybe it had been too much, too soon.

She had Hunter to think about. That little boy was the only thing that mattered. His happiness and safety would *always* come first. She had no business pursuing this passing attraction to Mark Shepherd.

None whatsoever.

The next afternoon, Shepherd was putting up the nativity scene on the church lawn when Hunter got home from preschool.

The boy got out of the minivan. Backpack slung over his shoulder, he climbed the steps of the Victorian, turned and waved good-bye to the driver. Instead of going inside the house, he tumbled back down the stairs and came skipping over the sidewalk to the church.

"Hi!" Hunter exclaimed.

Shepherd dusted dirt from his palms. "Why, hello."

"Whatcha doin'?"

"Putting up the nativity scene."

"Like the one in ouw yawd?" He pointed to the Victorian.

"Just like that."

"Can I help?"

"Shouldn't you let your aunt know you're home from school?"

He screwed up his mouth, wriggled like a caterpillar. "P'obably."

The door to the Victorian opened and Naomi stepped out onto the porch. He'd seen her leave that morning in Pastor Tom's van and return just after lunch. He'd called to her, asking if she needed help unloading the vehicle.

She'd firmly turned him down.

Okay. She needed her space. No problem. He needed his too. Yesterday had been pretty intense.

"Hunter," she called down the street. "Come inside for milk and cookies."

"C'mon." Hunter reached for Shepherd's hand. "Let's go."

"The milk and cookies are for you."

Hunter grinned and shook his head vigorously. "No." He laughed and pointed at Shepherd. "You too!"

"I think I'm gonna hang back."

"C'mon," Hunter insisted, tugging on his hand.

Naomi had come down the steps. She was standing in front of the house, her hands on her hips. A welcoming smile on her face.

Shepherd melted. He'd gotten a keep-away vibe from her last night. Wanted to respect it. But now? That smile said come-hither.

It's for the boy, you idiot.

"C'mon." Hunter tugged harder. It was funny, how hard the boy was working. His cheeks puffed out. His face turned red with the effort.

Shepherd relented and allowed Hunter to drag him toward Naomi.

Their eyes met.

Her smile deepened. "Look here, two of my favorite people in the whole wide world."

Shepherd's heart skipped a beat. Wow. Had she just said that? Why? Her cool greeting that morning left him feeling like he should give her a wide berth. Now here she was with honeyed words. What had shifted?

"Hey," he said, feeling awestruck.

"Hey." She tucked her fingertips in her back pockets. The movement rotated her elbows out behind her back. Lifted her chest.

He tried hard not to look at those uplifted breasts.

Refused to ogle her. But he did sneak a quick peek. He was only human.

"Thanks for looking after Hunter," she said, resting her hand on the boy's head.

"Hunter was looking for me."

She dropped her hand from the boy's head to his back. Took off the backpack, slung it over her shoulder. "Go on in the house, love bug. Pawpaw will get the milk and cookies for you."

"Daddy?" Hunter still hung on to Shepherd's hand. Looked up into his face.

"Mark and I will be along in a minute, sweetheart."

Hunter hesitated. Glancing from Shepherd to Naomi and back again.

"Go on." Shepherd nodded, sensing Naomi had something she wanted to discuss with him that she didn't want the boy overhearing.

"O. K.," Hunter announced, enthusiastically pronouncing the word like two separate letters, and skipped into the house.

"He obeys you better than he does me."

"That's not true."

"He needs a male role model." A pensive look came into her eyes, and she scratched her chin with her two fingers and her thumb.

"He's got your father."

"Yes, but he keeps calling *you* Daddy. He needs a younger male role model."

Shepherd didn't say anything. Wasn't sure what he was supposed to say.

"I heard you're going to play Santa for the toy drive," she said. "I'm so proud of you for volunteering."

Her words were a tonic. Juicing him up. Puffing out

his chest. Lifting his spirits and his hopes. Ahh, those dastardly hopes.

"Where did you hear that?"

"Patsy Crouch. She said you're making toys too."

"Just whittling a few things." He shrugged. "Like I did that angel for you."

"Where will you find the time?"

"I don't sleep much."

"It's so sweet of you." She clasped both hands to her heart. "I'm touched."

"No reason to treat me like I'm a superhero. I just know what it's like not to have a real Christmas."

"I'm so sorry for that." Her eyes turned melancholy.

"You have nothing to be sorry for."

"All right, then I feel sympathy for that little boy who didn't get happy Christmas memories."

"I don't know," he teased, trying to lighten the moment. "Eating corn dogs and Cheetos in the car parked outside a 7–Eleven on Christmas Day is more fun than you might think."

"Oh, Mark." Sadness iced her voice and she reached out to touch his forearm.

At the contact, energy surged between them. Immediate and startling.

The air was warmer than it had been the day before. Overhead, the sun burst through passing cloudbanks. Simultaneously, they both glanced up at the sky. Peering through the branches of a thick old oak tree.

Hanging directly above them was a big clump of mistletoe.

The clouds shifted, changing the direction of the sun's rays. A halo of light poured down over Naomi.

Captivated, Shepherd held his breath.

"Will you look at that," Naomi said, head thrown back, bathing in the golden glow. "We're standing under the mistletoe."

Shepherd's heart clutched, downshifted. *Chug-chug-chug.* "So we are."

Her eyelids lowered and she sent him a sultry look that knocked his circuitry haywire. She leaned forward, went up on her tiptoes.

Huh? *Chug-chug-chug* went his ragged heart. Did she want him to kiss her?

He knotted his fingers into fists. Quelling the urge to sweep her into his arms and kiss her until neither one of them could breathe.

She puckered her lips, closed her eyes.

"Naomi," he whispered.

She opened one eye, whispered back, "What is it?"

"What are you doing?"

"We're standing under mistletoe in December. You're supposed to kiss me."

"Naomi Luther," he said, fully shocked. Delighted by her audacity, but shocked nonetheless. "Are you asking me to kiss you?"

"Not me." She pointed upward. "The mistletoe."

"We're standing on the street in front of your house. Where you live with your parents and nephew. In public. Where anyone and everyone can see."

"It's out of my hands," she said. "You have to kiss under the mistletoe at Christmas. It's the rules, and you don't break the rules."

He could kiss her. Yes, he could. He could obey the rules. Follow protocol. Stick to tradition. Do the expected thing. It was, after all, what he did best.

What had he become? Someone who followed the rules at all costs? A man who couldn't think for himself? In his desire not to end up like his parents, had he allowed fear to lead him into blind obedience? Had he surrendered his common sense in exchange for safety? Gone overboard in the opposite direction?

Yes, laws were there for a reason. He wasn't arguing that. But ignoring his gut when his instincts were shouting at him to go left when all the rules said go right was treacherous.

If he'd dared to question his values last year, and gone with Clayton to the orphanage, he wouldn't be here today. And Clayton would be alive to celebrate Christmas with his family.

A punch of sorrow over his failing slammed him squarely in the throat.

Yes, Shepherd wanted to kiss her more than anything in the world, but not here. Not like this. This particular rule was made for breaking.

Naomi closed her eyes, and puckered her lips into a smile.

"You might need mistletoe to justify wanting to kiss me," Shepherd growled. "But I don't."

Her eyes flew open. "Huh?"

He dipped his head closer, lowered his voice. "When I kiss you, woman, it's going to be because it's the right time and the right place. Not because you're standing under a clump of some parasitic plant. It's going to be hot and it's going to last a long time and your knees are going to buckle. No mistletoe required. Count on it."

Body shaking from the control it took *not* to plunder her sweet pink lips, Shepherd turned and walked away.

* * *

When I kiss you, woman . . .

His words rang in her ears. A blip-pulse of wondrous anticipation jumped through her. Naomi shivered from the inside out.

The look in his eyes had issued a sacred promise. *When.*

Naomi licked her lips. She'd been playing with fire. She knew it when she'd stepped under the mistletoe. Driven by an uncharacteristic recklessness. More akin to Clayton's personality than her own.

Why had she done it?

Yes, hearing that Mark had volunteered to whittle handmade toys for the toy drive, to play Santa to needy children, melted her heart. Yes, when she saw how Hunter came alive around him, her brain flooded with what-if fantasies. Yes, the fiery heat pushing through her body whenever she was near him had a whole lot to do with her urges. And yes, he was sexy as ten kinds of sin.

All valid excuses to kiss a man.

But in the long run, pursuing something with him couldn't pay off. He was a temporary employee. He'd be moving on after the holidays. He was a former Marine who was still lugging around a lot of baggage. She was in the process of adopting her orphaned nephew. She was caught in an eleven-year, on-again, off-again relationship with her high school sweetheart.

So many reasons why she should stay in her lane and mind her own business.

For the rest of the week, her thoughts vacillated. She did her work, came home, cooked dinner. Sat across from Mark at the table. Made polite chitchat. Kept her desires on a chain. Watched him leave every night as he limped back to the church. Cutting a figure so lonely it yanked at every one of her heartstrings.

If a machine could graph her shifting thoughts about Shepherd, it would scribble wildly, with crazy high spikes and low valley dips. Up and down. A jagged, saw-tooth rhythm.

She made sure to never be alone in the same room with him. In case she was tempted to do something wild and crazy again. She simply didn't trust herself.

No matter how hard she tried, Naomi couldn't stop yearning for him. Pining across the dinner table when their eyes met. And she was fed up with her lack of self-control.

She had plenty to keep her busy. Focused on her work and the upcoming First Love Cookie Club charity dance and taking care of Hunter. Each night, she climbed under the covers with him in his red racecar bed and read *The Magic Christmas Cookie* to him.

Afterward, she migrated to her own bed, where she had trouble falling asleep. Despite her efforts to the contrary, she kept thinking about Mark and his sad, unhappy childhood. No child should have to go through what he'd lived through. And some people just shouldn't be parents.

Children were a gift from God. More precious than gold. They should be treasured and protected and cherished.

To think he'd been so mistreated ate her up inside. She wished she had a time machine so she could go back to the past and rescue that little boy. But she couldn't. She would do the only thing within her control.

Make a loving, happy home for Hunter.

Of course, she didn't have to raise the boy alone. She had her parents and Samantha's parents, neighbors and friends to help, but she *was* Hunter's primary caretaker. And as such, she couldn't willy-nilly pursue relationships with enigmatic men.

That meant putting her attraction to Mark Shepherd on ice. No sense starting something that was bound to end quickly. No matter how enticing. There were simply too many obstacles in their path.

Mark accepted her withdrawal. Actually seemed relieved. He would smile and nod when he came for dinner. Make small talk with her father and mother. Insist on doing the dishes while Naomi tucked Hunter in.

But he disappeared as soon as the dishes were washed.

This was good, she told herself. Things had moved too quickly. Yes. Yes. Keeping him at arm's length was definitely the way to go.

Why, then, did it feel like she was losing something monumental?

CHAPTER 15

Shepherd avoided Naomi as assiduously as she avoided him. It seemed for the best. She was starting to like him too much. Hell, let's be honest. He liked her too much. There wasn't a future here. He knew it was better to keep his distance. It was for her own good.

For the rest of the week, he did all the chores Pastor Tom asked of him. During the days, he finished building the new wooden awning, put a fresh coat of paint on the church, caulked cracks, replaced lightbulbs, balanced the ceiling fans, and secured baseboards. And he took a long walk around the lake every morning. The cool air cleared his head. Plus, the neighbors were starting to learn his routine and they called out greetings as he passed by. It was nice. And he felt welcomed.

At night, still battling insomnia and his intense cravings for Naomi, he stayed up late carving toys in the barn behind the rectory, crafting a jewelry box with a pop-up ballerina, two nutcrackers, four toy cars, and a set of stackable blocks. He added to that a palm-sized rocking horse, and a dozen wooden puzzles. He was quick and proficient.

It got him out of his head. Therapeutic.

As the days ticked off, Shepherd kept waiting for the real handyman to show up and expose his lie. The worry sat like a lead weight in the bottom of his stomach. Always there. Heavy and hard. But no one ever showed, and he wondered what had happened to the real handyman. Why hadn't he appeared?

More than once, he took out the Christmas key left to him by Clayton. Traced the cool metal with his fingers. Wondered what lock the key opened. Considered taking it straight to Naomi and telling her everything.

But he never did.

Because as soon as he told her who he was, his silly fantasies of an impossible future would be finished.

By the time Saturday rolled around, he had an entire box of handmade toys to take to a drop-off station. The event organizers had several donation spots set up around town, including one on the courthouse lawn to catch the tourist crowd coming in for the Dickens festival.

Pastor Tom had tried to make him take the entire weekend off, but Shepherd argued that since he hadn't done any handyman work on Tuesday when he'd driven Naomi around town that he hadn't earned it. But Tom insisted.

He got the answer about the real handyman when he dropped off the toys on Saturday morning. Nate was manning the donation station, wearing a Stetson, boots, and a duster, and looking as badass as he had the night Shepherd first met him.

Nate examined the contents of the box and let out a whistle of appreciation. "You made all these?"

"You told me to."

"Damn, son, you're an artist." Nate shook his head. "And fast too."

"You were right," Shepherd said. "When I'm working on the toys I'm not thinking about anything else. It's play. Empties my mind."

"Freedom." Nate smiled cryptically.

"For a time."

"What have you been doing for the PTSD?" Nate asked.

"Exercise," Shepherd said. Along with the morning walks, he'd been keeping up the isometric exercises prescribed by his physical therapist. "And listening to iRest tapes. Journaling about my feelings." He winced at that last part.

"Journaling is a tough one." Nate grunted.

"Tell me about it."

"But it helps."

Shepherd nodded. "Yeah, it does." But lately, the topic of his journal entries had all revolved around one thing.

Naomi.

. . . and his growing feelings for her. He wrote about the chestnut color of her hair, the way she smelled like peppermint and happiness, the curve of her shapely calves, and the sway of her curvy hips.

"Nightmares?" Nate asked.

"No."

"Hey, that's good news." Nate chucked him on the shoulder. "Are you sleeping?"

"Not as well as I could . . ." But that had as much to do with his yearning for Naomi as the PTSD. More even. Every time he lay down to sleep, her beautiful face popped into his head and fantasies took off in sexy directions.

Gideon wandered up. Greeted Shepherd with a shoulder clasp. "Good to see you, Gunny."

"You too."

"Your shift is over, Nate," Gideon said. "I'm here now."

"Thanks." Nate lowered the brim of his Stetson. "I'll take what we've collected so far over to the fire station."

"Fire station?" Shepherd asked.

"That's where we're storing the donations until Christmas Eve," Gideon explained.

A woman came up with a box of toys and Gideon turned to help her.

Nate drew Shepherd aside, leaned in, and lowered his voice. "Just to let you know. I did a little digging and discovered what happened to the handyman Pastor Tom thought he was hiring when he gave you the job."

A chill chased up Shepherd's back. "Yeah?"

"The man got arrested in Sulphur Springs for assault and battery. He's cooling his heels in the Hopkins County jail. Can't afford to post bail. He won't be arraigned until January."

"How do you know this?"

"Sheriff Hondo Crouch is a good friend of mine." Nate chucked Shepherd on the upper arm. "You're in the clear."

Shepherd exhaled but he didn't feel relieved. Instead, fresh guilt flooded him. Stirring everything up again.

Nate must have read something on his face, because he said, "Look at it this way, things are working out in your favor for a reason. You're *supposed* to be here."

Shepherd wanted to believe that, but it was too woo-woo for him.

"Let go of the resistance," Nate said. "Suspend your disbelief. There's magic afoot in Twilight."

Canting his head, Shepherd angled the other vet a look. "Are you saying you believe in magic?"

Nate picked up one of the toy cars that Shepherd had carved. "You don't think this is magical?"

"How can it be magic? I made it with my own hands."

Nate tipped his hat back on his head, grinned slyly. "Exactly."

"I don't get it."

"Trust," Nate said, gathering up the big sack of toys and throwing it over his shoulder. "All you have to do is trust."

"In what?" Shepherd asked, frowning.

Nate opened the door to a big SUV, got inside. He closed the door and rolled down the window. Before he drove away, he called out, "The magic of Christmas."

In one hand, Hunter grasped an oversized cookie. In the other, he carried a copy of *The Polar Express* they'd just bought at Ye Olde Book Nook. His eyes were round as walnuts as he whipped his head from sight to sight, giddy and greedy with the holiday season.

Naomi directed Hunter through the crowd with a hand on the top of his head. Enchanted by his delight.

The sky was brilliant blue, buffeted with fluffy white clouds. The air was balmy. A lovely sixty-two degrees. Sunny, and though breezy enough for a jacket, there was no need to bundle up. Just off the square, Naomi could see the lake sparkling in the sun like polished silver.

It was the perfect morning for a festival.

People dressed in Victorian period costumes flooded the streets. Beefeaters and London bobbies. Queen Victoria and Prince Albert. Dickens characters were everywhere. They spied two Marleys, three Scrooges, and four Tiny Tims. There was Miss Havisham with her one shoe. Oliver Twist and David Copperfield. Parents pushed strollers. Grandparents walked arm in arm. Teenagers texted. Entire families wore matching, intentionally ugly holiday sweaters.

Wreaths hung from lampposts. Christmas music played from outdoor speakers. Delicious scents hung in the air. Peppermint. Candied pecans. Cinnamon. Vendors sold spiced apple cider, hot chocolate, eggnog, and mulled wine.

And everywhere they went, there were cookies. Gingersnaps and ladyfingers. Lorna Doones and thumbprint cookies. Animal crackers and wedding cookies. And always, the ubiquitous kismet cookies. Sold in every store and kiosk. Wrapped in festive blue foil, with a white ribbon. The kismet cookie legend was written up on the back of the packaging.

This was Christmas in Twilight as Naomi remembered. Filled with fun and joy.

But haunted by the ghost of last Christmas.

Every place she looked, she saw her brother. Climbing on the lamppost on the corner of Ruby Street and Bowie when he was ten and she was supposed to be watching him. But she'd been caught up in flirting with Robert and hadn't paid attention. Clayton got stuck on the lamppost because he was too scared to climb down again. Sheriff Hondo, who'd been a paramedic back then, had come to the rescue.

She saw Clayton on the steps of the Twilight Playhouse where Mom had taken them to see *Rudolph the Red-nosed Reindeer* when she was twelve and Clayton eight. He was there in the window at Pasta Pappa's where the family had celebrated his sixteenth birthday.

At each and every place on the town square his memory lingered.

Down Bowie Street was the funeral home where they'd had Clayton's service. She could see the limousine parked on the side street. Maybe it was even the same limousine she and her family had ridden in from the funeral home to the church graveyard.

A wave of grief so hard and hot she could taste it rolled over Naomi. It tasted like soured towels and headcheese.

She gagged. Stopped. Pressed a hand to her mouth. *Oh Lord, please keep me from throwing up.*

"N'omi?"

The sound of her nephew's sweet, innocent voice yanked her back from that dark place. But her knees were shaky and she felt as if she might faint. She shouldn't have eaten that cookie on an empty stomach. Or drunk so much coffee.

Hunter shifted his cookie into the same hand as his book. Reached out to pat her arm. "You O. K.?"

"I think . . . I need to sit . . ." Her head swam and her vision blurred. She saw the sidewalk rising up to greet her.

But she never hit the ground.

Instead, a strong arm caught her. A masculine arm. Mark Shepherd's arm. Bracing the back of her spine. Her head cupped in his palm.

Feeling feeble and ashamed, she lifted her head. Their eyes met.

The air left her body as surely as if her lungs were trampolines and the Flying Wallendas had just catapulted off them. Yearning fisted her soul, strict and punishing. Stabbing her deep. She touched the tip of her tongue to the back of her teeth. Her gaze fixed on his angular mouth.

"I've got you." He'd come out of nowhere like a superhero. Reaching her when she needed him most.

She stared into that face, felt both salvaged and savaged. His hair was dark brown, almost black, and so thick it made her think of a magnificent forest, lush and vibrant.

"What happened?"

She wasn't about to tell him that she'd been overcome by grief. Didn't want to admit it even to herself. "Too much sugar, caffeine, and excitement."

"You okay?"

"I'm fine now. Thank you."

He righted her.

"Hunter," she said, her first clear thought going to the boy.

"Right here," Mark said, putting a hand to the boy's back and pushing him forward to her.

"N'omi?" Hunter looked worried. He tucked the book under his arm. Gnawed his cookie.

"I'm fine, sweetheart." She took a deep breath. Sent a grateful glance Mark's way. "Thank you."

"Do you need me to get you anything?" he asked. "Water? Something more substantial to eat?"

"No, no. I'm fine. Honestly." She put on her brightest, can-do smile. Smoothed down her hair.

"Can we still see Santa?" Hunter asked.

"Why yes!" she said, sounding like a gleeful Disney princess on steroids. Anything to get her joy back. "Of course!"

"Yay."

Mark's eyes met hers. "You sure you're all right?"

"Never better. Thanks again for your help," she chirped, ignoring the vacuum sucking a hole in her heart. Why had memories of Clayton fallen on her all of a sudden? It was unsettling and scary. "Let's go see Santa."

Hunter gave Naomi his book and cookie to hold. Reached out and took Mark's hand. "Come."

Led him to where kids and parents were lining up to see Santa at the North Pole exhibit set up on the courthouse lawn.

Mark looked at Naomi, raised his eyebrows. "Is it okay if I come along?"

"You want to stand in line with us to see Santa?" she asked, hoping he'd say no. She appreciated him for being there, but she still felt too discombobulated to deal with him.

Hunter squeezed Mark's hand. Nodded. "He does, N'omi."

She crouched to Hunter's eye level. "Are you sure he wants to come along? Did you ask his permission?"

Hunter tilted his face up to Mark. "Daddy?"

"I'm sorry," Naomi mumbled. "I don't know why he keeps doing that."

Shepherd peered down at the little boy who was looking at him as if he'd created the entire universe. "There's nowhere else on earth I'd rather be."

He sounded so genuine and sincere it rocked Naomi to her core.

"My, my," said an older woman with two little girls who came to stand in line behind them. "Don't you have the most beautiful family, sir."

Instead of correcting the woman, Shepherd beamed, slid his free arm around Naomi's shoulder, and said, "Why, thank you, ma'am."

And Naomi couldn't decide if she liked that or not.

They were leaving the North Pole exhibit after Hunter had his picture taken with Santa, and they ran into Terri, dressed as an elf and passing out flyers advertising her Hot Legs Gym and Day Spa.

"Good to see you again," she told Shepherd.

"You too." He nodded.

"Naomi," Terri said. "Just wanted to let you know everything's straightened out with the caterer for next Saturday night's dance."

"Thanks," Naomi said. "I do appreciate you picking up the slack. I know I haven't been at the top of my game."

"Paah." Terri waved a hand. "My pleasure. Glad I could help."

"I feel like I've let the committee down."

"Not at all." Terri glanced at Hunter, who was rubbing his eyes and yawning. "We understand."

Hunter tugged on Shepherd's hand. "Up!"

Without even thinking about it, Shepherd didn't miss a beat. He reached down and hoisted the little boy onto his hip.

Hunter buried his head against Shepherd's neck, yawned again. The kid smelled of cookies and exhausted little boy.

"Looks like someone is ready for a nap." Terri smiled at Hunter. A big hug of a grin, full of kindness and Christmas cheer. She switched her gaze to Shepherd. "You're a natural."

"Thanks." He was anxious to get Hunter and Naomi

home. She needed a nap as much as the boy. He didn't know why she'd almost fainted earlier. She seemed fine now, but he was still concerned. She'd been pushing herself far too hard.

"You're coming to the dance next weekend, right?" Terri said.

Shepherd glanced over at Naomi. "I haven't been invited."

"Naomi," Terri scolded. "You didn't invite him?"

Naomi flushed, stuttered. "I . . . I didn't think he'd want to come." She shifted her gaze to his knee.

He'd left his cane back at the rectory. His knee had been feeling stronger the last couple of days, and he'd come here only intending on dropping off the toys for the toy drive. He hadn't expected to hang out on the square with Naomi and Hunter.

"You absolutely must come," Terri invited. "Naomi needs an escort. I want to see her out on that dance floor. She's been spending far too much time making sure other people have fun and not having enough of her own."

"I agree with you completely, Mrs. Longoria," he said.

"Please," she said. "Call me Terri. I'm so glad you've come to Twilight."

"I'm pretty glad about that too, Terri," he said, and meant it. The reason he'd come here was a sad one, but the people he'd met were friendly and welcoming.

"And *you*, Miss Naomi . . ." Terri pointed a finger. "Need to take advantage of the day spa gift card we gave you as a thank-you for heading our committee."

"I'm sorry, Terri. I just don't have time for a massage." Naomi ruffled Hunter's wind-tousled hair. "I've got to chase after this little one."

"Make time," Terri said. "It's like the oxygen mask on the airplane. You have to take care of yourself first before you can help anyone else."

Naomi shook her head. "I appreciate the gift card, I truly do, but I'm just too busy. I haven't even had time to put up the Christmas tree yet. I hate for the gift certificate to go to waste. Can I give it to someone else?"

"I'll watch Hunter for you if you want to go for a massage," Shepherd offered. "I'll put up the tree for you too."

"I knew I liked you." Terri poked him gently in the ribs with her elbow. "Yes, Naomi, do what he said."

Naomi glowered at him.

He took in the dark circles under those big blue eyes. She might not want to take time for herself, but she needed it. Badly.

"See you at the dance next weekend," Terri called over her shoulder as she turned to greet newcomers. "And you . . ." She pointed a finger at Naomi. "Redeem your gift card and get that massage."

"You don't have to go to the dance." Naomi leaned in closer to whisper.

"But I want to go," Shepherd whispered back, inhaling her wonderful aroma. She smelled like holiday cheer. Cinnamon and vanilla. Just being near her boosted his spirits. "Unless you don't want me to go."

"It's a free country." She drew back. Her shrug was quick and prickly. All cactus. "Stay. Go. Suit yourself."

Why was she upset with him? Shepherd didn't get it. He thought they'd been having a good time. All he'd done was offer to watch Hunter so she could go get a massage. Was that a mistake? He was missing something.

"Where are you parked?" Shepherd asked, shifting a sleepy Hunter to his other shoulder.

"Here." She held out her arms. "I'll take him."

"I'll carry him to the car for you." He put starch in his voice and steel in his stare.

She looked as if she might protest, but then nodded. A curt little bob, stiff and out of sorts.

"Have I done something to upset you?" he asked.

"No," she denied.

"Then what gives?" he asked. "Why have you been giving me the cold shoulder?"

"I didn't . . . I haven't . . ." She blew her breath out through puffed cheeks.

"Does it have anything to do with me being ex-military?" he asked, navigating around a gaggle of women dressed as serving wenches, dancing on the sidewalk outside the wine store, Fruit of the Vine. "Does my being here stir up the grief over losing your brother that you haven't dealt with?"

"I'm dealing with my grief just fine," she snapped. "Thank *you* very much."

"Are you?" He didn't know why he was pushing her. This wasn't the time or the place. He had a sleeping boy on his shoulder and they were dodging dancing street wenches.

"Yes." Her eyes were full of bristles.

"Are you mad?"

"Yes."

"Good. I like seeing you this way."

That confused her. "What? Why are you trying to tick me off?"

"I just want you to know you don't have to constantly be in an up mood."

"This is me. It's my personality," she said, her smile sharkish. "I'm a happy, happy person."

"You don't look very happy right now. Which is okay, by the way. You shouldn't have to cover up your sadness or your anger."

"I. Am. Happy." She ground her teeth. "Oh. So. Happy."

"Then tell me about your brother." Shepherd wasn't sure what he was trying to accomplish. What was his end goal? Honestly, other than getting her to open up to her emotions she'd been tamping down for a year, he didn't have an agenda.

Don't you? The key you've been carrying around in your pocket says otherwise.

"I get it." She shook a finger at him. "You're trying to get a reaction out of me. Well, it's not going to work. This is Christmastime and I'm not going to let anything or anyone spoil it."

"Tell me about your brother," Shepherd pushed. "What was he like? What was his favorite breakfast cereal? Was he a Star Wars fan or did he prefer Star Trek? Did he like math? Or English? Did he ever break his arm? Could he swim?"

He saw the flash of anger in her eyes. Watched her fold the anger up and smile it away. Big. Stretchy. You're-not-gonna-get-to-me smile. She was seriously mad at him, but determined not to show it. He admired her stubbornness. Her jaw was a steel bear trap snapping closed.

"If I were going to tell you about Clayton, it wouldn't be here. Not like this."

"Where?" he asked. "When? Let's set a date."

In that moment, he understood why he was pushing her. He couldn't continue lying to her. For one thing, he was miserable keeping the secret. For another, he seriously liked her. She deserved the truth.

And when you tell her, if she hates you, what then?

Then she would just hate him. He didn't have any other option. No, he couldn't continue to lie to her, nor could he let her continue to lie to herself. She thought if she just pretended everything was fine, then she could make it so.

"Tell me about Clayton," he murmured.

"Oh look!" Naomi pointed. "They've got the snow throw up."

"Snow throw up?" he said, confounded. "Snow vomit?"

Naomi laughed, and the corners of her mouth crinkled. But he could see past the happy façade to the pain lodged deep in those blue eyes. "Not snow vomit, silly. That came out wrong. Let me try again. They've put up the snow throw."

He knew she was dodging the topic of her brother. He didn't know whether to keep pushing and ruin the moment, or let it go and enjoy himself.

And he *was* enjoying himself. Whenever he was with her things felt lighter. Brighter.

"C'mon." Naomi plucked the sleeve of his coat, dragging him along with her.

A colorful booth had been erected on the square. The booth was decorated with blinking, multicolored twinkle lights and blared Christmas music. Currently "Jingle Bells." It reminded him of a carnival midway booth at the fair. The game was similar to the one where the object was to knock down milk bottles with softballs.

Except the milk bottles were shaped like flat-topped

bowling pins with images of elves on them. And instead of softballs, you bought a bucket of snowballs to chunk.

"This was Clayton's favorite game," Naomi murmured so softly that Shepherd could barely hear her. "He killed at it."

"Competitive, was he?"

"You have no idea." She laughed, but it was a hollow sound, filled with suppressed grief.

"So tell me."

"I . . . I . . ." Something flashed in her blue eyes. Fear.

He understood now why she didn't want to talk about Clayton. Why she refused to accept her grief. She was terrified that if she gave in to it, she would fall apart and there would be no putting her back together again.

Shepherd got it. He'd been there.

But because of that, he knew something she didn't know. As long as you resisted the grief, as long as you ran from it, feared it, no matter how hard you tried, you could never heal.

"I can't talk about Clayton," she said. "Can you please just give me Hunter so I can take him home?"

"You miss your brother," Shepherd said. He missed Clayton too. He'd known the young Marine only a short time, but it had been easy to fall for Clayton's eager enthusiasm and open heart. They'd been friends. As good friends as rank had allowed them to be.

"Terribly," Naomi confessed, the soft pillow of her bottom lip trembling.

"You don't have to pretend to be happy with me. It's got to be a grind."

"No, no," she denied, trying to force another smile. "I *am* happy."

"Here's something I've learned," he said. "Whatever you resist persists. You keep tamping down that grief, eventually it's going to take a big toll. On your health, on your relationships, on your future."

"I'm not resisting my grief."

He stared at her. "Denial of a problem isn't healthy."

"Please." She held out her arms, the lines of emotional pain tightening her lips. "Give Hunter to me."

She was trying so hard not to fall apart. Straightening her shoulders. Setting her jaw. Thrusting out her chin.

Watching her shut down her emotions touched him to his core. She was so brave. He wanted to fold her into his arms and tell her that everything was going to be all right if she just let herself grieve.

But this was not the time or place to hold her feet to the fire. They were in a public space, surrounded by a throng of revelers.

He'd planted a seed. For now, it was all he could do. Giving her his most tender smile, Shepherd placed the sleeping boy into her waiting arms.

CHAPTER 16

The following day was Sunday, and Shepherd had been in town since Monday. Almost a week spent in the company of Naomi's loving family. The more he was around them, the more he liked them.

Pastor Tom invited Shepherd to attend church services. "Please come. It won't be the same without you."

How could he say no to that?

Shepherd couldn't remember the last time he'd attended a sermon. He wasn't entirely comfortable. He tugged at his tie. Sat up straight in the wooden pew. Wished he could take out his pocketknife and start whittling.

But Naomi was here, and that's all that mattered.

He sat next to her in the front row, which wasn't his seat of choice, but she was the pastor's daughter and expected to sit front and center. So here he was. Because there was nowhere else he wanted to be except by her side.

Irene sat in her wheelchair on the opposite side of the aisle. Hunter was back in the nursery with the other kids.

Pastor Tom's sermon was on forgiveness and it hit

close to home. Shepherd wondered if the minister had somehow discovered who he was, for it seemed as if Tom was looking straight at him.

And speaking of the truth . . . He'd intended on telling Naomi who he was yesterday at the festival, but she'd asked him to take her home. Begged off from cooking dinner, claiming she had a headache, and spent the evening in her room. He'd eaten take-out pizza with the rest of the family and spent most of the dinner trying to figure out if his pushing Naomi to talk about Clayton had caused her headache, or if she just couldn't face him across the dinner table.

Either way, he'd been miserable.

This morning, at the church, he'd come over to apologize for upsetting her. She'd smiled that sweet smile of hers and said, "Don't be silly. You don't have a thing to apologize for."

Then she'd patted the seat beside her in the pew, and here he was.

He glanced over at her. She was so beautiful it took his breath away. She was dressed in a long-sleeved blue velvet dress that matched her eyes. The material draped luxuriously over her curves, the wide circle skirt covering her knees. Her dark hair curled to her shoulders, gorgeously unbound. She looked like an angel perched atop a Christmas tree.

Maybe he should tell Tom who he was before he broke the news to Naomi. Especially since the pastor was talking so animatedly about forgiveness.

"Once you take the time to get to know people," Pastor Tom said, "you'll come to understand that we are all driven by our fears and wounds. That everyone is doing the best they know how in the moment. Once you understand, you can forgive them. Just as others forgive you for your mistakes."

It sounded so good. Like a reprieve. Shepherd wanted to believe it, but he didn't trust the ability of people to forgive. Would Pastor Tom be able to forgive him if he knew Shepherd could have saved Clayton, but hadn't?

Guilt overwhelmed him. Stronger than ever. He almost mumbled an excuse to Naomi and scrambled out of the church.

But then Pastor Tom finished up his sermon and the music started. The congregation sang from hymnals. Quaint and old-fashioned in this era of electronic prompters spelling out the lyrics on an overhead screen. Naomi held up her open hymnal so he could read from it and sing along with her.

Which was nice, because he had an acceptable excuse for moving closer to her.

Naomi's voice was sweet and pure. He heard it above all the others. Even though she was not singing any louder than anyone else. His ears were tuned to her and only her.

She sang and her song filled him. *He* was inside her. Resonating. Vibrating. Humming.

Enrapt. More present than he'd ever been in his life. Not even in war had he been so focused. Her rendition of the hymn opening up a whole new world of sound.

They were not separate, the two of them. They were one in her tower of song. Naomi sang, and because he heard her voice, he was part of it. Part of her.

It was the odd and intimate and exciting. This stunning knowledge. He felt suspended in time and space. Surrounded. Submersed. Utterly alive, and aware of his aliveness right in the middle of the ordinary and mundane.

Beautiful.

It was easy to feel alive on a battlefield when a man knew he could die at any moment. But to feel this alive, teeming with life in the most common of places?

What a gift!

He wanted to grab the feeling with both hands and hold on to it for dear life. But as soon as he had the thought of clinging, the feeling disappeared.

But he'd caught a glimpse. Seen a glimmer of what could be.

Shepherd was bowled over. Mind-blown. A mystical, mental union in song.

Naomi sang the last note, tilted her head toward him, and slanted her eyes up at him. A secret smile playing at her lips. As if she felt exactly the same thing.

If he'd left, he would have missed one of the most moving moments of his life.

Something shifted in Mark Shepherd after Sunday's church service.

Naomi didn't know what it was, but he seemed calmer, less edgy. After dinner, he didn't immediately run back to the rectory as he had the previous week. Instead, he lingered every evening all through Monday's game of Chutes and Ladders with Hunter and Tuesday's double feature of *Frosty the Snowman* and *Miracle on 34th Street*.

The week went on and except on Wednesday, when he mentioned he had a PTSD support group meeting, he joined in all the family fun—driving around town to see the Christmas lights, caroling with church members, and just . . . talking . . . together.

They talked and talked and talked. The conversations

light and easy. Nothing deep. Nothing unhappy. Just getting-to-know-you-better chitchat, all about music and art, books and food. The stuff you would say on a date.

Yes, she saw Mark every day, but they were never alone, and whenever Naomi tried to maneuver him away from the family for a private conversation, he'd steer her back to the group.

He wasn't avoiding her. He sat next to her on the couch. Helped her do the dishes. Put his hand to the small of her back and guided her over thresholds when he held the door open for her.

Not avoiding her. No. Rather, it was as if he was afraid to be alone with her.

Why?

Was he worried about losing his self-control?

Or about Naomi losing hers?

She'd finally made contact with Robert. He called her on Monday morning to say he'd been out doing fieldwork in the Colorado Rockies and hadn't gotten her text messages. They talked for a bit, but he'd seemed distracted, and when they hung up, neither one said, "I love you."

Naomi wasn't surprised. They'd been drifting apart for some time.

And she was feeling things for Shepherd that were quickly letting her know that while she loved Robert as a person, she was no longer in love with him.

Realistically, there wasn't a future with Shepherd, but she couldn't keep going on cruise control in her relationship with Robert. She had to break up with him.

After Christmas.

Get past Christmas and she'd deal with Robert.

Until then, she'd keep a smile on her face and a song in her heart. It was the only thing she knew to do.

* * *

Shepherd couldn't stop thinking about Naomi.

Or stay away from her.

Everything about her drew him—her hearty smile, her brilliant blue eyes, the soothing tone of her voice, her comforting homey scent.

His time in Twilight was limited, and all he wanted was to be near her. Soak up her sweetness. Wallow in her good cheer. He was desperate to make memories to sustain him in the gloomy days ahead.

Because those days were coming.

He felt it like a heavy wind pushing at the back of his neck. Isolation. Loneliness. It was his future. Even if the Luthers found it in their hearts to forgive him, he didn't belong here. This sweet place was as surreal as a storybook fairy tale.

And he was a man who'd never really had a home.

He wanted to tell her who he was, but every time he tried, the confession would have spoiled a beautiful moment. He told himself that Nate and the gang were right. Just keep his mouth shut until after Christmas. Let the family have a happy holiday.

Don't be selfish. Shoulder the guilt. Live with it.

The hard part about hanging around Naomi was twofold. One, he wanted to kiss her more than he wanted to breathe. And two, he yearned to confess his sins. Beg her forgiveness. Get her absolution. It was all he thought about when he tossed and turned in his bed at night with Jesus looking down at him from the picture on the wall.

Well, that and what Naomi looked like naked.

She would be shocked if she knew just how many times he imagined her without clothes on. He sort of shocked himself. He was really creative. Naomi naked underneath a waterfall. Bungee jumping. Nude house-keeping. Floating buns bare on the international space station. Stretched out on a '57 Chevy. A grand piano. A library bookcase.

It was fun to daydream. But it made things worse whenever he was around her. At the most inopportune times—playing board games, singing carols, sitting across the dinner table—those exciting fantasies would pop into his head.

Keeping his hands off her was almost impossible.

He reached down deep for self-control and took a cold shower every night to cool his ardor. It didn't help.

Everything about her inflamed him.

By the time Saturday rolled around, he was a walking bundle of unchained lightning. Suppressed sexual energy oozing from his pores.

Tonight, they were going to the First Love Cookie Club charity ball. There would be alcohol and dancing. And touching. And mistletoe.

Ah, crap. He was in trouble.

They planned to arrive separately at the party venue—the high school gym turned ballroom. As the committee chairperson, Naomi had to be there early to make sure everything was going smoothly.

And Shepherd had to go borrow a suit from Gideon. He'd pared down his life after rehab and he'd tossed out his suit. Luckily, Gideon had several and they wore the same size.

"You should always own a suit," Gideon said when he went to pick it up. "For funerals."

"Aren't you just a little bundle of sunshine?"

"I call 'em like I see 'em." Gideon handed him the suit on a wooden hanger. "Do you need dress shoes too?"

"Yeah."

Gideon gave a slight eye roll. "What size do you wear?"

"Twelve."

"Me too." Gideon reached into his closet for a pair of black dress shoes. "Here you go."

"Thanks."

"You planning on dancing?" Gideon nodded at Shepherd's cane.

"It is a dance. That's kind of the point."

"Just wondering," Gideon said. "I had a tough time adjusting to losing my hand. I had trouble doing normal things. Just wondering if you were having the same issues over your knee."

Shepherd shook his head. "You lost a limb. That's a much bigger deal than a bunged-up knee."

"Is it? In my book, it's a loss either way."

"Thanks for all this."

"Someday you can return the favor," Gideon said, as if he expected Shepherd to be around for a good long time. "See you at the dance."

When Shepherd got to the high school, most of the people going inside were dressed in Dickens-era clothing. Gingerly, he climbed out of his Jeep.

"Look at you," a passerby said, pointing at his cane. "Tiny Tim twenty years later. Creative."

He didn't know whether to be amused or insulted. He decided to channel his inner Naomi and laugh.

The passersby laughed with him.

Man, but he loved this town.

"Hey, cowboy."

Behind him, knuckles rapped against the side of his Jeep. He turned to see the sassy barista from Perks, dressed in steampunk garb. Goggles. Top hat. Knee-high black boots. Brown bustle skirt and corset. Trust her to give Dickens a Jules Verne twist.

She pooched out her bottom lip in an exaggerated pout. "You never did call me."

"You wrote your number on my palm, and I washed my hands." He held up his palm for her to see.

"Convenient."

"Truth?"

"Of course."

"I like Naomi."

Mia sighed. "I figured. Although I don't know why. Don't get me wrong. She's pretty and all that, but she's just so darn *sweet*. That chick'll give you cavities."

"Don't disrespect her." Shepherd sharpened his tone.

"I meant it in the best possible way." Mia clucked her tongue, eyed him up and down. "Does Naomi know that you're head-over-heels?"

"I'm not—"

"You are."

"Does that ploy ever work, by the way?" he asked. "The writing-your-phone-number-on-a-man's-palm thing."

"Honey," she said, lowering her eyelashes, "you're the only one who never called."

"I'm sorry if I hurt your feelings."

"Think nothing of it." She waved a hand. "Even the best batters strike out seven times out of ten. You flying solo tonight?"

"I'm meeting Naomi inside."

"Curses," she said, like a cartoon villain. "Foiled again. Walk me in?"

"Sure." He took the elbow Mia extended, and escorted her into the building.

There was no music playing. People were milling around looking lost.

"There you are." Naomi appeared in front of him, breathless. One look in her eyes and he forgot all about Mia. Dropping the other woman's arm, he stepped closer to Naomi.

Naomi was dressed in a long Victorian-era skirt and a high ruffled collar. She eyed Mia. A disgruntled expression flitted across her face, but she quickly cloaked it with a smile.

Was she jealous? That thought lit him up like a Christmas tree.

"I don't want to interrupt," Naomi said. "But could you come look at the sound system? The DJ isn't here yet, and we've got an input problem."

"Or . . ." Mia crossed her arms, her voice taking on a singsong tease. "Maybe it's an output issue."

"Why do you think I would know anything about stereo input?" Shepherd asked, his heart mushy with the idea that Naomi was jealous.

"Or output," Mia whispered.

"I dunno." Naomi's eyes sparkled in the holiday lighting. "You're good with your hands?"

"He is?" Mia looked at Shepherd's hands. "How would *you* know?"

"Personal experience," Naomi said. "I know what he can do with those hands."

"Whoa ho." Mia laughed. "Maybe it isn't an output problem. But just in case, do you want me to write my number on your palm again?" Mia winked at him.

"No," Naomi and Shepherd said in unison.

"Rats," Mia muttered. Shrugged. "Win some, lose some. Ooh, there's Jeff Perry. See ya. Hey, wait up, Jeff."

"She's sweet," Naomi said as Mia waltzed off with Jeff.

"Not at all." Shepherd shook his head.

"Sassy then."

"That's putting it mildly."

"About the stereo . . ."

"I *do* know how to fix your input." Shepherd wriggled his eyebrows.

She crooked a finger, her smile a radiant hook, hips swaying. "This way."

I'd follow that swing anywhere, he thought and went after her.

She took him backstage where the control base was located. "I'm praying you can get this fixed. I don't know when the DJ will get here, and what's a dance without music?"

He liked being her white knight. "Got your phone with you?"

She whipped her phone from her pocket.

"Switch on the flashlight and hold it over here," he directed.

She flicked on the flashlight. Leaned over his shoulder to illuminate the control panel. Her scent filled his nose. She smelled like Christmas, all peppermint and pine needles.

His mouth watered and he thought, *God, I'd love to taste those lips*.

"You need more light?" She inched closer. Her breasts brushed against his shoulders.

Shepherd gulped. He felt a little light-headed. Well, it was warm back in this corner, behind the stage curtain. He tried to focus on the wires, but damn if he couldn't stop thinking about the soft, high breasts pressing into him. She felt ripe, juicy. Pluckable.

Knock it off.

Yeah, right. That was like trying to stop ice from melting in the Sahara Desert.

He exhaled, jiggled wires. Music blared.

Simultaneously, they gasped. Jumped.

"Turn it down, turn it down." She stuck her phone in her pocket, dampening the light, and clasped both hands over her ears.

He grappled for the volume. Got things under control. At least as far as the sound system was concerned.

"Thank you." She blew out her breath. "Whew. Crisis averted. You've saved me again. I'm going to have to tell Dad to give you a raise."

"No need," he said. "I'll do anything for you. Gratis."

They were facing each other in the shadows. In the gym, they could hear people starting to dance to the music. "Please Come Home for Christmas." The Eagles version.

"*Anything?*" A mischievous note crept into her voice.

"Say the word, butterfly. Your wish is my command."

The side door opened, letting in light from the parking lot.

"I'm here, I'm here." A twenty-something guy in a Santa suit and fake beard burst through the door, carrying his equipment. "Sorry I'm late. I've got everything under control now."

Naomi looked skeptical.

Shepherd put a hand to her shoulder. "Let the man do his job. I want to hear more about what *you* need."

"I need to make sure the music keeps rolling."

"I'm on it, I'm on it," the DJ promised.

"He's on it." Shepherd reassured her. "You don't have to ride herd on everyone all the time."

Again with that skeptical stare. This time fixed on him.

The DJ took charge. Handling the music and the microphone. Drawing back the curtain. Going out on stage. Hollering, "Let's get this party started. For realz."

"See?" Shepherd held out his hand.

A sidelong glance. Her half smile. Small hand sunk in his.

Shepherd led her down the backstage steps and out to the gym floor. Couples were dancing. Party lights blinked festively. The central strobe in the middle of the room was loaded with mistletoe.

"So," he said. "What was that anything?"

"May I have this dance?"

He shook his head. "You don't want to dance with me."

She nodded. Confirming. Yes, she did. "You. Me. The dance floor."

"You've forgotten." He held up his cane.

"Don't give me that Tiny Tim routine. I've seen you crawling around on the rectory roof. I've felt you catch me when I almost fainted. I watched you carrying Hunter on your shoulder for half an hour. It's not easy. That boy gets heavy."

Yeah, in all those cases, it was after he'd downed anti-inflammatory pills. "You also saw me fall off the curb."

"Those sidewalks are notoriously trippy."

"You're not letting me off the hook."

"*Anything.* That's what you said."

He shook his head, laughed. "Indeed."

"I want to dance."

"Punch first?" He tried delay tactics.

"You can do this," she said in that way she had of challenging people. She would have made a good nurse. "You can dance with me. We'll take it easy. No competition."

"I'm a lousy dancer in the best of conditions, and this isn't that."

"I don't care." She held out a hand. "I want to dance . . . with you."

His knee was yelling at him, *Don't do it, fool, I might collapse and you'll end up on the floor.* But his heart said, *The woman of your dreams is asking you to dance. Be strong. Be brave.*

Her smile was the deciding factor. Those sweet, beguiling lips seduced without intent. Moist and pink and glistening in the light from the mistletoe-laden chandelier. He felt the same sense of fate that had swept over him the day she'd first gotten into his Jeep by mistake.

He took the hand she offered, using his cane to hold him steady so that he didn't put much weight on his bum knee. What a prize dance partner he was.

But his lameness didn't bother her. In fact, she looked inordinately proud to be squiring him onto the dance floor. Her shoulders were straight. Chin up. Her bearing regal and relaxed.

"Leave the cane," she said. "I've got you."

"You're going to lead?"

"Whatever it takes to dance with you, Mark." She said his first name as if it was a precious natural pearl she'd found while shucking an oyster. And she was polishing it up to a high sheen.

"I'm supposed to lead."

"Throw those silly, antiquated rules out the window." She gently tapped his temple with her small fist. "Who cares who leads? The point is to have fun."

Part of him felt liberated. Another part disadvantaged. *He* wanted to lead. Wanted to give her the fantasy of Cinderella dancing at the ball. But reality and fantasy were two different things.

It was all he could do to walk without limping, much less dance.

He stuck out his hand. "If I tumble, we go down together. As long as you're good with that . . ."

"Deal." She took his hand.

He held her close. Her lovely scent surrounded him. He peered into those blue eyes the color of a warm summer sky. His heart bounced off the trampoline of his stomach and into his throat. God, she was gorgeous, and he was the luckiest man on the face of the earth.

"Thank you," she whispered. "For dancing with me."

"Thank you for forcing me." He chuckled.

"Stick around, you'll figure out I'm pretty good at coercing people into doing things they don't want to do."

"I've already started putting two and two together."

"And yet, you're still here."

"Yeah." His voice came out husky. "I guess I am."

She laughed. Music to his ears. A tonic for his bedraggled soul. Because of Naomi, he'd come back to life.

The DJ put on "So This Is Christmas."

A slow song that sent several couples off the dance floor. But slow was his top speed, and he couldn't help feeling the DJ had picked something down tempo just for them.

Naomi wrapped her arm around his waist. She was his crutch. Holding him up. "Now," she said. "Put your arm around me."

It was as easy as that. His arm went around her waist, and he was holding her. She was holding him. They were holding each other.

Emotions tumbled in on him. He felt like the loner high school kid who'd by some miracle gotten lucky enough to escort the prom queen to the dance. He didn't trust it, the glorious feeling of hope. Why was she dancing with him? Out of pity? Or because she got satisfaction from taking on fixer-uppers?

Then she rested her head on his shoulder, quelling his self-doubts. All he could think of was her. The smell of her—shampoo and moonbeams, vanilla and mist. The sight of her hair—silky and smooth. The sound of her breathing—slow and controlled.

Startled, he recognized the pattern: 4–7–8 breathing. She was trying to steady herself. Who'd taught her that? Her brother?

"Are you all right?" he asked.

"Fine," she murmured, struggling to hide the shakiness in her voice, but he heard it. Loud and clear. She was unnerved.

So was he.

"Are *you* all right?" she asked, pulling her head back to look him in the eyes.

He'd never in his life felt righter. "I'm good."

"Your leg?"

"It's—" Heck, he'd forgotten about his knee. "Great."

"Really?"

"Better than I expected."

"That makes me happy."

She rested her head on his shoulder again and his knee wobbled a little. Not from pain, but from the realization that she wanted to be in his arms as much as he wanted her there. This was not just a rescue mission. Sure, she might feel sorry for him. But she was feeling more than that. He could tell from the pressure of her head against his shoulder.

He tilted his own head toward her, until his ear touched the top of her head. It was a perfect moment.

And then . . .

"Friends and lovers," the DJ called out over the microphone. "Are you ready to play mistletoe roulette?"

CHAPTER 17

"What's that?" someone in the crowd called out.

"Here are the rules . . ." the DJ explained. "You dance around the floor, switching partners every time the strobe light turns colors. When the music stops, you have to kiss whomever you're dancing with."

A few people shook their heads and left the dance floor, but several more couples walked out onto the floor.

Shepherd shifted his gaze to Naomi, ready to leave too. But she sent him a look so naughty it could earn coal in her stocking. "Sounds like fun."

"You already know how I feel about mistletoe," he grumbled.

Her cheeks reddened, but she met his gaze and whispered, "*Anything*."

"You're asking a lot."

"Fine. I'll find another dance partner."

He should have walked away. Just turned and got off the dance floor, but he didn't want her dancing with someone else. Didn't want her kissing anyone else.

The music started. The Bruce Springsteen version of "Santa Claus Is Coming to Town." Naomi interlaced their fingers. The strobe light was green. They danced two turns around the gymnasium.

The light turned purple.

"Bye." Naomi waved and turned to Jeff Perry.

Leaving Shepherd to dance with Mia. She purred a little growl, like a Jaguar engine. "We meet again," she said, with her cartoon-villainess laugh.

The light turned red and he was off with someone else. He kept trying to steer his partner near Naomi, who was dancing with Gideon Garza. Unfortunately, Gideon was just as intent on getting across the other side of the room where his wife, Caitlyn, was dancing with someone else.

Shepherd chased after them, dragging his partner along with him.

"Wow," the woman said, red-faced and perspiring. "You sure are lithe for a man with a limp."

"Where there's a will, there's a way," Shepherd said.

"What?" The woman blinked. But then the strobe changed colors again and he found himself face-to-face with Lily.

"You want near Naomi," Lily said.

"Yes."

"Let's cut across the middle. You've been sticking too close to the edge."

The middle looked daunting. What if he fell? But Lily was right. It was the quickest route to Naomi.

"You're a good friend," he said.

"Just so you know." Lily leveled him a cool stare. "I'm *her* friend. She seems to like you. Which is the only reason I'm helping you. But hear this, you hurt my friend, and I'm coming after you. Got it?"

"Roger that." Damn, but he liked Lily.

The music stopped.

Lily dragged him the last few steps to Naomi. Slipped in to whisk Naomi's partner away. Planted a big kiss on the startled man's lips.

Leaving Shepherd standing in front of Naomi in the middle of the dance floor.

"It's the rules," she said, pointing up. "We're together when the music ends and we're standing under the mistletoe again. We *have* to kiss this time."

"What is the deal with you and mistletoe?"

"It's fun." She beamed a spotlight of joy. "It's a Christmas tradition."

"I think you're just too afraid to claim your desires without an excuse," he said. "Blame it on the mistletoe."

"I . . . I . . ." she stammered.

They were being watched. Everyone else had already exchanged smooches. The crowd was clapping their hands and calling out, *Kiss, kiss, kiss.* The DJ got into the act, picking up the chant over the microphone.

"To hell with this." Shepherd locked his hand around her wrist, tugged her toward the exit. "Come with me."

She did not resist.

Heart thumping like mad, Shepherd dragged her out the side door and into the parking lot. Pressed her back against the side of the building.

He looked into her face. *Do it. Kiss her. You want it. She wants it. Do it.*

Shepherd loved everything about her—the smile on her lips, the twinkle in her blue eyes, the sweet sheen of perspiration dotting her brow. The way her chest hitched and fell in time to her jagged breathing. Her pure lightness of being.

God, he wanted what she had. The ability to roll with the punches and come back grinning. Her lips promised contentment beyond anything he had ever known. He wanted to kiss her.

Needed to kiss her.

She did not move away.

The toes of his shoes butted up against the tips of hers. Her feet were so delicate. Fine and fragile. But they anchored her to the ground like tree roots. She was not a girl who let the whip of life's winds break her branches. She swayed with the troubles, lithe and surefooted.

Shepherd lowered his head.

Naomi lifted her chin.

His eyes were wide open.

So were hers.

Thoughts tangled around his brain. Twirling and twisting. Was this stupid? Would kissing her only make things harder on him?

Walk away. Just go.

If only he could. For one thing, his legs were shaking so hard he couldn't walk. For another thing, he had the overwhelming fear that if he did not kiss her here, kiss her now, kiss her long and hard and deep, that he would never find true happiness.

Illogical. Sure. Don't get him started. But nothing had been logical since he'd driven into this magical town. Since this adorably sweet and kind woman had mistakenly jumped into his Jeep.

Maybe it hadn't been a mistake. What if fate had put him in that exact spot at that exact moment just so they could meet?

If he kept thinking like that, he'd have to move to Twilight. No rational community would take him in.

Snap to, Marine. He was disassociating from the very thing he wanted most.

Those lovely pink lips. Before he ever brushed his mouth against hers, he knew what she would taste like.

Peppermint candy canes. Refreshing. Sweet and tangy. Uplifting and wholesome.

She puckered her lips. Closed her eyes. Waited.

Shepherd gulped. This was his last chance to bail out. It was going to be okay. He could kiss her and it wouldn't wreck things. He wouldn't lose his head . . . or his heart . . . over just one kiss.

Denial is not just that river in Egypt, Gunny.

He could feel her breath on his chin, warm and inviting. He leaned in closer, his mouth almost upon hers.

From the gymnasium, the music was up tempo and loud. Outside, they were in the shadows, not completely hidden from view, but passersby would have to really hunt to see them. The air was cold, but not uncomfortably. Just enough bite to make things interesting.

His arms went around her.

She pressed her heart forward, and her breasts grazed against him.

He captured her lips.

No, not captured. Not really. She surrendered. White flag. Towel thrown. Her lips softening. Jaw loosening. Body melting into his.

Naomi's hand fluttered upward, and she skimmed heated fingers over the nape of his neck.

Inflamed, he deepened the kiss, tugging her closer, touching his tongue to her lips. She opened her mouth, and let him in.

Ah, he was right. Peppermint.

He slipped a palm to the small of her back, dipping her slightly, latching on to her securely. He experienced the kiss not just in his mouth, but throughout his entire body. His tongue. His teeth. His skin. His very bones.

He tasted her. Smelled her. Absorbed her.

Felt her lodge into the center of him. At his gut. And his heart. In his throat. In his brain. In his blood.

He closed his eyes, engrossed. Poured everything he had into that kiss. Telling her with his lips what he didn't dare put into words. *I want you. I need you. I think I might be in love with you.*

That last part was a surprise.

But it was true. He had feelings for her. Strong feelings.

He'd never been in love. Not really. He'd had girl-friends. Flings. Affairs. He'd had fun. He'd enjoyed himself. He'd made memories.

But that was all.

Shepherd had never felt the need to commit. He had looked around at his friends and fellow Marines who were falling in love. Getting married. Having children. He couldn't recall thinking—not at any wedding he'd attended, not at any birth announcement he'd received— *this is what I want.*

But he was thinking it now. *This. This. This. Her. Her. Her.*

Naomi.

She was *the one*.

Shepherd savored the kiss. Knowing this bliss could not last. Blessing himself with the taste of her. Committing her flavor to memory so he could remember it in the future when he was lonely and missing this special moment.

She made a quiet noise and snuggled closer. Wrapped her arms around his neck. Drew his head down. Pressed her body into his.

He groaned. Overcome. Overwhelmed. Overstimulated. And loving every second of it.

She was the rainbow after a storm. The climactic movement of a symphony. The light in a child's eyes on Christmas Day. She was everything he'd never had, and all that he'd ever wanted, rolled into one glorious package.

"Mark," she murmured. "Mark."

"Naomi," he answered, and they kissed each other so hard and long they stopped breathing.

"Okay," she gasped. "Quick break for air."

They inhaled deeply, and then went right back at it. Exploring each other with their lips, teeth, and tongues.

"You," she whispered when they broke for another breath, "are the best kisser ever."

"It's you," he said, feeling sappy and happy and not caring one whit that he sounded like a sentimental fool.

"It's us." She rested her forehead against his and closed her eyes. "It's us together."

He couldn't deny that, so he kissed her again.

"Mmm," she murmured, and licked his lips. "Mmm."

He pulled her upper lip between his teeth, sucked on it lightly. She giggled. He kissed the tip of her nose. Her cheeks. Her forehead. Her chin. Her earlobes. The pulse throbbing at her jawline.

"Better watch out," she said. "You're starting a fire I'm not sure you can put out."

That stopped him in his tracks, because he had a fire of his own burning through his solar plexus, searing his nerve endings, blasting away all common sense. He wanted her. It was the driving thought in his primal brain. Wanted their bodies joined.

Now!

But she was the minister's daughter and he was the man who was ultimately responsible for her brother's death. She hadn't dealt with her grief and he was still healing from PTSD. There was no getting around any of that.

Shepherd eased away from her, his breath coming in short, hard pants.

"We should go back inside," she said, pressing a palm to her lips, and shivering in the cold. It had been inconsiderate of him to drag her outside without her coat.

"Yes." He kept his voice firm. Steady. Belying how shaky he felt inside. He took her hand. She was trembling.

"Are you okay?" he asked.

"Just chilled." She rubbed her hands over her upper arms.

"Let's get you warm." He opened the door, put a hand to the small of her back again, and escorted her inside.

The contrast from the quiet intimacy of the parking lot to the boisterous Christmas party jolted him. He took her hand. Tucked her into his embrace. Swayed there with her in time to the music, while others danced around them.

He could feel the thudding of her heart, heard it beat in time with his own. She rested her head on his shoulder.

And for one split second, the world was absolutely sublime.

"May I cut in?" a masculine voice rumbled behind them.

Shepherd stopped. Glanced over his shoulder.

Spied a lean, good-looking man with chiseled cheekbones, pressed slacks, and a cashmere coat. Snowflakes dusted his hair, and he looked like he'd just stepped off the set of some sentimental holiday movie. He had a package under his arm, and eyes for only Naomi.

"Robert!" she exclaimed, and peeled away from Shepherd, her eyes feverishly alight. "When did you get here?"

"Right this minute." Robert was staring at Naomi and Naomi was staring at Robert and Shepherd felt like a third wheel that had sprung a leak.

"Why didn't you tell me you were coming home?" She sank her hands on her hips and eyed him up and down.

"I wanted to surprise you. Are you surprised?"

"Get a feather and knock me over." She lightly swatted Robert's shoulder, in the intimate way of lovers.

Couples two-stepped around the three of them. They were gumming up the flow.

Robert took Naomi's elbow as if he'd taken it many times before, and guided her off the dance floor, completely ignoring Shepherd.

Who was this guy? Waltzing in as if he owned the place. Owned Naomi.

Shepherd wanted to sit down, but the tables and chairs were all the way across the room and his knee was throbbing. Feeling exposed, and unsteady, without his cane to lean on. Where had he left his cane?

"Where are my manners?" Naomi asked, turning back to him. "Robert, this is Mark Shepherd. Mark is a former Marine, like Clayton. And he's the church's new handyman. Mark, this is Robert Bellamy."

Robert stretched out a hand to shake Shepherd's. "Nice to meet you, Mark. I'm Naomi's boyfriend."

CHAPTER 18

The two men sized each other up like roosters at a cock-fight.

"I need to talk to you," Robert said to her, his voice taking on an urgent quality. "Alone." He stared pointedly at Mark.

Naomi could feel the electrical charge of hostility crackling in the air. Robert and Mark did not like each other. She needed to talk to Robert, but she wanted to make sure that Mark was okay. She could tell the dancing had taken a toll on his knee. His eyebrows were furrowed, his mouth tightly drawn.

Plus, and here was the part that really confused her, when she thought of going off with Robert and leaving Mark, her heart sank.

Why?

Because Mark needed her.

Yeah, what about how much you enjoyed kissing him?

She shouldn't have done that. Not until she'd ended her relationship with Robert. After kissing Mark, she knew there was no future with her high school sweetheart. She needed to let Robert know that too.

"Could you give us a sec?" She held up one finger to Robert. "I need to help Mark find his cane."

"I don't need any help." Mark's voice was gravel, his dark eyes darker still. He turned and started back across the middle of the dance floor. She assumed because that was the quickest way to a chair.

But maybe it was the quickest route away from her.

Her stomach churned. She should have told him about Robert. Why hadn't she told him about Robert? Why? Because she'd known Mark for only two weeks and, well, okay, here was the truth: she'd wanted to break up with Robert before she told Mark about him.

Whoa! It was only just this minute she realized it. And?

The kismet-cookie-dream-fated-to-be thing was pretty powerful, but scary as hell. She'd been with Robert since she was sixteen. He was the only man she'd ever been with. That was a lot of history to throw away.

Had she been hedging her bets? Dueling legends. Kismet cookies versus high school sweethearts? Weren't both myths silly things to base relationships on?

Yes. Absolutely.

Shame filled her. She would like to think she wasn't the sort of woman who kept a man on a string. But apparently that's what she'd been doing with Robert by continuing this long-distance relationship when her heart wasn't in it. Any man who couldn't get fully on board with Naomi adopting Hunter had no place in her life.

Watching Mark limp away tore her to pieces.

The song had changed, the DJ breaking into "Jingle Bell Rock." People were grabbing partners and pouring onto the dance floor. Getting in Mark's way.

He zigzagged to miss a couple that darted out in front of him, and his knee buckled.

Naomi's stomach leaped into her chest. Instantly, she was shoving people aside to get to him. And she managed to grab his elbow just before he went down. They seemed to keep saving each other.

His mouth pressed into a stern line and his body turned to steel against hers. "I've got it."

That stubborn masculine pride.

"I know you do," she soothed, and let go of his arm.

She went ahead of him, making shooing motions. Clearing a path. She spied his cane propped against the stage. Snagged it, and brought the cane back to him. "Here we go."

"I don't need *you*." He snatched the cane from her hand, leaned heavily against it.

Ouch. Okay, his pride was wounded and he was taking it out on her. He had a point though. She should have told him about Robert before she kissed him. There had been time. Two weeks' worth of it. But, she'd been scared that if he knew about Robert he wouldn't kiss her, and she'd been so hungry for his kiss.

And that was the *real* truth of why she hadn't mentioned she had a boyfriend.

Dear Lord, please forgive me. She'd been selfish and inconsiderate. She deserved Mark's anger.

Undaunted, she pulled out a chair for him.

He grunted. Didn't meet her eyes.

Okay. She exhaled through pursed lips.

Mark took care with each placement of his cane. When he reached the chair, he dropped down hard onto the seat.

"You're in pain," she said. "Shall I get you some ibuprofen?"

"No. I don't need anything." He cast a glance back across the dance floor. "Go on. Robert is waiting for you."

Naomi looked to where Robert was standing, giving her an impatient, hurry-up stare, and then she looked back at Mark.

His mouth tightened as though he was fighting off pain.

"I have time for you," she said. "We can talk."

"Go." It was a bark, a command. He scowled.

Something more was going on here. Yes, they'd kissed. But it *was* just a kiss. It wasn't as if they'd had sex. She could see why he would be irritated or upset with her, but he was flat-out angry. The vein at his temple jumped, and his jaw clenched.

Naomi inhaled sharply. Could he be jealous of Robert? But if he was jealous of Robert, that meant Mark had feelings for her. Did he? Her pulse sped up. Oh gosh, she had feelings for him too. Big, scary feelings.

"Why are you so huffy?" she asked.

"I'm not huffy."

"You are." She nodded to where he'd knuckled up on the cane. "What's this all about?"

"You." His tone was blunt, but his eyes held unfathomable depths of gentleness.

"Me? What did I do?"

"You didn't leave me alone when I asked you to," he said.

"All I wanted was to help."

"No, all you want is to be needed." His stare was steely. "It's an issue with you."

Naomi notched up her chin, hurt. "And what's wrong with wanting to be needed?"

"You tell me."

"Well, I don't like it when the people I'm trying to help turn testy." Her chest squeezed tight, forcing a snort of air from her lungs. "Is that what you mean?"

"That's because you expect to get something out of helping."

"Excuse me?" She rested her hands on her hips, felt her temper push against her throat. They were about to have their first fight. What a location for it, right in front of her community.

"You expect people to be *grateful* because you swoop in and save them. Naomi to the rescue."

"I do *not*." But even as she said it, she knew there was a grain of hard truth in his words. Weren't people *supposed* to be grateful when you helped them? It bugged her when she went out of her way to lend a hand and folks didn't thank her. Okay, he was right. She did expect a thank-you. Was that so wrong?

He raised both eyebrows, sent her a cool appraising glance.

"You're impossible," she said, exasperated and confused. Was this about Robert? Or something else?

"Most likely," he agreed with a grunt.

"And irritating."

"I am. But you have to ask yourself, Naomi, why are *you* getting triggered?"

"I . . . um . . ." She snorted again, tossed her head. "*You've* been to therapy."

"I have," he said mildly. "And I've learned that when I'm upset for no good reason, it's generally because I've allowed something, or someone, to push my buttons. It's about me, not them. Or as my psychiatrist says, take it vertical."

"What does that mean?" Her skin chilled. Goose bumps sprang up.

Mark had been seeing a psychiatrist. Was this part of the secret he'd wanted to confess the first day he'd shown up at their dinner table? A secret her father had quashed with his message of forgiveness and acceptance. But that was a good thing. He had PTSD. He was working on healing. Why should that be a secret?

"Look inside yourself for the answers to what's bugging you," he said. "Not to the behavior of others."

"Well . . . well . . ." she sputtered. He was right. She was triggered and it ticked her off that he was calling her on it. "La-di-da."

He grinned then. Looking thoroughly amused that he'd gotten her goat.

"You know what I think?" She swished her head from side to side.

"I have absolutely no idea."

"I think you *like* pushing people away. You believe it keeps you from getting hurt," she challenged.

"Oh ho?" His eyes narrowed, glittered darkly in the colored lights.

"But it doesn't."

"No?"

"Loneliness is just as painful as putting yourself out there. You gotta pick your poison. That's up to you. But me, I'd rather go with people than without them."

Having said everything that she needed to say, her heart racing, Naomi turned and marched away.

* * *

Feeling like a bumbling idiot, Shepherd fumbled for his cane, desperate to get out of the ballroom. His gut pitched, and the muscle at his temple ticked. What a fool he'd been to kiss Naomi.

Discovering too late that she had a boyfriend.

He put all his weight on his bum knee, perversely needing to feel the pain. Punishing himself for daring to think he had a chance with her.

The problem wasn't just the boyfriend.

He was the real problem. He had too much childhood baggage he was still dragging around. And a white Christmas key in his pocket that had belonged to her dead brother. That enigmatic key that had brought him to this town. To her.

The woman of his dreams.

He lurched forward. Headed for the door. He didn't look back at Robert and Naomi. Couldn't bear to see her wrapped in another man's embrace.

His heart tightened, a lonely instrument. *Thump-thump-thumping.*

The Christmas music, which earlier had sounded so cheery, grated on his nerves. He gritted his teeth. Narrowed his eyes against the onslaught of "All I Want for Christmas Is You."

Up ahead, the exit sign glowed red. He moved faster, anxious to get out of here, anxious to breathe.

The dance floor was crowded. He had to wend a circuitous path to his destination. Out. He had to get out.

Panic pushed up through his lungs and he flashed back to the Kandahar orphanage. Where he'd found Luther in a chokehold. The wounded terrorist, Ackmed Talid, pressing his handgun against Luther's temple. That stupid

Christmas light lei around Luther's neck blinking cheerful colors.

Shepherd slammed through the exit door. Stumbled out into the alley. Panting. Sweating. Shaking.

"Gunny?" Nate Deavers's coal-black gaze was acute. "You with me?"

Where in the hell had the former SEAL come from? Where were they? Shepherd blinked, glanced around. Christmas lights. Laughter from inside the gym. Music. In the distance, the dark shimmer of the lake. Snowflakes. It was snowing.

He was in Twilight. Not Kandahar. This year. Not last. Clayton Luther was dead. He was alive.

And Naomi had a boyfriend.

Disappointment was a rat, gnawing a hole through his belly. Why hadn't she mentioned she had a boyfriend? There'd been plenty of opportunities.

No. He wouldn't blame her. Take it vertical. This was his fault, not hers. He'd just assumed she was single. If he had asked, he wouldn't have been blindsided.

Here was a bigger question.

Why *was* he blindsided? She was smart, single, and attractive. He should have *assumed* she was in a relationship. Why hadn't he asked? That gave him pause. The answer was obvious. He'd *wanted* her to be available. Hadn't wanted to know if she wasn't.

Well, now you know. Hands O-F-F.

"Gunny." Nate gripped his shoulders. "Snap to."

Shepherd shook his head.

"Where are you?" Nate grunted.

"Twilight, Texas." Shepherd gripped his cane, leaned heavily on it. Felt the solidity of the earth through the tip of it. Grounded himself.

Nate nodded. Dropped his hands. Stepped back. "C'mon, let's hit the Waffle-O-Rama."

Shepherd wanted to say no. He wanted to be alone, but the part of him that had struggled so hard to come back from Kandahar nodded.

"My pickup is this way."

"Where's your minivan?"

"I was in town taking more toy donations to the fire-house. I saw you tumble out the back door of the gym." He paused. "You had a look on your face . . . well, let's just say I recognize that look."

Blowing out his breath, Shepherd ran a hand through his hair. "I'm falling apart."

"That's good."

"It is?"

"Yes, now we can put you back together, better than ever."

"I'm beginning to think you're my guardian angel."

Nate's eyes twinkled. "Maybe I am."

They reached a battered green Ford parked at the curb. Nate opened the passenger door and let Shepherd in.

Shepherd hoisted himself up. Placed the tip of his cane on the running board. Used it as a fulcrum. Landed hard in the seat. Buckled up.

Nate got in and started the engine. Drove to the waffle place.

Without saying a word, they went inside. Sat at a table in the corner where they could both have their backs to the wall and watch the door. Old habits of self-preservation died hard.

They ordered coffee and apple pie.

It was early, and with so much else going on in town, there was hardly anyone inside the restaurant.

"Flashback?" Nate asked.

Shepherd nodded, unfurled the paper napkin from around the silverware.

"The trigger?"

He shrugged. Spread the napkin on the table. Lined up the fork, spoon, and knife so that the bottoms were evenly spaced.

"Shepherd?"

"Who knows?" He liked having Nate with him. But at the same time, he found the other man's presence taxing.

"*You* know."

Bombarded by so many emotions that he did not want to feel, Shepherd pulled a palm down his face. "The flashback was about Clayton."

Nate nodded, a reassuring bob of his head. "I figured."

"Be honest. Tell me the truth. How long before the flashbacks go away?"

Nate lifted one shoulder, leveled him a pitying stare.

Angrily, Shepherd glowered at him. He hated being pitied.

"Depends," Nate said.

"On what?"

"How willing you are to let go."

"Let go of what?" His voice came out waspish, but Nate stayed even-keeled.

"Guilt. Shame. Regrets. Blame . . ." The former SEAL tapped the table with an index finger. "Anger."

"Well, isn't that a basket of Post Toasties?"

Nate laughed and reached for the cup of coffee the waitress set in front of him. "Glad to see you've hung on to your sense of humor. That's one thing you don't want to let go of."

A few minutes passed. They sipped coffee in silence.

"I've got a question for you," Shepherd said when the waitress was out of earshot and he leveled a hard stare at the other man.

"What's that?"

"How come you didn't tell me that Naomi Luther had a boyfriend?"

"She and Robert have been on again, off again for years. I can't keep up." Nate raised an eyebrow, lifted his cup, and settled back in his chair. "Honestly, I didn't know you were interested or I would have mentioned it."

"I think I'm falling in love with her." Shepherd chuffed out his breath.

"That's a lot to process." Nate took a sip, studied Shepherd over the rim of his cup. "You. Naomi. The ghost of her brother hanging over your relationship."

"Tell me about it."

"You got a lot of obstacles."

Yep. Stacked up like cord wood. "I know."

Nate shook his head. "She's a wonderful woman. Generous as the day is long."

Shepherd stirred his coffee. He didn't know why he stirred it. He took his coffee black. Hadn't added any sugar or cream. Maybe just to see the coffee swirl.

"Does she feel the same way about you?"

Shepherd snorted. "That's the impression I got when I kissed her. But then here comes this guy announcing that he's her boyfriend."

"You're going to let someone like Robert Bellamy stop you from going after what you want?"

"I dunno." Shepherd pulled both palms down his face this time. "I should just leave town. This whole thing is doomed."

"How so?"

The past was a hammer, pummeling him from every direction. "Her brother died because of me, Nate."

The other man tilted his head. "Is that *really* true?"

"If I'd gone back—"

"Put the blame where it belongs. On the terrorist who killed him. This is what I'm talking about. You've got to let go of feeling like it's your fault. You can't save the whole damn world, Shepherd."

"I can try."

"No, no you can't. Not if you want a sane life. You *do* want a sane life?"

"More than anything," he whispered. Clenched his hand into a fist against his knee. Nate was right.

"You're not responsible for other people's actions. You can't be. Hell, man, it's hard enough being responsible for your own."

More truths. More great advice.

Shepherd picked up his fork, and cut into the slice of warm apple pie.

"Got a question for you," Nate said.

"What's that?"

"Why are you here having pie with me instead of talking this through with Naomi?"

"I'm not the kind to trespass on another man's land."

"Well, if Naomi is kissing you, rest assured all is not well in Robert Land. She is not a fickle woman."

Shepherd felt hopeful for the first time since he'd learned about Robert.

"Sometimes you have to break the rules to get what you want. Go to her. Trespass. Tell her what she means to you."

For a man who'd learned to honor the rules, Nate's words were a caldron of intrigue, tempting and dangerous. Did he keep quiet and stay out of Naomi's life? Or did he go for it. Break the rules. Tell Naomi what was in his heart.

Following the rules keeps you safe, whispered the teenage boy who'd lost so much because of the people in his life who broke the rules. If he kept quiet, he wouldn't get hurt.

But if he didn't take a chance, he'd never know if their kiss had been monumental for her too.

If only things were that simple. He couldn't tell her how he felt without first telling her who he really was. His flashback tonight was clear. Their relationship could not move forward as long as he was holding on to his secret.

Nate came to the same conclusion because he said, "If you tell her how you feel, you have to tell her about Clayton."

"I know." Shepherd stared down at his hands cupped around the coffee mug.

"It's all part of letting go. The secrets. The lies. The misguided beliefs."

"It's hard."

Nate's nod was slow, filled with empathy and meaning. "It is."

Shepherd might be a rule follower, but he wasn't a coward. The time had come. He'd put this off for too long. He had to come clean. If Naomi forgave him, okay. If not, that was okay too.

And Robert? What about him?

Well, that was up to Naomi.

He pushed his pie aside, met Nate's gaze, and said, "Take me back."

CHAPTER 19

"Let's take a walk." Robert held his arm out to Naomi.

She took his elbow because it was familiar. Something she'd done hundreds of times. But even as she linked her arm through his, her mind was chewing on her argument with Mark. Was what he'd said true? Did she go around helping people simply because she had a deep-seated need to be needed?

Was that why things had gone south with Robert when he'd left Twilight first for graduate school, and then for his job in Colorado? He hadn't needed her any longer? Was *that* the reason she hadn't gone to Denver with him? Did that also explain her attraction to Mark? He was a man in need and Naomi loved to be needed?

What an eye-opener. These were tough questions and it took courage to look at them. And honestly, she felt blindsided.

What was so bad about wanting to help? Caring for other people made her happy. She loved the everyday, behind-the-scenes stuff that turned a house into a home—cooking, taking care of Hunter, assisting her mother. She enjoyed her job, but only because it too was about doing things for other people.

Was Mark suggesting she was wrong?

Nothing is wrong with helping people. The answer popped into her mind. *But it can't be a one-way street. You've got to let people help you too.*

Ahh, there it was. The rub. Her downfall.

Robert squired her around the town square. The place was alive with tourists and fun activities. Karaoke poured from the Fruit of the Vine. The line for Santa's North Pole workshop was twice as long as it had been last weekend. A group of carolers sang on the street corner. It was magical, fun, sweet.

And she couldn't enjoy it.

Her emotions were lava, bubbling beneath the surface. Churning and hot, ready to spew and boil over.

"I love your costume," Robert said.

"What?" Naomi blinked, looked down at her dress that she'd sewn herself. "Oh. Thanks."

He led her from the square to Sweetheart Park, his steps quick and jubilant. Outrunning her. Leaving her behind.

"Robert, slow down."

"Naomi." He chuckled. "Speed up."

That was their relationship in a nutshell. He'd always been on the fast track, wanting more. Grasping. Reaching. On the hunt for never-ending improvement.

To Naomi, it seemed like just so much pointless rushing around. The real action was right in front of you, life unfolding in the blooming of a Christmas cactus or a little boy's smile. In the washing of dishes and making of sandwiches. In holding the hand of a sick friend, in the rocking of a cradle, in the whisper of the wind through the trees.

She rushed to catch up with him, knowing that if she had never met Mark Shepherd, she would still be doing what she was about to do. She looked at Robert's face. He was so handsome. More handsome than Mark when you got down to it. But there was shallowness to his chin. Softness in his cheeks. While she'd found him appealing at sixteen, now, at twenty-seven, she found him lacking in some fundamental way.

Not a solid man. Not a man you could count on when the chips were down.

Robert stopped underneath the Sweetheart Tree. The same spot where she and Mark had sat the day he'd taken her shopping.

"Please," he said, dusting off the concrete bench. "Have a seat."

Her stomach tightened all the way up to her chest. Naomi settled down on the cold bench. Wiggled to warm her bottom.

He had something in his hand. A small black velvet box. He went down on one knee.

Panic flared through her. Her pulse jumped. "Rob—"

He held up a hand. "Shh."

"I—" She started to stand up, but he reached out a hand and pushed her back down.

"Naomi Luther." Robert cracked open the box, revealed an engagement ring. "Will you marry me?"

Fear knocked Naomi's heart sideways. For so many years she'd dreamed of Robert's proposal. Now here it was. Coming as she'd often imagined it might. In Sweetheart Park, underneath the Sweetheart Tree where their names were carved. In December, surrounded by twinkle lights and Christmas music, the air frosty and festive.

Naomi looked down. The diamond was impossibly huge. Easily worth two months of his six-figure salary. Nausea swamped her.

She didn't want it. Hadn't wanted this, she realized, in a very long time.

Robert, having grown tired of waiting for her to leave their hometown behind, had moved on without her. They'd broken up and gotten back together half a dozen times over the eleven years they'd been going out. Their breakups had always been over the same thing.

He wanted more from life than what Twilight had to offer. And Naomi couldn't leave her family and community behind. Her happiness was here. The fact that her love for Robert wasn't strong enough to lure her away was telling. She had loved him as her high school sweetheart. And on some level, she would always love him for what he'd been to her. But she knew in her heart that he was not her soul mate.

Not *the one*.

She thought of Mark Shepherd. She barely knew the man, and yet she knew him in a way she'd never known Robert. She'd dreamed of Mark and he'd appeared. Whenever she was around him, she felt fully accepted and understood. Her feelings for Mark were heady, thrilling, and she wanted more.

Tears formed in her eyes, and she put both trembling hands to her mouth.

"Are those tears of joy?" Robert asked, his voice shaky.

"Robert," she whispered, "please get up. Please put the ring away."

Confusion scrambled his handsome features. To most people, on paper, he was a much better catch than Mark Shepherd. Master's degree. Solid career. Good family.

But he hadn't wanted children.

And that's all Naomi had ever really wanted—a home and family of her own.

He wanted to see the world.

Naomi's world was right here in Twilight.

"What's wrong?" He snapped the ring box closed, hopped to his feet.

"This is . . . too sudden."

"What do you mean, sudden? We've been going out since high school."

"We haven't even seen each other since summer. You could have called. Texted that you were coming at least."

"I've been busy . . ." He pressed his mouth into a thin line. "Working overtime to pay for your ring. You're busy too. Running your own business, helping your mom, taking care of Hunter. You could have called just as easily as I could have."

"I wasn't buying a ring and making wedding plans."

"No? What was that I walked in on at the gym with you and—"

"Robert," she interrupted, standing up. This time, he did not push her back down. "You're asking me to marry you, but what about Hunter? How does he fit in with your plans?"

"What do you mean?" His breath fogged in the cold night air. He curled his fingers around the velvet ring box. Jammed his hands into the pocket of his coat.

"I'm Hunter's legal guardian. I'm in the process of adopting him."

"I know that."

"He's going to be my son—*our* son—if we were to get married."

"I understand what adoption means, Naomi." His tone turned sarcastic.

"You're willing and ready to become a father?"

"If it's what I have to do to win you, then yes, I am."

Alarmed, she took a step back. "You can't give lip service to being a father to get me to marry you. You have to *want* to be Hunter's dad."

"I'll get there, Naomi. I'm sure of it. He's a nice kid."

"You have to *love* him."

"You gotta give me time. Love doesn't happen overnight."

But it was happening overnight between her and Mark, she realized. Surprise was a spike stabbing right through her spine. Was she falling in love with Mark? After experiencing his kiss, she'd have to say yes. "Nor when you're hundreds of miles away. How can you fall in love with him when you're never around?"

She thought of Mark and the way he looked at Hunter with adoring eyes. The way Hunter kept calling him Daddy. How tender Mark was with the boy. How good the two were together.

"Love can happen overnight," she said. "It does."

"Look," Robert said, shifting his weight. "I'm being honest here. I'll do the best I can with Hunter. I accept that you and he are a package deal."

She stared at him, wondering if she'd ever really known Robert. "I'm sorry. That's just not good enough. Hunter deserves parents who love him with all their hearts and souls."

"You're living in a fantasy world," Robert said. "I promise to provide for the boy, and treat him well. But that's *all* I can promise."

"I appreciate your honesty," she said, a cascade of emotions tumbling through her—sadness, regret, irritation, hope. "And your position. I hope you understand that under the circumstances, I can't marry you."

He looked like a mule had kicked him in the gut. His mouth dipped down, eyes shuttered. "Naomi . . ."

"We missed our moment. If you'd proposed five years ago . . ." She shrugged. "I would have said yes in a heartbeat."

"Five years ago, I was starting grad school."

"There's always been something keeping us apart, Robert." She gentled her voice. "Perhaps there's a reason for that."

"It's the guy, isn't it? The one you were dancing with." He hitched in a deep breath and his eyes narrowed. "The cripple."

She bristled. The hairs on her arms stiffened and her spine straightened. "That's unkind, and I won't tolerate it."

"You're the one being unkind." He hurled the words at her like a snowball packed around a rock.

Was she?

"This isn't easy for me," she went on. "We've shared a lot. We've had good times and bad times and I will always have fond feelings for you—"

"You always did champion lost causes." His tone was brittle. His eyes flared with hurt and anger.

Guilt wrung her out. She felt worn and bleary.

"That's why you'd rather have a cripple than a whole man."

"Oh, you did not just say that!" She gasped, cheeks flaming.

"Truth hurts, huh?"

"You're making this so much easier," she said, clenching her hands into fists. "When did you get so cold?"

He backtracked, raised a placating hand. Looked ashamed. "I'm sorry. You're right. I'm hurt. I didn't expect you to reject me. You threw me for a loop."

"Seriously? The longer you were away, the easier it was for me to be without you. You're not even a big part of my life anymore."

He grimaced, his face chiding and sad. "I tried to get you to move to Denver with me."

"Without the benefit of marriage."

"I wasn't ready for marriage then." His nose was turning red in the cold. She supposed hers was too.

"And my father is a pastor. I couldn't move to Denver without being married."

"Which is why you didn't." He jammed his hands in his pockets.

Heart aching, she met his eyes. "We missed our window."

He shook his head, looked petulant. "We're high school sweethearts."

"That doesn't mean we're right for each other at this point in our lives."

He took a coin from his pocket, flipped it into the fountain. "There. I wished to be reunited with my high school sweetheart."

"It's just a legend, Robert. We're not Rebekka Nash and Jon Grant."

"The legend has worked for other people. Jesse and Flynn, Emma and Sam." He swept his hand at the tree carved with names. "Caitlyn and Gideon. Sarah and Travis. Dozens of people."

"But not for Naomi and Robert."

Memories flooded her. So many happy memories. The good times with Robert. Sharing a banana split at Rinky-Tink's before it went out of business. Canoeing the Brazos River. Fourth of July picnics. Prom night. Making love for the first time underneath the stars in his parents' backyard when they were out of town. They'd both been seventeen. Robert had been her one and only lover.

She was throwing it all away for a stranger.

Because with those happy memories came the unhappy one. Robert cheated on her when he was in college, causing their first serious breakup. He begged her forgiveness, and she'd given it to him. Everyone makes mistakes and he was so contrite. And for a time, things had been really good between them again. But Robert had gotten involved in grad school and then later his job in Denver. He told her his career had to take the front seat for a while, and she'd tried to be understanding. But she couldn't shake the feeling his career meant more to him than she did.

Then Clayton and Samantha died and *everything* changed.

"What does this crip—" He stopped himself before he finished the inflammatory word. "This guy have that I don't?"

"He's not the reason I'm saying no."

"Don't lie to me. I saw the way you looked at him. Is it because he's military and you haven't dealt with your grief over losing Clayton?"

Was it? Naomi placed a hand to her heart.

"Are you attracted to him because you feel like you can fix him? And if you fix him, that it will somehow make up for losing your brother?"

His insight blew her away. He was normally a bit self-absorbed, but in that moment, it seemed as if he could see right through her. Maybe she did try to "fix" everyone, and maybe he was right about why she was attracted to Mark.

Sobering thought.

But just because he might be right about that didn't mean Robert was right for her. She could see that now.

"Nothing will make up for losing Clayton." She gulped, determined not to cry.

Robert sank his hands on his hips, broadened his stance. "If it's not pity, and you're not trying to make up for Clayton's death by taking on this damaged Marine, then what is it?"

How could she explain the power of the connection she had with Mark? "I dreamed of him," Naomi confessed. "Before I ever met him."

"What?" Robert looked at her as if she'd taken leave of her senses. "When?"

"Last Christmas Eve. I put a kismet cookie underneath my pillow because I wanted to dream of *you*, but instead I dreamed of a man I'd never met. Then he turns up and I felt something I never felt with you." Her voice cracked. She interlaced her fingers. Clasped them to her heart. This was so hard.

"What's that?" he asked, tears misting his eyes.

"Fate," she whispered, his pain overlaying her own. She did love Robert, just not in the way either one of them deserved. "One look in his eyes and I *knew* we were destined. I can't explain it beyond that."

"You believe in the damn kismet cookie legend, but not the sweetheart legend?"

"It's got nothing to do with legends."

"You just said it did."

"No, I said when I look at him, I feel a rush of love and destiny that I never felt for you. I love you, Robert. Don't get me wrong. But it was *never* like this. Like it's meant to be."

"Fine." He barked a harsh sound, hurt and disappointment etched on his face. "I hope you have a happy life."

"I wish the same for you."

"I won't be back. This is done, once and for all."

"I know."

"Are you sure this is what you want?" His mouth was grim. His eyes bleak.

She nodded, her heart in her throat. Every muscle in her body tense and sore.

"All right then. This is it. Good-bye." Robert hunched his shoulders, burrowed deeper into his coat, turned and walked away.

Naomi watched him go, realizing she'd professed to Robert what she'd been trying to deny to herself since the day she hopped into the wrong Jeep.

She was in love with Mark Shepherd.

CHAPTER 20

Spurred by a force so strong that he could smell it, Shepherd drove to the Luthers' house. His body tensed. His head hummed a one-word mantra. *Naomi. Naomi. Naomi.*

It was after ten-thirty.

She was probably in bed.

He didn't care.

But when he got there, he almost drove past the house. Convinced himself to wait until morning. Then he saw that someone was sitting on the front porch swing.

He slowed.

It was Naomi.

His heart leaped. It was as if she'd just been waiting for him. Huddled in a down coat that was too big for her. He knew with unshakable certainty that it was Clayton's coat.

His heartstrings jerked.

He pulled up to the curb and got out. Left his cane behind. He was tired of having a crutch. He was going it alone.

"Hello," she called to him as he came up the sidewalk.

"Why are you sitting out here?" he asked, easing up the porch steps.

"I needed some air."

"Why?"

"Robert just asked me to marry him."

Sucker punched. He tasted bile in his throat. His heart chugged. He was too late.

She scooted over, making room. Patted the seat beside her. Because he wasn't so sure that his knee could support him, Shepherd sank down. Sent the swing rocking and the chains creaking. She turned toward him, torso swiveled, but with her feet planted firmly on the ground facing forward.

"I said no."

"No?" he echoed, not sure he understood what she was saying.

"I told Robert I couldn't marry him. I turned him down." Her gaze locked on his.

For several seconds, he stared at her in awe. He felt as if the world had shifted permanently on its axis and he could never again look at things in the same way. In his wildest dreams, he could not have imagined feeling this way.

"Aren't you going to say anything?" she asked.

"Why?"

"Why did I say no?"

He didn't trust his voice. Simply bobbed his head. But he did not drop her gaze.

Her eyes were nervous. The tip of her tongue darted out to moisten her lips. "Robert is the only boyfriend I've ever had. The only man I've ever . . ." She didn't finish the sentence, but he got the gist. "He was my high school sweetheart, and I told you how this town is about high school sweethearts."

"These all sound like good reasons to say yes."

"I couldn't accept his proposal. Even though once upon a time, I longed for it desperately."

He didn't ask her why again. He just sat there. Hand wrapped around the swing chain. Rocking gently. Waiting.

"I thought I loved him," she said. "Or what passed for love. Robert was easy to be with—"

"That's because he lived in another state."

She laughed, a hearty sound of relief. "Most likely."

"Long-distance relationships are difficult."

"I didn't really realize that until . . ." She trailed off, her gaze glued to his.

"Until what?"

"*You.*"

Shepherd opened his mouth, but no words came out.

"Could you say something?" Anxiety pulled her brows into a frown. "I'm out on a limb here."

"You . . . you . . . broke up with Robert because of me?"

"You kissed me and I melted. I never knew a kiss could make you feel that way. Robert's kisses never made me feel like that—" Her eyes misted with emotion. "Oh, please don't tell me you don't feel it too."

"I feel it." He lowered his voice. "Like an earthquake."

She caught her breath, an audible gasp in the dark. He wanted to kiss her again. Right here. Right now.

"Naomi," he whispered.

"Mark," she whispered back.

He felt like an animal that had been let out of a cage. He scooted closer.

She met him halfway.

He wrapped an arm around her waist. Peered into her eyes.

She gulped, moistened her lips again.

Shepherd lowered his head.

Her gaze darted away for a moment, looking at the door, then back into his eyes. "This is happening so fast."

"Too fast?" he asked.

"We barely know each other."

"And yet," he said, "it feels like I've known you all my life."

"Yes." She curled against him. "Like a hundred life-times."

He needed a moment to process this. He'd come here fully expecting to be shot down, and now that the exact opposite was playing out, he had to take a breath. Make sure he was grounded. That this was really happening, and he hadn't lost touch with reality.

"I get it," she said. "It's overwhelming."

"But in a good way."

"There's something I have to tell you," she said.

Wow, okay. Here was his opening, a way in. She'd tell him what she needed to tell him. A secret, from the hooded way she was looking at him from underneath lowered lashes. Then he could open up about Clayton.

"What is it?" he asked, feeling his muscles tense.

"This is going to sound crazy . . ."

"I've got two good ears and an open mind."

She smiled at that, a shaky smile, but still a smile. How bad could her secret be if she was still smiling? He didn't care. No matter what she told him, he wouldn't judge her. Who was he to judge anyone?

"I'm listening." He drew her closer. "Tell me."

"Long before I ever knew you . . ." She blew out a long breath through pursed lips. "I dreamed of you."

Dazed, dazzled, he matched her smile. He reached for her hands. They were cold, but she latched on to him tight. Could she feel the power of his emotions for her? "Guess what?"

"What?" she whispered.

"This is going to sound crazy . . ."

She touched her ears. "Go ahead. I'm listening."

He dipped his head, going in for a kiss, and whispered, "I dreamed of you too."

His arms went around her waist and her arms slipped around his neck. He kissed her, or she kissed him. Naomi wasn't quite sure which. Didn't matter. It was some kind of cosmic, simultaneous kiss.

As if the heavens were yanking them together like old-fashioned magnetic kissing dolls. A sign from above that they belonged.

Gratitude filled her heart.

His lips were warm and soft and moist. He tasted of apple pie and cinnamon, and smelled of pine, sandalwood, and soap.

Her heart fluttered like a shaken snow globe. Her pulse surged in a way it had never quite surged before. Excitement. Hope. Joy.

Yes, *joy.*

His kisses were joyous things. Alive and beautiful. He was so good at kissing. As good at kissing as he was at whittling toys. He must have kissed a lot of girls to get this good. But she didn't care how many girls he'd kissed before her. All she cared about was his mouth on hers. Right here. Right now.

Her entire body tingled just as it had in the parking lot outside the gym. From the top of her head to the soles of her feet. Tingled. Strummed. Vibrated.

She cupped his face between her palms, brazenly wanting more.

He laughed, a throaty sound from deep inside his chest, but he did not stop kissing her. Good. She did not want him to stop until their lips were chapped and they were gasping for breath like landed fish.

She closed her eyes, letting him sweep her away.

Mark deepened the kiss, taking her with him.

Her mind spun lazily, crazily. Was this really happening? Could she be dreaming again?

His hands were in her hair. Stroking her with a tender caress. She felt so special. She wished they could stay on the porch swing. Kissing. Forever.

She might have plotted a way to make that happen if the front door hadn't cracked open and a bright little voice said, "N'omi, I thwisty."

"Motherhood calls," Shepherd whispered against her lips.

"I'm sorry."

"Don't be. Hunter comes first. There will be time for me later." He looked into her eyes, and she read the unspoken word, *Right?*

She smiled, nodded to his unasked question.

"N'omi?" Hunter stuck his head farther out the door. "Bwww."

"Back inside, little man. I'll be right there."

"Go." Mark patted her on the shoulder. "I'm headed for the rectory."

She stood, lapped up his lingering smile. "I'll see you in church tomorrow?"

"Wouldn't miss it for the world."

Oh the yearning!

Sleep did not come. Naomi could not stop thinking about Mark and his kisses. It wasn't just that she was falling under his spell, but rather he seemed as enchanted as she.

And he'd dreamed of her as she'd dreamed of him. Unbelievable. A stunning turn of events.

She wished they'd had more time to discuss it. How and when he'd dreamed of her. What his dream had been about. She had so many questions. How could she sleep when she had no answers?

Around midnight, she got up to go to the bathroom, and caught sight of herself in the mirror. Her cheeks were flushed, her eyes shiny, her hair a mad tangle. She looked as feverish as she felt. She pressed a palm to her brow, was almost surprised to find her skin cool and dry.

Inside, she was hot and damp and thirsting for the forbidden.

Mark.

Two doors down.

Sleeping in the rectory.

She had no conscious plan. No purposeful intention.

But she washed her hands and left the bathroom. Tiptoed downstairs to the coat closet. Shrugged into her winter coat, and jammed her feet into her boots sitting at the mudroom door.

Quietly, she slipped outside.

On the street, a soft silence lay over the neighborhood. Not even Christmas music from the town square.

Her breath chuffed frosty in the chilly air. She bundled her coat more tightly around her and started off down the sidewalk.

When she reached the church, she hesitated outside the rectory. Did she just go in? Knock? Why was she here? What was she doing? This was a mistake. She should go.

Turning, Naomi started down the steps.

Heard a guttural scream come from inside the rectory, a great primal sound of pain.

She jumped, startled. Terrified. Flung herself back around, grabbed the door handle. It was locked. Instinctively, she yanked on the knob, as if by doing so the lock would simply fall off.

Another electrifying yell.

Heart slamming into her chest, she flipped over the welcome mat, snatched up the spare key, and with trembling hands struggled to jam it into the lock.

A raw howl so chilling that the sound seized Naomi by the spine and shook her. The hairs on the back of her neck stood up.

She finally got the key into the lock, turned it, shoved open the door, and tumbled over the threshold.

The hallway was completely dark, but she didn't linger to search for the light switch. She'd grown up in this church. She knew the way.

Running her hand along the wall, she bulleted to Mark's room.

Found him curled in the narrow twin bed in a fetal position, clinging to his pillow and crying out. "No! No! Don't go, don't go!"

Unnerved, she paused at the door, a glint of moonlight falling through the curtains. He was having a PTSD nightmare. Should she wake him?

He batted the air with his fist, gritted his teeth, sucked in air with a hiss. His eyes were squeezed tightly closed.

She knew better than to touch him. Could feel despair rolling off him.

"Watch out for Talid! Run, run!"

Talid? Her blood ran cold. Talid was the terrorist who'd killed Clayton. She'd had a few nightmares about the terrorist herself. But why was Mark dreaming of Talid?

It's a common name over there, she told herself.

Mark let out another blood-curdling scream. "I'm sorry, so sorry!"

Naomi rushed across the room to him. Hovered near the bed. "Mark, Mark," she called, and then to make sure she got through to him, "Shepherd. Wake up. You're home. You're safe. You're with me."

He grunted. Blinked. Stared up at her as if peering through a fog.

"Mark, it's me, Naomi."

"Naomi?" he whispered.

"You're here, in Twilight with me."

"Twilight?"

"At the rectory of my father's church."

His eyes sharpened. She noticed tears on his lashes, and that his hands were trembling. Her heart jerked. He was suffering.

"Mark," she whispered, drawing closer. "Would it be okay if I got into bed with you?"

He nodded, and in that moment, she saw exactly what he'd looked like at Hunter's age. This man had not been nurtured the way he should have been nurtured.

She slipped behind him, scooped him into her embrace, and stroked his hair while he shivered in her arms. Felt the warmth of his body seep into hers. "Shh, shh."

He curled against her, his head on her chest. The weight of him was exquisite in a forlornly beautiful way.

"Go back to sleep." She hummed a lullaby. Brokenhearted for the sorrows he'd been through.

He clung to her arms as she rocked and swayed him. Her chest clenched so tightly it hurt.

Naomi bent her head and pressed her lips to his temple. "Shh, shh, I'm here, I'm here. You're not alone. I've got you."

Slowly, he drifted back to sleep.

She stayed with him until she was sure the nightmares were gone. Wishing she could stay the entire night, but knowing she could not, she eased from the bed inch by inch, careful not to awaken him. She tucked the covers over his shoulders. Placed one more soft kiss on his forehead, and then slipped out the door and walked home.

In the darkness of that solitary night, she felt profoundly changed.

Holding him while he was broken and vulnerable peeled back the layers of her feelings, drilling down to her core. Exposing everything.

She loved him.

It was as simple and as complicated as that.

And Naomi knew in her heart of hearts that she was bonded to this man on a level so deep that nothing could ever break it.

CHAPTER 21

Following church services later that morning, Shepherd pulled her aside. "We need to talk."

"Now?"

He shook his head. "This is going to take a while."

"Oh," she said, wondering if he remembered his nightmare. Anxiety set her stomach fluttering. "Is it that thing you wanted to tell me about last night?"

"Yes. That."

"Can it wait until tomorrow?" she asked. Not wanting to put him off, but her to-do list was longer than her arm. "We have out-of-town guests coming over for a late lunch and I have online orders to prep and get ready to ship out tomorrow, and then bedtime routine for Hunter."

"I can help with some of that."

"No, I've got—" She stopped. Remembered what he'd told her about thinking she had to do everything herself. Recalling how vulnerable he'd been last night in her arms. "Okay. That sounds good. Do you want to help me prepare lunch?"

He started rolling up his sleeves. "I've got your six, butterfly."

Together they cooked the meal and had so much fun doing it, Naomi could see them doing this every day. And my, but it was so much easier with two.

Getting ahead of yourself. What had happened in the rectory had been beyond special, but they had a long way to go. Issues to work through.

Yes, she knew that, but she couldn't stop herself from dreaming about making room for this good man in her life.

They didn't get a chance to talk privately that day. Her mother invited the out-of-town guests to stay the night, and Naomi had to sort all that out. Shepherd offered to help, but her father sent him on a mission to borrow a rollaway cot from a neighbor and by the time everything was squared away, Naomi was yawning so big she had to cover her mouth with a palm.

"Rain check on the convo?" She yawned again.

Shepherd nodded. "Get some sleep. It'll keep."

She walked him out to the front porch. Shrugged repeatedly, and kneaded her shoulder blade. Winced.

"Something wrong?" he asked.

"Sore muscles from wrapping packages. Job hazard." She waved away his concern. Didn't tell him that her shoulders were mostly sore from holding him for hours after his nightmare. He didn't seem to remember it and she didn't want to embarrass him by bringing it up.

"You should use that spa gift certificate Mrs. Longoria mentioned," he said. "Get a massage tomorrow."

She shook her head. "No time."

"What are your excuses?" He grinned, shook his head.

She rattled off her to-do list, and ended with, "I told Hunter we'd put up the tree tomorrow when he got home from preschool. It's the only time I have a moment to spare and we've got to get the tree up. It's already the fourteenth."

"That's when you'll get your massage," Shepherd said firmly. "You go to the spa, I'll put the tree up with Hunter."

"But—"

"No buts."

"I want to enjoy putting up the tree with Hunter," she protested.

"You do plenty of other things with him. This will be guy bonding time."

She considered that a moment. Rubbed her shoulder again. He made a good point. "It would be nice to get a massage."

"Self-care," he said.

"You really did go to a lot of therapy, huh?"

"Yes, so consider me the expert. Tomorrow. Three o'clock. You've got a date with a masseuse." He leaned down to give her a peck on the cheek.

Her heart swelled with joy and she playfully snuggled closer. "Hey, hey, is that all I get?"

"One of your out-of-town guests is peeking through the curtains at us."

"Rats," she muttered.

"Good night, butterfly," he called, and headed back to the rectory.

Leaving her sighing longingly for more.

When Shepherd arrived at the Luthers' house the next afternoon at two-fifteen, Naomi was still trying to get out of going to the spa. She'd come up with half a dozen excuses why it was selfish for her to take ninety minutes out of her day to take care of herself.

"Look at this." She took a mass of tangled Christmas lights from a big cardboard box. A Gordian's knot of lights. Dropped the twisted mess in the middle of the living room floor.

"I'm good at puzzles." Shepherd eased down on the carpet, sitting with his bum knee straight, the other bent in front of the snarled wires. "I'm going to straighten this out before you get back from picking Hunter up from school."

"Oh goody, a competition. If you don't have them untangled by the time I get back in six minutes, I stay here." She leaned over, patted his shoulder, and headed toward the door.

"Oh, butterfly," he hollered after her. "It's on like Donkey Kong."

Exactly seven minutes later, she was back from the preschool with Hunter. Shepherd had ten strands of a hundred and fifty lights all separated and lined up in a row, ready to dress the tree.

"Seriously?" she said. "How did you manage that?"

"Told you I was good."

She stuck out her tongue at him.

"I'm even better at that." He wriggled his eyebrows at the sight of that lovely pink tongue.

She rolled her eyes.

"Get a move on," he said, tapping the face of his watch. "Your appointment is at three."

"I need to make Hunter an after-school snack."

"On it. Go."

"You don't know what he likes."

Shepherd looked at the boy. "What do you like?"

"Peanut buttew and jelly sammies!" Hunter sang out.

"There you go." Shepherd picked up Naomi's jacket

off the back of the couch where she'd draped it when she'd come in.

"I—"

"You're going," he insisted, pressing the jacket into her hand. "No argument."

"I'm too bus—"

"We've been over that."

"You—"

"Shh." He hushed her.

"It's—"

"No excuses." He scooped up her purse from the coffee table, slung it over her shoulder. Got a thrill from his fingers brushing against her skin.

"But—"

He opened the front door. "Out."

Naomi balked, digging in her heels and wrenching her arm from his bum's-rush grip. "Hunter can be a handful. He—"

"I'm an ex-Marine. How hard can it be?"

"Harder than you think. You don't know anything about kids."

"Go. Relax. Enjoy being pampered. We'll be fine." He shoved her out the door, closed and locked it behind her.

"Okay." Shepherd stared down at the boy once Naomi was gone. "It's just you and me, kid."

"Daddy." Hunter grinned at him and raised his arms to be picked up.

"We gotta get something straight here," Shepherd said, hauling the kid up onto his hip. "I'm not your dad."

The boy stared at him with serious dark eyes.

"Not that I wouldn't want to be your daddy. Don't get me wrong. Any guy would be lucky to have you for a son. It's just that's not who I am."

"Daddy." Hunter bobbed his head.

"Shepherd."

"Daddy."

"Shepherd."

Hunter giggled. "Daddy."

"Mark," he said. "If that's easier. You can call me Mark."

"Daddy."

"Mark."

"Mawk?"

"Mark," he confirmed.

"Daddy Mawk?"

"Just Mark."

"Just Mawk," Hunter mimicked. "Daddy Mawk."

Shepherd decided to let it go. He couldn't control what the kid called him.

"Here's the deal. Naomi's got a list—"

"Mama." Hunter threw back his little head and laughed as if it was the funniest thing he'd ever heard.

"Yes, I suppose she is your mother now. Anyway, Mama's got way too much on her plate, so I thought while she's relaxing at the spa, we could set up the Christmas tree."

"Mama."

"Uh-huh."

He touched an index finger to Shepherd's cheek. "Mawk."

"You've got it now. Smart boy."

"Mama and Mawk."

"No, Mama and Mawk are not a couple . . ." But he sure wished they could be. Not just wished it. Longed for it. But there were a lot of landmines between here and there. He was afraid to hope.

He thought about the night she'd climbed in his bed and held him as he trembled from the PTSD nightmare. It had been a touching moment. But he hadn't mentioned it to her. In fact, told himself he'd dreamed that too. He was embarrassed that she'd seen him in such a state. And humbled to his bones.

The memory, while sweet, made him uncomfortable, and he shoved it aside.

"Your mission," Shepherd said, leveling the boy a look that set off peals of fresh giggles, "is to stay out of the way while I put the tree together. Got it?"

"Got it!" Hunter clapped his hands.

The boy did not, however, get it. Shepherd dragged the big tree box in from the mudroom where Tom had taken it down out of the attic. And there was Hunter padding right behind him.

"Twee." Hunter pointed.

"Yes, it's a tree." Shepherd picked Hunter up and sat him on the couch. "You sit there and watch."

He turned back to the box, took out the branches, started dividing them into piles arranged by the color-coded order in which the branches went on the tree.

Whoosh.

Here came Hunter. Picking up one of the bigger branches and marching around the living room with it, humming "Santa Claus Is Coming to Town."

"C'mon here." He grabbed the boy by his belt loop and towed him over. "Clearly, having you sit and watch isn't going as planned. Let's put you to work instead."

Hunter studied him as if trying to parse out what Shepherd was saying.

"See this?" Shepherd pointed to the metal end of the

branch that Hunter was holding. "It's got a red dot on it. That matches the red dot on the tree base. See here?" He showed the boy. "Do you know your colors?"

"Wed," Hunter announced, dropped to his knees on the rug, and matched the red dot on the branch to the red dot on the circular metal rod that served as the artificial tree's spine.

"Good boy," Shepherd encouraged. "Here, let me help you get it in the hole. Sometimes you have to jiggle it."

Hunter watched intently as Shepherd slipped the branch into the spine.

"Now, can you find more red branches?" Shepherd asked, showing him the red dot on another branch.

Hunter took his task seriously. Picking out the branches with red dots and giving them to Shepherd so he could fit them into the spine, building the tree from the bottom up. Shepherd was surprised by how helpful the kid was. But then they finished up with the red branches and Hunter got distressed.

He threw around the remaining branches, a worried frown on his little forehead. "No wed. No wed."

"It's okay," Shepherd said, gently guiding him. "Look here, we've finished with the red. Next comes orange."

"Owange?"

Shepherd showed him a branch with an orange dot on it.

"Owange," Hunter said, getting the picture, and went after the orange branches. They finished the orange and then went for the yellow, then the green. Going from color to color until they'd erected the entire tree.

After Shepherd affixed the final branch that became the tree's crown, Hunter tipped back his head and stared up at the whole thing. "Whoa."

"Whoa is right," Shepherd agreed. "It's a pretty big tree."

His cell phone dinged with a text message. Shepherd pulled his phone from his pocket, grinned. It was from Naomi.

How R things going?

Shepherd texted: Don't tell me U took your phone into the massage room.

NAOMI: Oops.
SHEPHERD: Powering off my phone now.
NAOMI: Hunter?

Shepherd snapped a picture of the boy still gawking at the tree and texted the photo to her.

NAOMI: U got it up already?
SHEPHERD: Yeah, sexy woman.
NAOMI: Pervert.
SHEPHERD: U R the one with the dirty mind.
NAOMI: Ha. Ha.
SHEPHERD: Hunter is a good helper. Great kid.

She sent a series of smiling, applauding emojis. Then added: Don't decorate it without me.

SHEPHERD: Turn off your phone. That's an order.
NAOMI: I'm not in the military.
SHEPHERD: Still an order.

She sent a smiley face emoji sticking out its tongue.

He meant to send an eye-rolling emoji, but punched the wrong image and pasted up a smiley face blowing a kiss.

She sent a kiss emoji right back to him. Followed by a gif of a beating red heart.

And Shepherd couldn't help falling for her just a little bit harder.

CHAPTER 22

When Naomi arrived home, the entire family decorated the tree, making a party out of it, complete with Christmas music, hot chocolate with mini-marshmallows, and a roaring fire in the fireplace. She was determined to make things perfect. Keep up the family traditions no matter what.

Everything was going so well as Pastor Tom went outside for more firewood and Shepherd placed the last of the ornaments on the tree. Hunter had fallen asleep on the couch, and Naomi was crouched looking for the best spot to hang the angel Shepherd had carved for her. After they found it, they knew they were finished and stepped back to admire their handiwork.

"Something's missing," Naomi said, surveying the tree, rubbing her chin with her fingers and thumb.

"Looks good to me."

She cocked her head. "No, there's something off."

"We've got the lights, tinsel, garlands, ribbons, a star at the top . . ." Shepherd ticked off the items on his fingers.

Naomi circled the tree, looking high and low. "Where's Clayton's ornament?"

"What's it look like?" Shepherd asked.

"It's a blue hound dog popping out of a stocking. He got it when he was Hunter's age, and he loved that thing."

"I didn't see it when we were taking the ornaments out of the box," Shepherd said.

"Mom." Naomi turned to Irene. "Did you put it up someplace special after last—" Naomi broke off.

Shepherd heard the sorrow in her voice, and it was all he could do not to pull her into his arms and hug her tight.

"The neighbors took down the tree last year." Irene's voice was as heavy as her daughter's. "Remember?"

"That's right. Do you recall who it was?"

Irene shook her head. "That whole time was a blur. I have no idea."

"Could it have been Terri?"

"Maybe. Honestly, it could have been anyone," Irene said.

"We *have* to find it."

"Don't worry yourself about it, sweetheart. It will turn up," Tom added.

"What if it doesn't?"

"Maybe it fell out of the box in the attic," Irene said.

"Good idea." Naomi scrambled out of the room. She returned a few minutes later with cobwebs in her hair, and a forlorn look on her face. "Nothing. Unless it fell in the insulation."

"Don't go digging around in the insulation." Tom's brow furrowed. "It's fiberglass."

"I'm sure it didn't fall into the fiberglass," Irene said.

"We have to find it!" Naomi's voice had taken on a shrill quality that was unlike her.

"Maybe it's in Hunter's room," Irene suggested.

"How could it have gotten into his room?" Naomi asked, but she was already headed toward the boy's bedroom.

"I'll help you look," Shepherd said.

Hunter had awakened, and he was sitting on the couch rubbing his eye. "What's w'ong?"

"Sweetie, did you see your daddy's ornament? The blue dog in the stocking?" Naomi dashed back over to kneel in front of the boy.

Hunter slowly moved his head back and forth.

Naomi hopped up and tore into Hunter's room. Concerned, Shepherd followed her. She dropped to her hands and knees on the floor, looking under Hunter's racecar bed. She dragged out toys. Stuffed animals. Puzzle pieces. Hot Wheels.

"Search the closet," she told him, moving on to the toy box.

"I help!" Hunter cried, and ran to Naomi's side. In less than a minute, the two of them had emptied the toy box. The contents were scattered around the room.

"It's not here," Naomi said, tossing the toys back in the toy box. "How are you doing?"

The closet was neat. Orderly. Clothes hung up. Shoes on a rack.

"I don't see it."

Irene and Tom had come to the doorway. Irene in her wheelchair, Tom standing behind her.

"It probably got lost in the . . ." Irene's jaw tightened. "Aftermath."

"It can't be lost." Naomi shook her head. Her mouth flattened and her eyes widened. "It can't be." Her voice climbed an octave on that last word. She scooped up the remaining toys in her arms, dumped them into the toy box. Jumped to her feet.

She started pacing, distress rolling off her in waves. Tapped her forehead with her index finger, mumbled, *"Think, think, think. Where can it be?"*

Shepherd had never seen her like this. She was wound up. Normally, she was the calm one. The steady happy presence. Why was she so distressed over the ornament?

Looking alarmed, Irene pushed up out of her wheelchair. "Honey, it doesn't matter. We can leave off the ornament this year."

"No we can't. No we can't." Naomi's voice was a string now, vibrating at a fast, high rate. "This year has to be *perfect*."

"There's no such thing as perfect, sweetheart." Irene wavered on her feet. Shepherd could see her torn between needing to sit back down and wanting to go to her remaining child.

Naomi stood in the middle of the room. Her legs splayed wide. Her hands moving everywhere. First on her hips. Then at her throat. Her mouth. Her heart. Her eyes. She looked as if she were on the verge of a panic attack.

He wanted to tell her to breathe, but he had a feeling that would upset her even more.

"I can try." She hardened her chin.

"You're making yourself crazy with all the trying. We'll buy another ornament in honor of your brother."

"No! No!" Naomi shook her head, the cobwebs floating above her hair like a halo. "It *has* to be Clayton's ornament. Hunter needs something to remember his daddy by."

"There's plenty of things he—"

"Don't you get it? He's already forgetting his daddy," Naomi went on, unchained. "Hunter already thinks Mark is his daddy." She waved a hand at Shepherd.

"Really, Naomi, it would be fine to buy a new ornament."

"But Clayton's blue hound dog and my pink hound dog ornament are a matched set. It's tradition."

"We'll make a new tradition."

"If it's new, it's not tradition."

Shepherd didn't know what to do. If he got in the middle of this family situation, he might make things worse. It took everything he had in him to keep his mouth shut and stay out of it.

"It's not really about the ornament, is it, sweetheart?" Irene's tone softened and she eased back down in her wheelchair.

Naomi dropped her chin to her chest. Was she crying? Probably a good thing if she cried. The holidays were bound to bring up unresolved emotions, especially since Clayton had died at Christmas. Shepherd's gut churned. He hated that she was hurting.

Irene wheeled her chair over to her daughter, touched Naomi's shoulder.

Naomi hauled in an audible breath, and raised her head. A big, bright smile graced her face. Artificial. Forced. "It's okay, Mom. You're right. I made a big deal out of nothing. I apologize for having a meltdown."

"Shh, shh. It's okay. It's all right."

"It's not. I shouldn't have taken my emotions out on you."

"You didn't. You're fine. More than fine. You're wonderful. Amazing. We are all so fortunate to have you. I don't know how you manage to hold it all together."

Naomi's chin tipped up, determination hot in her eyes. "I *will* find that ornament."

"Honey, please don't make yourself crazy."

"I'm not going to." That forced smile again. "I just need to take a break." She held up her hands.

Naomi might have smoothed things over with her mom, but she didn't fool Shepherd. He'd been where she was. Overwhelmed with powerful emotions. She'd been holding it together for everyone else for so long, she'd never had a chance to fully grieve.

He could see it in her body language. She was a caldron of unexpressed feelings, waiting to boil over. She *needed* to boil over. Needed something or someone to take out her rage and grief on.

It should be him. He should be her target. He *was* the target.

Tell her. Tell them all. Right here. Right now. He should get the truth off his chest. Let the chips fall where they may.

And ruin the Christmas that Naomi was trying too hard to make merry?

No. That was selfish. The guilt was his to carry. He had to keep quiet. He couldn't tell them who he was until after Christmas.

"Okay, the meltdown is officially over." Naomi was smiling so hard he feared her beautiful face would crack wide open.

This wasn't right. If she kept up this forced happiness, this punishing pace, she was going to get sick.

Oh Lord, he'd gotten her brother killed. He was back to that. *Always.* It was all his fault. Clayton. Samantha. The Luthers' grief. The lost Christmas ornament. He was responsible. The buck stopped with him. There was no one else to blame.

Um . . . Shepherd heard Dr. Fox's voice in his head. *Terrorists might have played a small part in it.*

Okay. Granted. A terrorist might have been the instrument of Clayton's death, but Shepherd was the catalyst. If he'd only listened to his gut instead of insisting on following protocol. If he'd gone to the orphanage with Clayton, the story would have had a different ending.

And then, after he'd gone after Clayton, when he might have saved him . . . he'd left him behind.

The guilt was a hot stew. Bubbling. Burning. Raw as ever. The last few days with Naomi had made him start to forget the real reason he was here. He'd let the warmth of her family seduce him into thinking he could have a future with her.

Foolish. So damn foolish of him.

The Luthers were the fallout. A nice family thrust into a war thousands of miles away. Sacrificed their son and brother. For what?

Until last Christmas, Shepherd had never questioned the military. It had been his home. His family. Like all families, it had its pluses and minuses. Its strengths and flaws. When he was living in the middle of the system, the flaws had seemed minor in comparison to the strengths.

But now? Here? On the other side of it? Swamped in the aftermath? All he could see was the destruction of war.

Somehow, he had to make amends, and doing handyman work simply was not going to cut it.

Naomi lifted her head and met his gaze, grief swimming in her eyes.

In that moment, Shepherd knew what he had to do. Knew it as surely as he knew his own name. If he did not intervene, Naomi was going to keep pasting that fake smile over her grief until she lost touch with the truth.

Naomi was completely ashamed of herself. She was the glue of the family, and here she'd come completely undone.

Unacceptable.

She straightened her shoulders and her spine. Mark had been so great today, helping out with Hunter so she could go have a massage. She should be calm. She should be chill. Instead, she was agitated as hell. Distressed beyond reason at the loss of Clayton's ornament.

Smile. Smooth it over. Merry and bright. Put on a happy face for Hunter.

Hunter was what mattered. He was the *only* thing that mattered.

She glanced over. Saw Mark watching her with worried eyes. She turned up the wattage on her smile. She knew exactly what would give her an attitude adjustment.

Mark's red-hot kisses.

She inclined her head toward the kitchen. "Help me start dinner?"

"Sure." He nodded and joined her.

Out of view from her parents and Hunter, she slipped her arms around his neck. Pressed her mouth to his for a kiss.

He did not kiss her back. Instead, he untangled her hands from around her neck. Whispered, "Not now."

That hurt her feelings a little, but she understood. He was right. This thing they had going on was so new. They didn't know where it was going or if they could work past their issues. What if Hunter walked in on them? This wasn't the time or place.

"Right," she said.

"It's not just that." His tone was somber, his brown eyes darkening to almost black. "We need to have a serious talk. This thing between us can't go any further until we do."

"Ouch." She drew back, tried not to show how much his words distressed her. "That sounds ominous."

"Not ominous. No." He shook his head. "But there's something you should know about me."

"Please don't tell me you have an STD," she said, trying to make a joke, but it came off weird.

"No STD," he said. "But PTSD. Please make time for me as soon as you can."

"It's not something you can tell me quickly?"

"No. Let me know the next time you have the evening free."

She bit her bottom lip. "Okay."

Her cell phone dinged in her back pocket. She grabbed for it, happy to have something else to focus on. The text was from the Woolys, Samantha's parents. They wanted to know if they could have Hunter the following night. They hoped to take him to see a school Christmas play that his cousin was in.

"Well," she said. "You're in luck. Hunter will be with his other grandparents tomorrow evening. Looks like we've got ourselves a date."

CHAPTER 23

The following evening, Mark picked Naomi up at five. She wasn't sure where he was taking her. It seemed to be more confession time than an actual date. She wore jeans and a sweater and hoped he hadn't been planning anything fancy.

She couldn't get a read on him. His expression was impassive, unshakable—the face of a military man in full control of his emotions.

Her anxiety was off the charts. She'd barely slept. Worrying about what he was going to tell her. Her mind played with a hundred different scenarios. Each more terrible than the last. He'd made no secret he'd been in therapy. He was ex-military. She'd just assumed he had PTSD. What if it was something much worse?

Oh gosh. What had she done? Going for a guy she didn't know. Based on nothing more than physical attraction, and the fact she'd dreamed about him.

Was she losing her mind?

"You look pretty," he said, when she shut the door and buckled her seat belt.

"Thank you."

"How are you feeling?"

"Nervous," she admitted.

"Me too," he said.

She didn't know if she was comforted or bothered by that admission.

He reached across the seat, gave her arm a reassuring squeeze. Drove across the train tracks to the other side of town. Pulled into a vacant strip mall. Parked in front of an empty building with a faded red sign on the roof that read "Twilight Lanes." Giant twin bowling pins framed the sign.

Gideon Garza had inherited the old bowling alley from a cousin, and he hadn't been able to find a buyer for the building. It had sat in disrepair for years.

"What's going on?"

"I'll tell you inside."

"You're not planning on buying the place, are you?" she asked. Joking. Mostly. But part of her perked up. If he was buying the place, it meant he was staying in Twilight.

"Gideon let me have it for the evening." He took a key from his pocket.

"You know Gideon?"

"He's in the group therapy sessions I've been going to," Mark said.

"Is it helping with your PTSD?" she whispered.

He met her gaze. "More than I ever dreamed it could."

"I'm happy for you."

He didn't drop her gaze. "Me too." He paused. "Thank you for being there the other night when I . . ."

"Do you have nightmares like that often?"

"Some, less often now."

"About the war?"

He nodded, his eyes darkening. "I'm told it will get better with time as long as I do the things I need to do."

"Like what?" she said.

"Develop a routine. Eat healthily. Get plenty of exercise. Talk it out with people who've been there. Work on mindfulness practices."

"And you're doing all those things."

"I am."

She smiled, so happy he was making progress, and shifted her gaze to the vacant building. "We're going bowling?"

"Not exactly."

"What exactly?"

He got out of the Jeep. Went around to help her out. "Let's go see."

"You're freaking me out a little." She chuckled.

Mark wrapped his arm around her shoulders, drew her close. "I want to assure you of one thing."

"What's that?"

"No matter what happens, you're absolutely safe with me."

"Okay now, see. That right there? That just doubly freaked me out." Her laugh was shaky. What was up?

He stopped outside the door. Cupped her face in his hands. Kissed her soft, sweet, and slow. "Does that help any?"

"A little," she admitted.

"Then let's try that again." He deepened the kiss, held her close.

She leaned into him, sighed dreamily. His kisses were the stuff of romantic movies. "I'm somewhat reassured. But do it again, just to be sure."

He kissed her again, and then, grinning, opened the

door. He went first to turn on the lights. With a gentle hand on her shoulder, he waved her over the threshold.

The inside of the building was covered with tarps. As if someone was intent on painting the ceiling and protecting the walls.

"What is this all about?" Naomi turned to look at Mark.

"It's not as creepy as it looks," he said.

"I wasn't creeped out until you mentioned it. But now that you did, it does have a *Dexter* vibe. Good thing I trust you implicitly."

"You sure?"

"If I didn't, I wouldn't be here." She peered into his eyes. Saw nothing but honor and honesty.

"I'm glad that you trust me," he said. "Because I'm going to ask you to do something that might initially make you uncomfortable."

"If it involves latex suits and ball gags, I'm out of here," she said, only half teasing. Her pulse jumped from a canter to a sprint. Was he sexually . . . um . . . adventuresome? She'd only been with Robert and their sex life had been normal, ordinary. Rather humdrum in fact. If he was looking for something kinky, she might have to take a pass.

Depending, of course, on what it was.

She did have a curious streak.

"Hey, me too," he said. "I'm not into the rough stuff. Too much of the hard side of life when you're a Marine on the front lines."

His sincere and gentle expression relaxed her. She smiled at him and he smiled back, and she did feel totally safe.

"What *is* this all about?" She swept a hand at their surroundings.

"Wait right here." He walked across the room. Opened a door where the owners used to store bowling shoes. Wheeled out a metal cart stacked high with various colors of glass plates.

Taken aback, she frowned at the cart full of dishes. "What the heck?"

"We're going to throw these," he explained. "Or rather, *you're* going to throw them."

She glared, not tracking. "At what?"

"Down the lanes." He pointed.

"Why am I going to bust perfectly good plates?"

"They're not perfectly good. They've got hairline cracks or chips."

"Where did you get them?"

"Various places. Pasta Pappa's, school cafeteria, thrift store. Terri Longoria hooked me up."

"Terri knows about this?"

"Yep, and she's fully on board. She agrees this will be good for you."

"Why are you two talking about me behind my back?"

"We're both worried about you."

"Again, why are we throwing these?"

"*You're* throwing them to get in touch with your anger."

She backed up. The last thing she wanted was to get in touch with her anger. She wanted as far away from her anger as she could get. "No thanks."

He leveled her a chiding stare. "You need to do this."

Naomi crossed her arms over her chest. "I don't."

"You do," he said, sounding really certain. "You've tamped your anger way down inside and covered it up, but it's still there. Simmering."

She snorted and rolled her eyes.

"Aha. A symptom of suppressed anger right there."

"I don't see the point."

"I told you it was going to make you uncomfortable."

"You were right."

"You're used to building stuff, preserving things. You're not one to destroy."

"That's right. Let's go." She turned for the door.

He grabbed her arm, towed her back to face him.

She couldn't meet his gaze. Her stomach was knotted and her heart was a thoroughbred racing the final furlong. She closed her eyes.

"Remember that analogy you told me about sweeping dirt under the rug."

Oh crap. Bitten in the butt by her own advice.

"Naomi," he whispered.

She opened one eye, peeked at him. He was still hanging on to her wrist.

"They have to tear down this old building before a new one can be built in its place."

"Or they could restore the old building."

"Not if the foundation is crumbling. The old has to fall away in order to make room for the new. Cycle of life."

"If you start singing songs from *The Lion King*, I seriously am going to belt you."

"There it is," he crowed. "That's it. Reach right on down and grab hold of that anger."

"*You're* the one making me angry."

"Good. Be angry. Get mad. Throw a fit. You don't grow when you're comfortable."

"You want me to take a wrecking ball to my life?" she wailed, startled by how upset her voice sounded. Why did this idea scare her so much?

"No," he said. "I just want you to smash a few plates."

"I don't want to do this." She tugged against his grip, but he would not let her go.

"Naomi." His tone was calm, but firm. "Do you trust me?"

It might sound stupid, but she did.

"Trust," he murmured, his voice low and reassuring. "Trust."

"Fine. Okay. Give me a damn plate." She didn't cuss often, but he was pushing all her buttons.

"Thatta girl." He produced a pair of goggles. "First put these on. Safety first."

Snorting, she put on the goggles. Part of her felt cornered, but another part of her was strangely excited.

He grabbed a white dinner plate off the cart and passed it to her. Naomi balanced the plate in her hand, saw the hairline crack running through the middle. She wasn't destroying a usable plate. She felt better about that.

Mark studied her with encouraging eyes. "Go ahead."

"You want me to just hurl it at the wall?"

"That's why I put the tarps up."

"You did all this?"

"Yep."

"Why?"

"To help you."

"I don't need—" She cut herself off. Maybe she did need help. He'd gone to all this trouble for her.

Once upon a time, she'd pitched for the church softball team. Back before her life got so complicated. Heaving in a deep breath, she wound up her arm and sailed the plate down one of the tarp-covered alleys.

It whizzed through the air and hit the wall with a satisfying *smack*. Busted into fragments.

The air rushed from her in a cannon breath. Hard and all at once. *Whoosh.*

She remembered the pickle jar Hunter had broken. How Mark had cleaned up the mess. He had that quality about him. The guy who picked up the pieces.

"How do you feel?" he asked.

A wiggle of relief squirmed through her. "Give me another."

Mark passed her a second plate.

Crash.

The china exploded into smithereens.

She smashed a third, then a fourth.

Mark fed her plates.

She threw them.

They got into a rhythm. Mark handing her dishes. Naomi breaking them. Systematically, they moved down the alley. Naomi filling the lane with busted glass. Mark pushing the cart over to the next lane.

The deserted bowling alley rang with the sound of shattering glass. They ran out of white plates. Switched to blue. Red. Lemon. Green.

At first, throwing the dishes was about breaking the rules. There was a sassy daring to it. Out of the ordinary and unexpected. It was bold. It was disrespectful. It was *fun*.

She liked it. Laughed. Threw more plates.

"Now really get mad," Mark told her. "Think of all the times you wanted to throw a fit but didn't."

Ugh. Uncomfortable. She spent her life avoiding confrontation. Fought to keep things light and happy. Intentionally calling up her anger scared her.

"What are you afraid of?" Mark asked, sounding like the Marine gunnery sergeant he'd once been, all the tenderness gone from his voice. "Get mad, *dammit*."

"You want me to get mad?" she yelled.

"Yes. Get furious. Don't hold anything back. Become the Incredible Hulk. When was the first time you remember getting angry?"

"When I was Hunter's age, and I saw a man kick a dog."

He put a plate in her hand. "See that man now. See that man kick the dog. Throw this plate at his head. Make him stop hurting the dog."

She closed her eyes, latched on to that memory. Felt a surge of dark red anger pulse through her. She let out a ferocious warrior cry, flung the plate with all her might.

"Good job," Mark coached. "Again!"

He pushed another plate in her hand. She curled her fingers around it. This one was a platter, bigger and heavier than the others.

An image popped into her head. This one of a boy who'd once poked her in the butt with a straight pin on the school bus when she was eight.

Drawing on every bit of strength she had in her, Naomi gave a strangled war cry, and hurled the platter. It exploded into white glass powder.

She had no time to recover. There was another plate in her hand, Mark whispering, "Make it bigger. Feel the rage. Live it. Breathe it. Own it."

He wanted it bigger? She'd give him bigger. This time, she let loose with a string of curse words along with the plate.

"That's it! That's it!"

She didn't wait for him to give her another plate. She was grabbing at them with both hands. Rage boiling up inside her, furious at everything and everyone who had ever hurt her. The pervert who'd exposed himself to her on a jogging trail when she was in college, the rheumatoid arthritis that robbed her mother of her mobility, the mother-trucking Marines for leaving her brother behind to die in Kandahar.

No man left behind? Ha. What bullshit. The Marines had run away. Left Clayton in enemy hands. She grabbed plates faster than she could throw them. Some fell to the floor, shattering around her.

Naomi didn't care.

She was sobbing and flinging, surrounded by glass and pain. So much damn pain. Years of repressed anger came rolling out of her. She smashed and smashed and smashed until she stood trembling, and sweating, all the dishes shattered.

All the energy drained from her body. Salty tears flowing from her eyes, dribbling down her cheeks, over her lips.

She was exhausted. Wrung out. Muscles twitching. Shattered glass everywhere.

Naomi glanced over at Mark.

He came to her. Crunching across broken glass in his combat boots. Swept her into his arms. Picked her up as easily as if she were Hunter. Carried her from the circle of broken glass. Held her tightly. Took off the goggles. Kissed her forehead. Murmured soothing words.

Finally, finally, she stopped jerking and trembling and panting.

"Now," he whispered. "When you're ready. We build a tribute to your brother."

CHAPTER 24

Shepherd had brought a folding table, two camp chairs, a square of plywood, and glue. He also had bottled water and snacks.

They sat at the table. Shoulders hunched. Sorting through glass shards. Looking for the right pieces to create a mosaic image of Clayton. From the photos on her phone, Naomi selected her favorite picture of her little brother.

The photograph had been snapped a few days before he joined the military. In it, Clayton had hair that curled about his ears, and a neatly trimmed goatee. And he wore that teasing grin that could both inspire and irritate, little-brother style. His blue eyes sparkled with inherent mischief. He was a young man in love with the world.

This was how Naomi wanted to remember him.

They worked for hours. When they finished the mosaic—made of shards of shattered glass—it was a decent rendition of the photograph. Good enough to keep. Good therapy. Surprisingly, a good memory.

"How do you feel?" Shepherd asked.

Naomi exhaled in two parts. "Better. Thank you."

He looked at her with such tenderness. Her heart skittered. "Now for the hard part," he whispered.

"Cleaning all this up." She sank her hands on her hips. Surveyed the plate carnage. Wow, she had been pretty ticked off. Who knew?

"I'm not talking about that." He reached for her hands. "We need to have a serious conversation."

"Do we have to?" She wrapped her arms around his neck. "I'd rather kiss."

"Nao—"

She closed her mouth over his. Kissed him.

"Not now." His voice vibrated against her lips.

Ticklish. She laughed. "Yes. Now."

"Naomi, we *must* talk."

"So talk," she murmured, moving her mouth down his chin to his throat, where she playfully sucked on his neck.

Shepherd groaned. "I mean it."

"Your mouth says no, but your body says yes," she teased, pressing her hips against his erection.

"Are you sure you're a pastor's daughter?" His breathing was heavy, hot.

"Wanna know a secret?"

"What?" he gasped.

"The pastor's daughter has a tattoo," she whispered.

"Really?" He breathed. "I do too."

"You're supposed to have one. You're a Marine."

"That's stereotyping."

"I'll show you mine if you show me yours," she said, not caring one whit how brazen she sounded.

"Cheeky." He lowered his eyelids, sent her a seductive glance. Licked his lips.

Had she successfully derailed him from that "serious" conversation? She hoped so. "Let's see it, Gunny."

He rolled up his shirtsleeve. Revealed a muscular arm roped with strong veins. The material of the shirt stretching tight against his biceps.

Her mind went arid with lust. Her insides twitched. *Holy smokes, what guns!*

Shepherd showed off the *Semper Fi* navy blue ink on his left upper arm. The tat was simple, understated. But artfully done. Just those two words in script font.

"Are you?" Naomi stared into his eyes.

"Am I what?"

"*Semper fi.* Always loyal?"

He flinched as if she'd stuck a knife into his solar plexus. Mark dropped her gaze. Glanced over the bowling alley. His breath quickened.

"Mark?"

He didn't answer her question. Instead, he said, "Your turn."

She slanted her eyes to the side, a sly smile sliding across her lips. "Um, the ink is in a naughty spot."

He rubbed his palms together. Laughed. "I want to see."

Here was the deal. The tattoo was on her fanny, and she wasn't sure she was brave enough to moon Mr. Shepherd. Not when she found him so irresistibly sexy. Why had she started this?

It had all the earmarks of a Bad Idea.

Yes, she definitely wanted to have sex with him. But not in a vacant bowling alley filled with busted-up plates and a heartfelt mosaic of her dead brother. Not exactly high romance.

And they were supposed to be having some major talk. His secret confession, she feared.

Was that why she'd told him about the tattoo? She was forestalling the inevitable? Terrified that his revelation would irrevocably change things?

"Are you going to make me guess?" he asked, his voice lowering along with his eyes, his gaze sweeping down over her breasts.

"Not there," she said.

"Hmm." His gaze flicked lower. To her belly.

"Not there."

Down went his gaze.

Lightly, she swatted his shoulder. "Mind out of the gutter."

"Hey," he said. "You're the one making me guess."

Feeling shy, she reached for the top button on her jeans. Undid it.

Mark's eyes widened, and he gulped so hard his Adam's apple bobbed like a flag on a pole.

Slowly, she turned her back on him. Eased her waistband down. Showed him her hip.

He bent for a closer look. She could feel his warm breath against her cool skin. Goose bumps.

His laughter filled the bowling alley. Big and rich. "Well, well." His finger traced the ink on her bum. It was a small tattoo. No bigger than a quarter. "Will you look at that? A butterfly for my butterfly."

My butterfly.

Her heart fluttered. Unnerved, she pulled her jeans up. Buttoned them.

Mark got to his feet. Took her by the shoulders. Gently, turned her around to face him.

Her backside still tingled where he'd touched her. Vibrated with energy. She was trembling again. This time from a completely different emotion than anger or grief.

"When did you get the ink?" he asked.

Too shaky to meet his gaze, she stared at the hollow of his throat. Noticed a blue vein pulsing there. "After Clayton died."

"As a symbol of resurrection?" he guessed.

She nodded. Raised her head.

Their eyes met.

She reached for him. Tugged his head down toward her. Kissed him with every cell vibrating through her body.

He didn't kiss her back.

She stopped. Confused. She wanted him so badly, and from the hardness of his erection pressing into her leg, he wanted her too. Determined, she caught his bottom lip between her teeth. Sucked lightly on it.

"Naomi," he murmured, sliding his hands around her waist. Moving her off him. "No."

Shame whipped through her. A whirlwind of embarrassment. Had she misread the signals? "What's wrong?" she whispered.

"I can't," he rasped.

"I want you." She wriggled closer. He grew harder still. "I can feel how much you want me. We're both consenting adults . . ."

"No."

"Why not?" she cried, feeling peevish, and thwarted by how honorable he was being.

"Because . . ." He hauled in a deep breath, stared her straight in the eyes. Saw everything he was about to lose.

It was a shattering sound. The moment when he heard his heart break.

He might be falling in love with her. But no matter how powerful the kisses, she couldn't be falling in love with him. Not the true Mark Shepherd. Because she did not know him. How could she when he'd been so deceptive?

Face it. Once she learned who he was, it was over. She would never forgive him. How could she? He shouldn't have kissed her. The genie was out of the bottle.

Too late.

Please, Lord. He surprised himself by praying. Bargaining. *Please let her forgive me. Please let this turn out all right.*

"Because what?" she asked, jamming a frustrated hand through her hair. "Why can't we have sex?"

"Because *I'm* the reason your brother is dead."

That stopped her. Cold.

Naomi splayed a palm to her chest, stumbled backward. "What?"

Shepherd saw it in her eyes. The look he'd feared. Horror. Anger. Loathing. Disgust. This was it. His moment of reckoning. The rubber meeting the road.

"Clayton was in my platoon." He paused. "Under my command."

Dead silence filled the bowling alley.

Naomi's eyes grew wide in disbelief, and her jaw unhinged. "How?" She shook her head. "I don't understand."

"I was in Kandahar with Clayton. I was his commanding officer."

Her mouth rounded into a startled O. "You . . . you're the one who didn't go back for him?"

Shepherd winced. "It wasn't as simple as that, but yes. Your brother died because of errors in judgment. *My* errors."

Naomi pressed a palm to her forehead. Started to pace. Boots crunching over broken glass. She pivoted, came back toward him. *Crunch. Crunch. Crunch.*

Her face drained of color. "You're no handyman."

He shook his head. His stomach in knots. His heart was a ham-fisted pump. Heavy and thick. "No."

She moved the palm from her forehead to her mouth. Looked as if she was going to throw up. "All this time, you've been lying to us."

"It was never my intention—"

"It doesn't matter your intention. It's what you've been doing."

"I tried to tell your father when he hired me. He told me he didn't want to know about my past. I tried again the first night I came for dinner. You remember that."

"You didn't try hard enough," she said. Her voice was an iceberg. She was pacing again. Grinding the glass to sand beneath her footsteps.

He wanted to reach out. Take her into his arms. Beg for her forgiveness. But he left her alone. She needed time to process.

"I've tried to tell you several times," he said. "But something always got in the way."

"If you really wanted to tell me, you would have found a way." Her voice was icicle-cold.

"You're right. I didn't want to ruin your Christmas. You were trying so hard to make everything perfect. I decided to wait until after Christmas to tell you. And that's true. But I also had a selfish reason for not telling you."

She folded her arms over her chest and stared at him as if he'd disappointed her in a most fundamental way.

"I knew if I told you, I wouldn't stand a chance of

getting to know you better. I was hoping if you got to know me that by the time you found out . . ." He trailed off. It sounded impossibly stupid now.

"You took advantage of my ignorance."

"I'm not proud of myself."

She spun around. Put her back to him. Plowed both hands into her hair. Her shoulders jerked up and down. Was she crying?

"Naomi?" He moved toward her.

She ducked her head. Held up her hand behind her. A stop-sign palm. *Don't come any closer.*

Wretched, he inhaled deeply. Clenched his jaw.

When she turned back around, her face was expressionless. But her eyes were red-rimmed. "Tell me what you came to Twilight to tell me."

"Let's sit down." He motioned to the camp chairs.

She hesitated.

Alarmed, he was afraid she wasn't going to sit. He didn't want to tell her the story while she was standing on broken glass.

"Please." He moved to the chairs. Pulled one out from under the table for her.

With stiff, robotic steps, she minced her way over to the chair. Sat down. Eyes unreadable.

Heart in his throat, Shepherd sat down across from her.

On the table in front of them was the mosaic of her brother. Built from glass shards of her grief and anger.

He pulled the white key strung with a Christmas ribbon from his pocket. Settled it on the table in front of her. "This was found among your brother's things, and a note directing me to bring the key to your family in

person. You could say Clayton sent me. His note said
your family would know what to do with it."

Naomi stared at the key as if it were a poisonous
snake. "I have no idea what that is about."

"You've never seen this key before?"

She picked it up. Turned it around. Studied it. "No."

"Maybe your parents know what the key symbolizes.
I just brought it."

She tucked the key into her coat pocket. The room
was cold now. Frost puffed from her mouth when she
spoke. "You came all this way. Lied about your identity. Took a job you weren't qualified for. Stayed for two
weeks. Because a dead Marine told you to?"

Shepherd nodded.

"Why?"

"I owed it to him."

"Then why did you wait so long? Why not come right
after it happened? When we needed to hear from you the
most?"

He winced. "I just received this key upon my discharge at the end of November."

"Who gave it to you?"

"My psychiatrist."

"Why did they wait to give it to you?"

"The military didn't think I was ready to act on Clayton's message. They held it back from me until my health
was more stable."

"You could have just ignored the key. Stayed away.
Left us alone."

"I could not."

She stared at him. Drew the collar of her coat up to
her ears. "Go on."

"Your brother was new to my unit," he said. "Clayton had only been there a month."

Naomi reached out a finger. Touched the mosaic. Traced her brother's face. Her pain was raw. Staggering.

"Everyone in the platoon liked him. Me included."

"He had such a lovely spirit." Her voice floated high. She touched her mouth.

"Yes, but he was impulsive too."

"I know," she said. "He decided on a whim to join the military. He was having trouble finding a job that paid enough to support his family. He'd gotten married too young. And Samantha got pregnant right away. We thought the military would help grow him up." Her voice cracked.

Shepherd crawled his hand toward her, but she moved away. Quickly, he dropped his hand into his lap. "Last Christmas Eve, your brother received a tin of cookies from home."

Bit by bit, he told her the story. How Clayton begged Shepherd to go with him to the orphanage to pass out toys and cookies. How he'd refused, even though he and Clayton both had Christmas Day off, because leaving the base was against protocol.

How his gut was screaming at him to go. All his instincts pointing him in that direction. How if he'd just gone, Clayton wouldn't have been AWOL. But most importantly, if he'd followed his gut and gone, Shepherd would have recognized the wounded terrorist who was hiding out in the orphanage. He'd been briefed. Had seen Ackmed Talid's picture. Clayton had not.

"I should have gone. It's my fault. My instincts told me to go. If I hadn't been such a stickler for the rules, I would have gone. I could have prevented Ackmed from taking your brother hostage."

"What would you have done if you'd gone?" she asked. "If you'd seen Talid?"

"I would have neutralized him."

"You mean you would have killed him?"

"I would have done whatever it took to keep your brother safe."

"So yes?"

"I know it sounds ugly. Especially to a pastor's daughter, but yes. War is an ugly business."

She stared at him as if he was a stranger. That look in her eyes was a bullet to his gut.

Hauling in a deep breath, he told her the rest of the story. How he'd discovered Clayton was AWOL. How he'd taken two other Marines with him to retrieve her brother. How when they'd gotten there, they discovered Talid was holding Clayton hostage in the orphanage.

How Talid's confederates, who'd come to pick him up, had opened fire on them. Hitting one of Shepherd's men in the throat. Shepherd had been torn between getting help for the man who was bleeding out, and trying to save Clayton.

He'd taken off back to the base. But the idea of leaving a man behind tore a hole in his soul. He'd spun the Jeep around, determined to rescue Clayton. But then Shepherd had taken a bullet in the knee and another bullet had struck his helmet. He hadn't even realized he'd been shot in the head.

His remaining man, who was holding pressure on the wounded Marine's throat, had said, "Gunny, we're gonna lose him if we don't get to medical ASAP. You gotta make a choice."

"In the end," Shepherd told Naomi, "I had to decide who was going to live and who was going to die."

"You chose the other man over my brother." Her voice was icy.

"Only because trying to rescue Clayton was so tricky, and the other man was going to die if I didn't get him help."

"Did he live?" Naomi asked. "The other man?"

Shepherd nodded. "He did."

She said nothing. Her gaze was glued on the mosaic. Her hands knotted into fists. Knuckles white.

"I hated having to leave him. Hated myself for not saving them both." He cleared his throat. "For the past year, it's all I've been able to think about. How I failed Clayton. How I failed your family. And then when I got here, I found out about Samantha and I knew I was indirectly responsible for her death too."

"That's a heavy burden to carry." She got up. Moved away from him.

He rose to his feet. Grappled for his cane.

She tucked her fingers into the back pockets of her jeans. Her face was full of sadness. "I can't imagine life has been easy for you."

He barely moved his head. His neck muscles were strung tight as a tennis racket. "Please forgive me," he said. "I know it's asking a lot. And I understand if you can't. But I've never been more sorry for anything in my life."

"I'm sorry," Naomi whispered. "I can't forgive you."

Her words were a sledgehammer. Delivering to Shepherd everything he'd feared. He was too broken to fix. His sins were too grave for forgiveness.

Yes, it was harsh. A blow. If he hadn't been holding tightly to his cane, he would have staggered. Lost his balance. Fallen.

His heart *had* fallen. Fallen off the lofty perch of hope, and onto the cold, concrete ground of reality.

Her eyes, however, were soft. Her expression filled with compassion. She looked as if *her* heart was breaking for him, and it was tearing her apart that she could not help him.

"No one can forgive you," she murmured.

It was just as he'd suspected. He was unforgivable. Unlovable. His own parents hadn't loved him. Not in the way all children deserve to be loved.

No salvation.

Not for him.

"No one . . ." Her eyes were lasers, locked onto his. Burning hot. Twin blue flames of truth.

Yeah, yeah, he got it. His fingers locked around the cane, and he held it tightly, feeling that if he let go he would die.

". . . can forgive you," she repeated, moving toward him. "Until you forgive yourself."

Huh?

"You've locked yourself in a prison of your own doing." She reached up and tapped her fist gently against the side of his head as if trying to knock some sense into him. "*You* must forgive *you*. Until you do that . . ." She trailed off again, shrugged as if it was the saddest thing on earth. "Well, I can't be with you."

She struck to the core of him, like the cold steel of a sharpshooter's bullet lodging in his chest. "Don't you see? I *can't* forgive you."

He stood there trembling, willing himself not to react. To take it. To listen. To hide his pain from her.

"Oh," she went on, "I could say that I forgave you. Tell you my truth. That in my heart . . ." She laid her palm over the left side of her chest like she was saying the Pledge of Allegiance. "I feel nothing for you but deepest mercy."

I feel nothing for you.

That's what his mind heard. It was the shabby raft that his fears and self-doubt clung to. Even as he realized that raft had a hole and was sinking fast.

I feel nothing for you.

Why would she? How could she? Her brother was dead because of him. Not just her brother, but her sister-in-law too. She was the surrogate mother of an orphaned four-year-old because of him.

"You know what I think?" she asked.

"What's that?" He restlessly shifted his weight, off the cane and onto this good leg. Pulled up his spine, tucked in his shoulders. His bum knee tingled. Pins of pain poking through him.

"I think that deep down inside, you don't want to be forgiven. That you want to be punished."

"What?" His voice rasped against his throat.

"You heard me."

"That's crazy."

"Is it? If no one held anything against you, if everyone accepted you for who you are, you couldn't wallow around in this pity blanket you've wrapped yourself in."

"I don't feel sorry for myself." He glowered. "Quite the opposite. I don't give a *damn* about myself."

"Really?" She sank her hands on her hips, glared right back at him. "I think you've gotten so used to beating yourself up. So used to being miserable. You're afraid to be happy."

"That's ridiculous."

"Yes," she agreed. "Yes, it is."

Anger was a noose around his neck, hot and itchy. He balled his right hand into a fist. Bit down on the inside of his cheek. Felt a dull, throbbing ache in the center of his chest.

Her features softened, her tone growing quiet. "You've got to stop believing that everything is your fault. It's time to forgive *you*. You had a screwed-up childhood. It messed with your head. You came out of it with some illogical ideas about the world. Believe it or not, you *are not* responsible for everything. You are not responsible for the grown adults in your life. You are not responsible for my impulsive brother who decided to disobey orders. Do you really think things would have turned out differently if there had been someone else in command?"

He barked out a short, hard laugh. Heard the snap of anger in the pointed, brittle sound. "Oh, that's rich. She who takes care of everyone. Even people who don't appreciate her. She is telling me *I'm* not responsible for everything. Well, right back at ya, sweetheart."

Naomi's jaw went slack. She stared at him, her eyes owlish and hurt.

Immediately, he regretted lashing out at her. "I . . . I . . ."

"You don't have to snarl at me. I was only trying to help."

"That's just the thing," he said, feeling the rope of anger still whipping around inside him like a downed power line. Writhing and sparking. Electric. "You're always sticking your nose in where it doesn't belong. Even when people clearly don't want your help."

Her gasp was a high sound, thin and short. Her eyes darkened. Her mouth pulled down.

"I . . . I didn't . . ." *I'm sorry.* The thought sprang into his mind, but he couldn't form the words. Why not? Why couldn't he apologize? Was she right? Was it true? Did he actually *not* want forgiveness?

Of course he did. That was why he'd come here. Delivering Clayton's Christmas key might have been his outer mission, but inside, where it counted, all he'd really wanted was to be absolved of his guilt.

It was a lightning-bolt moment.

She *was* right. If he didn't have his guilt to drag around like an albatross, he would be free, and if he were free, where would he go? What would he do?

Who would he be?

"You've followed the rules for so long in an effort to protect yourself that you have no idea who *you* are. You've got a lot of inner work to do, Mark Shepherd. I could forgive you until the cows came home. My parents could forgive you. Hunter—when he's old enough—could forgive you, but here . . ." She pointed an index finger into his chest, into his heart. "If forgiveness doesn't come from inside, from where it counts most, you'll never be happy. And I can never be with you."

With those parting words, Naomi turned and walked out the door.

Leaving Shepherd with a gaping wound inside him so big and wide, the military could have driven a tank through it.

CHAPTER 25

Shaking with anger, hurt, grief, and a surprising hit of relief that she didn't understand, Naomi raced home. It was three miles away. It was almost ten o'clock at night. She didn't care. Her legs pumped hard beneath her as she ran, eating up the sidewalk.

If she lived to be ninety, she'd never forget the look of wounded shock on his face. The last thing she'd wanted was to cause him pain. But he needed something to jolt him out of the web of self-blame he'd gotten ensnarled in.

She knew that web all too well. She'd gotten caught up in it herself. When someone close to you died tragically and unexpectedly, it was so easy to get hauled into the cruel loop of self-recrimination. If only she'd done this or that differently, Clayton and Samantha would still be alive.

The thing was, she didn't possess that much power. God was in control, not her. The sooner she let go of the need to be in charge, the better.

She'd lost herself in helping people. In taking responsibility for things that were not her burdens to carry.

Mark had done the same thing. She could see her mistakes now. He could not.

It had taken every ounce of strength she had in her not to absolve him. She wanted to absolve him. In her heart, she *did* absolve him.

But she'd realized with a clear and true certainty that the best help she could give him was not to help him.

This was a radical notion, a startling conclusion.

She had to let Mark heal himself. And he had to start the healing before she could be in a relationship with him. It didn't matter that he was her soul mate. She could not be with him until he could forgive himself. Trust himself.

And she had no idea how long that would take.

Or if he would even take the steps necessary.

That thought killed her, the idea that he might not be able to reconcile his pain. Might not be able to move past his horrible childhood.

She was almost home.

Naomi stopped running. Breathing heavily, she walked the rest of the way back to her house. Mark had not come after her. She'd expected him to come after her. Had been prepared with a speech for why she would not get into the Jeep with him.

A stitch caught her side. Hand to her abdomen, she went up the porch steps. She was going to have to have a conversation with her parents about Mark Shepherd. A conversation destined to ruin the merry Christmas she was struggling so hard to create.

Defeated, Naomi wrapped her hand around the Christmas key in her pocket, took a deep breath, and stepped over the threshold.

* * *

Shepherd followed Naomi at a distance. He did not try to pick her up. Knew she would refuse. He had to let her deal with her emotions the way she needed to deal with them. Her community was safe. People would help her if she got into trouble.

Still, he could not let her run home alone in the dark.

Once he saw her go inside the Victorian, he pulled into the church parking lot. Went into the rectory, to his lonely bedroom.

Stared at the bed where she'd held him and rocked him while he was in the throes of a PTSD-induced nightmare. A nightmare about her brother.

Jesus stared down at him from the picture on the wall, golden halo above his head, and a beatific smile on his face.

"Sorry to let you down," Shepherd apologized. "I did the best that I could."

Jesus kept on smiling.

"I suppose I could ask you to forgive me. I'm not very good at this praying stuff."

But maybe he could be. He wanted to be.

Naomi's words sprang up in his mind. *If forgiveness doesn't come from inside, from where it counts most, you'll never be happy. And I can never be with you.*

How did he forgive himself? How did he get to the bottom of his issues? How did he start on the road to self-discovery and recovery? How did he learn to start trusting his gut?

Shepherd knew only one thing for sure. If Naomi couldn't be with him, there was no reason to stay in Twilight.

* * *

Mom was already in bed when Naomi walked in. Hunter too, was asleep.

For that, Naomi was grateful. She wanted to spare her mother as much pain as possible. And she didn't know if she had enough emotional strength to put her nephew to bed if he'd still been awake.

It was after ten. Her father was puttering around the kitchen. Starting the dishwasher. Wiping down the cabinets.

"Hey, sweetheart," her father called. "How was your evening?"

"Daddy," she said.

He raised his head, and met her eyes. Could see at once something was wrong. He was across the kitchen in a heartbeat. Pulling her into his arms. "What's wrong, sunshine?"

She hadn't meant to cry. Didn't know she was so close to tears. But the minute she was in her father's comforting embrace, tears sprang from her eyes.

"What is it?" he asked, concern lacing his voice.

"Mark," she sobbed.

"Is he hurt? Are you hurt?"

Yes, yes! He was broken. She was broken. *They* were broken.

Her father directed her to a kitchen chair. Produced a tissue. Pressed it into her hands. "Tell me what's wrong."

Naomi sat down, shook her head. "Dad, Mark Shepherd lied to us. He's not a handyman. Joe did not recommend him."

She expected her father to be horrified. Or at the very least upset. "Sunshine, Joe *did* recommend him."

"Then he lied to Joe too. Mark Shepherd was Clayton's commanding officer. He came to town to give us this." She pulled the white key adorned with the Christmas ribbon from her pocket. Settled it on the table. "Mark claims Clayton left the key for him and the message to bring it to us. That we'd know what it meant. That's why he's here."

"Ah," her father said, and picked up the key.

"Do you know what it means?"

His smile was round and happy. His eyes filled with love and forgiveness. "Indeed I do."

She waited.

He said nothing.

"Are you going to clue me in? I don't remember this key at all."

"That's because the key didn't come from Clayton."

Confused, she frowned. "Where did it come from?"

"Joe."

"Pastor Joe Trammel? He's the one who recommended Mark for the handyman job, right? How did Mark get hold of a key from Joe Trammel?"

"No."

Naomi shredded the tissue into tiny pieces. Strewing paper fluff onto the table. "I don't get it. Mark swore to me that Clayton had left this key for him. It's the reason he came to Twilight. Why would he make that up?"

"Not Joe Trammel," her father said. "Joe Fox."

She kneaded her brow, flummoxed by her father's cryptic smile. "Who is Joe Fox?"

"Mark's psychiatrist."

"Back up." Naomi raised her palms, watched tissue dust drift from her hands. "I'm completely lost. How do you know this key came from Mark's psychiatrist?"

"Because I asked Dr. Fox to find a skeleton key, spray paint it white, and tie a Christmas ribbon around it. And give it to Mark Shepherd upon his discharge from the Marines."

Weary and ragged from her exhausting evening, Naomi frowned. "But why?"

"I wanted Mark to come here."

"So why the subterfuge? Why not just call and invite him?"

"Because Joe didn't think he would have come. Mark's the kind of man who needs a mission."

"Okay, Dad. I'm not tracking." Naomi hitched in her breath. "You've got to start from the beginning. None of this makes sense to me."

Her father took her hand. "Dr. Fox contacted me a few months ago. He was concerned about Mark's recovery."

Naomi moistened her lips. "How so?"

"Shepherd kept blaming himself for Clayton's death, and Joe couldn't find a way to break through to him. He thought if Mark came to Twilight and met us, learned that it was possible for him to be forgiven, that he could start to heal."

"What about us?" she said, her voice coming out shriller than she intended. She was still stunned and hurting by Mark's revelations. She couldn't deny that. "Did Dr. Fox consider that having Mark here would stir up a lot of *our* pain?"

Her father cupped her cheek with his palm, held her eyes with a steady gaze. "He believed that having Mark here would be healing for us too. Forgiveness is a powerful tool, sunshine. You know that."

"Does Mom know who he really is?"

"Of course. Your mother and I have no secrets from each other."

"But you kept it a secret from me?"

"We felt Mark needed the opportunity to open up in his own time. You might have . . ." Her father paused. "How can I put this delicately . . ."

"I would have rushed in to rescue him and spoiled what you were trying to do."

"Ahh." Her father's smile deepened. "Being self-aware is the first step toward change."

"So you didn't mistake Mark for the handyman that Pastor Trammel had recommended." She knew Joe Trammel had recommended a handyman to her father. She'd been doing her father's books when he'd taken the call and she'd overheard their conversation.

"That was a stroke of luck," her father said. "I was already worried about how we were going to get Mark to hang around and see what a loving community we had after he brought us the key. Then two days before Mark was discharged and Dr. Fox was to give him the key, Sheriff Hondo called to tell me that the handyman Joe Trammel had recommended had been arrested in Sulphur Springs on assault and battery charges."

"Oh my! Thank heavens we didn't end up with that handyman."

"If we had, we would have forgiven him too," her father reminded her. "None of us are without sin."

"Weren't you worried that Mark would refuse to be mistaken for the handyman?"

"It was a gamble. But Dr. Fox told me how important a sense of community is to Mark and that he has a need to be needed. Then every time he tried to set me straight about who he was, I cut him off at the pass."

"Did you ever think that letting him live the lie and not telling him you knew the truth might be equally jarring to a soldier with PTSD?"

"I talked to Dr. Fox about it once Mark kept quiet. And he felt this might just be the kind of jolt Mark needed to fully snap him back to reality. We actually brought Nate Deavers and his group of vets in on it too. He had support all around him, even if he didn't know it. We weren't taking any chances."

"So *you're* really the reason he lied."

"He didn't lie. He just didn't share his identity with you. His motives were pure. He didn't want to ruin our holiday. You're trying so hard to make it perfect."

"So he doesn't know the key is bogus? He truly believes Clayton left him the key."

"Dr. Fox found an envelope that Clayton had left for Mark with a leave request in it. He took the envelope, typed up a letter from Clayton, and put the key in the envelope."

"This feels very underhanded."

"I thought the same thing, but Joe . . . Dr. Fox felt the step was necessary in order to lift Mark out of the despair he'd fallen into."

"I wish you'd let me in on this," she murmured.

"I'm sorry you got hurt," her father apologized. "I deeply regret it."

A bit of anger went through her. "You left me wide open. Vulnerable."

"I am so sorry, sunshine."

She couldn't stay mad at her father. He was her rock and he was looking so guilty. Instantly, she forgave him. "It's all right, but I need some time to process all this."

"You have deep feelings for Mark?"

"I love him, Daddy."

Her father nodded, didn't seem the least bit surprised.

"He's a good man. Flawed like us all. But he has a huge heart."

"It's more than that." She met her father's gaze. "I dreamed about him before I ever met him. And he dreamed of me." She told their story about the Christmas cookie dreams. "He's my soul mate."

"God works in mysterious ways," her father said. "What dreams may come."

"But it happened so fast. I'm worried it happened too fast."

"When it's right, sunshine, it's right. Have you prayed on it?"

"I have. I'm still confused."

"God operates on his own timetable."

Naomi chuffed. She felt exhausted. Wrung out. Tonight had been an emotional assault on every front. Draining. "Mark's not ready for a relationship. He's still beating himself up. Still hasn't learned how to trust his own instincts."

"Give him time."

"I was harsh with him," she said. Guilt sat heavily on her shoulders. "I said some cruel things."

"Was it something that he needed to hear?"

She didn't hesitate. "Yes."

"Then it wasn't cruel. He knows that you're not cruel."

"How can you be sure?"

"Ultimately, I can't know. But Mark's a reasonable person. Grounded. Down to earth. He's a man who strives to do the right thing."

"Even when the 'right' thing isn't necessarily the correct one," she said, remembering what Mark had told her about following protocol when his gut instinct had begged him to accompany Clayton to the orphanage.

"He's tormented by what happened. I don't know if he can ever let it go."

"He's strong."

"I don't know if he's strong enough to overcome this. I love him, but I have Hunter to think about. Hunter must come before everything."

Her father pushed back his chair. "It's late. You need to get some sleep. Things will look brighter in the morning."

"I won't sleep with this weighing on my mind. I have to go talk to Mark. Apologize for being so harsh."

"All right." Her father leaned down. Kissed her cheek. "Whatever you decide, know that your mother and I are always behind you."

"Thanks, Dad. I'm so lucky and grateful to have you both." She stood up, hugged her father tight.

He went off to bed.

She put her coat back on. Walked over to the rectory, and the closer she got, the faster her pulse raced. By the time she knocked on Mark's door, her heart was lodged firmly in her throat. She almost convinced herself to turn and go back home. Wait until morning like her father had said.

From behind her, she heard footsteps. Out of the darkness, a rough masculine voice said, "What do *you* want?"

CHAPTER 26

"We need to talk." Her voice was a string, tight and thin.

"Then talk." Shepherd folded his arms over his chest.

"It's cold. Can we go inside?" She inclined her head toward the rectory.

"We already talked. It didn't go so well."

"That's why we need to talk again."

He shook his head. What was there left to say? She was right. Until he got to the bottom of his issues, they had no future together.

"Please."

He wanted to say no, but he couldn't refuse those big blue eyes. He moved past her to open the door. Held it for her to enter.

She stepped from the hallway into his bedroom, flicking on the light switch as she went past. He followed, every muscle in his body tensing.

Naomi turned to him. "I'm sorry. I was too harsh."

"You were honest. The truth hurts." He gave a loose, rebellious shrug, trying to look cool and tough.

She didn't fall for it. She came across the room.

Parked her cute little self right in front of him. "I want to pick up where we left off."

He arched an eyebrow. "Meaning?"

"I want you."

She looked at him, her upturned face incandescent and vulnerable. And close. So very close. Close enough for him to see where her tears had dried salty tracks on her cheeks. Her eyes were on his. Enthralled. Her head tilted back slightly. Ears cocked to the sound of his voice.

His fingertips tingled, anxious to touch her. His blood chugged sluggish and hot.

Just like that, it felt as if the world had become quicksand and there was no solid ground left in the universe.

He reached for her hand, threaded his fingers through hers. Drew her tightly against him. Lowered his head.

Her lips met his. Eager.

She yielded. Gave everything over to him. Held nothing back. Kissed him with a fire and passion that robbed his breath.

There were a hundred reasons why this was not a good idea. Never mind that she now knew his secret. She was still raw from the anger and grief she'd expressed that evening. She hadn't had time to absorb her new knowledge about him. No time to integrate. This was pure reaction. Neither one of them had had time to consider the consequences of going to bed together.

But his body was overriding every bit of his common sense.

Her smell invaded him. Lit him up like a Christmas tree. Her taste was his undoing. The way she parted her lips lured him in. Pushing him beyond reason.

"Make love to me, Mark," she begged. "I want you. I *need* you. Please."

He burned with yearning. Not just for her body, although there was plenty of that. But the physical stuff wasn't enough. Not with Naomi. He was in deep. Deeper than he'd ever been. Never mind the danger he'd faced in the Middle East. Nothing felt as weighted, as monumentally life changing as making love to this woman.

She wriggled against him. Fierce and hungry. Kissed him again.

Now he'd done it. Struck the match. Lit the flame.

He knew he'd been swimming in treacherous waters. Understood there were riptides and wild currents, and yet he'd waded in.

But he was a sucker for the Christmas magic and he was just too damn weak-willed to resist temptation. He nibbled her earlobe. She moaned, a soft little sound of ecstasy.

His heart was a drum. *Thump-thumping* with red-hot desire. "Why are you here, Naomi?"

"Isn't it obvious?" She ran a hand underneath the hem of his shirt. Laid her palm against his bare skin.

"Why now? What's driving you? Are you trying to shut down your darker emotions again? Whitewash them with pleasure? Is that really why you're here? You want to use me as a salve for your wounds?"

"Would that be such a bad thing?" She fiddled with the buttons on his shirt.

He folded his hand around hers. "I don't want it to be like this."

"Why not?"

He pressed his forehead to hers, looked her in the face until both their eyes crossed. "Do I need to get some more plates and take you back to the bowling alley, butterfly?"

"I've dealt with those feelings," she said. "The plate smashing. Making the mosaic. It was very therapeutic. Healing. I thank you. But there are other kinds of healing, Mr. Shepherd."

"If you start singing Marvin Gaye, I'm going to tickle you." He moved a hand down to her side. Hovered over her ribs.

Naomi hummed a few bars of "Sexual Healing."

He made a light scratching motion against her skin with his fingers. "I'm serious," he warned.

"Me too." She kept humming. Raised her eyebrows. Daring him.

He cupped her chin, peered into her eyes. "Why are you here?"

"Because I know you're leaving. I came over to apologize for being so harsh to you at the bowling alley and I saw the Jeep packed with your things. And I just can't let you go without spending one night with you."

"I have to leave. You were right. I've got to face my past and untangle that mess. I have to figure out why I can't trust my gut. Why I can't forgive myself."

"I know." She reached for the buttons on his shirt again, and this time he did not stop her.

"You still want me?"

"We're here now," she whispered. "This is where the healing begins."

"Naomi."

"Mark." She stripped his shirt off his shoulders. Her eyes lit up at the sight of his bare chest. "Oh. My."

"You've only been with one other man."

"All the more reason to have a taste of something new." She licked her lips.

"This is a big deal."

"Quit stalling, Mr. Shepherd. It's time to put out."

What a delight she was. For Shepherd, Naomi was a refuge from normal life. A haven for his mind. She was hallowed ground. Being with her was play. Sacred. Salvation. She was smart, insightful, inspirational, devoted. With her, *because* of her, he was fully engaged. Alive in a way that he'd never before lived.

He laughed and hugged her.

"Hey, hey," she said. "That's affection. I want *heat*. Got it?"

"You mean like this." He swept her up. Planted a hot, hard kiss on her lips. Used his tongue to ignite and incite.

"Exactly like that!" she crowed breathlessly when he finally let her go. "Now the big question. Do you have condoms?"

"Packed in my Jeep."

"Well." She made shooing motions. "What are you waiting for? Go get them."

While a bare-chested Mark raced out to the Jeep for the condoms, Naomi took the picture off the wall, turned it facedown on the dresser. She went to the bathroom. Fluffed her hair. Pinched her cheeks. Good enough.

"Naomi," Mark called. "Are you still here?"

She popped back into the bedroom.

"There you are." He looked relieved. "I thought you took off."

"You're not getting rid of me that easily."

"Look what I've got." He waved a roll of condoms. "Three."

"Feeling pretty sure of yourself, huh?"

"I live to please you."

The humility of his statement, the sincerity in his eyes, told her everything she needed to know. He loved her. Even if he hadn't said it, she knew he did. "We both need this."

"Yes." His voice was dusky. He stood in the doorway. She was in the middle of the room, a few feet away. She remembered the first time he'd come into her kitchen to find her sopping up pickle juice in a field of broken glass.

Overcome by how quickly things had moved with them, she put a palm to her mouth.

"Are you scared?"

"Of you? No, not ever." She understood him. Knew what a gentle giant he was beneath the warrior's heart.

He looked reassured. Happy.

"Are you scared of *me*?" she asked.

"Butterfly, I'm quaking in my boots."

"Why?" She laughed at the idea of it.

"I'm terrified of messing this up."

"You won't."

"What if I can only last sixty seconds?"

"You do have three condoms. We go again."

He reached over to tuck a strand of hair behind her ear. "I want you desperately. More than I've ever wanted anything in my life. But this has to be right for both of us. There's no need to rush into something you end up regretting."

"Divine timing," she whispered. Oh no, had he changed his mind? "It feels right to me. How about you?"

"It's felt right from the moment you climbed into my Jeep."

"We're completely alone. It's just you and me. Now, take me to bed." She flung her arms around him.

He captured her in his brawny embrace. Lifted her up.

"Whoa. Wait. Can you carry me?"

"Hell yes."

"What about your knee?"

"I've got you, butterfly. Don't ever doubt it."

Convinced, trusting him, she enfolded her legs around his waist. Entangled her arms around his neck. Nuzzled his chest. Faith in him parted the sorrow of the past year and she was right where she belonged.

He carried her the four steps to the bed. She could feel the sturdy, steadfast thump of his heart beating against her chest.

This was so easy. Who knew that being with him would be this easy? Effortless as a bird gliding on the breeze.

She tilted her head back to get a good look at him. Those dark eyes, that strong chin and masculine nose. Skin nicked with scars. Some people might think he looked scary.

To Naomi, he was the most handsome man in the world. How had his face become so familiar to her in such a short time? It felt as if they'd known each other their entire lives.

He was good with Hunter, a natural father. She'd thought he was sexy from the very beginning. But the more she came to know him, the more her attraction added deeper layers. What she felt for him was much more complicated than simple sexual chemistry. Although there was plenty of that too.

She could not wait to be with him, to feel his body inside hers.

He laid her back on the mattress. Stepped back. Sent an appreciative stare strolling over her body. His eyelashes lowered in a totally beguiling manner. His face whetted into a sly grin that said, *I'm about to see you naked.*

"You are so gorgeous," he murmured, his voice catching on the final word. Hushed and reverent.

She was feeling pretty reverent herself. Her hands were trembling. Again. This was a big step. Their first time together. Her first time with someone other than Robert.

If she'd had time to prepare, this would have gone down differently. Not in the rectory for sure. Or her bedroom at her parents' house. Maybe she would have booked a room at the Merry Cherub. But no, everyone in town would have known what they were up to. Maybe it was best not to be prepared.

Just let it happen. Roll with the flow.

But if she'd planned this she would have reapplied her makeup after the bawl fest at the bowling alley. Gone to Terri's spa and waxed in places he was about to see. She would have worn sexy undies and a bra that matched her panties. Candles. Music. Snacks.

Mark didn't need any mood setting, if the bulge in his jeans was any indication.

"Don't worry about a thing, butterfly," he said, seemingly reading her mind. "Everything is going to be just fine."

He came closer again, his knees bumping against the end of the mattress.

Feelings flooded in on her. Excitement. Anxiety. Elation. Fear. She lay on her back staring up at him. He was the most magnificent man she'd ever seen.

He unbuckled his belt. Yanked it free from the belt loops. It made a sexy, slithering sound. He unsnapped his jeans.

She froze. Ensnared. Barely able to breathe.

"You want to see what's behind the zipper?" he teased.

Naomi nodded. Yes, she did.

"I'm already half-naked. It's your turn now. Take off your top."

Naomi sat up. Reached for the hem of her shirt, arms crossed. Taking her time, like raising the curtain on a stage show, she peeled the shirt upward and over her head. She wadded it into a ball and threw it at him.

He caught it. One-handed. Tossed it over his shoulder. What was behind him was not important.

The room was cold. Her nipples beaded hard beneath her teal bra.

"Keep going."

But instead of taking off her bra, she boldly hooked her arm around his waist. Pulled him to her. On top of her. Until the erection inside his jeans nestled against the zipper of her jeans.

Slick as satin, he reached behind her for the snap on her bra. He fumbled a bit. So much for his smooth operator vibe. Beneath the shadow of dark stubble at his jaw a muscle twitched.

"Naomi." He breathed her name. "This is the first time I've made love to a woman since before Clayton . . ."

The mention of her brother stopped everything cold.

"I'm sorry," he said.

"Don't be."

"After last Christmas—"

"You didn't feel you deserved pleasure."

His eyes widened. Apparently the thought hadn't occurred to him before, but from the muscle tic at his jaw, he was thinking of it now. "Maybe."

"You deserve all the pleasure in the world, Mark

Shepherd. That's why I'm here tonight. To prove that to you."

She kissed him lightly. On the cheek. Moved to his temple. Forehead. The bridge of his nose. Kissed his nose all the way down the tip.

He sat still. Letting her kiss away. It was weirdly sexy. Showering him with endless kisses while he stayed motionless. More healing. A ritual. A rite. They were inventing it as they went along.

When he lowered his head to kiss her breasts, she let out a soft sigh.

They were both still wearing their jeans, both naked from the waist up. They touched each other. Exploring every spot. Tender caresses. Slow massages.

He clasped her in his arms. Those vast sturdy arms. She prayed he would never let her go. *Please, God, please.* She rested her head on his shoulder. She wasn't very experienced in lovemaking.

This was new.

And scary.

She reached up to stroke his face. Her hands trembling.

"Are you absolutely sure you want to do this?" he whispered. "We can turn back. Anytime. It's not too late. You're a pastor's daughter."

"I'm twenty-seven. And I have a tattoo."

"Oh," he teased. "That makes all the difference. Let me see." He reached for the button on her jeans. She did not resist.

Leisurely, he tugged off her pants. She raised her hips off the bed. Helping him. He took her panties off with her jeans. Let out a low whistle of appreciation. His eyes fixed on her.

Feeling shy, she reached for a pillow to put over her thighs.

"Did I embarrass you by staring?"

"A little," she admitted.

He kissed her. She was sitting in his lap. He still had his jeans on and the denim was rough against her bare bottom.

It was the sweetest of kisses. Gentle and kind. She ran the tip of her tongue along his bottom lip. Tasted his special, Mark Shepherd flavor.

His mouth was a plume. Skimming against hers. The quietest of torments. His peppermint breath warmed her skin.

Good man. He was a good man inside and out. Considering his background, she didn't know how he'd gotten that way, but he was. If only he could recognize his own goodness.

She shut her eyes. Leaned her head back. Felt his hot lips scorch her throat. A froth of heat fizzed between their lips. She swallowed his radiance. Absorbed him. Felt it slip down her throat. Bubble in her stomach. Slide lower with rowdy insistence.

With him, she felt reborn. Shiny and new. Fresh and clean. Healing. They were healing each other.

"Are you cold?"

"No."

"Do you need to shift? Move? Go to the bathroom?"

She opened her eyes. Stroked his dear face with her fingertips. "I have no needs other than to be with you."

He stretched out on the bed. Pulled her down beside him. The luxurious sweep of his long, dark eyelashes softened the angular lines of his tanned cheekbones.

His cocoa-colored eyes searched hers, full of awe and adoration.

No man had ever looked at her quite that way. As if he'd found his North Star and it was she.

Mark looked so unguarded. It was a touching moment. She placed three fingers to her lips. He might be a strong, brave Marine, but he was also quite fragile. She had the power to break him, and that realization rocked her to her bones.

He trusted her. He might not trust himself, but he trusted her.

Honored beyond speech, she felt her heart turn to butter in her chest. She was toast. This man had her heart forever. If they never spent another moment in each other's company after tonight, it didn't matter. She would always love him. He was her soul mate, and nothing could ever change that.

Mark lowered his head to kiss her breasts. Paying special attention to her nipples. Kissing first one, and then the other.

She writhed. Overcome with need. "Get out of those jeans!"

"Yes, ma'am." His smile broke open like a sunrise. And he stripped off his pants and underwear.

"Finally."

"Greedy little thing." He laughed.

"Make note of that."

"I'll file it under Important Things to Know About Naomi."

They were sitting in the middle of the bed. Cross-legged. Peering into each other's eyes. It felt cosmic.

They couldn't seem to get enough of staring into each

other. Savoring every moment. Every smell. Every sight. Every sound. Taste. Touch.

His touch was light at times. Firm at others. He seemed to know exactly when to ease up on the pressure, and when to push. Everywhere he landed—her ears, her palms, her elbows, her knees—she tingled. As if he had lightning bolts in his fingers and they could stir magic.

After an hour or more of exploring each other's bodies with hands and tongues, he eased her onto her back. Straddled her.

He checked in with her again. "How you doing, butterfly?"

"If I get any better I'll explode."

"Well, that's promising," he said.

She could feel his erection between them. A massive, hard shaft she could not ignore. It was there. Up. Big. Proud.

He kissed her. Her entire body swamped with heat. His mouth moved down her body, taking a road trip from one set of lips to another.

When he reached the most secret part of her, she contracted. Worried. Afraid. Not knowing what to expect. Robert had not ever gone down there. He'd told her that he didn't care for that particular sex act.

Mark, on the other hand, was enthralled. He smooched languorous trails of moist heat and she was mesmerized. Her sensitive skin incredibly responsive. Her body a throbbing magnet of electrical light.

He tenderly parted her knees. Tickled his fingers over her inner thighs as if he was playing heavenly music on a celestial keyboard. All thoughts fled her mind. Body awareness claimed her concentration. This was why she'd gone to bed with him. To feel fully alive in this moment. To live her kismet cookie dream.

Those incredible lips of his pressed hot, fervent kisses up the inside of her leg, inching closer and closer to her feminine core.

"Do you like this?" he murmured. "Do you want more?"

"Yesss," she hissed through clenched teeth. "Yesss, yesss, yesss." A sublime snake of yesses. A streaming steam of yesses. A never-ending circle. Yes-yes-yes-yes.

The closer he got to her entrance, the tighter her muscles tensed. By the time his tongue touched her most sensitive area, her fists were clenched. Her eyes squeezed closed. Her entire body stiff as a drum skin. Her breath coming in short, gulping staggers.

"Relax," he murmured against her skin. Sent a sweet vibration buzzing through her.

As if that was so easy to do when he was doing the most incredible things to her. She gasped. Arched her back against his eager tongue.

Heat and moisture. Sensation layered on top of sensation. She couldn't think. Couldn't breathe. All she could do was surrender to this man. Her beloved.

He took his time. As if savoring the world's most sumptuous meal. He had her giggling and gasping. Panting and praying. Clutching his head and crying for more. The man was a sex magician.

His fingers slid into the game, stretching and teasing, taking things up another notch. She had no idea there were so many levels of arousal. How was this even possible? Naomi felt like a rosebud blossoming in the heat of a nurturing sun. Opening up. Flowering wild and free. Blooming to her full potential. She was a nymph, a goddess, a queen. She was a glistening, glittering galaxy!

Time hung suspended. In amber. In honey. In treacle. Languid and warm and rare. A golden moment that stretched out limitlessly and teased her with the thought that this was how the universe secretly existed.

In the immutable vastness of *now*.

It seemed fated. As if from the moment she'd mistakenly hopped into his Jeep, they'd been building toward this encounter.

Toward each other.

His touch, his skill, his reverence, pushed her closer and closer to the edge. Sensation built, grew, swelled. Pushed down on her.

And when she gasped, wide-eyed and startled, shivered, shook, Mark laughed.

"What . . ." She gasped, her body rippling in riotous joy. ". . . was that?"

"Butterfly, don't tell me that was your first orgasm."

CHAPTER 27

"So that's what all the fuss is about." She breathed. "Wow."

He shifted his body away from her, but his hand was still stroking her gently.

"No," she whispered. "Please."

"What is it? Are you okay?" His hand stilled, his voice filled with concern.

"Not at all. I just . . . it's just . . . I'm not ready for this to end. I want this night to last."

"Ah, butterfly." He laughed, kindness in his chuckle. "This is only the beginning."

Her heart did a trippy little hope tap—*tat-tat-tatty-tat-tat*. Did he mean the first of many orgasms or the first of many nights like tonight? She so wanted to believe it was the latter.

She sneaked a peek at his face. He was at the foot of the bed, gazing at her over the tops of her bent knees.

His lips curled into a naughty-boy smile. Glistened in the muted light. He looked smug and so handsome she didn't know if she could survive many more nights like this one.

"I want you to have fun too," she said.

"Believe me, darlin'," he drawled, "I'm having the time of my life. It's okay. Just let things flow."

She was about to protest that it wasn't fair for her to get her jollies while he went without. But then he lowered his head and went back to doing what he did so masterfully.

That amazing mouth burning her. Branding her. Banishing her to the outer reaches of reason. Her body was alive. Electric. Tingling. Throbbing. Ticking. Jolt after jolt of sensation hit her. Robbed her of thought. Of sanity.

She was an animal. Wild. Hungry. Desperate.

"Mark," she shouted, not even aware she was calling his name. "Mark!" A punctuation. "Mark, Mark, Mark." A chant. Maybe it should be her new mantra. No more faith of a mustard seed. In this moment, he was her hope. Her faith. Her everything. "*Mark, Mark, Mark, Mark*."

His hands and tongue performed wily wizardry.

She arched her back off the mattress. Her fingers latching into his hair. Not letting go. She cried out. A mad, tumultuous sound. The growing heat flared, flamed. Consuming her in rhythmic waves of vivid yellow starbursts.

He slowed.

Teasing.

"More," she whispered between adrenaline giggles. "Please more."

He was one hundred percent in charge. She was at his mercy. But while he teased, he didn't torment. Not much, anyway. Just enough to make it more pleasurable than uncomfortable. He knew how to walk the fine line. Escalating the tension. Holding back in order to push her into more thrilling heights.

Naomi didn't fight it. Just let him be in charge. Allowed him to blow her away. To cast his magic spell. Body. Mind. Soul.

Five seconds in and Naomi was fairly certain she was going to pass out if something didn't give soon.

And then, oh God, she was gone. So gone. Disappeared. Vanished. She gasped, grasped, panted, quivered. Transformed from regular old Naomi Luther, personal shopper and soon-to-be officially a mom, into a high priestess. Venus. Aphrodite. Clíodhna. One of those incredible goddesses.

Whimpering, she clutched a pillow to her chest. Struggled to fully absorb what was happening.

She opened one eye. Got a good look at Mark. Sighed. If she died now, she'd die a happy, happy woman. She dropped her knees in opposite directions to the mattress. Motioned him to her with come-hither fingers.

He climbed onto the bed between her splayed legs. Watched her with inquisitive brown eyes. He paused for what felt like a week, his eyes searching her face. "How you doing, butterfly?"

Butterfly.

His special word of endearment for her. The first thing he ever called her. The word that matched her tattoo. Her symbol of resurrection. He was resurrecting her.

"Fine." She bobbed her head. Realized belatedly he was checking to make sure she was ready to continue. "Oh yes. That. Finer than fine."

He stretched out beside her. Raised up on one elbow. Looked down at her in an expression of such acceptance and tenderness that her heart floated up out of her chest and into her throat. Bobbling like a helium-filled balloon.

Balloons could burst. Or float away. They didn't stay bright and cheery forever. That's what she was afraid of. Worried that tonight wouldn't be enough to transform him. To heal him. To heal *them*.

Discreetly, he put on the condom. Leaned toward her, his big body parallel to hers. "Is it okay if I kiss you now?"

"You don't have to ask permission," she said. "I want this as much as you do."

"Naomi." He said her name simply and gathered her against him. Inhaled the scent of her hair. Pressed his mouth against hers.

He tasted of her. Salty and sexy. What a turn-on!

She tugged his head down, deepening the kiss. Letting him know it was okay to share. She loved the mingling. The merging. The beautiful magic of two soul mates fully enjoying each other's bodies. In her heart, she was fully and completely committed to him. Without a doubt, she knew he was her one and only.

Wondered if he knew it too. Prayed that he did.

"Mmm," he moaned. "You taste so good."

They laughed together. And kissed. Long and slow and creatively. Taking their time. Rolling in the specialness.

When they were both panting and desperate, he flipped her over on top of him. Her knees fell to either side of his hips. She straddled him the way she did that day on the sidewalk in the town square. That harbinger of a moment.

He spanned his hands around her waist. Held her poised over this straining shaft. Let her dangle there.

"Look at me," he whispered.

They exchanged glances.

"Do you feel it?"

"What?" she whispered back.

"Our combined energy."

Oh boy, did she feel it! The heat and vibration surging from him into her before they were even joined.

Slowly, he lowered her. She reached down to touch him, to guide him inside her.

"No hands," he commanded. "Let our bodies find their way. They know where to go."

His control was amazing. Millimeter by millimeter he eased her down. She could feel the throbbing of him pulsating at her entrance. Full of life force. She wanted to engulf him. Absorb him.

She wriggled, trying to get lower quicker. Desperate to connect with him. But his hands held firmly around her waist. Suspending her at that exquisite level of almost having what she wanted. But not quite able to get there.

"Tease," she said, and he laughed.

But he relinquished his hold, let her body sink down to envelop his. She gasped, joyous. He grinned and patted her butt as she settled in. Her body stretching over his girth.

She shifted, savoring the pressure of him inside her. He hissed a you-feel-so-good sound that vibrated throughout her being. Shivers of pleasure tripped over her.

They were fully connected. No separation.

She stared down at him. He peered up at her. For a sweet, blissful moment, they didn't move. Then he cupped her breasts and she rocked forward and he groaned. And everything went wild.

This may be our first and last time together. The thought bounced around in her head. But of course, she would see him again. *He might not be able to change.* To give her what she needed.

Pinch. Twist. Ah yes. The truth.

Her heart skipped a beat. Was this a one-time affair? She'd been swept away by need and desire. Hadn't really thought this through. Her emotions had been crazy tonight, swinging from low to high. Back and forth. She'd been through the whole spectrum of feelings in one endless evening. She wasn't thinking rationally.

Mark pulled her head down and kissed her thoroughly. A kiss that offered promises of happily-ever-after. Could she trust that? Could she trust him?

He seemed so trustworthy, but he didn't know how to trust himself. How could she trust a man who couldn't trust his own judgment?

Momentary panic flared inside her. Too late. It was too late to backtrack. He'd given her every opportunity to say no. To back out.

They were already joined. Merged.

Like it or not, this night meant something. The paradigm had shifted and she was committed. The way she looked at love would never be the same. She was changing. He was changing her—from a girl who chose to see the world through rose-colored glasses, into a woman who could see clearly human beauty in all its faults and flaws.

Life wasn't about ignoring the problems and hoping for the best. Rather, she was growing in the knowledge that saw those problems as opportunities. And tackling those opportunities with her eyes wide open made her stronger, tougher, and more independent. She didn't need anyone to save her.

She could save herself.

If this relationship crashed and burned, losing him would not destroy her. No matter how much she loved him. No matter that he was her soul mate. Her destiny. She'd survived so much loss already. She would survive whatever rough seas life dished out. There was a little boy next door depending on her.

She could handle come what may.

Right now, she was going to handle *him*. In the best possible way. Naomi smiled in the darkness.

"What's so funny?" he asked.

"You," she said, reaching around to grip his hips and sink even deeper onto him.

"Woman," he gasped, and dug his fingers into her buttocks. "You're driving me out of my ever-loving mind."

She rocked back and forth. Giggling.

He wrapped his arms around her back and partially sat up. Sending his body somehow sliding impossibly deeper inside her. He fisted one hand around her hair, holding her in place while he captured her lips and kissed her hard and long.

They were rocking together now. A single unit. Bouncing on the mattress, squeaking the bedsprings.

Drunk with the wildness of it. Of him. Of them. She closed her eyes and let the eclipse slide over her.

"That's right, butterfly," he said, using that lovely nickname again. "Just let go. I've got this. I've got *you*."

His voice was a fleece blanket, warm and soft. Carrying her away. Keeping her safe. He nuzzled her neck, nibbled her earlobe. His tongue licked her tender flesh. Goose bumps rose on her skin, spread down her body.

Without preamble, he tucked his arm around her

waist and flipped them over in one smooth motion. He was on top. Cradling her head in his hands. Peering into her eyes.

Naomi felt him grow harder inside her, and a little moan of pleasure escaped her lips.

"You are so beautiful. I've imagined you naked in my bed from the minute you landed in my Jeep."

"Really?" She smiled, feeling a bit self-conscious. She never thought of herself as particularly beautiful. Pretty, okay. But beautiful? Not by a long shot.

In his eyes, she saw her reflection, realized that he truly found her beautiful. That touched and humbled her.

Mark stroked her cheeks with his fingers, planted kisses everywhere he touched. Her forehead. Her chin. The tip of her nose. "Do you have any idea how sexy you are?"

When he said it like that, she *felt* sexy. Naomi lowered her lashes, smiled serenely.

He tugged her closer. Moved inside her. Slowly at first, getting a leisurely rhythm going. He tilted his pelvis against hers. Rubbing the spot that sent electric sensation flooding her pelvis.

Their mouths, their bodies, their minds united. Creative. Expressive. Instruments of physical love. But it was more than that. Higher. Rarer. Art. They were creating art with their bodies. With each other. A magnificent, timeless dance of love.

This was why people called it lovemaking. She felt cherished, and she cherished him in return.

But along with the cherishing came the charging heat and fiery desire. The blistering, crackling, sizzling need. They were caught in a swirl of lips and tongues. Arms and legs. Tangled. Entangled. Enmeshed.

It was a dance of penetration and retreat. Of ebb and flow. Profound. Complex. Tricky. Sticky. Wet and willing. Sensitive.

Her entire body was hypersensitive to his touch. Receptive. She was aware of every brush of his fingers, every breath he took. The taste of his mouth. The sight of his bare skin. The throb of him.

Her cells tingled and glowed. It seemed a top-secret message from the universe. Confidential and hush-hush. Just the two of them in on this great and powerful answer to the mystery of life.

Love. She thought it. Felt it. And in that moment, knew it.

A breathless whirl. Visions of possibilities. Shadow and light. The world was inside her and she was inside the world. Vast. Endless. No limits.

Falling. Oh, she was falling.

While at the same time, rising. Surging up on energy and passion. Soaring to the apex of something big. A comet shooting across the sky, high, arcing . . .

Headed for a beautiful, shattering plunge into un-mapped territory.

Mark was pushing her to those majestic heights. His body thrusting into her. She writhed with pleasure beneath him. Her hands fisting the sheets. Toes curling in ecstasy.

"You okay?" he whispered, his voice husky and brusque with urgency. Checking in with her again. "You ready?"

"Yes, oh yes." She pushed against him. Urgent for more. Ready to share the ultimate with him.

He responded. Quickening the pace. Intensifying the pressure. Rocking into her hard and swift. The world tilted. The universe rattled. The galaxy split.

Every part of her turned electric indigo. Icy hot. Fiery cold. Dichotomy. Yin and yang. Opposites coming together to form the perfect whole.

Miraculous oneness.

Their sweaty bodies clung. Climbed. Climaxed. Crashed. She cried out his name. He groaned hers.

She had never felt so magnificent. So sexy. So much like a woman.

A final thrust. That last stroke and she cracked wide open. The deep shudder of release cleaving through the middle of her. Robbing her breath. Sapping her strength. Draining away all the tension.

She sucked in a mouthful of sheet, laughed. Sighed. Cried.

Mark made noises of his own. Male, guttural, earthy.

She grinned, feeling erotic, exotic, and powerful. She had reduced him to a quivering mass. Ha ha.

Mark fell to one side. Gathered her in his arms. Cradled her in the crook of his elbow. Kissed her cheek. Tightened his grip as if he intended on never letting go.

His face was shiny in the light from the hallway. His satisfied smile so incredibly sexy she could hardly stand it. She had just made love with this strong, gorgeous, flawed, complicated man.

And it was the best night of her entire life.

CHAPTER 28

The next morning, Naomi uncurled awake in the pre-dawn darkness. She stretched luxuriously, remembering the glorious night just past. Glanced to the other side of the bed.

Found Mark watching her, lying on his side with his hands stacked under his chin. His dark eyes aglow with what looked exactly like the happiness bubbling inside her.

He gave her a diamond-studded smile. "Morning, butterfly."

She smiled back, her heart on overflow.

"You are so beautiful." He reached out for her hands, took them in his. Brought them to his lips. Kissed each knuckle one by one.

His warm mouth on her skin sent sweet shivers up her spine. This moment was special. The morning after they first made love.

Still holding her hands, he drew her closer to him, his soft smile turning sexy and beguiling. The smile that said she was the only woman in the world for him. That charming sweet smile, that she had loved from the time she'd accidentally climbed into his Jeep.

The smile she'd seen in her kismet cookie dreams.

Kindred spirits.

Soul mates.

He kissed her, tenderly at first, then slowly deepening it.

Her body responded immediately, heating and tightening. She moaned low in her throat, desperate for him. When it came to him, she had zero self-control.

His control was pretty shaky too, because when she slid her hand down his chest to his belly and lower, he tossed back his head and let loose with a guttural sound.

He was hot and ready for her. When she touched the most masculine part of him, he shuddered and called her name. "Naomi."

Fumbling, he grabbed for the condom on the bedside table, and once he got it on, he pulled her against him and nuzzled the curve of her bare shoulder. Pressing kisses up and down her throat, while he shifted her onto her back and tenderly eased into her.

Just as they did the night before, they clung to each other, rising together to the summit of pleasure. Made for each other.

And no one else.

Afterward, they lay in each other's arms, breathless and perspiring. Filled with the joy of this special moment.

"I love you," Mark whispered, cupping her face with his palms and staring into her eyes. "I love you, Naomi Luther."

She gasped at his words, a slight sound, but distinct.

She knew he loved her. Saw it in his eyes. Felt it in his touch. But his words surprised her. She didn't expect him to say it so readily and with such heart.

He kissed her again, full of enthusiasm.

I love you, Naomi Luther.

Music to her ears. Her head swam, dizzy and delighted. She had no idea how this had happened so fast. Three weeks ago, she hadn't even known him. But she had dreamed of him a year ago, and now he'd turned her life upside down in the best possible way.

They had so much to sort out. Details to discuss.

It was thrilling and scary. This leap into the abyss of love.

Naomi dragged her mouth from his. "Mark?"

"Yes?"

"I love you too."

The corners of his mouth lifted in a hallelujah smile. She reached up to trail her fingers along his hard jaw, marveling at his handsome face. Traced his cheekbones and then his lips.

He kissed her fingertips.

She shivered. With desire. With love. With hope. So much hope.

Was she being a fool to think things would be this easy? The part of her that was afraid all this would disappear, as quickly as it came, chewed on that piece of fear.

A rich sadness crept over her. Last night, as wonderful as it had been, was over. In the past.

And the future? Well, that was pretty uncertain, wasn't it? She had no idea what last night meant in terms of going forward. Things might not work out. This had happened so fast, and she came with a ready-made family. Was this what he really wanted? Or had he just gotten carried away?

Doubts pressed into her brain, tightened her chest. Yes, she was terrified this wasn't going to work out.

But oh, how she loved him.

A tear slid down her cheek, surprising her. Her body melancholy for something she was afraid to want so desperately.

She wasn't upset. There was a special kind of beauty in the uncertainty. Her heart was open. Ready for what lay ahead. It was okay. She was okay. No matter what happened between her and Mark, she would survive this. After losing Clayton and Samantha, she could survive anything.

But she couldn't help praying for their happily-ever-after.

"Hey, hey." He brushed her tears away with this thumb. "What's wrong?"

"I . . . you . . . us." Her bottom lip trembled.

He kissed the tip of her nose, peered into her eyes until they were both cross-eyed and giggling over it. "Us," he said, and squeezed her tightly. "Can you imagine it? Us. We. You and me."

The melancholy feeling was back, settling into her bones in a new way. She wondered how growing up with the parents he grew up with had molded him. It couldn't have been easy. She admired how he had come through that upbringing with such honor and integrity. He was a rare man.

One in a million.

"I want to marry you," he said.

Her heart skipped a beat. Two. She blinked at him, stunned and giddy and scared. So scared. "Wh-what?"

"This isn't an official proposal. When the time comes, I'll do it up right. Bended knee. A ring. Ask your father for your hand in marriage. The whole shebang."

"Mark—"

"I'm just putting it out there. I think we should get married."

"I—"

"I know you've been proposed to before . . ."

Just last week. By Robert. She was having a heck of a December. Two proposals in one month.

"But I've never asked anyone to marry me before."

"I believe you." She felt a little sad about that. He'd gotten all the way to thirty without loving someone enough to want to propose to her. "But this is marriage we're talking about."

"You don't want to marry me?" He sat up, with pillows supporting his back against the headboard.

"I want to marry you very much, Mark Shepherd." She peered deeply into his eyes, cradled his cheek in her palm. "But it's not that simple."

"Why not?"

She told him then about the Christmas key. How her father and Mark's psychiatrist, Dr. Fox, had set up the whole thing. "It was all a ploy to get you to Twilight. They thought once you got here and met us that we could all start to heal."

He didn't seem upset by her revelation. She was more irritated by the manipulation than he was. His smile turned wistful. "I'm so very glad they did. If they hadn't, I would never have met you."

"It wasn't honest."

"But it did the trick."

"You should be mad. I'm mad for you."

"How can I be mad about anything that led me to you?" He drew her into his arms and she rested her head on his chest. Listened to the strong beat of his steady heart.

"Your feelings about Dr. Fox and my dad sending you on a wild-goose chase with a fake Christmas key aren't the issue."

He lowered his eyes and his voice, caressed the top of her ear with his thumb. "You're calling yourself a goose."

"Stop trying to make fun, I'm being serious here." She swirled her fingers through the small patch of dark hair between his nipples.

"Okay," he said, stroking her hair. "What *is* the issue?"

"You didn't have time to transition from the military to civilian life. You went from being discharged to showing up on our doorstep. You haven't had time to figure out what you really want."

"I want you," he said, his voice turning mulish.

"Is it because you believe in following the rules? You made love to the preacher's daughter so now you have to ask her to marry you. Is that it?"

"No! Not at all," he growled.

"Are you sure?"

"I love you, Naomi. That's why I asked you to marry me."

She thrilled to his words, but they needed to be absolutely sure this was what they both wanted. "You need time away from me. Clear your head. Get some perspective. Go back to see your psychiatrist. Find out why he thought it was necessary to play mind games with you."

He tightened his arms around her. "I don't want to go."

"Which is precisely why you should. If you marry me, you'll be an automatic daddy."

"I know that. Hunter calls me Daddy already. I love the little guy as much as I love you."

"That might be true," she said. "But you didn't have good parental role models. And you don't know how difficult raising a child is. You need to think about this before jumping in with both feet."

"I want to marry you. I want to be Hunter's father."

"This is complex stuff here, Shepherd," she said, calling him by his last name so he would know how serious she was. "Heavy-duty psychological stuff. You've fallen in love with the sister of the man whose death you feel responsible for. I want you to find out if it's truly love you're feeling for me and Hunter, versus a need to make amends."

His breathing deepened, lengthened. "That's what you want?"

She lifted her head from his chest, moved around on the bed so they were face-to-face and she could look him squarely in the eyes. "No, that's what *you* need. Time and space."

"How much time and space?"

"Let's say Christmas. You come back by Christmas, then we'll talk about getting married. If you don't come back . . ." She lifted a shoulder, steeled her jaw. "I'll understand."

"That's a week away."

"Do you need more time? We could make it New Year's Eve."

"No, no," he said. "I'm having a hard enough time imagining what I'm going to do without you for a week."

"You'll be fine."

"I won't."

"You will."

"You're worrying for nothing," he said.

"Then it shouldn't be a problem." She got out of bed and started putting on her clothes. "I need to get back home before the family gets up."

He grabbed her by the wrist and hauled her back into the bed for a long, hot farewell kiss.

"Go," she panted, pulling away. "If I see you on Christmas, then I'll know this was truly meant to be."

"And if you don't?" he said, looking worried for the first time since she insisted he leave.

A jolt of worry shook her too, but she schooled her face not to show it.

"Then know this, Mark Shepherd, wherever you go in this world, whatever you do, right here"—she drew a heart shape over her heart—"you will always be well and truly loved."

"How are you feeling?" Dr. Fox asked.

It had been two days since Naomi sent Shepherd away. He'd driven his Jeep to DFW Airport and caught a flight to Maryland, rented a car there so he wouldn't have to do all that driving. He'd been replaying the last few weeks in his head. Remembering everything about Naomi. The sound of her kind voice, the scent of her natural fragrance, the way she moved, that cheerful smile. How quickly he'd fallen in love. Was she right? Were his feelings for her somehow muddled with guilt and a sense of responsibility toward her and Hunter?

But how could a deep, abiding sense of love and rightness be wrong?

He'd gotten a motel room near Walter Reed and had managed to talk Dr. Fox's receptionist into squeezing him in for an appointment.

Shepherd glanced to the windowsill. The dying plants he'd watered when he was last in this office almost a month ago were thriving. Their leaves were shiny and green, reaching for the light. It didn't take long to turn things around. All they'd needed was attention.

"The plants look good. You started taking care of them?"

"Bought a little plant food," Dr. Fox said. "How do *you* feel?"

"About you faking me out with the Christmas key?" Shepherd raised an eyebrow.

"If that's bothering you."

"Why did you do it?" Shepherd asked, leaning against the sofa and draping his left arm over the back. "I'm sure you had a point."

"You needed a mission."

"Why the subterfuge with Pastor Luther? Why pretend Clayton left me the Christmas key?"

Dr. Fox shifted, setting his chair casters to squeaking. "You'd stopped making progress. I needed to do something to snap you out of your mistaken beliefs."

"And what beliefs are those?"

"That the world is a dangerous place, and for the most part people can't be trusted. That if you just follow the rules, you'll stay safe." Dr. Fox leaned forward, rested his palms on his thighs. He peered at Shepherd over the rim of the reading glasses perched on the end of his nose.

The man had hit the nail on the head.

Shepherd's lifelong doubts and fears distilled into a quick summary. Albeit reductive and a bit dismissive of his suffering, but Dr. Fox was right. Shepherd's childhood had been dominated by dangerous situations and parents he could not trust. The military—his salvation, with its rules, rank, and regimens—had formed the last triangle of his belief system. The Marines gave him structure. Structure gave him stability. Stability gave him peace.

Until last Christmas in Kandahar when everything he'd come to trust and depend on imploded.

"This particular set of beliefs is not uncommon in PTSS sufferers," Dr. Fox went on. "It can lead to feelings of alienation. These beliefs can arise from not having enough emotional support. It's been theorized that strongly held negative beliefs predict soldiers' vulnerability to developing post-traumatic stress symptoms following a traumatic event. It also explains why two people can go through the exact same experience, and one will develop PTSS and the other will not."

Shepherd sat there, absorbing this.

"Whereas," Dr. Fox went on, looking like a professor delivering a lecture from a podium, "an optimistic belief system can actually be a buffer against the effects of trauma."

That made a lot of sense.

"Bottom line? Pastor Tom and I felt the deception was worth the risk to get you to examine your belief system." A grin crept over Dr. Fox's face. "Then when the opportunity came up for Tom to pretend to mistake you for the handyman, he just went with it."

Shepherd curled his hands into fists. "Lying to the Luthers caused me a lot of emotional conflict. What if that had made my condition worse?"

"Tom was in contact with me. I guided him."

"Lucky coincidence," Shepherd muttered. "What if I hadn't gone along with Tom's mistaken identity ploy?"

"Sometimes it does really feel as if Jung was onto something about synchronicity."

There was more synchronicity than Dr. Fox knew—kismet cookies and Christmas Eve dreams. He wasn't going to tell the psychiatrist about that. It was too special to share.

Plus, he didn't want the man dismantling his feelings with logic. His love for Naomi was real, no matter the whimsical story behind it.

"Do you think it was bad that I didn't insist on telling Tom who I was?"

"Actually"—Dr. Fox's eyes brightened behind his glasses—"I was proud of you."

Shepherd cocked his head, confused. "For lying?"

"No." The psychiatrist sent up a self-satisfied grin. "For not following the rules. You listened to your gut instinct and rolled with the situation instead of staying stuck in the 'rule' of honesty is the best policy. I was excited for your progress."

Shepherd cocked his head, studied the doctor with a flinty gaze. "Your methods are unorthodox."

"I tailor the method to the patient. I wouldn't have used this approach with anyone else. But you needed to learn to trust yourself above any rule." Dr. Fox set his notebook down on the desk, ran two fingers over his upper lip. "Besides, it worked, didn't it?"

"I'm back for a reason."

"And why is that?"

Shepherd told him then about the situation between him and Naomi, about how they'd fallen in love in such a short time. "She thinks my feelings for her can't be real because it happened so fast."

Dr. Fox tapped his chin with his index finger. Said nothing.

"She thinks by asking her to marry me I'm just following the rules. In other words, I made love to her, now I have to marry her."

"Are you?"

"No."

"Are you sure?"

Shepherd scowled. "Absolutely."

"How can you be sure?" Dr. Fox's gaze turned cagey.

"How can anyone be sure of anything?" Shepherd hardened his chin.

Dr. Fox lifted his shoulders and his hands in a no-one-can-know gesture. Well, that was unhelpful.

"So I'm supposed to spend the rest of my life measuring my decisions on whether I'm following the rules or not?"

"No," Dr. Fox said. "You're supposed to learn how to trust your gut so implicitly that acting on it becomes second nature."

"Is that what you do?"

The psychiatrist grinned. "How do you think you ended up with a Christmas key in your pocket?"

Irritation burned his nape. "How do I get to the place where I instinctively know when I should break the rules and when I should adhere to them?"

Dr. Fox spread his fingers wide, pressed the fingertips of his hands together. Rested his index fingers against his lips. "When you finally drill down to the source of your beliefs and start unraveling them."

"Meaning?"

"Confront your mother."

Shepherd's blood ran cold. He hadn't seen his mother since she received a twenty-five-year sentence for armed robbery when he was twelve. "Is that really what it takes?"

"How much resistance are you feeling to the idea?"

"One hundred percent."

Dr. Fox leveled him a hard stare. "What we resist persists."

"More Jung?"

"What can I say?" Dr. Fox cracked open a smile. "I'm a fan."

The idea of facing his mother soured his stomach, but in his heart Shepherd knew the psychiatrist was right. He'd closed the door on that part of his life, but his relationship with his mother remained unresolved.

Maybe visiting her in prison was exactly what he needed to really put the past to rest so he could move on into a whole new life with Naomi.

"I've given it some thought," he told Dr. Fox.

The psychiatrist nodded and they talked for a little while longer before ending the session. "You've made amazing progress in less than a month," Dr. Fox said. "I'm impressed."

It was all because of Naomi, and Dr. Fox and Pastor Tom's little manipulative ploy that got him to her. He held no grudges. He could feel the effects of posttraumatic stress slipping away. Dr. Fox was right. He had one last thing to do before he could let go of his past completely.

Confront his mother.

He left the psychiatrist's office feeling both elevated and anxious. Limped out into the lobby. Saw a familiar face waiting in reception.

It was the red-haired private. Dressed in blue jeans, a

bright green shirt, and a brown bomber jacket. Calmly whittling. And smiling.

An inexplicable sense of joy seized Shepherd. Expanded his heart.

The kid looked transformed. His eyes were bright. His skin was clear. He radiated self-confidence.

What a change.

"Gunny!" The kid leaped to his feet, embraced Shepherd in a bear hug.

"Hey."

The kid stepped back, eyed Shepherd up and down. "You're looking good."

"I could say the same about you."

"No cane?"

"I need it less and less."

"That's awesome."

"You look happy," Shepherd said. "What happened?"

The kid met his eyes. "You."

"Me?"

"That day we met and you gave me the knife and the wood." The kid shook his head. "Who knew whittling was exactly what I needed?"

"I'm glad it helped."

The kid picked up the wooden soldier he'd been carving. "I'm making this for my nephew for Christmas."

Shepherd turned the carving in his hand. "Wow, that's really good."

"Turns out I'm a natural. Who knew?" The kid's eyes glowed with inner excitement.

"How are the nightmares?" he asked, handing the toy soldier back to the private.

"Few and far between." The kid's smile was radiant. "I think I'm gonna be okay."

"I know you are." He chucked the kid on his shoulder.

The receptionist nodded at the kid. "You can go in now."

The kid picked up his belongings. "Have a merry Christmas."

"You too," Shepherd said, and headed for the door.

"Gunny," the kid called out.

Shepherd stopped, turned. "Yes?"

"You're gonna be okay too."

Shepherd smiled and walked out, praying that the kid was right. He wouldn't know for sure until he did the thing he'd been avoiding for eighteen years. Don his emotional armor and go into battle with his past. And end his mother's influence over him once and for all.

Then he could return to Naomi unfettered and ready to accept her love.

CHAPTER 29

At eight o'clock on Christmas Eve morning, Shepherd limped up the steps to the assisted-living facility in Lexington, Kentucky.

He'd driven the rental car from Maryland to Kentucky, needing time to collect his thoughts. He'd driven past the old places where he used to live. Visited one of his foster families who were still in town. He'd kept up with them through Christmas cards and friendships on social media. They welcomed him with open arms. Reminded him how he had his own moral compass separate from his parents. How he'd carved his own way in the world. They sounded proud of him. And he saw himself through the lens of a different perspective.

The takeaway, added to what he'd learned from his session with Dr. Fox, was that because he'd grown up in such a chaotic situation, he'd developed a hypervigilant need for safety and security.

His foster mother told stories of how he would get out of bed at night to double-check that all the doors were locked. Recalled how he had driven her berserk with a dozen what-if questions during disaster drills. Mentioned how suspicious he'd been of strangers. Constantly questioning motives. But once he finally trusted someone, he was intensely loyal. They were his friends for life.

Given his pattern, was it any wonder he'd become such a rule follower? That he'd gravitated toward the military—a structure that fed community, loyalty, and adherence to hierarchy?

The only problem with all that?

Just as Dr. Fox had said, he hadn't developed the ability to trust his gut and common sense over the rules.

On the front lawn of the assisted-living facility, someone had built a family of snowmen. A resident? he wondered. Or visiting family members? Maybe the staff?

Papa Snowman sported a corncob pipe beneath his carrot nose and hairbrush mustache. Mama Snowman had a red-and-green-checkered bandana tied around her head. And Baby Snowman had a pacifier as a mouth.

Whimsical. Cute.

Too bad his mood was anything but.

Shepherd's gut was a churn, sloshing emotions thick as butter. For the first time in eighteen years he would see his mother.

He barely remembered her. He was five when she went to prison the first time. She'd spent a year inside that time for identity theft. She'd been in and out on a revolving door of prison sentences throughout his childhood—six months for writing hot checks, ten months for shoplifting, three years for credit card scams.

He recalled her scent—cigarettes and hairspray. And that she loved Starburst candy. She usually carried some in her pocket, and if he was good, she'd give him one. Usually, it was the orange flavor because they were her least favorite.

Inside, the building was blazing hot. The furnace

hummed loudly enough to be heard above the TV in the main room tuned to the DIY Network. On the screen, a picky young couple were turning their noses up at a kitchen because it didn't have granite countertops.

Several residents were ringed around the TV in wheelchairs. Sheets were tied around their waists like seat belts. Most of them were asleep. A Christmas tree stood in the front window. Halfheartedly decorated with sparse ornaments and minimal strands of multicolored twinkle lights. The place smelled of citrus-scented antiseptic plied over the underlying odor of urine, burned oatmeal, and hopelessness.

Shepherd gulped.

A woman in her mid-forties sat at a computer desk in the living room area. She stopped keyboarding and glanced up. She wore hospital scrubs. Her name tag said: "Angela Barton L.P.N." She offered him an efficient smile. "May I help you?"

"I'm looking for Virginia Shepherd."

She studied him a moment, her gaze lingering on his cane. Nodded. "She's in the south wing. Go through those double doors." She motioned toward the back of the room. "And across the courtyard. She's in apartment 4B."

"Thank you."

"I'm glad to see she's got a visitor," the nurse said. "I've been here for two years, and in all that time, Virginia's never once had a visitor."

There was a reason for that.

"She doesn't have much family," he explained. "And what she does have she alienated a long time ago."

"Her chart says she had a son," Angela's voice softened. "But no one knows anything about him."

Yeah, there was a reason for that too.

"I'm glad you came to visit her," Angela went on. "She's having a good day."

His throat closed off and he couldn't even say thank you. He nodded and followed Angela's directions to apartment 4B.

For the longest moment, he stood at the front door. Working up the courage to knock. Now that he was here, he had no idea what he was going to say to her.

Before he could raise his fist and rap on the door, it opened and a young dark-haired woman emerged. Her badge identified her as Lola Lopez, a social worker.

"Oh." Her eyes widened in surprise. "You're here to visit Virginia?"

"Yes."

"And you are . . ."

"Her son."

"Oh," Lola said again and then, "oh my."

"What does that mean?" Shepherd asked.

"I . . . well . . . we . . . that is, I, and the rest of the staff"—she waved her hand in a general, inclusive way—"hoped this day would finally come before Virginia lost her memory completely."

"She's got Alzheimer's," he said, repeating what he'd learned when he'd called the prison system and discovered she'd been released two years earlier. "That's why she's out of prison early."

"Yes." Lola's fading smile looked as if she was about to offer him tea and sympathy. "Compassionate release. That plus prison overcrowding."

Shepherd knuckled up on the cane.

"She's in a good place today, but there's one thing you need to know about relating to someone with advanced dementia."

"What's that?"

She leveled him a serious stare. "We avoid confronting them with the truth."

"You mean lie to her?"

"The preferred method is distraction. Get the patient interested in something else. Usually, they easily forget what you were talking about."

"And if that doesn't work?"

"We enter their reality."

"In other words, lie."

"Bend the truth."

"You're saying don't bring up the fact that she was a horrible mother, and a miserable human being." He said it matter-of-factly. It was the truth and he wasn't feeling bitter or resentful. If anything, he just felt sad.

"I'm saying there's a reason she was released. Have compassion." Lola's eyes were full of empathy, as if she'd been down a similar road.

"You want me to lie to her, and forgive her?"

"Isn't that why you're here?"

Was it?

Lola stepped to one side. "Come on in, I'll introduce you to her. Your name is . . ."

"Mark," he said, his voice scraping against the back of his throat.

"So glad you're here. What a lovely present." Lola clapped her hands, a short, quick gesture of approval. "Come in, come in, and merry Christmas to you."

"Merry Christmas to you too," he mumbled, feeling out of step and out of place. But who would feel comfortable and relaxed in a situation like this?

"She's in the living room." Lola ushered him into the apartment that was no larger than four hundred square feet. Small living room and a kitchen he could see from the doorway when he walked in. Simply furnished. Functional. Clean.

It reminded him of the military.

"Virginia," Lola said. "You have a visitor."

The woman sitting on the plain brown couch turned to him. She was only fifty-seven, but she looked at least ten years older. Her hair was short and silvery gray. Her face lined with wrinkles. The TV in front of her was on. It was the same DIY program. The picky young couple had progressed to the backyard. This time they were bemoaning how much work it would take to keep up the big lawn.

"Who are you?" his mother blurted, her eyes narrowing suspiciously. He remembered that look.

"Virginia," Lola said, her voice soft and careful. "This is Mark."

His mother's eyes took on a dreamy expression, as if she'd drifted off into the past. "Mark? I once had a son named Mark."

Lola's gaze met Shepherd's and she made a motion that said, *I'm just going to go*, and she slipped out the door.

Leaving him alone with the woman who'd left him so many years ago.

Pulse quickening, Shepherd approached. He sat down in the chair across from her. They would be on eye level, and he could rest his knee.

"Tell me about your son," he said, surprised. He had no idea he was going to say that.

Her eyes grew misty, tears glistening. "I lost him a long time ago."

"What happened to him?" Was it cruel? Not telling

her that he was her son? He held back because just blurting it out seemed too jolting. He remembered what Lola had said. Go against the traditional rule of always telling the truth. Here the rules were topsy-turvy. Bending the truth was not only acceptable, but encouraged.

His mother was so frail, her body thin, face gaunt. Whatever she'd done in her life, it had taken its toll. "I . . . went to jail and he went . . . somewhere." One tear rolled down her cheek. "I loved him so much. But I was not a good mama."

"I'm sure you did the best you could." He shocked himself with that. Where was all the resentment and blame he'd harbored for so long? He reached down inside, trying to find it. Came up with nothing.

"I did." She nodded. "But it was not good enough." She sat up straighter. Stared him in the eyes. "Do you have children?"

He thought about Hunter, and his gut twisted. "I'm in love with a woman who has a son."

She considered him with a long, measured expression. "It's not the same. Not unless you marry her, and adopt the boy. When you're a parent, then you'll understand."

For the first time since coming to Lexington, a flash of anger passed through him. "Understand what?"

"The things you'll do for your kids."

He almost laughed in her face over that one. "What did *you* do for your son?"

She looked at him, puzzled. "Do you know my son?"

"Yes," he said. "I do."

Her eyes rounded and she brought her hands to her mouth and made a small noise of despair, and in that moment, Shepherd was certain that she recognized him.

"Do I know you?"

"My name's Mark Shepherd."

"Mark." Her eyes lost their clarity, went foggy again. "I had a son named Mark."

He let out his breath through clenched teeth. There would be no resolution here. He did not know what he'd come here seeking from her. An apology? He wasn't going to get that.

"Would you walk with me in the garden, Mark?"

"It's cold outside."

"I have a good winter coat."

Why not? Moving was preferable to sitting here in this cramped little room with the woman who'd given birth to him, but had never been a real mother.

"I'll get your coat for you," he said. "Where is it?"

Her smile brightened her weathered face. "In my bedroom closet."

He levered himself off the couch with his cane, ambled into the bedroom. It was clean and plain in here as well, not many personal items—a red knitted blanket thrown across the foot of the bed, a pair of black ballet slippers, a small framed photo on the bedside table.

Shepherd hadn't intended on snooping, but the photograph drew his attention. He stepped closer to her bed. Picked up the photograph.

It was a faded Polaroid of a child—a little boy wearing a baseball cap and high-top sneakers. The moisture left his mouth and his heart careened into his chest. It was a picture of him when he was four or five. One of the last pictures taken of him when he lived with both parents. In the photograph, he was eating an ice cream cone, sitting on the back porch of the little house they'd rented on Vine Street. Chocolate. His little face was smeared with it, but the kid looked happy.

He looked *happy*.

Shepherd remembered his childhood as a dark, dreary existence. Something to escape from. Something to forget. Something to strive to get beyond. His childhood had not been a happy one. But here was cold, hard evidence that there had been happy moments.

"That's my favorite picture of you," his mother said from the doorway.

He put the picture down on the bedside table, turned to look at her. "Mom?"

"It is you, isn't it?" she said, her voice high and breathless.

"Yes."

She rushed across the room, stood in front of him in the dim gray light seeping through the open curtains. "Mark."

"Mom," he repeated, everything in his body clamped down like a vise. His stomach. His throat. His heart.

They stared at each other. His thoughts were a restless tornado, dark, fast, and hard to track.

"You found me," she said.

"Yes." It was all he could manage. His stance was rigid. He held the cane in front of him. A flimsy shield.

She dropped to her knees. Wrapped her arms around his legs. Tilted her head back to look up at him. "Please forgive me," she begged. "Please, please."

A roil of pain and grief knotted up in his gut. Spread through his veins like a poison. Infecting him with unexpected thoughts. He felt deeply sorry for her. For all the wrong decisions she'd made. The wrong turns she'd taken. She'd wrecked her own life far more than she'd wrecked his.

"C'mon," he said gently. Took her under the arm and eased her to her feet. "It's okay."

"*Please forgive me. Please forgive me. Please forgive me.*" She didn't say for what. She didn't have to. He knew and she understood that he knew.

"I forgive you," he said. Suddenly feeling as if his heart—which had been tied in cable wire and dropped with an anchor into the middle of the ocean—had been cut free. He was a buoy on the water. Bouncy and resilient. Then he said it again. "I forgive you."

She looked at him and he could see the confusion stealing over her once more. A blank expression in her eyes. Confusion. Fear. A bucket load of fear.

"Who are you?" she cried.

Quick as a finger snap, she'd lost her perch on reality.

"I'm Mark," he said patiently, drawing on a reserve of strength he thought he'd lost forever outside that orphanage in Kandahar.

"Mark," she said. "I had a son named Mark."

"I know." He smiled kindly and took her hand. "You told me."

"That's his picture." She pointed to the Polaroid. "He was a very happy boy."

"I can see that. Here," he said. "Let's get your coat. I'll walk with you in the garden and you can tell me all about him."

"Oh, would you?" She clapped her hands like a child. "That would be so very nice. Thank you, thank you."

Mark took his mother's hand, and with forgiveness swelling in his broken heart, helped her on with her coat and led her outside.

CHAPTER 30

Shepherd had no more gotten back into the rental car than his cell phone rang.

"Where are you?" It was Nate Deavers.

"Kentucky."

"What! You're supposed to be here at five to stuff yourself into a Santa suit, and give out presents. Were you planning on letting us down, Shepherd? Don't let us down."

"Relax," Shepherd said. "I have a plane ticket. My Jeep is in the parking lot at DFW. My flight touches down at three. I'll be there in time."

"Whew. You're a good man. When I heard from Naomi that you'd left town, gotta tell you, I was ready to track you down and strangle the life out of you."

"Good to know our support group leader is homicidal."

Our support group leader. Nate said it as if he were part of the Twilight community. He was. Or he could be. If he wanted. All he had to do was claim it.

"How are you?" Nate asked.

"I'm coming home," Shepherd said. "What do you think?"

"Get your ass back here," Nate said. "And all will be well."

Shepherd grinned, and for the first time in his life, he truly believed that. "Do me a favor, will you?"

"What is it?"

"Don't tell Naomi I'm back in town."

"You want to surprise her?"

"Something like that."

"You need a place to stay?"

"You offering?"

"I am. What are you waiting for?"

With that invitation, Shepherd shut off his phone, started the car, and headed to the airport.

On Christmas Day, the Luthers' house was filled with people. Parishioners. Neighbors. Friends. Family.

Food and conversation flowed.

Naomi bustled about, happy to be of use, happy to have something to take her mind off Shepherd. Or the lack thereof. She hadn't heard a peep from him since she'd sent him away.

She topped off drinks, turned down the thermostat as the fire in the fireplace, and the crowd, overheated the room. Refreshed the canapés tray and did the dishes.

And tried not to dwell on the fact that Shepherd was gone and she had no idea if he would ever come back.

And she'd been the one to send him away. Telling him that she couldn't be with him until he learned to trust himself. Why had she done that?

It was for the best, she told herself. She had too much on her plate for a relationship. Adopting Hunter. Running her business. Helping her mother.

But surely he wasn't going to let Christmas Day go by without at least calling and telling her what he'd decided.

A knock sounded at the front door, and she flew to throw it open. Smile on her face. Pulse strumming. Hopes lifted.

Her best friend, Jana, stood on the porch, presents in her arms. Wearing a tall green steampunk hat with mistletoe dangling from the brim.

"Oh," Naomi said. "It's you."

"Well, merry Christmas to you too," Jana said, and thrust the packages at her.

"Sorry," Naomi apologized. "Didn't mean that the way it sounded. How's your mom?"

"Her recovery is going great. She'll be out of the rehab hospital next week. I celebrated with her this morning, then got on the road to come home to see how this thing between you and Shepherd works out."

Naomi had been texting with Jana every single day since Mark left.

Jana studied her face. "Shepherd hasn't shown up," she guessed.

"No." Naomi clutched the packages to her chest. Wished that Jana did not know her so well.

Jana made a *tsk-tsk* noise. Took off her coat and hung it on the rack in the foyer. The mistletoe in front of her face bounced jauntily.

"What's this all about?" Naomi flicked the mistletoe.

"I'm tired of leaving fate up to those damn kismet cookies," she said. "Come hell or high water, I'm getting kissed today."

"Jasper Winters is sitting in the rocker in front of the fireplace," Naomi teased, referring to the church's oldest parishioner. Jasper was pushing one hundred, but still had an eye for the ladies. "I'm sure he'd be up for it."

"Shut your face," Jana quipped. "You're just being tacky because you don't have a boyfriend either. Finally, we're in the same boat."

"I have a boyfriend," Naomi said, feeling a bit defensive. She'd had sex with Mark. He'd wanted to marry her. But in the face of no communication from him on the holiest of holidays, it was an empty claim.

"I know. And *you*, foolish woman, sent him packing."

"I had to," Naomi said. "He had a lot to think about."

But just as she said it, she realized something monumental. She'd sent Mark away not just so he could have time out to think, but so that she could too. Because she truly did have a lot to consider before she jumped into a relationship. Namely, that for her entire life she'd put on a happy face whenever things got challenging and pretended that nothing was wrong. Not so much because she was afraid to face her heavier feelings, but because in the caretaker role she'd assumed, she tried to keep her loved ones from suffering.

She had to stop taking on everyone else's pain and let them work through their issues on their own. Sending Mark away had meant great progress on her part. In the past, she would have smoothed over the lump of dirt beneath the rug and pretended it wasn't there. This time, she'd thrown back the rug so they both could examine and clear out what was under there.

But what if he didn't return?

He had been important to her from the moment she jumped into his Jeep and he called her butterfly.

Jana leaned over to give Naomi's arm a comforting squeeze. "Did you sleep with a kismet cookie under your pillow last night?"

"Did you?" Naomi said, evading the question.

"I did." Jana lowered her eyes.

"And?"

"There's a reason I climbed the live oak in my back-yard this morning and snipped some mistletoe off the branches."

"Really?" Naomi linked her arm through Jana's and drew her down the hallway and into her bedroom. "Who invaded your dreams last night?"

Jana slanted her gaze to the floor and smiled. "Wouldn't you like to know?"

"Someone here? At the party?"

Jana bobbed her head, sent the mistletoe dancing.

"What! Tell me more."

"Not until you tell me who *you* dreamed about last night."

Naomi shrugged, felt a leaden ball of sadness settle in her throat. "Mark. He's the one. He'll always be the one. But Jana, what if he doesn't come back?"

Jana sank down on the end of Naomi's bed. "He'll come back."

"I'm not so sure."

"If he's *the one*, he'll be back."

"I wish I had your confidence. I told him not to come back until he can forgive himself for Clayton's death. But that was before we . . . well, you know."

"Maybe he hasn't forgiven himself."

"Maybe he hasn't. Maybe he can't. Maybe . . ." And this was what she feared most. "Mark doesn't love me the way I love him."

Jana snorted. "The man is crazy for you."

"You think?"

"I know."

The doorbell rang.

"Honey," her mother called out from the living room. "Can you get that?"

"Could be him," Jana said.

Naomi jumped up. Raced for the door.

It was Samantha's parents. They were there to pick up Hunter for their turn. She had his things ready. Kissed him good-bye. He was excited to see his other grandparents and barely waved at her as they carried him off to their car.

Naomi stood on the front porch. Shivering in the cold. Watching them drive away.

"I can guarantee that little man will be back." Jana slung an arm over Naomi's shoulder. "And he's the *real* love of your life."

Naomi sighed. Jana had a point. No matter what happened with Mark. She was Hunter's mother now, and the boy was indeed her heart and soul.

That was enough.

It had to be.

"You sure you don't want to come to evening Christmas services with us?" her father asked. Irene sat at the door, swaddled in warm clothing, ready to propel her wheelchair two doors down to the church.

"I'm exhausted, Dad." That was true enough. But the real reason she didn't want to go was that the optimist in her held out hope she might still hear from Mark. "And with Hunter out of the house, this is my chance for a nap."

"Okay, sunshine." Her father kissed her forehead. "You get some rest."

She watched them leave, her heart heavy.

Instead of napping, she went into the kitchen and

started cleaning up. Christmas music played from the kitchen speakers. "Silent Night."

Naomi snorted. Yep, Mark was silent all right.

But honestly, when she compared it to last year? This was a piece of cake. This time last year, the doorbell had rung and they'd opened it to find two Marines standing there. Samantha had started screaming before the men uttered a word.

Blinking back her grief, Naomi sighed and scrubbed the pan she was cleaning extra hard. *Don't think, don't think, don't think.*

The doorbell rang.

For a surreal moment, she thought she'd been jettisoned a year back in time, and they were about to get the terrible news about Clayton all over again.

But the house was empty. She was home alone.

She dropped the scouring pad and pan. Dried her hands off on a dishtowel. Went to the door.

Mark stood on the front porch steps, a woolen cap on his head. His cane in his hand. Snowflakes drifting down around him. "May I come in?"

Her heart was a racecar piston, running fast and hot. Naomi stepped aside. Waved him in. "Please."

That smile was all she needed to know that she'd made the right choice.

He limped inside. His grin grew wider the closer he got. Genuine happiness was on his endearing face that she'd missed so much.

Dusting off his boots on the welcome mat, Mark stopped a few feet away. Watching her as if wanting to make sure she wasn't punking him before he came closer.

"Hi," he said, his eyes searching hers.

"Hey."

"Why aren't you in church? I went to the church first. I thought you'd be there. You weren't there." He was nervous. Talking too much. It was sweet, really.

"It's the first anniversary of Clayton's death." She waved a hand in the direction of her father's church. "I needed some time to myself."

"To mourn?"

She nodded. "The grief doesn't stop. You just learn how to live with it. Have you learned how to live with it, Mark?"

"I'm working on it," he confessed. "I'm a work in progress."

"That's all that matters. We're all works in progress."

An awkward silence fell like a black velvet curtain between them.

"You came back," she said.

"I had to. I'd promised Nate I'd hand out gifts to needy kids."

Disappointment scooped her insides out. He hadn't come back for her after all. "I'd forgotten about that."

"I don't break my promises," he said. "Not if I can help it."

"One of the things I like about you."

"What else do you like about me?" His eyes twinkled.

"Fishing for compliments?"

"I'll take what I can get."

"Your sense of divine timing," she said, "is impeccable. Hunter's with his other grandparents, and Mom and Dad are at church."

"So we're home alone."

"For an hour or so."

"Hmm," he said, moving closer. "Hmm."

"What's the humming all about? You sound like a bee."

"You're the butterfly, I'm the bee," he said.

"Where have you been?" she said. "Why didn't you call or text me? I dumped one boyfriend because he didn't call or text me regularly."

"Is that a threat?"

"It's a promise." She grinned and he grinned right back.

"You called me your boyfriend," he said.

"I didn't."

"You did. In a roundabout way, but you said it."

"I implied it. Not the same thing."

"It's the same thing."

"It's not, but I'll let it go. We have the house to ourselves, but there's a ticking clock . . ."

"Got it," he said. "Time's a-wasting."

With a song in her heart, she took him by the hand and led him to her bedroom.

Fifteen minutes later, sated and satisfied, they lay snuggled together.

Shepherd's long, lonely journey ended here. In Naomi's bedroom. In her arms. He closed his eyes. Absorbed her warmth. Fed off the glow of her unconditional love.

He took her into his arms, folding her close to his chest. His heart leaped with happiness.

"Where did you go when you left here?" she whispered. Lightly peppering his chin with quick, sweet kisses.

"First to see Dr. Fox."

"Got things sorted out?"

"I did."

"Where did you go after that?"

"Kentucky."

"Back to the beginning."

"Yes."

"What did you find there?"

"My mother. They let her out of prison early. Compassionate release."

Naomi froze in mid-kiss. "Oh, Mark. Do you want to talk about it?"

He didn't, not really. But he needed to talk about it. So he did, detailing for Naomi what had happened in that assisted-living facility in Kentucky.

"I'm so sorry." She squeezed his hand. "I can't imagine how hard that must have been."

"I want to move her," he said. "I want to bring her to an Alzheimer's facility here."

"To Twilight?"

"Yes."

"Why . . . why?"

"Because I'm moving here. I'm hoping to make Twilight my home." He took her chin, turned her face in his direction. "It all depends on one thing."

"What's that?"

He got out of bed, put on his jeans, pulled a ring box from his pocket, got down on one knee. "Naomi Luther, will you marry me?"

"What?" Naomi sat up. Sheet clutched around her bare breasts.

"I love you, Naomi. This week away from you showed me just how much. I can't imagine my life without you and Hunter in it."

"Oh, Mark," she cried. "I love you too!"

"Is that a yes?"

"Yes, yes."

He slipped the ring on her finger and she flung herself into his arms so forcefully, she knocked him onto his back. She was straddling him, eyes misty with happy tears.

"I want you more than I've wanted anything in my life and I want to be a real father to Hunter."

"I know Clayton would approve," she said. "If he can't be here to raise his son, this is the next best thing. I also know that Clayton doesn't blame you for the way things turned out. He was the most forgiving person I ever knew."

Briefly, Shepherd closed his eyes. He exhaled, opened his eyes, and tugged her against his chest. "I hated being away from you."

"Shh, shh. We had to fall apart to find our way back to each other." She stroked his cheek. Her soft fingertips like velvet against his day's growth of scratchy beard. "It's part of the process, I'm learning. My family was shattered after Clayton's death." She hitched in her breath. "But so were you."

Tears pushed at the corners of his eyes. No. He needed to be strong. For her.

She cupped his face in her hands. "It's okay to fall apart. Not just okay, but necessary. *You* taught me that."

"Naomi."

"Cry. Grieve." She kissed his forehead. "Grieve for your mother. For your father. For your lost childhood. For the terrible things you've seen in war. Let it all go."

A tear slipped down his cheek. Hot and slender. Ran down his face. Hit his chin with a hot plop.

He'd tried so desperately to build a foundation in the military. Had followed the rules. Had believed it was the answer to what he'd spent his life searching for. In his effort to find roots and anchor himself, he'd clung to the "rules," thinking that could save him.

What he had failed to see until he learned to be in the present moment with Naomi was that he was *already* saved. Everything was within reach. All he'd had to do was stand still and accept it.

The Christmas key had brought him here. That key held the answer to their transformation. Through coming here and finding Naomi, Shepherd understood that he was not responsible for the actions of the men who'd murdered Clayton.

He'd followed orders, done the best he could do. No one blamed him. It was time he stopped blaming himself for circumstances beyond his control.

Naomi looked at him, tears running down her face, not even trying to staunch them. He smiled at her. Proud of her.

"Look what you've done to me," she sobbed. "You've unleashed *all* my emotions." She smiled at him through the tears. "Thank you for that."

Tenderly, he cupped her cheek. Kissed her lightly.

Life was complex and bittersweet. Filled with joy and sorrow. Laughter and tears. It was all part of the great, messy mystery.

That Christmas key had given them the most precious gift of all.

Love.

EPILOGUE

"Mom, Dad, wake up, wake up, Santa's been here!" Hunter danced around their bed, whirling like a little dervish.

"It's five DIP ." Naomi groaned, covering her head with a pillow.

"You sleep a bit longer," Shepherd said, leaning over to place a gentle hand over her rounded belly. "I'll put the coffee on."

"Decaf for me."

"I remember." He kissed her gently, then took Hunter's hand and led him from the bedroom. "Let's go make pancakes for Mommy and then we'll open presents."

"Aw man," Hunter said, but went along with him.

Pastor Tom had married them on Valentine's Day, with their friends and family in attendance. Hunter had been ring bearer and Jana the maid of honor. Shepherd had even brought his mother to the ceremony. While she'd been confused about what was going on, she had been in a pleasant mood. He'd gotten permission to move her into an Alzheimer's facility in Twilight, and he visited her twice a week.

Even Robert had come to the wedding with his new girlfriend, and Naomi had been thrilled to see them so happy. Robert wasn't the one for her, but he had been a big part of her life for a long time and she wished him all the best.

Shepherd had gone to work for Hutch, who had a business making custom cabinetry, putting his woodworking skills to good use. They'd bought a house one block over from Naomi's parents, making the down payment with money Shepherd had saved as a single man in the military. In the sunroom, they'd retiled the floor, inserting into the tile the mosaic they'd made of Clayton that night in the bowling alley. Cementing him into their hearts and minds forever.

Naomi's adoption of Hunter was finalized in April. Then Shepherd put in the paperwork to adopt him as well, and in September, Hunter had officially become his son. But in Shepherd's heart, the boy had been his from the moment he'd wrapped his arms around Shepherd's legs in the Luthers' kitchen and called him Daddy.

And now, a new little bundle of joy was on the way. Samuel Clayton Shepherd, named in honor of his aunt and uncle, was due to be born at the end of April.

Shepherd couldn't wait. His heart was full. By coming to Twilight, he'd gained not only a wife and children, but a thriving, loving community of friends and neighbors.

And by facing his past, and the misguided beliefs that sprang from his childhood, he'd learned how to trust his instincts. He'd been able to find peace with his mother and balance in his life.

"Dad," Hunter said, coming into the kitchen holding a brightly wrapped package to his ear and shaking it. "Can you wrap up a puppy?" The boy had talked nonstop about wanting a dog for Christmas. They'd led him to believe he wasn't getting one.

"Hunter," Shepherd said, not wanting to spoil the surprise waiting for him in the garage. "You know that you can't."

"Aw man." He looked disappointed.

Shepherd suppressed a smile.

Yawning, Naomi shuffled into the room in her bathrobe and slippers. Her hair was mussed, sleep creases on her cheek. She looked absolutely adorable.

Shepherd pulled her to him, kissed her long and soft. Then handed her a cup of decaf coffee and one of the banana nut muffins that Terri Longoria had brought over the day before. "Morning, butterfly."

"You ready for this?" she asked, smiling at him over the rim of her mug.

"Got fresh batteries in the camera." He picked up the camera on the counter.

Hunter was bouncing around, popping in and out of the kitchen, bringing and shaking a different package every time he reappeared. "Can I open them now? Canna, canna, canna?"

Naomi ruffled his hair. "Lead the way."

"Yay!" Hunter bunny-hopped into the living room ahead of them.

Shepherd slipped his arm around Naomi as they entered the room. His gaze landed on the beautiful Christmas tree that he and Hunter had erected together. This year, instead of the usual ornaments, they decorated the tree entirely in white skeleton keys hung with red velvet ribbons.

It painted a striking picture. A hundred white keys honoring their love.

They sat on the couch, watching Hunter open his presents. Shepherd filming as he tore into them, one after another. It seemed he was on the search for that one special present. When he'd gone through all the gifts, Hunter turned to his parents, his bottom lip pooched out in a pout.

"Something wrong, son?" Shepherd asked.

"I didn't get a dog." Hunter blinked rapidly. "I wanted a dog."

Naomi called the boy over, whispered in his ear. "Go look in the garage."

Hunter's eyes widened and a sweet grin overtook his face. He darted to the garage. Shepherd and Naomi got up to follow him.

Hunter threw open the door, dropped to his knees at the sight of the golden retriever puppy. "C'mon 'ere, boy."

The puppy flung himself into Hunter's arms, licked his laughing face.

"Mom, Dad," Hunter gasped between helpless giggles. "Thank you, thank you. This is the best Christmas ever!"

While Hunter romped with the puppy, Shepherd tugged Naomi into his arms for a long, soulful kiss.

She took his hand and placed it on her belly, and for the first time, he felt their son growing inside her kick.

"Oh!" he exclaimed, feeling as wide-eyed as Hunter did when he spied the dog.

"Yes." She smiled and rested her head on his shoulder.

Standing there with all the dreams of his life coming true, Shepherd sent up a prayer of heartfelt gratitude.

For this was indeed the best Christmas ever.

**And now a sneak peek to Lori Wilde's upcoming
Avon Books release, coming in spring 2019!**

TO TAME A WILD COWBOY

Available soon at your favorite bookseller!

CHAPTER 1

Mrs. Bean's white nondescript sedan pulled up outside the duplex. Followed shortly by a familiar bronze Ford King Ranch one-ton dually pickup truck.

Distressed, Tara stood at the living room window, arms wrapped securely around Julie. Her heart skipping crazily.

This was it. The moment she'd been dreading since she'd learned who the baby's father was. Mom, Kaia, and Aria had offered to be here for the showdown, but this was Tara's battle. She needed to fight it alone. At least for now.

Afterward, her family could help her pick up the pieces.

Always a good hostess, she had set out a teapot and coffee carafe on the coffee table, along with finger sandwiches and scones. At the last minute, she'd bought pink strawberry wafer cookies because she remembered that they were Rhett's favorite. As if this were some kind of silly garden party instead of a serious meeting that could end all her hopes and dreams for the future.

Mrs. Bean got out of her car. She wore a strange little pillbox hat over the top of her bun, a beige suit dress, low-heeled pumps, and a strand of pearls, looking as if she'd raided the Jackie O collection of a vintage clothing store. Her outfit added to the surreal quality.

But it was the man stepping from the expensive pickup truck that drew Tara's attention.

His hair was the color of aged whiskey, private select, and on the sexy side of shaggy. He wore a straw Stetson cocked rakishly to the left. His heavily starched jeans clung tight to his muscular thighs, and a gold rodeo belt buckle glistened in the afternoon sun like the Holy Grail.

He walked with a lanky roll, his hips lean and loose. A leisurely stroll that said, *I've got all the time in the world for you, babe.* Tara understood why women fell over themselves to get next to Rhett Lockhart. He possessed that undeniable *something*.

Tara steeled herself. Denying it. Denying him.

That bowl-'em-over charm didn't work on her. She knew all his mischievous tricks. She'd been the baby-sitter standing outside his bedroom window, fourteen to his ten. Arms crossed over her chest, catching her impish charge as he slipped to the ground, incorrigible and unrepentant. Even then. Now, eighteen years later, she was foster mother to his infant daughter.

Fate was a fickle wench.

Mrs. Bean crossed over the lawn to speak to him, holding out her hand, tote bag hoisted up on her shoulder. He shook the woman's hand, but his eyes stayed trained on Tara's front door.

Instinctively, Tara clutched Julie closer.

Rhett and Mrs. Bean turned, moved up the sidewalk in lockstep. They cut an uneven picture. Five-foot Mrs. Bean in her Jackie O duds, placing a hand on her pillbox hat to hold it in place against the wind. Five-foot-eleven-inch Rhett, sporting designer boots, sweeping off his Stetson, and resting it against his chest by the crown.

The closer they drew, the harder Tara's heart pounded.

Julie squirmed, made a soft mewling sound. Tara hitched her higher, kissed the baby's cheek. "It's going to be okay, sweetheart. You're about to meet your daddy."

This was a good thing, Tara tried to tell herself, the best thing for Julie. Every girl deserved to know her daddy.

But what if Rhett wanted custody?

Tears clogged Tara's throat. Maybe he wouldn't want the baby. Maybe he would understand he wasn't equipped to care for an infant with ongoing health issues. Maybe he would agree to relinquish his parental rights so Tara could adopt her.

Please, she prayed silently, *please*.

She'd spent the past three days planning how to lobby her case. She could rally the Alzate and Lockhart clans. Get them to convince Rhett he wasn't in any position to raise a child. He didn't have the skills or, let's face it, the constitution for fatherhood. He was a party-hardy type with wanderlust, a single-minded rodeo cowboy driven to win at all costs. Not the ideal environment for child-rearing.

They passed Tara's view from the window, climbed the front steps, and for the first time she saw Rhett was sporting a black eye, bruised lips, and a stitched cut over his left eyebrow. Bull riding casualty? Or barroom brawl? Either was highly probable.

She whisked from the living room, down the foyer to the door. Got there just as they knocked.

Still holding Julie close to her heart, Tara took a deep breath. Opened the door. Meant to say hello, but couldn't find the words. Terrified that if she spoke, she'd start crying.

Mrs. Bean stood on the welcome mat, a tight little smile on her face. She turned to Rhett. "Mr. Lockhart, this is your daughter Julie's foster mother, Tara Alzate."

Behind Mrs. Bean, Rhett's face paled as his battered eyes met Tara's gaze, and he said in a voice choked with stunned shock, "My God, it's *you*."